SHATTER THE SILENCE
Harmony Grove Series, Book 2

Copyright © 2020, by Carol J. Post

ISBN: 978-0-9863802-5-9 (ebook)
ISBN: 978-0-9863802-6-6 (print)

All rights reserved. Except for use in any review, no part of this book may be reproduced, scanned, or distributed in any printed or electronic form without express written permission from the author. The scanning, uploading, and distribution of this book via the Internet or any other means without the permission of the author is illegal and punishable by law. Please do not participate in or encourage piracy of copyrighted materials in violation of the author's rights. Purchase only authorized editions.

This is a work of fiction. Names, characters, places and incidents are either the product of the author's imagination or are used fictitiously, and any resemblance to actual persons, living or dead, business establishments, events or locales is entirely coincidental.

Cover Design and Interior Format
© THE KILLION GROUP, INC.

SHATTER THE SILENCE

Harmony Grove Series

CAROL J. POST

ONE

SHEET-COVERED SHAPES LOOMED like ghosts in the dim light.

Tia Jordan pushed the door open further and entered the room, stirring up dust and setting off a series of sneezes. A half brick lay on the hardwood floor, along with shards of glass, but other than the broken window, the room looked much like the others she'd viewed—lifeless, dirty and neglected for nearly half a decade. The huge old house had all kinds of potential. It would just require weeks of work to make it livable.

But she wasn't one to look a gift horse in the mouth.

When she'd gotten the call from the attorney saying she needed to be present for the reading of Elizabeth Sloan's will, she'd been pleased but not surprised. She'd met the woman only a handful of times, when she'd participated in the services her church had held at Mrs. Sloan's adult living facility. In the three years since opening her emergency abuse shelter, Peace House, Tia had benefited from numerous fundraisers organized by the citizens of Harmony Grove and been the recipient of several grants.

She'd gone to the lawyer's office expecting to be ushered into a conference room with family members and possibly representatives from some other charities to receive a small cash donation. Instead, she'd sat alone with the attorney and learned that she was the primary heir to the estate. A son, George, would inherit ten dollars, and a grandson, Jason, would receive the personal effects inside the house, if he could be located within six months of her death.

Tia flipped the switch, and a floor lamp came on, its glow chasing the shadows into the far reaches of the room. Along the back wall, heavy drapes hid a bank of windows. She pushed one aside to peer out. A blanket of steel-gray clouds hung low in the sky, the midday sun somewhere behind.

She swiped a hand down one of the dirt-coated panes and squinted at the back yard. Actually, *yard* wasn't the right word to use. *Yard* implied at least a loose sense of organization—grass, shrubs, flower beds, with some kind of defined edges for each.

Instead, the landscape looked as if someone had come in with a bush hog every few months and mowed down thigh-high growth. It was currently overdue.

Ten minutes ago, she'd stepped from her car onto the cracked concrete drive, then made her way up the front walk, an unruly blend of weeds and grass encroaching from both sides. She'd been nervous. There'd been too good of a chance of running into a snake. Or two. Central Florida rarely got cold enough to slow down the creepy-crawlies, even in early December.

She let the drape fall and moved away from the window. The yard had a lot of potential, just like the house. It was large, with plenty of room for outdoor living, places where tormented souls could find serenity. That potential was what she'd focus on—the end result. Not all the work it would take to get there.

Of course, she'd have help—volunteers from local neighborhoods and businesses, high schoolers doing their community service for scholarships, even some of the battered women she took in. Some who came through her doors threw themselves into activity, hoping to outrun the demons that pursued them. Others sat alone, quiet and withdrawn, temporarily disconnected from life.

Tia had done both.

She moved back through the room, toward the open doorway. Judging from the shapes of the sheet-covered furniture, the space had been used as a den. It would be her office. With its location at the end of the hall and its own exterior door, she'd be able to bring in new clients without traipsing them through the living areas until after she'd spoken with them and they felt ready to face the others.

Finished with her tour of the first level, she turned off the light and headed toward the grand stairway. With as long as the place had been abandoned, she'd been surprised but relieved to find the power on. Leaving a house closed up in Florida without the A/C running at least occasionally was a sure-fire way to end up with a moldy mess.

She'd almost reached the entry when the ominous creak of hinges sent a chill up her spine. She froze, then backtracked into the den, her sneakered steps soundless against the wood floor.

She'd locked the front door after entering. She *always* locked her doors. The practice almost kept at bay that ever-present sense of vulnerability. Did someone pick the lock or enter with a key? A caretaker maybe?

No, there hadn't been any caretaking done at the place in months. It wasn't the grandson, either. After leaving the lawyer's office, she'd come straight here with the key, anxious to see what had just been dropped in her lap. The preliminary search for the grandson had so far turned up nothing.

Whoever was inside the house with her had entered without ringing the bell or knocking. That made him a threat.

Footsteps sounded, moving closer, and she squatted behind a sheet-covered object. It was probably a desk, judging by its shape and size. Particles of dust sifted into the air around her, and it started again—that tell-tale tickle in her sinuses.

No, not now. She pressed a shaking finger to the space above her upper lip. Wasn't there supposed to be a pressure point somewhere, something that could hold off a sneeze?

The sensation passed, and she released a silent sigh. She'd remain hidden until she was sure her unwanted visitor posed no threat. Running a home for abused women and children had made her wary. More than once, an irate husband or boyfriend had railed outside the shelter, threatening to kick in the door if she didn't open it. On both occasions, she'd called the police. With her location a block from Main Street, they'd arrived almost immediately.

Now, she was a good ten minutes from the outskirts of Harmony Grove. But that wasn't her only problem. With her purse sitting on the kitchen island and her cell phone inside, calling for help wasn't an option.

Screaming wouldn't bring assistance, either. Since she was closed up in the house, the nearest neighbor a quarter mile away, no one would hear her. She'd be hard-pressed to defend herself, too, if the need arose. Her rifle was locked in its case back at the shelter, and her pepper spray was in her purse, along with her cell phone.

The footsteps stopped. "Hello? Anyone here?"

The voice gave her pause. He didn't *sound* threatening. With that warm, smooth baritone, he could be hosting a late-night radio show...or singing love ballads.

Of course, that didn't mean anything. Neither did good looks, charm or a charismatic presence. All too often, those were just tools used to con unsuspecting, naive women. And once those men got them where they wanted them, they had all kinds of ways to keep them there.

Tia pressed her hand against the silk scarf draped just below her throat and ducked even lower. Her safest bet was to remain hidden until the man left, or if he ventured upstairs, she could grab her purse, slip out and drive away. The footsteps began again, heavy male ones, and that sneeze she'd successfully stifled erupted with almost no warning. She clamped a hand over her nose and mouth, trying to seal off any spaces where noise might escape. It didn't work. Instead of a full-blown sneeze, she ended up with something between a snort and a half-hearted raspberry.

"Hello?"

She rose from her hiding place. Whoever he was, he wasn't going to find her cowering in the corner, plastered behind a desk. She'd worked hard to shed that "victim" label. It had apparently worked. People described her as having a lot of spunk, bold and fierce.

She put on a good front.

She crossed the room and stepped into the hall. Not ten feet away stood the man behind the voice. He had her beat by a good eight or nine inches. Of course, at five foot two, she didn't meet many people who didn't beat her height. He far outweighed her, but she couldn't guess by how much. He was well-muscled, athletic—someone large enough and strong enough to inflict some pain, especially with no one to come to her aid.

Except there was kindness in his eyes, and though he wasn't smiling, his jaw was relaxed. Dark brown hair curled over his ears and against his shirt collar, and the end of his nose was just shy of straight, as if it had been broken at some point. Maybe he got hit in the face with a softball during Little League.

He lifted his eyebrows. "Who are you?"

She frowned. "Who are *you*?"

"Jason Sloan."

She nodded slowly. The long-lost grandson. The attorney must have found him. Or more likely, he'd heard his grandmother had passed away and had come hoping to get something. It was amazing how kids and grandkids could ignore their elderly relatives for years, then come out of the woodwork when there was possible money or valuables to claim. He probably wasn't happy, thinking she'd swooped in and stolen his inheritance.

Let him think what he wanted. She wouldn't lose any sleep over it. The fact that she'd just moved to Harmony Grove four years ago, and she'd seen his grandmother more times than he had, spoke volumes. He didn't deserve any more than he was getting.

She didn't, either. But the women and children who would benefit did. If he hoped to talk her out of anything she'd been left, he was in for a rude awakening. She had a legitimate will and needed every bit of her unexpected inheritance. Her rented ranch-style home was filled to capacity and bursting at the seams. With a much larger facility, she'd have the means to help so many more women and children.

He stared down at her. "And you are?"

She squared her shoulders, ready to do battle. "Tia Jordan. Of Peace House." If he hadn't heard of the shelter before, he'd know it now since it had been listed in the will.

Jason stood studying her, as if expecting some kind of explanation. Finally, he shook his head, confusion etched into his features. "Did you work for my grandmother or what?"

"No, I didn't."

"So what are you doing here?"

Was he serious? Did he really not know? "Have you read the will?"

"I have. A copy has been in my mother's possession for some time."

A sliver of her defensiveness slid away. "I guess you're here for the personal effects."

That look of confusion returned. "I *will* be going through the personal effects, but I plan to get the place cleaned out and sold as quickly as possible."

Her chest heated as irritation shot through her. Maybe he was used to pushing people around and getting his way. It wasn't going to work this time. She had a will and that decided it, regardless of what *he* thought was fair.

He was named; his grandmother had included him. His father was named also. There was no oversight. Both men could fight it all they wanted, but they didn't have a leg to stand on.

Except Jason didn't seem combative. She'd gotten much better at reading people, and the only emotion she was picking up from him was confusion.

She narrowed her eyes. "You do know that, except for the personal effects, your grandmother left everything to Peace House?"

He shook his head, one hand planted firmly on his hip. "That's impossible."

"Why do you say that?"

"Because I have a copy of the will, and she left everything to me."

Jason maintained a white-knuckled grip on his Ram's steering wheel, tamping down the urge to roar. No one would hear him if he did. He was flying down the four-lane road that led into Harmony Grove, and all his windows were up. Releasing that bellow he was restraining wouldn't accomplish anything, but it would probably make him feel better.

A second will. No way.

But it was true. When he'd refused to believe it, that Tia woman had taken him out to her car, the little white Fiat he'd seen parked in the drive. Then she'd handed him the document she'd supposedly just received.

It wasn't prepared by his grandparents' lawyer or any of his partners in the large Lakeland law firm. This copy of the will had the name and address of a local Harmony Grove attorney.

He was probably Tia Jordan's lawyer and represented Peace House, someone who was biased, even though he wasn't supposed to be. What was Peace House, anyway? Some kind of religious cult? A commune where everybody lived together in peace and harmony?

He knew nothing about Peace House, but he'd sized up Tia Jordan quickly. She was tiny, more than a head shorter than he was, with wispy blond hair that fell just to her shoulders, expressive blue eyes, and a vulnerable air that made a man want to go instantly into protective mode. But he was far past being swayed by a pretty face and innocent airs.

He knew Tia Jordan's type. She was one of those greedy, gold-digging women who befriended older people solely to convince them to change their wills and leave everything to her. She'd beat him out of his inheritance. He hadn't been able to hide his shock, but he'd restrained the anger until he was safely away from his grandparents' place. What should now be his place.

Instead, he would inherit some personal effects while Tia got everything of value. Even the furniture was going to her. Maybe relying on an almost twenty-year-old will had been stupid. But he hadn't considered the fact that someone might swoop in and steal his inheritance.

He drew in a cleansing breath, steeling himself against the fury coursing through him. What he needed to do was go for a run. It was something he'd learned long ago, the effectiveness of physical activity in soothing anger.

And prayer. Except today, prayer alone wasn't working.

He'd been near the end of his rope, with months of bills to get through and savings almost depleted. Though he hadn't rejoiced over his grandmother's death, for a few hours, he'd believed he could tunnel his way out, and a weight he'd carried for the past eight months had lifted from his shoulders. It had lightened, anyway. Now it was back.

At least the woman hadn't gloated. She'd stared up at him with strength and determination. Judgment, too. Fine. Let her judge. It was easy to disparage others when one didn't know their circumstances.

The speed limit dropped as he neared the outskirts of Harmony Grove, and he lifted his foot from the gas. The little town held good memories, as did the house he'd just come from. It had been his refuge, his grandparents his saviors. Until his dad no longer allowed contact.

He pulled into a parking space at the aptly named Tranquility Inn. Catty-cornered across Main Street lay the park where concrete paths wove past a basketball court, playground and picnic area and finally around Lake Mae. He and his mom had regularly joined his grandparents there for Saturday lunch. His grandmother always supplied the basket of food. After eating their fill, the adults would talk while he played in the playground or, when he'd outgrown that, circled the lake on his roller blades.

Yeah, Harmony Grove was the backdrop for his best childhood memories. It was nearby Winter Haven that was the source of all his bad ones.

He stepped from his truck, glancing back at the park. It called to him. His run would have to wait. He hated to be the bearer of bad news, but he had a phone call to make.

Once inside his room, he pulled up his recent calls and made his selection. His mom answered on the first ring.

"You got in to see the attorney?" Her voice held enthusiasm, energy. It was the first she'd shown in some time. Though she tried to put on a good front, each treatment seemed to suck more life from her. Or maybe that was the cancer.

"I did." He strode to the back of the small room and looked out the French door at the garden beyond. "Got a key and went by Grandma and Grandpa's house."

"How is everything?"

He released a deep sigh and walked back to the tiny kitchen area. Pacing didn't take the place of running, but it was better than standing still. "I ran into someone there and learned about another will, prepared July 5th of this year." Less than five months ago.

"What?"

"Grandma left almost everything to a local girl and some organization called Peace House."

In the heavy silence that followed, Jason's chest squeezed. His mother was never at a loss for words.

No matter the situation, she didn't just have the words, she had the *right* ones. It was one of the things that made her such a good counselor, along with her empathetic nature and the fact that she had her own traumas to draw on. This time, there weren't any words.

He gripped the wooden back of one of the two kitchen chairs. "She left me her personal effects, not to include the furniture." Sarcasm crept into his tone on the last few words. The furniture wasn't important to him. He had no need for it and wouldn't have wanted the hassle of shipping it back to his place in Groton. But the provision seemed to add insult to injury.

"Don't be angry with your grandma." His mother spoke in that calm way of hers. "We've had no contact with your father's family since you were thirteen."

"Out of necessity. And Grandma understood that."

"She didn't know where we were, how to get in touch with us or if you were even still alive. She and your grandpa didn't want your father to inherit. She told me that when she gave me a copy of the will."

The will. The one that left everything to him, except ten dollars that was to go to his father. The Lakeland lawyer had located him. He was living near Biloxi, Mississippi and didn't indicate any plans to return. That was fine by Jason.

He resumed his pacing. "She apparently decided she didn't want me to inherit, either." That decision likely involved some persuasion from Tia Jordan.

"I'm sure it wasn't that. She probably wanted to make sure she had everything nailed down, someone to fight your father if he came back and tried to contest the will." A heavy sigh came through the phone. "Maybe you should have made contact with her."

"And risked Dad finding out where you'd gone? No way."

He'd missed his grandparents over the years and thought about them a lot. After becoming an adult, he'd considered making contact. After all, several years had passed. His father had had plenty of time to move on. But in the end, it was a risk he wasn't willing to take. His mother had given up a lot to disappear.

He stopped at the front door and rested his forehead against it. "We need this money."

"We're in no different of a place now than we were forty-eight hours ago."

He frowned. What she said was true. His mom had maintained contact, albeit infrequent, with only one person in Central Florida, the neighbor responsible for helping them get out. The woman had called Monday afternoon with the news of his grandmother's death. He'd left Connecticut at two a.m. Tuesday and had arrived in the wee hours this morning. After grabbing a few hours of sleep, he'd visited the lawyer in Lakeland and gotten the key.

Then Tia Jordan had kicked the foundation out from under him.

Yeah, his situation was no different than it had been forty-eight hours ago, but his mood was. It was as if someone had given them a life-saving gift then promptly snatched it away.

He pushed himself away from the door. "If Tia Jordan thinks I'm going to walk away without a fight, she's going to be disappointed. I'm nowhere near ready to concede this battle. I'm going to do some checking while I'm here."

He had the time. He'd put in an emergency request for three weeks of the vacation he had banked. He'd already planned to be off for the last two weeks of the month, when the company shut down for the Christmas holidays.

"I'll talk to people, see what I can find out about Grandma's mental state. The will I saw today supersedes the one we have, but if I can prove Grandma wasn't of sound mind when she signed it, there's a chance I can get it thrown out."

He softened the determination in his voice. "Has Marci been there yet?" Marci was his mother's best friend and had promised to check on her every day.

"Yeah. We had lunch together, then played a game of Scrabble."

"Good."

When his mom had first gotten sick, he'd moved her in with him to assist with her care. The choice had been a no-brainer. His mom had needed him. Five years earlier, though, it wouldn't have been that easy. Singleness had its benefits.

He finished the conversation with a promise to keep her posted. Then he changed into some tennis shoes, gym shorts and a T-shirt. The next thing on his agenda was the run in the park.

As he pulled the door shut, some of his tension seeped out with the breath he expelled. What circled through him now felt less…toxic. His mom had that effect on him. Actually, she had that effect on everybody.

After checking traffic both directions, he made

a diagonal path across Main, sneakers slapping the asphalt. Regardless of his conversation with his mom, he wasn't ready to forego his run. He wasn't ready to raise the white flag of surrender, either. He was a fighter, not a quitter, and this was a battle he'd see through to the bitter end.

He wasn't fighting for himself. He was in it for his mother.

And it was literally a matter of life or death.

TWO

THE MID-AFTERNOON SUN shone from a cloudless sky as squealing children sailed down the slide. Every swing was occupied, the creaks of the chains a rhythmic backdrop to all the happy sounds drifting through the playground.

Tia smiled at the carefree air that permeated the park. Two of the boys were mirror images of each other and were in her care. So was their mother, sitting next to her.

Katie Burch had come to her on Monday, her little blond angels in tow. When the crisis center had called to place her, Tia had almost turned her away. Now she was glad she'd made the space, even though she'd had to vacate her bedroom and set up a cot in her office. Besides Katie and her boys, Tia currently housed three women who occupied single beds in the master bedroom and a mother with two children who stayed in the second bedroom.

"You're doing a good job with your boys."

Katie looked at her, and one side of her mouth turned upward in a half smile. That side looked good. On the other, her lip was busted and swollen. Her eye had obviously been the target of an angry fist as well, the surrounding skin a sad shade of purple.

"Thanks. I try."

"I know it's hard."

Katie's gaze shifted to where one of the boys was climbing the ladder on the slide. Ethan or Aiden? Tia wasn't sure.

"I should have done this a long time ago." Katie's tone was flat, emotionless.

Tia waited for her to continue. Katie had told her story during the intake interview. While one of Tia's volunteers had entertained her boys elsewhere in the house, the young mother had sat in Tia's office and poured out her heart through a flood of tears.

Katie stared straight ahead, the pain in her eyes evidence that she was no longer observing the activity on the playground. Her gaze hadn't moved, even though her son had sailed down the slide and had run to the merry-go-round to join his brother.

"I thought that as long as he didn't lay a hand on the boys, I could put up with it. What choice did I have? I got pregnant at the beginning of my senior year of high school, dropped out and got married two months later. I have no marketable skills."

"We'll help you with that." Along with counseling, finance classes, personal living and more, as long as she stayed with the program. Unfortunately, the statistics were sad—victims returned to their abusers an average of seven times before embracing healing. Reconditioning after years of having one's self-esteem stripped away wasn't easy.

Katie sucked in a breath and released it in a slow sigh. "I didn't want him scaring the kids so I kept telling him he shouldn't hit me in front of them." Her eyebrows drew together, as if she sensed something was wrong with what she'd said but she wasn't sure what it was.

Tia put a hand on her shoulder. "It's never okay for him to hit you, no matter who's around."

"I know." It was just two words, but the conviction behind them was lacking. Katie had a long, difficult road ahead of her. "I didn't tell you what led to my leaving."

No, she hadn't, beyond that she'd done it for her boys. As with every new client, Tia had let her relay as many or as few details as she was comfortable sharing.

"My neighbor told me something that opened my eyes. My boys and her girls were outside and she was sitting in the porch swing watching. Her little girls were playing with Barbies and had given Ethan and Aiden Ken dolls."

She hesitated, and her expression darkened. "Everything was fine until Aiden's Ken accused Barbie of burning his dinner and started hitting her, telling her she's a worthless piece of trash and doesn't deserve to live." She lowered her head and her shoulders drooped. "Aiden was acting out a scenario he's seen at home so many times, and my neighbor knew it."

Tia's heart twisted. She recognized the dejected pose, as well as the emotion behind it—discouragement, defeat, hopelessness. And humiliation. As if there was something wrong with the abused rather than the abuser.

Katie picked at a hangnail on her left ring finger until it bled. Less than three inches away, a gold band provided a reminder of the vow it represented—to love and to cherish—a vow that had never been kept.

"The boys have seen their father hit me so many times that, though I've told him otherwise, I'm afraid they think it's okay, that this is how men handle conflict and anger." Katie's eyes filled with tears. "Have I ruined them by not leaving sooner?"

Her gaze locked with Tia's, eyes pleading for encouragement, some magic words to assure her that she would be all right and so would her boys.

But Tia didn't have a crystal ball. Children that grew up in abusive homes often became abusers. Many didn't, though.

"Your boys are young." Just turned six, according to the representative from the crisis center. "Stay with the program. Counseling will be available for all of you."

Before Katie could respond, Tia's ringtone sounded, and she pulled her phone from her back pocket. The number wasn't familiar. The 386 North Florida area code was. A vise clamped down on her chest.

No. She'd gotten the six-month notification in September. She still had another three months before she would have to start looking over her shoulder.

After excusing herself and stepping away, she swiped the screen and breathed a shaky *hello.*

"Tia Jordan?" The male voice was deep and professional.

"Yes?"

"This is Sergeant Rick Bateman from the Florida Department of Corrections."

The vise tightened, and she waited in silence for him to continue. She had no choice. Her throat had closed up.

"I'm calling to inform you that Victor Krasney is scheduled to be released this Friday."

She closed her eyes as dread spiraled through her. *Two days.* "But I was told March. He can't be released yet." The words were pointless, but they spilled out anyway. As if her feeble protests could alter the course of the justice system. "I still have three more months."

"I'm sorry. He's being released early."

After disconnecting the call, she leaned against a lamp post, trying to slow her breathing and ward off a full-blown panic attack. Nearby, the thud of a basketball against concrete and the stampeding of a half dozen teenage boys formed the backdrop for the alarms going off in her head.

As soon as she was alone, she'd warn her younger sister. Randi hadn't disappeared like Tia had, but she wasn't a sixteen-year-old girl anymore. She was a mature, independent woman. Like Tia, she'd changed her last name, but for different reasons. She'd gotten married.

At the time, though, the things Victor had promised to do to Randi if Tia tried to leave had kept Tia exactly where he'd wanted her—under his cruel control.

Twinges passed through her chest, just painful enough to remind her that no matter how hard she tried to escape the past, some traumas lingered. She pressed a hand to the scarf draped there. Was she feeling the scars on the surface or the ones that resided much deeper?

When she headed back toward the playground, a lone jogger moved down the concrete path toward her. Below his gym shorts, his sneakered feet pounded the pavement, and a black T-shirt stretched taut across his muscular chest. The bill of his cap cast his face in shadow.

He drew closer and lifted his head. Brown eyes met hers for a brief moment before shifting away.

Jason Sloan.

She dropped her hand and squared her shoulders. When he jogged past her without saying a word, she heaved a sigh of relief. They'd have to speak eventually, but thank God, it wouldn't be this afternoon.

Although he'd hidden it, he'd been angry when he left his grandparents' house. Given the circumstances, she didn't blame him. He'd shown up thinking he would come away with everything—lock, stock and barrel.

She didn't begrudge him the personal effects, especially anything that held sentimental value. If there *was* anything with sentimental value. Not likely. If he had fond memories of his grandmother, he wouldn't have ignored her for the past however many years. But he was entitled to whatever he wanted to take.

He hadn't said where he was from, but the blue Ram she'd watched back from his grandmother's drive had a Connecticut plate on the front. When he rifled through the contents of the house and packed up whatever he wanted to take home, she preferred to supervise. He didn't seem the type to seek revenge by vandalizing or booby trapping the place, but she didn't put her trust in anyone who hadn't earned it. Even then, it didn't come easy.

When Tia reached the playground, Katie rose and called her sons. Tia released a sigh, fatigue creeping into her bones. In the span of a few hours, she'd inherited a house, encountered an irate heir and learned that the fragile sense of security she'd enjoyed for the past five years was about to come to an end.

Katie fell in next to her, and they followed the path out of the park, the boys skipping ahead. After crossing Main, they turned left toward Tranquility Inn.

She didn't have business there. In fact, she hoped to slip past, unnoticed by its guests. One guest, anyway. Since she'd just seen Jason Sloan running in the park and Tranquility Inn was the only motel in Harmony Grove, that was likely where he was staying. As they drew closer, the dark blue Ram sitting in one of the inn's parking spaces confirmed her suspicions.

Katie looked over at her. "I know I already said it, but thank you for taking us in. And thanks for listening. I haven't told many people my story. In fact, I hadn't told anyone until I called the 800 number." She pursed her lips. "There wasn't anyone I felt comfortable talking to. He didn't let me have friends and kept me isolated from my family, not that they would have been much support."

Tia nodded. That was a common tactic for abusers—to take away the victim's support system, so she'd feel she had nowhere to turn.

In the silence that followed, Tia watched the boys bounce along several yards in front of them, still on an energetic high from their time at the park. When the small family had arrived at the shelter, Aiden's and Ethan's eyes had held the same fear and uncertainty that had filled their mother's. Maybe it was temporary, but for the past hour, both of them had been able to set aside their traumas and be normal, carefree boys. The resilience of kids was amazing.

At the corner, they took a right to follow Tranquility Drive, which ran along the inn's left side. Tia didn't know whether the inn had been named after the street or vice versa, since both had been there long before she arrived four years ago. But from the moment she'd rented a room in the older three-bedroom home that shared the inn's rear property line, she'd envied the establishment's garden. A tall viburnum hedge blocked the view from her own yard, but a wrought iron gate on the side gave the guests access to Tranquility Drive and offered passersby a peek into the lush surroundings.

By the time she'd left the Sloan place this afternoon, she'd already had big plans for the overgrown back yard—flowering plants, stone paths, a fountain, maybe even a fishpond. There was something healing about strolling through a garden. The beauty of nature had a way of soothing the soul.

Until she could make the move, she'd continue to be thankful for where God had placed her. She'd moved into the home when she'd first arrived in Harmony Grove, sharing expenses with two roommates. Her landlord, Sonya Garrett, shared her vision for helping women and children in need of safe shelter, so when Tia had announced her desire to go from volunteering at a Lakeland shelter to starting her own shelter in Harmony Grove, Mrs. Garrett had jumped in with both feet, introducing her to a Winter Haven lawyer who would set up the nonprofit pro bono, then helping with grant writing and fundraising. When Tia's roommates had obtained other lodging,

Mrs. Garrett had allowed Tia to stay on for a little more than what she'd paid for just her share. She still served on her board of directors, along with two men and two other women in the community.

The neighbors had been supportive, too, except for one. Harold Reynolds, two doors down on the opposite side of the street, had been pretty vocal with his objections to having "that kind of place" in the neighborhood, that it would bring in all kinds of riffraff. Fortunately, both times the "riffraff" had arrived, he'd been at work.

As Tia and the Burch family headed up the walkway leading to the wooden porch, sounds of life drifted through the open windows. Two conversations were going on simultaneously, while kids played nearby. A television droned in the background.

When she opened the door, one voice stood out from the others. Not that it was louder, because it wasn't. It was hushed, but tense, the tone pleading. The woman stood with her back to the others, the phone's receiver pressed to her ear. Its cord dangled from the base mounted to the wall, resting against her arm before disappearing in front of her.

Tia moved closer. Danielle had come to her a week ago, sad and withdrawn, ready to burst into tears if someone so much as looked at her. Not much had changed. Her shoulders stayed curled forward, and she avoided eye contact. She'd changed into a pair of jeans and sweater that she'd chosen from the clothes closet but didn't look like she'd brushed her hair since she'd arrived.

Danielle drew in a shaky breath, the mass of light brown tangles resting against her upper back. "Please don't be angry." During the pause that followed, she flinched. It was obvious who she was talking to and what constituted the other side of the conversation.

This was why Tia had never removed the old phone and replaced it with a cordless. The lack of privacy kept most of the women from breaking the rules. Some of them did it anyway.

"David, please." Her voice broke. "I know it was my fault. I should have kept my mouth shut. I promise it won't happen again."

Tia stopped next to her, but the woman kept talking, apparently unaware she was no longer alone.

"I know. You're right. You're always right." The sarcasm that should have accompanied those words was absent. "I shouldn't have left. I'm sorry."

Tia pressed the button to disconnect the call, and the woman's face jerked toward her. Shock filled her eyes then turned to chagrin. Tia didn't give her the opportunity to offer a defense.

"You know the rules." Her tone was as low as the woman's had been, but with a steely edge. "You agreed to them before you moved in."

"I'm sorry. It's just that I've had a lot of time to think. I know he hit me, but it was my fault. I need to try harder."

Tia heaved a sigh, trying to rein in her frustration. "It doesn't matter how hard you try. There'll always be something to set him off."

"He doesn't do this all the time, only when I make him mad. Then he's really sorry and makes it up to me."

Tia shook her head. No amount of sweet words or gifts could atone for what she saw. Discoloration marked the left side of Danielle's jaw and the opposite cheek, old enough to have faded but too new to have disappeared altogether. And even though the December day was a comfortable seventy-five degrees, she was wearing a turtleneck sweater. She'd arrived in something similar. She claimed she got cold easily.

Tia didn't believe it. The woman wasn't wearing sweaters to stay warm. They were there to hide the bruises. Or cuts. Or burns.

"There are acceptable ways to handle anger." Tia's tone was compassionate but firm. "Violence is never one of them. Things with David aren't getting any better. In fact, I'd guess they're getting worse. You need to get out before children come along."

Her face crumpled. "But I love him."

Tia heaved a sigh. How many times had she heard that?

The woman's gaze dipped to the ground. "What are you going to do to me?"

"I don't know yet. You didn't just put yourself in danger. You put everyone here in danger."

"I didn't tell him where I was."

"You broke the rules."

"I'm sorry. Please don't send me away. He's really mad that I left. I should have stayed, tried to work things out. But now that I'm here, I'm afraid to go back, at least until he's had more time to cool down."

If Danielle was telling the truth and hadn't given away Peace House's location, Tia would consider letting her stay. Another option would be to arrange with another shelter director to have her moved. The last option wasn't an option at all—discharging her from the program and having her return home.

Tia expelled another sigh. "I don't know yet. I'll think about it." And she'd pray about it.

She understood the struggle the women faced—the battle with depression and anxiety, the belief that they couldn't live without their abuser, the trauma of trying to adjust to a new normal, no matter how safe and supportive, when remaining in the familiar situation would be more comfortable. But calling him from the shelter was inexcusable.

Twice since opening Peace House, Tia had been put in the position of standing in her living room, rifle cocked, praying the police arrived before she was forced to do something with lasting consequences.

So far, she hadn't had to pull the trigger, but if it came to that, she wouldn't hesitate.

She would do whatever she had to do to protect herself and the women and children in her care.

Jason pulled onto Main from the parking lot of the general store. Pole lights dotted both sides of the street, their circular glow spilling over the decorations attached to their posts. Two bags of groceries sat in the passenger seat. After his run in the park yesterday afternoon, he'd picked up a frozen dinner, a couple of breakfast burritos and sandwich stuff for lunch. He now had another one-day supply of food. The kitchenette in his hotel room included a mini-fridge, with the emphasis on "mini."

When he'd made the trip to Harmony Grove, he hadn't planned to spend several weeks in a motel. Whatever disrepair the house may have suffered, he figured he could get it livable in a day or two, even if he had to rough it. That had been before he'd learned he didn't have a Harmony Grove house.

At the inn, he stopped in the space in front of door number eight. Today hadn't been very productive. He'd visited his grandmother's facility and spoken with the staff there. No one had hinted at confusion or any reduction in his grandmother's mental capacities. Several had used the worn-out phrase "sharp as a tack." With that kind of testimony, he'd never be able to contest the new will.

At least he'd gotten his grandmother's room cleaned out, the personal possessions, anyway. He still had the furniture to remove. That would involve a future trip or two.

Tomorrow he'd make another call. This one would be to a BethAnn Benson, the owner of the local fabric and craft store. According to the people he'd spoken with at Winter Gardens, BethAnn's church did weekly services for the residents there. She'd apparently spent a lot of one-on-one time with his grandmother, sitting and visiting with her after the services ended. Her grandmother was also his grandmother's best friend. Since the older lady was in the hospital with a recent broken hip, he'd start with BethAnn. She probably wouldn't have anything to add to what the others had told him, but he wasn't giving up until he'd investigated every angle.

He looped the two bags over his arm and reached for the Ram's door handle. Running into Tia at the park yesterday afternoon had caught him off guard. He'd jogged through the area, circled the lake, and was heading past the playground back toward the inn. He'd seen her from a distance, standing next to the lamp post, her phone pressed to her ear.

As he'd drawn closer, she'd ended the call. All the confidence and determination she'd shown when they'd initially met was gone. Instead, fear-filled eyes had stared out from a pale, drawn face. An unexpected sense of protectiveness had surged through him, and his step had faltered. If he had a soft side, that was the quickest way to it—a woman in need, frightened and alone.

Then her eyes had met his, and she'd slipped back into confident mode, making the change as swiftly and easily as one dons a mask. Her size was deceiving. What she might lack in physical strength, she obviously made up for in grit and determination. She was going to be a formidable foe.

If he could find someone who'd observed signs of dementia in his grandmother, he'd have the Lakeland attorney subpoena her medical records. Otherwise, contesting the will would be a waste of time and money. He'd have to torpedo his plans and let Tia Jordan walk away with his inheritance.

As soon as he swung open the truck's door, shouts drifted into the cab, an angry male voice. He climbed out and listened. The words were slurred, but he got the gist. The man was demanding to be let inside somewhere. Pounding punctuated the voice, the sounds of a fist against a wooden door.

He dropped the two bags into the bucket seat, then slammed and locked the Ram's door. The voice came from behind the inn. He jogged toward the road that ran along its side. The words were clearer now.

"Danielle, get your butt out here right now before

I bust down this door."

Jason broke into a full run as a wave of red-hot fury shot through him. He'd been here before. Not exactly *here*. Ten miles away. But the situation had been the same. A drunk, angry man making threats. Threats he always carried out. Back then, Jason hadn't been big enough to do anything about it. Now he was.

He turned the corner and ran along the wrought iron fence that bordered the sidewalk and framed the inn's luscious back yard. As he passed the tall hedge, a ranch-style home came into view. The porch light was on, and a glow shone around drawn blinds at the nearest window, but the rest of the house was dark. Whoever this Danielle was, she was probably hiding. It wouldn't do any good.

It never did any good.

The guy standing on the porch was big, built like a linebacker. He raised a burly fist and beat on the door again. "You've got five seconds to open this door. If I have to come in and get you, I'll drag you out by the hair and give you a beating you won't forget."

Another jolt of fury charged through Jason with all the heat and power of a lightning bolt. He made a diagonal path through the front yard, headed straight for the porch.

The guy lifted a foot and thrust outward, the crack of splitting wood like an explosion in the quiet evening air. The lower hinge came loose, leaving the door jammed into the opening at an awkward angle. A second kick splintered the frame, rendering the locks useless. One more kick and the door would be lying inside.

Jason hit the porch at a full run and crashed into the

intruder with the force of a locomotive. The impact sent both of them hurtling across the hardwood floor, the damaged door an obstacle for only the briefest moment.

The guy struggled beneath him. Jason raised himself up enough to flip him over, then straddled him, trapping the man's arms beneath his knees. Booze-scented fumes assaulted his nose.

The intruder's face blurred and faded, and another image took its place—a squarish jaw clenched in anger, dark eyes filled with disdain, pinched lips that never cracked a smile unless it was tinged with cruelty. Jason raised a fist. The man would pay for all the pain he'd caused.

Movement in Jason's peripheral vision penetrated his madness. Someone was there, someone small and slight. Danielle?

He jerked his gaze upward. Wispy blond hair cascaded over one shoulder, and blue eyes stared down at him, a mixture of fear and determination. Not Danielle. Tia. She held a rifle, finger on the trigger. The barrel was aimed at him and the man whose face he'd been ready to smash two seconds earlier.

He raised his hands. Sirens sounded, drawing closer. Someone had called the police. That was what he should have done, rather than charging in and almost getting himself arrested for battery. Or worse.

No one moved as the sirens grew louder. One, then the other abruptly ceased, and a deathly silence fell over the scene.

Moments later, two police officers charged through the open doorway, both dressed in the dark blue

Harmony Grove PD uniforms. One man was young, likely brand new to law enforcement. Judging from the salt and pepper hair and matching goatee on the other officer, he was likely mid-fifties. Both had their weapons drawn. Jason was as much a target as the creep he was restraining.

He stood slowly, hands still raised, and Tia stepped forward. She'd lowered her weapon as soon as the police arrived. "This guy's all right." She indicated Jason with a tilt of her head. "I met him yesterday. Jason Sloan, Elizabeth's grandson. He caught this creep kicking in the door and tackled him."

She looked down at the man on the floor as the younger officer clicked a set of handcuffs around his wrists. "That would be Danielle's boyfriend, soon-to-be ex if she has any sense."

Disdain filled her tone. She was obviously put out with her roommate's choice in men.

"I'll go get her. She can make the identification and give you any information you need."

After putting the weapon aside, she pivoted on one foot and strode from the room. A minute later she returned, half leading, half dragging someone behind her. The grip she maintained on the woman's upper arm didn't look at all gentle.

Jason shifted his gaze to the woman's face. Rivulets of tears streamed down both cheeks. When she reached up to wipe them away, her hand trembled.

Jason's heart twisted. He was well-acquainted with the haunted eyes, the beaten-down posture, the fear that wrapped around her like a cloak. He'd heard people ask in that condescending way of the ignorant, why women put up with abuse. But escape wasn't always possible. And it was never easy.

Tia didn't seem to be burdened with the sympathy he felt for her roommate. Compassion apparently wasn't part of her character. She would probably boot the woman out on the street as soon as the police left.

Maybe he was being unfair. He had no idea what had led to tonight's events. He was ignorant of Tia's situation, too.

The younger officer helped the suspect to his feet and led him outside. Tia followed, so Jason did, too. He'd have to hang around. Though she'd told them what had happened, they'd probably have questions for him.

By the time the officer had the cuffed man loaded into the back of the patrol car, the older one had exited the house also. Danielle remained inside.

Tia smiled at the older officer. "Thank you, Tommy."

His name plate said *Willis* but Tia seemed to be on a first-name basis with him. One of the nice things about living in a small town.

As she began to relay her side of the story to Willis, the younger officer approached Jason. He introduced himself as Alan White, then pulled a notepad from his shirt pocket.

"Let me start by getting your information. Tia said you're Jason Sloan. Address and phone number?"

Jason provided the requested details, then relayed how he'd heard the commotion from the inn's parking lot and had run over to see if he could assist. "The guy kept demanding that Danielle come out, or he was going to break down the door. That was what he was doing when I tackled him. You guys arrived right after that."

He left out what had happened between the tackle and the arrival of the officers, how he'd almost come unhinged and done something he'd be sure to regret. Looking up and seeing Tia standing there with her rifle pointed at him had forced him to pause long enough to rein in his anger. *Thank you, God.*

As he talked, Officer White wrote feverishly in his pad. He was young, but he exuded competence, and his eyes held intelligence. That sharp gaze probably didn't miss much. At the officer's prompting, Jason relayed the specifics of what the suspect had said and filled in a few other details.

White put away his pad and handed Jason a card. "If you think of anything else, let us know."

He watched the two men walk to their vehicles, then looked at Tia. Whether she wanted his help or not, he wasn't leaving until he secured her house.

"Are you going to be okay?" She was hiding it well, but she had to be shaken up.

"I'm fine. This isn't the first time I've had an irate husband or boyfriend show up at my door, threatening bodily harm."

What? This was a regular occurrence? What kind of life did the woman lead?

Realization slammed into him. "This is Peace House." It was a statement, not a question. Tia Jordan ran a shelter for abused women.

"We don't broadcast the location. We don't even have any signs. Tonight is a great example of why."

He looked back through the gaping opening into the living room. "You can't even lock the house."

"I'll board it up. I can get the women to help me."

"There are others?"

"Four other women and four kids."

Jason lifted his eyebrows. "They're quiet. I didn't know anyone else was here."

"As soon as Danielle's boyfriend arrived, I told everyone to get in the back and hide until I say it's okay to come out. With their backgrounds, fleeing conflict comes naturally. So does fear."

"I understand."

She cast him a doubt-infused glance. That was all right. She didn't need to know his family history.

He frowned. "Let me help. Lowe's will be open for another twenty minutes. If I leave right now, I can grab some plywood before they close."

"No need. There's some in the shed, left over from boarding up the windows before our last hurricane." She gave him a wry smile. "I'll put Danielle to work. She's the reason we're even dealing with this tonight."

He pursed his lips. "Is it right to lay the blame on her for someone else's actions?"

"I'm laying the blame where it belongs. She called him. That's something they agree to before they come to Peace House—no contact with their abuser, and no revealing their location."

She crossed her arms. "When I got home from the park yesterday, she was on the phone with him. She claimed she didn't tell him where she was, but when I went back to get her tonight, she admitted that she *might* have said something about Harmony Grove and Tranquility Inn."

Jason shook his head. No wonder Tia had shown no sympathy.

After she turned down two more offers to help secure the house, he headed back to the inn and put his groceries away. Then he slipped out the single French door into the garden behind. One of the small bistro tables called to him. This one sat in the middle of a circle of three queen palms, a matching chair on each side.

He sank into one of them and leaned back. The sky was cloudless, the moon a few days past full. Its glow spilled over the garden, bathing the landscape in soft light. Sitting outside at night in December, wearing jeans and a polo shirt, wasn't something he often did in Connecticut.

When he and his Mom had hopped on the bus that terrifying night seventeen years ago, with nothing but the clothes on their backs and cash donated by a kind-hearted neighbor, the brutal winters were just one of the changes he'd had to adjust to.

There were also the months of homelessness, in and out of shelters until his mother got on her feet. And the constant fear that his father would somehow find them and bring them back to Florida.

He rested his arms on the table and intertwined his fingers. Besides enjoying the temperate winter evening, he had another reason for sitting outside. Tia wouldn't let him help, but until he knew that she and her women were safely back inside, he'd keep himself parked in that chair. At the first sign of trouble, he could be out the side gate and on her property in a matter of seconds.

They were still working. Soft feminine voices reached him through the hedge, along with the scrape of plywood against the porch surface as they wrestled the sheet into position. The whine of a screw gun followed. He had to admire Tia's strength and self-sufficiency, even if she *was* somewhat of an adversary.

Tomorrow he was going to pay BethAnn Benson a visit in the hopes she'd have information that would give him grounds to contest the second will. Except now he'd lost some of the passion for his quest.

Tia wasn't a gold-digging woman intent on beating him out of his inheritance. She was a kind-hearted soul who was giving everything she had to help abused women and children escape the hell that was their life. According to what she'd said, that small home currently housed nine people, including Tia. His grandmother's place could accommodate two to three times that many—women and children with nowhere to turn, desperate for safety and security.

Until an hour ago, he'd wanted nothing more than to wrestle his inheritance back and was willing to use any means at his disposal to accomplish it. Now he wasn't so sure. If everything went to Tia and Peace House, could he really begrudge her that?

How could he choose between his mother's life and a cause that was so close to both of their hearts?

THREE

TIA SWUNG OPEN the shed door, her screw gun in one hand, the box of screws tucked under that arm. She'd managed tonight's project on her own with the assistance of two of her ladies. Danielle hadn't been one of them.

Tia had had good intentions—Danielle needed to take some responsibility for her actions. But when they'd selected the two pieces of plywood and brought them to the front of the house, Danielle had still been such a nervous, blubbering mess that Tia had sent her inside.

After stepping into the shed, Tia flipped the switch, and light filled the small space. Her push mower occupied its spot along the left wall, and miscellaneous yard tools stood in the corner next to two bags, one containing fertilizer and the other potting soil. Instead of using the shelter's resources on a lawn service, she maintained the yard herself with the help of a volunteer.

On the right wall, plywood cut to various sizes stood against the shed's wooden studs. There were two fewer pieces than had been there an hour ago. None of the sheets had been tall enough to cover the door opening, so she'd secured the lower half, then the upper portion. There was also a door that hadn't been there an hour ago, standing next to the plywood. Fortunately, all the damage had been confined to the frame.

Ignoring the items against the side walls, Tia walked to the back, where a black case lay open on a small work table. The drawers beneath held hand tools—a hammer, tape measure, screwdrivers and wrenches.

She didn't have a well-equipped workshop, but the items she'd accumulated over the past three years enabled her to make small repairs without having to bother her landlord. Some projects she'd tackled on her own, with the help of instructions she'd found on the internet. With others, she'd accepted the help of a local handyman who'd donated his services.

After returning her screw gun to its place, she secured the latches on the case and slid it onto a shelf next to her jigsaw. Jason had offered to assist, but she'd refused. He'd have gotten it done a lot faster, but she didn't want to feel indebted to him.

She was also afraid of him now. She hadn't been before, but seeing the raised fist and the unrestrained fury in his eyes, her guard had gone right back up.

Not that she didn't appreciate what he'd done. The instant Danielle's boyfriend had shown up, she'd hit one of the three panic buttons hidden inside the house, automatically summoning the police. But the intruder had gained entry before they could arrive. Had Jason not tackled the guy, she might have been forced to pull the trigger.

His actions were over the top, though. Rather than simply playing protector and restraining the guy, she'd feared he would kill him. His lips had curled back in an angry sneer, and his eyes had burned with vengeance, as if he'd somehow made the whole thing personal.

With the help of her ladies, she'd managed to secure the place without him. The result wasn't pretty. The two pieces of plywood were different sizes, overhanging the bottom of the opening more than the top. Doing the job right was going to involve rebuilding the jamb. Besides the fact she didn't have the right materials, the project was beyond her skill level, even with YouTube videos.

She stepped from the shed and slid the padlock into the hasp. The others had gone back inside a few minutes ago. As she walked toward the back door, the hum of a car engine reached her, growing louder as it moved down Tranquility Way. She rested a hand on the doorknob and listened. Instead of fading, the sound died abruptly, as if someone had just stopped out front.

Uneasiness sifted through her, and she shook it off. She was just on edge. There was nothing to fear. Her neighbor across the street had probably gotten home. When she stepped around the side of the house, her chest tightened.

A white van was parked at the end of her driveway, the call letters of one of the local news stations painted on its side. Two people had already exited. One held a microphone while the other fiddled with a camera.

Tia had a good rapport with the local media. They offered free advertising for her fundraisers and had always been discreet about the shelter's location. But hitting the news made her nervous. Even more so, now that Victor was being released tomorrow.

Tia approached them. "I'm afraid you missed the action." What little action there was. She wasn't even sure why they were there. Surely they had bigger stories to chase than that. The two other times an irate ex had shown up, Tia hadn't even made the local paper.

The woman with the microphone smiled at her. Tia had never met her. Sporting a smart suit, her shoulder-length hair cut in a style that complemented her face, she was poised, confident and beautiful, someone who obviously looked good on camera.

"We hear the police were called out to the shelter tonight."

"Yes, one of the residents got in touch with her boyfriend." She frowned. "Sort of let our location slip."

"Not good. What happened?"

"He demanded that she come out, and when she didn't, he kicked in the door."

"Was anyone hurt?"

"No. The women and children were all hiding. A neighbor heard the commotion, ran over and restrained him until the police got there."

"Do you have this neighbor's name?"

Tia hesitated, then shrugged. "Jason Sloan." If he didn't want any notoriety for his good deed, he could refuse the interview.

"Where can we find him?"

"He's staying at the inn, but I don't know the room number."

"Do you know anything about the guy that was arrested?"

"Nothing, other than that he was the boyfriend of one of my clients."

After a few more questions, the reporter thanked her and the camera clicked off, the red "record" light going dark. Tia followed them to the van.

"As always, you'll edit out anything that might reveal the location of the shelter?" If the story would even air. It was doubtful.

"Of course."

"And blur my face and keep my name a secret?" Some directors could afford to be public. Tia couldn't.

"Yes."

As the cameraman loaded his equipment into the van, Tia shifted her gaze to the right. A figure stood two doors down on the opposite side of the street, bathed in the glow of a nearby streetlamp. Harold Reynolds.

Great. He'd likely witnessed the entire altercation and would be happy to add his two cents to the reporter's account. Whatever he said, it wouldn't paint the shelter in a positive light. He'd wanted her out of the neighborhood from the day she opened Peace House. He didn't know how close he was to getting his wish, thanks to Elizabeth Sloan.

When she moved out, maybe Mrs. Garrett would rent to a couple of wannabe death metal musicians who conducted their practice sessions in the living room. With the windows open. No, she wouldn't wish that on the rest of the neighbors or Tranquility Inn's guests. Actually, wishing it on Harold Reynolds wasn't the Christian thing to do.

The van pulled away from the curb. Two doors down, the brake lights came on and it eased to a stop.

Whatever. Reynolds could say what he wanted.

When Tia walked into the living room, all but one woman and her thirteen-year-old son had gone to bed. The woman, Pam, sat on one end of the couch reading a novel. It was one she'd taken from the bookcase that occupied a spot on the opposite wall. The shelves boasted a good variety of choices, both fiction and nonfiction, thanks to Kevin Burgess. He and his grandfather owned Harvey's New and Used Books and kept the shelter well-stocked with reading material.

Thirteen-year-old Damian hadn't touched a book since he and his mother had arrived four days ago, even though there were some young adult offerings on the shelf. When Tia had made the suggestion, all she'd gotten was an eye roll. Instead, he'd kept himself occupied with his Gameboy or whatever the device was that stayed glued to his hands almost every waking hour.

He was the kind of kid mothers tried to protect their own children from—one that exuded attitude and wore a boulder-size chip on his shoulder, ready to lay out anyone who might think of knocking it off. Tia empathized with the women who came to her fearful, battered and beat down. She had a heart for the children, too, every one of them. She just didn't know how to relate to the adolescent and teenage boys.

It wasn't that she hadn't tried. She had. And it wasn't that she didn't care, because she did. Often the kids who were the most unlovable were the ones who needed love the most.

Damian was no exception. He'd been yanked from

everything familiar and didn't even have any kids his age to vent to. His eight-year-old sister wasn't a good candidate. Neither were Katie Burch's six-year-old twins. To an adult, five or seven years was nothing. For a kid, it was a lifetime.

When Tia walked farther into the room, Pam looked up from her reading. She was one of the two women who'd helped with boarding the door.

She gave Tia a half smile. "You look tired."

"I'm beat." She regularly burned the candle at both ends. The last couple of days, there'd been a few flames in the middle, too.

Pam closed the book and stood. "Come on, Damian, let's hit the sack."

Damian didn't look up from his game. "I'm not ready to go to bed."

"Tia is. So take it into the bedroom. And don't wake up your sister."

He sprang from the chair with an irreverent twist of his shoulders and stomped down the hall. His footsteps echoed through the house. Seconds later, a door creaked open then slammed shut. So much for not disturbing his sister.

Pam heaved a sigh. "He hates me. I took him away from his father."

"You did the right thing."

"I know that up here." She tapped her temple. "But I don't feel it here yet." She pressed a fist to her chest.

"It takes time. You're making a total life-change."

Pam shook her head. "I don't understand it. His father doesn't beat him like he does me, but he's so harsh with him. He says he's trying to make a man out of him. He's been so intent on stamping out any weakness, he's never let Damian be a child. The meaner he is, the more Damian tries to please him."

Tia put a hand on her shoulder. "He craves his father's approval. That need is hard-wired into him."

"Thank you. I can't tell you how much I appreciate what you're doing. For all of us."

Tia watched her walk down the hall, her posture burdened but not defeated. Pam possessed a strength that was lacking in so many of the women who came through her shelter. But her story was just as sad.

This wasn't the first time Pam had left her home. There'd been two others. The last time, her husband had agreed to her condition that he get counseling for anger management. He'd started then quit a month later, and the cycle had begun again.

After trudging into her office, Tia opened the cot that stood in the corner, a blanket and sheet trapped in the folds. When she finally climbed under the afghan she'd laid out on top, she released a long sigh. The fatigue she'd tried to hold at bay seeped into every bone.

God, please bless the women and children you've placed in my care. Meet each of them where they are. She rolled onto her side then added another prayer for protection.

So often, what she did was heartbreaking. On nights like tonight, it was terrifying.

It was also the most rewarding thing she'd ever done in her life.

Jason leaned against the passenger door of his Ram, undecided whether to get back in and return to

Tranquility Inn or go ahead with his plans. He was parked between BethAnn's Fabrics and Crafts and Harvey's New and Used Books.

The bookstore had been there when he was a kid. His grandmother had taken him shopping during one of his and his mother's visits and had told him he could select any four books. He'd chosen J.R.R. Tolkien's *The Hobbit* and *The Lord of the Rings* trilogy. Advanced material for a nine-year-old, but the series had begun in him a lifelong love of reading.

He was pretty sure BethAnn's was new. At least it hadn't been there when he and his mom had left. Not that a fabric store would have been on his radar.

Now it was. He didn't expect to get any useful information. For all he knew, Tia and BethAnn were friends. If that was the case and he plied BethAnn with questions, Tia would be sure to find out. She wouldn't be happy.

Last night, he'd remained sitting at the small wrought iron table until the women on the other side of the hedge had secured the broken door and gone back inside. He'd almost reached the rear entrance to his room when the creak of a shed door had broken the silence, and he'd guessed Tia was still outside, putting up her tools.

Then the news van had driven past the side entrance. He'd almost walked over to intervene. Being featured on TV didn't seem like a good thing for Peace House. But Tia had had the situation under control. She and the reporters had seemed to share a mutual understanding—she'd allow them to do their job, and they wouldn't compromise the safety of her or her clients.

An irate boyfriend breaking down a door didn't seem worthy of the six o'clock news. Apparently, what constituted big news in Harmony Grove was a little less impressive than the newsworthy topics in New London.

He pushed himself away from his truck. A block away, a white SUV sat at the curb in front of C.J.'s Garage, the driver still inside. The mechanic's shop was open, the doors raised on all three bays, but instead of going inside, the guy looked as if he was waiting for someone and was taking the opportunity to squeeze in a nap. His head was tilted all the way forward, the wide-brimmed hat hiding his face.

Jason turned to head down the sidewalk toward the entrance to BethAnn's. The hour was late enough that most of the shops had opened but early enough that no one had reached the peak of the day's business.

He stopped in front of the fabric shop and peered through the display window. It was decorated for the holidays, a Christmas tree at one end. At the other, lighted stars hung over a miniature fireplace, electric logs glowing a reddish-orange. In the middle, wooden cubby holes held a variety of craft projects. Swags of tiny white lights and pearl garland formed a glittering ceiling for the entire display.

Jason moved to the glass door and swung it open. When he stepped inside, voices drifted to him from the back of the store. A woman was planning a summer wedding and BethAnn, or someone who worked for her, was assisting with designs and fabrics for bridesmaids' dresses.

This could take a while. No problem. He didn't have anywhere he needed to be. He strolled across the front of the store. A U-shaped counter occupied the center of the space, its front portion holding a cash register and credit card scanner. A stack of sales flyers sat next to the register. Beyond the flyers was a gallon-size plastic container that had at one time likely held pretzels or other snacks. A computer-generated sign wrapped the front half, its edges affixed with tape.

Jason moved closer. "Peace House" stretched across the top in capital letters. Text below read, "Help make Christmas special for victims of domestic abuse." A graphic of a Christmas tree occupied the lower half.

In the picture, the space beneath the tree was filled to overflowing with wrapped presents. By Christmas Day, Peace House's real-life tree would be, too, if the donations in the container were any indication. It was more than half full. There were lots of dollar bills, but also some fives, tens and twenties. Even a couple of checks had been folded and stuffed inside.

Jason pulled a twenty-dollar bill from his wallet and tucked it through the slot cut into the lid. As it fell onto the pile inside, his chest clenched. What he'd just done seemed hypocritical, considering his reason for being there. He'd taken a small part in providing superficial gifts for Peace House's abused women and children, while planning to wrestle away the gift that would impact so many others long term.

He spun away. Tia's shelter needed the house. But his mother needed the money that selling it would bring. If she couldn't continue her treatment, he'd lose her.

He wandered into the bead section then turned the corner. The next aisle wasn't any more exciting than the first, with rows of yarn lining the shelves. After pacing two more aisles, he turned and retraced his steps, not wanting to disturb the two women at the back. From what he'd overheard, the bride-to-be sounded like more than a customer. The women's voices held the warmth of friendship.

Finally, footsteps sounded against the vinyl tile floor and the conversation grew louder.

"I appreciate your advice. I'm usually pretty decisive, but when I see all the colors and styles, I can't make up my mind."

"Hey, it's my job. After all, I *am* your maid of honor."

Yep, definitely friends. It made sense. In a town the size of Harmony Grove, everyone knew everybody and the residents were tightly knit. Tia would be in that group. If Jason opposed her, he'd probably have the whole town against him.

From his vantage point amid the skeins of yarn, he had a clear view of the women as they walked toward the front door. Both looked to be somewhere around his own age, maybe a little younger. One had long, dark hair woven into a braid. The other had blond curls that bounced against her shoulders as she walked.

Neither fit the image he'd created for BethAnn. Owner of a fabric and craft store and regular contributor to church services for elderly people—he'd imagined her to be older. He watched the brunette exit, then stepped from the aisle.

The blond turned then started. "I didn't realize anyone else was here."

"I came in while you were in the back."

She gave him a friendly smile. "I hope I didn't keep

you waiting long. Can I help you?"

"Are you BethAnn?"

"I am."

He nodded. The fabric store was definitely new. Now that he was seeing her up close, he guessed he had two or three years on her. She'd have been in elementary school when he left.

"I was wondering if you'd be willing to talk to me about Elizabeth Sloan."

BethAnn tilted her head to study him. "And you are?"

"Jason Sloan, her grandson."

Her eyebrows lifted. Was it surprise or judgment he saw?

"She mentioned you. I take it you haven't been here in a while."

Yeah, judgment. In the words, even though she hadn't allowed it to creep into her tone.

"Not lately. I live in Connecticut." That wasn't the reason for his absence, but he wasn't here to justify his apparent inattentiveness.

"I guess you're here for the funeral."

"Yeah." That was one of the things he'd do while he was here, now that he'd learned the time and place from the folks at the home.

"Her wishes were to be buried right away, then have a memorial service held at Winter Gardens, the adult living facility. It'll be at ten tomorrow morning, but I assume you already know that."

"Yes. Thanks."

"I'm sure it'll be nice. She was well-liked."

BethAnn walked to the U-shaped counter nearby and leaned against one long edge. It was wider than the others, likely a table for cutting her fabrics. A 36-inch ruler was mounted to the surface near the inside edge, a metal groove running perpendicular, providing a guide for her scissors.

He stepped closer. "I understand you knew Grandma well."

BethAnn smiled, fondness filling her eyes. "I did. She and my grandma have been best friends since Grandma and Grandpa moved here about fifteen years ago. I also saw her a lot at the adult living facility. My church holds services there every Sunday afternoon. I can't sing, play an instrument or preach, but I give great hugs."

He returned her smile. "I'm sure the residents appreciate that as much as the singing and preaching. Maybe more."

"I don't know about that, but it's nice of you to say so."

BethAnn exuded friendliness. She was just the type his grandmother would take to. Maybe he'd been wrong about her judging him.

"Have you heard that she willed her home to Peace House?"

"I hadn't heard, but I'm not surprised. From the moment I told her about what Tia was doing, she seemed fascinated with the shelter. She asked about it every time I talked to her."

"Did Tia visit my grandmother a lot?"

"No. She came with me a few times, but her ministry is the shelter. It keeps her busy."

He pursed his lips. The image he'd held of Tia scheming to scoop up his inheritance was wavering.

BethAnn's brow creased. "I just thought of

something. Five or six months ago, your grandmother asked me to write down Tia's full name and the name of the shelter so she could add them to her prayer list. Maybe she had another reason for getting the information."

He nodded. "The new will was prepared July 5th, so that fits."

"With how passionate your grandmother seemed about Tia's cause, it made me wonder if she'd been abused herself."

"My grandfather? No way." He took a breath to tone down the defensiveness that had crept into his tone. "He was the sweetest, gentlest man who ever lived."

Actually, Grandpa was her second husband. Her first had been killed in a car accident when Jason's father was young. His grandmother had never talked about him. If her first husband had been abusive, she'd never even hinted at it.

"I didn't mean any offense. It's just that this cause was so dear to your grandmother's heart. It's like it was personal for her."

"Maybe you're right. Grandma had been previously married. I don't know what happened before Grandpa came into her life."

He drummed his fingers against the countertop, catching himself after just two rolls. It wasn't impatience. It was tension, indecision. How could he get the information he'd come for without it being obvious to BethAnn what he was doing?

He gave her a sad smile. He didn't have to fake the emotion. He'd loved his grandparents and would always regret not being a part of their golden years, even though he'd had no choice.

A sense of loss stabbed through him. "Was she happy?"

"She was content. You couldn't be around her without feeling a sense of peace. It radiated from her. She had a lot of friends in the home. Everybody loved her. My grandma visited her regularly, too, even signed her out once or twice a month and took her to lunch."

"I'm glad to hear that." The thought of her spending her final years lonely and forgotten made his heart hurt. "The folks at Winter Gardens said your grandmother fell and broke her hip."

"Yeah. Her blood pressure's up, but as soon as they get it under control, they'll do the surgery. The recuperation time is going to drive her crazy." She shook her head. "Your grandma and my grandma both, you couldn't keep them down."

"So Grandma's health was pretty good to the end?"

"Excellent. We were all shocked when we heard about the stroke."

"Did she seem to have any pain, trouble getting around?"

"Not that I could tell. If she did, though, she wouldn't have mentioned it. She was super upbeat, never complained."

"Her mind was clear?"

"Totally. She always remembered what we'd talked about the week before. I'd tell her about something coming up, and she'd ask about it my next visit."

Definitely no signs of dementia. BethAnn's words confirmed the information he'd gotten from everyone else. The new will would stand.

What would have happened if he'd renewed contact with his grandparents when he'd become an adult? His grandmother wouldn't have chosen a different heir. The if-he-can-be-found phrase in the will said it all.

Making the decision to stay away hadn't been easy. In the end, his need to protect his mother had overridden his desire to be a part of his grandparents' lives. Now, the inheritance he'd counted on was going to someone else. In his determination to keep his mother safe, he'd ultimately sealed her fate.

"Thank you for talking to me. It's a relief to hear her final months were…" Were what, good? With no family around? "…weren't bad."

BethAnn gave him a sympathetic smile. "I'll see you at the memorial service tomorrow."

He thanked her again and walked from the store. When talking about friends and visitors, BethAnn hadn't mentioned his father. Maybe he'd severed ties with everyone in Harmony Grove.

Actually, that had happened several months before Jason and his mother had left. After years of arguments over his father's inability to stay sober and hold down a job, his grandparents had stopped enabling him and had shown some tough love. Jason's father hadn't taken it well. Not only had he severed contact with his parents, he'd forbidden Jason and his mother to communicate with them, too.

Jason climbed into his truck and shut the door. The white SUV was still there, framed in his side mirror. The guy had finished his nap. His head was up, angled toward the passenger side of the windshield. Jason gave him the briefest glance, another man consuming his thoughts.

Seventeen years had passed, and his father was still ruining his life. He'd thought his mother was well out of the way of any harm the man could inflict. He'd been wrong.

One night, thanks to a kind-hearted neighbor, they'd escaped. All the weeks and months and years since, they'd remained hidden to ensure his father would never find them. In the process they'd lost the inheritance that could have saved his mother's life.

He clenched both fists and brought them down hard against the steering wheel. Heat built in his chest and spread outward—anger at his father, at his mother's illness, at his circumstances in general. Maybe even at God.

Couldn't something go according to plan, just once? He worked hard, saved his money, set long-range goals and made good decisions, but no matter how diligently he tried, that coveted sense of control always slipped through his grasp.

As a child, he'd watched his mother suffer at the hands of his father and had been powerless to stop it. Now here he was, thirty years old and back in the same helpless position, his life spinning out of control. Except this time, the enemy was the cancer, and he had no more ability to stop it than he'd had as a child to stay his father's cruel hand.

Jason put the truck in reverse and eased backward in the parallel parking space. It was good his father planned to remain in Biloxi. If he showed up at tomorrow's memorial service, in Jason's current frame of mind, he wouldn't be able to restrain himself. Then his father would be the one on the floor unconscious, blood spewing from a broken nose.

When he pulled from the parking space onto Main, the traffic light a block away was red. One person likely to be at tomorrow's service was Tia. Regardless of how well she'd known his grandmother, she'd have to pay her last respects to the woman who'd made such generous provision for the shelter.

Maybe he could speak with her afterward. He needed to make arrangements to get the personal effects. He had a key, but since the house had been left to Tia, he didn't feel right coming and going as he pleased without talking with her.

As he eased to a stop at the light, he glanced in the rear-view mirror. The SUV's headlights had come on. The driver waited for a car to pass, then left the parking space.

Jason frowned. Was someone following him? The guy he'd tackled last night was locked up. He'd watched the Harmony Grove cruiser pull away with the creep in the back.

Maybe he'd already bonded out and was intent on revenge. Or maybe he'd gotten a hold of a friend who was willing to exact that vengeance for him.

The light changed, and Jason stepped on the gas. When he approached the inn, the SUV was still behind him, one vehicle between. They'd only gone two blocks. Neither vehicle was likely to turn off that quickly. But he couldn't ignore the sense of unease settling over him.

He drove past the inn, then turned down one of the side roads. The car behind him went straight. The SUV turned but held back. Jason's uneasiness intensified. He squinted in the rearview mirror at the emblem on the front. Toyota, either a Highlander or a RAV4.

Over the next few minutes, he made his way to Highway 17 and headed toward Bartow. The route took him past his grandparents' place, but he kept going. The SUV matched his speed, accelerating when he accelerated, slowing when he slowed. Maybe the driver had business in Bartow. After all, it was the county seat.

Jason leaned toward the door to remove his phone from his right pants pocket. Then he held it for several moments, lower lip pulled between his teeth. Was this a good reason to call 911? It wasn't exactly an emergency. No one was threatening him.

He dropped his phone into the cup holder, coming up with a different plan. He'd drive the rest of the way to Bartow, let the SUV's driver believe that was where he was staying, then try to lose him.

There was just one problem. If his pursuer returned to Harmony Grove, his truck would stick out like a neon sign. There were lots of Rams on the road, even blue ones, and he didn't have any bumper stickers or window decals personalizing his truck. But it was probably the only one sporting a Connecticut license plate.

Maybe he'd back in and remove the plate from the front. Florida only required rear plates. He'd probably get away with it.

As he glanced in the rear-view mirror for the dozenth time, he tightened his grip on the wheel. A pistol in the glove box would make him feel a little safer. But he'd never been one to possess a firearm, or even learn how to handle one properly. He'd always believed that anger and lethal weapons made for a bad combination.

Instead, he'd have to rely on his wits. If things turned ugly, he'd call the police and hope and pray they got there in time.

FOUR

TIA PUSHED A box toward an opening in the attic floor. "Christmas" stretched across one side in black magic marker. Several others were marked the same way. Once she opened them, she'd find out exactly what she'd packed into each one.

A pair of hands reached up, and the box disappeared a few seconds later. Before reaching for the next one, Tia wiped her face. She'd been up there only ten minutes, but already, sweat dotted her forehead and had soaked into her T-shirt in several spots.

She'd waited till almost seven to pull down the access ladder and venture into the space, hoping that with the sun set, it might cool down. It hadn't and probably wouldn't until the early morning hours. Whether temperatures reached the summertime highs in the upper nineties or the comfortable seventy-five degrees of a typical winter day, attics in Florida were hot.

Tia slid another box toward the opening. She and the women had a regular brigade going. Tia was in the attic, Pam two thirds of the way up the fold-down ladder, Katie a few steps from the bottom, and the others making trips back and forth between the garage and the living room to stack what they'd toted against the wall. Tomorrow she'd pick up the tree, with BethAnn's help. It was tradition—the first weekend in December, Christmas came to Peace House.

She grasped the last box as her cell phone rang in her back pocket. *Not another family.* She hated to turn anyone away, but at the moment, she had room for only one person, a space that had opened up when Danielle left.

After Tia had caught Danielle talking to her boyfriend, she'd delayed taking action. Last night's events had made the decision for her. She couldn't put her other women and children at risk, so she'd had her moved to a different shelter.

When Tia pulled her phone from her pocket, instead of the crisis center's number, the screen displayed BethAnn's name. Her friend dispensed with the greetings.

"Turn on the news."

"Why? What's on?"

"Right now, a commercial. But after the break, they're doing a story about some excitement at a local shelter."

"Seriously?" That little incident last night was actually making the news?

"They also said something about the capture of a Georgia fugitive who's been at large for the past three years."

"That's not my story. Different shelter." Unless... The reporter had asked her what she knew about the man who'd been arrested. Maybe she'd had information that Tia hadn't.

Her stomach filled with lead. Today was Friday. Unless there'd been some unexpected red tape, Victor was out of jail. Had he sat through his incarceration letting his anger simmer, thinking of all the ways he was going to make her pay? Or had he declared her disappearance "good riddance" and was planning to set his sights on someone else?

She hadn't had contact with him recently enough to know. The last time she'd seen him was the day of his trial. While she'd testified, he'd sat at the table with his attorney, dressed in the jail's orange jumpsuit, wrists and ankles shackled. He'd stared daggers at her the entire time. She hadn't seen him throughout the divorce, either. She'd served him with papers in jail, and he hadn't been at the final hearing.

She handed the box to Pam. While it made its way from one set of hands to another, Tia called down the stairs. "Turn on the TV. We might have made the news last night." Moments later, the sounds of a McDonald's commercial drifted through the house.

Once the steps were clear, Tia descended and walked to the living room. Katie's twins sat on the floor near one wall, a pile of Legos between them. Two neat stacks of boxes stood against another wall. Right after dinner, while the others had cleaned up the kitchen, Pam and Tricia had helped Tia rearrange some of the furniture, leaving a corner vacant. A metal stand sat in the space, ready for the tree she would bring home tomorrow afternoon.

Tia took a place on the sectional sofa with the other women. The scene on the screen switched from a family enjoying their big Macs and fries to a reporter standing in front of a news van. It was the same woman Tia had spoken with last night. She introduced a story about a suspect who'd committed a string of bank robberies in the Macon area, one that had resulted in the death of a teller. His mug shot went up on the screen, and Tia gasped.

Tricia looked at her. "Danielle's boyfriend?"

"Yes." She'd known the man was dangerous. She hadn't realized the extent of the danger at the time.

The reporter continued. "Tonight, this man is behind bars due to an unlikely series of events."

Moments later, the camera cut to Tia. Ethan rose and moved closer, his attention captured by the television. He was quieter and more serious than his brother, with sharp eyes that seemed to always be taking everything in.

He tapped Tia's leg. "Is that you?"

"Yes, sweetie."

"How come your face is all blurry?"

"So no bad people recognize me." It wasn't just Victor. It was anyone who knew him who might tip him off.

Ethan paused for several moments, apparently digesting what she'd said. "Is my dad a bad person?"

"Ethan!" Katie reached for him. "Come sit with Mama and stop bothering Miss Tia."

Ethan allowed his mother to slide him onto her lap, but he kept his gaze fixed on Tia. "My daddy hits my mommy."

"I know. We're going to try to make sure that doesn't happen anymore."

He wiggled free from his mother and plopped down next to his brother and the Legos. When Tia returned her attention to the television, her blurred image was no longer on the screen. Instead, two family members of the murdered teller expressed their relief that their loved one's killer would finally be brought to justice.

The station moved on to a report of a series of home invasions in Lakeland, and Tia breathed a sigh of relief. The focus of the story had been a fugitive's capture, not her shelter. As a result, Harold Reynolds had had zero airtime, probably a huge disappointment. He would have enjoyed his moment in the limelight.

Things couldn't have turned out more perfectly. Even Harmony Grove's grumpy chief of police wouldn't be able to find fault with the events that had taken place when they'd resulted in a violent criminal being taken off Florida's streets.

The first time an irate ex had shown up at Peace House, threatening to break the door down, Chief Branch and Alan had been the ones to respond. Alan had been his usual personable self. As near as Tia could tell, Branch didn't have a personable side. He'd informed her that, as chief, he ran a tight ship and that Harmony Grove had the lowest crime stats in the county. He'd assured her that he'd do whatever it took to keep his good reputation, so she'd better make sure everyone connected with her towed the line.

Katie pulled her lower lip between her teeth. "Aren't you concerned about the shelter being on the news?"

"They were careful. The local media has run stories before, covered fundraisers and such, and they've always been discreet."

Pam nodded. "There was a close-up shot of your

porch, with the boarded-up doorway, but nothing identifying it as yours. The two rockers were even outside the frame. They didn't mention Peace House or Harmony Grove, either, just said 'a Central Florida shelter.' That spans a lot of counties."

"True." They'd kept her face blurred, too. Maybe she should have asked them to distort her voice, an extra precaution.

Judging from the creases between Katie's eyebrows, the assurances soothed her concerns only slightly. Tia pursed her lips. Most of her clients knew she had personal experience with abuse, but she hadn't shared the details with any of them. Katie had more of an inside track than the others had. She'd been there when Tia got the call from Sergeant Bateman. Though the other woman hadn't been close enough to overhear the conversation, Tia's fear and panic had told its own story.

In spite of her assurances to Katie, Tia had concerns. She couldn't hope the report hadn't aired in North Florida. It would likely have hit all the stations between Harmony Grove and Macon. She could only hope that Victor hadn't identified her voice. Maybe he hadn't even seen the report. After spending the past five years in prison, he'd probably been out celebrating his freedom, drinking with friends.

There wasn't anyone she could ask. She hadn't maintained contact with any of their friends, because they'd all been *his* friends. She hadn't tried to reconnect with hers, either. Besides the possibility of putting them in danger, his finding her through her friends in their hometown of Madison would have been too easy.

Instead, she'd come three and a half hours south, making a new life for herself in Harmony Grove, and her mom and Randi had settled in Jacksonville after Randi's marriage. If Victor returned to Madison to track her down, he'd be out of luck. There was no one left for whom she was more than a memory.

Whether he tried to track her down or not, she wasn't naive enough to hope he'd had a change of heart. Men like him didn't change. At least not for the better. They only descended into greater depths of cruelty.

She would never wish what she'd experienced on another human being, but she couldn't help hoping that he'd moved on.

Whatever that entailed.

Tia walked from the garden center cash register, a receipt clutched in one hand, and BethAnn fell into step beside her. The sun was almost overhead, a dim glow behind a gray blanket. The weather forecast called for rain in the late afternoon and evening, which this time of year meant an approaching cold front.

Tia smiled over at her friend. "Thanks for helping me out."

"No problem. The Peace House Christmas tree is a tradition."

The first year, Tia had managed alone. A store employee had helped her secure the tree she'd purchased to the top of her Fiat. The trunk and lower part of the tree had jutted forward from her roof like the cannon barrel on a tank, extending beyond the front bumper by a foot or two. The upper limbs had drooped over her back window so far they'd almost dragged the road.

When she'd gotten to Harmony Grove, Tommy Willis had stopped his cruiser to help her unload the tree and made her promise to let him transport it with his pickup truck in the future. Last year, she'd made good on her promise, and he'd met her at Lowe's with his pickup truck. This time, BethAnn's company van would serve as the transport vehicle. Within a few minutes, a Walmart employee had the seven-foot tree tied to the racks, and they were pulling from the parking lot.

The first thing this morning, BethAnn had picked her up, and they'd gone together to Elizabeth Sloan's memorial service. Jason had been there, too. Tia had expected as much since he could no longer use distance as an excuse to stay away. After the service, he'd started to approach her several times, but someone else had gotten to her first. Finally, he'd given up and left.

At the first traffic light, Tia looked at BethAnn. "In a few minutes, we'll find out if anything blew up while I was gone."

She hadn't left the residents alone. Her part-time admin and accounting person, Monica, was there, working in Tia's small office. Her advocate was there, too. Kristina's expertise was children, and though she helped with the new client intake process if Tia was tied up elsewhere, Tia assigned her to work with all the young people who came through her doors. When Peace House expanded, she'd have to bring on more staff, both paid and volunteer. Acting as advocate for fifteen women instead of five or six, besides performing her duties as shelter director, wouldn't be doable.

BethAnn turned down Tranquility Drive. When she cleared the inn's back hedge, Jason was rounding the side of her house.

Tia narrowed her eyes. "What was he doing in my back yard?"

"Since your front entrance is boarded up, where else would he have gone? Either something happened while we were at Walmart, or he came to see you."

She hoped it was the latter. Not that she wanted to see him. It just beat the alternative. Any more excitement and Harold Reynolds would be circulating a petition to have her shut down.

BethAnn turned into the driveway. "Should I pull around back or do you think we can manage from here?"

"I'd rather not put ruts in Mrs. Garrett's lawn, so if you don't mind toting a tree that far, we'll do it from here."

"I don't think we'll be doing this alone." BethAnn's eyes were on Jason.

He greeted them as soon as they exited the van. "I assume the tree is going inside."

Tia nodded. This afternoon, she and the residents would decorate it. Anyone who didn't want to participate wouldn't be coerced. Usually the residents enjoyed the activity. For some, it was a much-needed distraction. For others, it was nostalgic, taking them back to happier times. Whatever their stories, Tia always tried to infuse her home with Christmas cheer, to create a bright spot in their otherwise dark worlds.

She rounded the van to untie the rope that ran from the top of the tree to the trailer hitch. Jason was already working on the others. She and BethAnn could have managed alone. They'd have opened the doors and stood on the seats to reach the top racks. But Jason could untie all the knots standing in the driveway and seemed intent on helping.

Soon the tree was down, and BethAnn nodded toward the house. "Jason and I have the tree. You can get the door."

When Tia swung it open, sounds of activity drifted out, accompanied by soft voices. Some of the women were preparing lunch. A dry-erase board hung near the doorway into the living room, chore assignments on one side and a menu on the other. Today's fare was submarine sandwiches, chips and fruit.

Pam turned toward them holding a butter knife streaked with mayonnaise. "Perfect timing. Tricia, Angela and I will have lunch ready in about ten minutes. Meanwhile, Katie's entertaining the kids."

BethAnn and Jason carried the tree into the living room while Tia closed the back door. When she followed, the room was vacant except for Damian who was sitting at one end of the sectional sofa, eyes glued to his game.

Jason picked up the hacksaw she'd retrieved from the shed this morning and started trimming the trunk, Damian's gaze fixed on him. Instead of that perpetual air of disinterest, the kid's eyes held curiosity.

Jason looked at him and smiled. "Hey, buddy."

The curiosity turned to disdain. "I'm not your buddy."

As the game reclaimed Damian's attention, Pam stepped into the doorway and gave Jason an apologetic smile. "This is Damian. I *have* taught him manners, although he seems to have left them at home."

Jason smiled. "Not a problem. We all have those kinds of days."

Pam disappeared back into the kitchen and Jason returned to his sawing. Soon a two-inch thick piece of the trunk lay on the floor.

Jason put down the saw and stood. "I could use a man's help getting this tree lifted and fastened into the stand."

Damian looked up at him with a sneer. "I hate Christmas." He stood and stormed from the room, likely headed out back.

Jason grinned at Tia. "Or you'll do."

The irreverent treatment hadn't fazed him. He was obviously better at relating to angry teenage boys than she was. Maybe he was a counselor or youth worker. Whatever his occupation, Tia had to give him credit. She wouldn't have even attempted it.

Jason lifted the tree, and she guided its trunk into the stand. As she tightened the bolts, BethAnn stood back to help them make it plumb. After directing them through a few adjustments, she brought a thumb and forefinger together in the OK sign. "Perfect."

Tia straightened and moved to stand next to BethAnn. Jason pulled out his keys and opened a pocketknife. While he cut the netting that wrapped the tree, BethAnn leaned toward Tia, her voice a whisper.

"He's cute."

Yeah, Tia had already made that observation, back

when he'd shown up at his grandmother's house on Wednesday.

"He's my adversary." Her words were as soft as BethAnn's. "He thinks I'm cheating him out of his inheritance."

Jason approached, a wadded-up roll of netting pressed between his hands. "Where is your trash can?"

Tia extended her arms. "I'll take it."

He passed off what he held, seriousness settling into his features. "Have you had any threats since Thursday night?"

"None. Did you see the news story?"

"What news story?"

"You tackled a fugitive. Wanted for bank robberies, even murder. Bad dude."

"Whoa." His eyebrows drew together. "You haven't seen anyone suspicious hanging around since then?"

A vague sense of dread sifted through her. "No. Why?"

He dropped his voice low enough that it wouldn't carry beyond the living room. "Someone followed me yesterday."

The dread intensified. "Followed you where?"

"All the way to Bartow."

She drew her eyebrows together, dread giving way to concern. "What were you doing in Bartow?"

The question escaped before she could filter it. Had he visited the courthouse to file paperwork contesting the will? No, he'd do that through a lawyer.

Her prying didn't seem to bother him. Maybe he didn't get annoyed easily. Angry, yes, if Thursday night's display was any indication. Anger was a different emotion from annoyance, one a lot more dangerous.

"I wasn't doing anything. I'd stopped at BethAnn's store. When I went in, a white SUV was parked in front of the mechanic's garage a few doors down."

Tia nodded. On the way to Winter Haven this morning, BethAnn had told her about Jason's visit. He'd likely been searching for ammunition to get the will set aside. BethAnn didn't think so. She wasn't naive, but she tended to give everybody the benefit of the doubt. It was only after someone had shattered her trust that they'd have to work hard to earn it back.

Jason continued. "I left about fifteen minutes later, and the SUV was still there. When I pulled away from the curb, the driver allowed a car between us then pulled out, too."

BethAnn pursed her lips. "Any chance he just happened to be leaving at the same time?"

"I considered that, but after he followed me through several turns, I knew that wasn't the case. I left Harmony Grove, headed toward Bartow on Highway 17. He followed me all the way there."

Tia frowned. "Did you try slowing down and letting him pass?"

"I did. He adjusted his speed to match mine. I didn't lose him until I got into town."

Tia drew her eyebrows together. This wasn't good. He'd just arrived a few days ago. He hadn't had time to make enemies. Except one.

Danielle's ex likely hadn't appreciated being body-slammed in her living room. Or having Jason on the verge of smashing his face. The man was being held without bond, but what if he had friends standing by to exact vengeance?

Tia's stomach churned with a toxic mix of worry, fear and guilt. The last she tried to squash. She hadn't asked him to get involved.

But he had. He apparently possessed a strong protective instinct, especially when women and children were involved. Maybe he was a cop or security guard instead of a counselor or youth worker.

"You're sure he didn't follow you back here?"

"I'm positive, so I'm hoping he doesn't know where I'm staying. I removed the Connecticut plate from the front and backed into the space in front of my room. So if he drives through town looking for my truck, it won't be so obvious."

Tia nodded. "That was smart." Maybe he had an occupation where stealth was important. FBI or undercover narcotics.

Pam stepped into the room. "Lunch is ready. Angela's getting Katie and the kids."

Tia looked at BethAnn and Jason. "You guys are welcome to stay."

BethAnn joined them occasionally. And Jason… well, the least she could do was offer him a meal after he'd set up the tree.

Jason smiled. "I'll take you up on that. Definitely beats a peanut butter sandwich alone in my room."

BethAnn held up a hand. "Thanks for the invite, but I've left Bonnie alone at the store long enough."

After BethAnn said her farewells, Tia led Jason through the dining room and into the kitchen. A large platter of subs lay on the counter, along with a plate of apple slices and halved bananas, peels on, and a bowl of chips.

Katie's twins stood next to their mother, holding their plates as she filled them. Pam's eight-year-old was old enough to handle her own. Her thirteen-year-old stood off to the side, waiting for the others to clear out.

After the four women had gone through, Tia motioned Damian over to the food. Her method for dealing with him was mostly ignoring him. Since that seemed to be what he wanted, she didn't feel guilty.

Jason was the last to dish up his plate. She waited for him to finish then tilted her head toward the door. "What do you say we eat outside?" She had two picnic tables in the back. One had been there when she moved in. The other had been donated shortly after she started the shelter.

Damian went out ahead of them. So had his sister and mother. The rest of the residents occupied the eight-seater table in the dining room, which left Damian with a table to himself. Jason started to move in his direction, and Tia shook her head. The man was a glutton for punishment.

She smiled at Pam. She and her daughter Julia sat facing the house, their backs to the yard. "Do you mind if we join you?"

"Absolutely not."

Tia sat opposite them and made introductions. "Jason is the one who tackled Danielle's boyfriend and restrained him until the police got there."

As he eased down next to Tia, Pam gave him an appreciate smile. "We owe you. Tia told us to go in the master bedroom and lock the door. Then she waited in the living room to face him alone. She's one brave lady."

Heat crept up Tia's cheeks, not as much from the compliment as the fact it was being given in front of Jason.

"I do what I have to, but this was a little more excitement than I prefer."

Jason grinned. "I agree."

Tia bit into an apple slice. "Where do you work?"

Or maybe she shouldn't have asked him that, in case he was FBI or something.

"Electric Boat."

She raised her eyebrows. "What is that? It sounds like a ride at an amusement park."

He grinned. "No amusement park rides. The full name is General Dynamics Electric Boat. We design and build submarines. We're not too far from the Navy sub base at Groton."

"So you're in the Navy?"

"No."

"You just build their submarines."

"I'm responsible for a small part of the process. I test the electronics after they're built."

"Interesting."

Damian apparently thought so too. He'd stopped eating and sat staring at Jason. That spark of interest Tia had seen in his eyes earlier was back, but stronger.

She smiled at Jason. "I made several guesses about what you might do for a living. That wasn't one of them."

"What kind of guesses?"

"Counselor, someone who works with youth, law enforcement, undercover narcotics, FBI agent."

Laughter burst from his mouth. "You have a good imagination."

"That's what I've been told." She grinned. "Maybe I should write a novel."

"Maybe you should. You'd have plenty of material to glean from."

What he said was true. Except using someone else's experiences didn't feel right, and she had no desire to relive her own.

She grew serious. "When do you have to be back?"

"Not till January."

"They let you go that long?"

"I have five weeks of vacation banked. The company shuts down the last two weeks of December. Employees can sign up to work if they want to, but most of them take vacation then. I tacked another three weeks on to the beginning. When I actually choose to go back will depend on how long it takes me to get things wrapped up here."

"It'll take time to go through all your grandparents' things."

"I know. Do you mind if I work there without you while I figure out what to do with everything?"

She took a big bite of her sub, buying herself some time before she'd have to answer. She'd felt before that he wasn't the type to vandalize the place. Judging from his actions Thursday night, she'd pegged him right.

He'd been angry then. Enough so, it had scared her. But the anger hadn't been directed at her. Instead, it had been aimed at the man who'd threatened her and her residents. Ever since, he'd seemed different, as if his attitude toward her had changed.

Or it could be a front, a way to get her to let down her guard, to lull her into trusting him. He had five weeks. Maybe he hoped to catch her unprepared. If that was what he was doing, he was wasting his time. Ten vacations wouldn't be enough time to gain her trust. She wasn't like BethAnn.

She finished chewing the bite she'd taken and swallowed. "Yeah, that's fine." Staying with him the entire time he worked wasn't feasible. "I'll be popping in and out, but you won't see me today." She had a tree to decorate.

She finished her lunch, then stood to take their empty plates. He followed her inside.

"Thanks for lunch."

"Thanks for your help with the tree."

"No problem. While I'm at Grandma's place, I'll check the shed and see if there might be a mower and weed eater."

"If there are, they've been sitting so long, the gas inside them has probably turned to sludge."

He smiled, showing white teeth that were straighter than his nose. That slight bend didn't look bad on him, though. Coupled with the strong jaw and those brown eyes enriched with golden flecks, he had an exotic charm that a lot of women would find irresistible.

Not that he was likely to try to use any of that charm on her. The walls she'd put up discouraged any men who thought about pursuing her. It was the surest way to avoid repeating past mistakes.

She watched him disappear around the side of the house. Beyond him, heavy gray clouds piled up on the horizon. Today's decorating would be restricted to inside. The exterior lights she'd leave for next week.

When she stepped into the living room, Tricia entered from the direction of the hall.

"Are we going to decorate the tree now?" She nodded toward the boxes stacked against one wall, each labeled *Christmas.*

"Sure. You want to round everybody up?"

Tricia nodded, then walked out to find the others. With high cheekbones, long eyelashes and a small, upturned nose, she possessed a delicate beauty. But she didn't recognize it. Her feet shuffled against the tile floor, and her shoulders were hunched forward, as if she was trying to be inconspicuous by occupying the smallest space possible.

Tia understood. That desire to be invisible could ingrain itself pretty deeply. So could the sense of worthlessness.

She didn't know Tricia's story. She didn't need to hear the details to put herself in the other woman's shoes. She understood all too well what it was like to live under the rule of a cruel man, to have her self-worth stamped out one blow at a time, her identity carved away until she no longer knew who she was.

Tia pressed the scarf to her throat.

She could almost feel the steel blade against her skin.

FIVE

A CHILLY BREEZE BLEW down Main street, picking up stray oak leaves and carrying them in lazy circles in some of the store alcoves. Yesterday's rain had come and gone, leaving behind temperatures twenty-five degrees cooler.

Jason walked down the sidewalk, his phone pressed to his ear. He'd called to check on his mother. She sounded fine. She always had a lilt to her voice—a sweetness underscored with joy. Sometimes she had to work at it. This was one of those mornings.

She'd chosen to watch her church services online instead of attending, a truer picture of her condition than the reassuring words. The chemo drug she'd been on previously had stopped working. This one worked but had more side effects. It also had a much higher copay.

"I started sorting the stuff at Grandma's house."

After leaving Tia's yesterday afternoon, he'd gotten through the master bedroom and bathroom. Currently the items to donate were piled on his grandparents' king-size bed, with the things he was taking back to Connecticut stacked on the dressers. After church, he would pick up boxes.

"Find anything interesting?"

"Nothing major. Some knickknacks and other odds and ends. I did finish clearing out Grandma's room at Winter Gardens, hauled the last of the furniture she had there to the house." He'd finished that yesterday. "I have her jewelry box, too."

"Your grandma had a lot of nice pieces."

"She did." Every Christmas and birthday had garnered another sparkly gift from Grandpa. "I'll bring the box to you. You can choose what you'd like to keep, and we'll sell the rest."

"You should save some pieces for your future wife."

Jason stifled a snort. His mother knew better, but her optimistic nature wouldn't allow her to quit hoping for a daughter-in-law—one who would return her affections this time—along with a grandchild or two. Her hopes were in vain. He'd been there, done that and had no intention of jumping back into that mess anytime soon.

She drew in a breath, signaling a change in subject. "It'll be interesting to see what you find at the house. I wouldn't put it past your grandmother to have stashed something of value there."

"I doubt it. Grandma wasn't one of those folks who didn't trust banks and kept her life savings hidden in coffee cans."

In fact, she'd used a local credit union. The Mid-Florida checking account was listed in the will, left to Tia and her shelter, along with the house and its furnishings. The odds of finding enough inside to keep his mother's treatment going for a few more weeks were pretty slim.

"I know her." There was conviction behind the

fatigue. "She loved you and would have wanted to provide for you if there was any chance the lawyers could locate you. Since she left you the personal effects, I believe there's something among them of value."

He didn't share her conviction. "She made the new will five and a half months ago. Considering she's spent the last five years in a retirement facility, she wouldn't have had the means to make any kind of provisions."

A gust blew, sending a slight chill through him. Fortunately, he'd packed a few sweaters. He wasn't complaining, though. This was nothing compared to winter in Connecticut. The sun shone from a clear blue sky, its heat penetrating his jeans and knit sweater.

"You sound like you're walking."

"I'm headed to church. It's such a gorgeous day, I figured I'd walk instead of taking the truck."

The nice weather wasn't the only reason he was walking. If whoever followed him last week was still lurking about, he was safest with his truck right where it was—sitting in front of his room, backed in, rather than parked in a public space.

"Enjoy that Florida warmth." There was a smile in her tone. "There's a foot of snow on the ground here."

"I wish I could bring you back." The cold bothered her, especially now. Those twenty extra pounds she'd carried for years had fallen away some time ago.

He wouldn't risk it, though. His father was no longer here. He hadn't even come to yesterday's memorial service. But until Jason got word that the man was dead, he and his mother would never be free.

"What church are you going to?"

"Hope Community Church. You wouldn't know it. It's a newer church."

He'd done an internet search and found only two in Harmony Grove. One was the church his grandparents had attended. The other one was closer to Tranquility Inn. It also boasted a contemporary worship style and a pastor who looked like he wasn't much older than Jason.

He didn't know anybody, but that wouldn't stop him from visiting. Church attendance had become a regular thing since his mom had dragged him pouting and protesting into the Connecticut church when he'd been fifteen. That decision, combined with a youth pastor who refused to be put off by an angry, rebellious teenager, had probably saved his life. It had kept him out of prison, anyway.

A soft sigh came through the phone. "I hope you enjoy your service. I'm going to lie down until mine begins."

His chest squeezed at the weakness in her voice. He pocketed his phone, then clenched a fist, anger building inside.

He couldn't direct it at Tia. From everything he'd gathered, she hadn't done anything to steal his inheritance. He couldn't even direct it at his grandmother. In her situation, he'd have done the same thing—anything to keep his father from inheriting.

That left one place for him to direct his anger—at himself. There had to have been a way to let his grandparents know he was alive and well without putting his mother in danger.

A pickup truck passed him and made a right turn at the next street. On a Sunday morning, traffic on Main Street was sparse. According to the signs on the doors, several of the businesses wouldn't open until the afternoon.

In the distance, a gold sedan approached. Behind it was a white SUV. As the vehicles drew closer, Jason squinted, his pulse quickening. The SUV bore the Toyota emblem. Was it the same one that had followed him? Maybe, maybe not. Both the RAV4 and the Highlander were popular models, and white was a popular color, especially in Florida where summer temperatures often hovered near 100.

He shielded his eyes against the sun shining from its mid-morning position ahead of him. The sedan continued forward at the same speed. The SUV seemed to be slowing down. It was close enough now for him to see the silhouette of the driver. He wore a hat, similar to the one on the person who'd followed him to Bartow.

Jason glanced around him, searching for an inconspicuous place to stand. There wasn't one. Twenty feet ahead was an awning, but the entry wasn't recessed. The business he'd just passed was the same way. There weren't even any trees or signs to duck behind.

He pulled his phone from his pocket and stopped to lean against a lamp post. He'd act as if he was texting someone, then record the license number as the vehicle passed. A block away, the SUV made a sudden left turn, disappearing behind a building before Jason could even identify the model.

The anger that had surged through him earlier returned full force. Or maybe it hadn't yet abated. Too many things in his life were out of his control—his Mom's health, his shaky finances, the life-saving inheritance he'd received then lost, and now a threat he didn't know how to combat, because he didn't know who or where it was coming from.

A few minutes later, Jason turned the same corner. Hope Community Church was two buildings ahead on the left. The SUV was gone.

When Jason stepped inside the church, he'd been wrong about not knowing anyone. BethAnn stood in the aisle about halfway up, in a small cluster of people. The moment she saw him, her face lit with a smile that was reflected in her eyes. She raised her hand in an enthusiastic wave. After he approached, she made introductions. Melissa was the bride-to-be that BethAnn had assisted the day Jason visited her store. Chris was her fiancé.

BethAnn continued. "Unless you're meeting someone, you can sit with us and Tia."

Tia? Jason looked toward the door as Tia started up the aisle. Morning sunshine streamed through the frosted side windows, bathing her in a soft glow. Silky waves framed her face, and her lightweight lavender sweater fell over fitted black pants. As she drew closer, full pink lips curved upward in a friendly smile.

He returned the gesture, tamping down the unwanted attraction. It was pointless. Besides, he was in church. When they all filed into the nearest row, Jason ended up seated next to Tia, probably BethAnn's doing. He couldn't say he minded.

Chris looked over at him. He was seated on Jason's

other side. "Are you visiting?"

"Sort of. My grandmother passed away and I'm here to clean out her house."

The other man smiled. "I can relate. A few months ago, my dad passed away and I came for the same reason. Ended up staying. Now I'm living in the house I grew up in and running my dad's marine store." His smile widened to a grin. "And I'm engaged to my college sweetheart. You never know where life will lead."

Jason nodded. How true. Two years ago, both his mom and his bank account were healthy. But regardless of the uncertainty of life, it wasn't likely to lead him to Florida. Not permanently, anyway.

Six people filed onto the platform in front and took their place behind instruments and microphones. As they led into the first song, he smiled. It was one he knew from his church in Connecticut. So were the next two, and he enjoyed singing along.

Tia obviously did, too. At one point, she glanced up at him. Something passed between them, a sort of connection. It went beyond their mutual affection for his grandmother. Even beyond Tia's cause—the fact that he'd lived it and she likely had, too. It was deeper than physical attraction.

He hadn't known about their shared faith. When they'd sat down to lunch yesterday, he'd bowed his head for a quick prayer of thanks. Maybe Tia had done the same thing. He hadn't looked.

He slid her a sideways glance. She was singing with her head tipped back and her eyes closed, the words flowing from her heart. Her faith was obviously as sincere as his own.

Not that he was perfect. He wasn't. Some bad habits died with the first "Forgive me, Jesus." Others dug in and held on, refusing to be uprooted. He'd come a long way since his angry teenage years. His fuse was longer now, his hot buttons less reactive. But he still hadn't mastered the concept of letting go and trusting God while his well-laid plans unraveled.

After the last song ended, the worship team exited the platform and the congregation sat. A man stepped behind the pulpit. Jason recognized him from his picture on the church's website. He looked even younger in person. As he proceeded with his message, there was nothing timid in his delivery. He'd titled the sermon *Joy in the Midst of Trials*.

His scripture text was familiar. As soon as he mentioned Matthew 6:33, Jason could have quoted the verse word for word. He'd memorized it as a teenager and reminded himself of the command several times in the intervening years—"Seek ye first the kingdom of God, and his righteousness, and all these things shall be added unto you."

He was trying. He thought he'd been doing a pretty good job of seeking God's will, at least during those periods when he wasn't obsessed with trying to figure things out on his own. He was still waiting for the last part of that verse. Any time God wanted to start doing some of that "adding," it would be fine by him.

A good place to start would be with answering some of those heartfelt prayers for his mother. No matter how many nights he'd paced the floor, he'd watched one treatment after another deliver disappointing results. Some glimmer of light at the end of the tunnel would be nice. He wouldn't object to some financial blessings, either. He sighed, dragging his thoughts back to the message.

The pastor was speaking with conviction, one index finger raised. "When you're worrying about things you have no control over, trying to finagle them to go your way, you're monitoring God's responsibilities."

What, had the guy read his mind? No, he knew better. It wasn't the first time God had used a sermon to nail him with exactly what he'd needed to hear. He just wasn't sure how to put this one into practice.

As the last strains of the closing song faded to silence thirty minutes later, the pastor's final charge echoed through his mind.

"God is in control. You are not. Accept the boundaries of your domain. That's where you'll find freedom."

Freedom. The thought was appealing. As he followed Tia toward the exit door, he rolled his shoulders, trying to release the ever-present tension.

He'd be the first to admit that he wasn't in control. It was driving him crazy. He couldn't do anything to lessen his mother's suffering. No amount of worrying was going to add a single dollar to his bank account. And no, he hadn't accepted it. He wasn't sure he could.

He stepped into the sunshine. The chill that had been in the air during his walk from the inn was gone.

BethAnn turned to face the others. "Where does everyone want to go?"

Melissa pursed her lips. "Is anyone else in the mood for Italian?"

Chris grinned. "I'm always in the mood for pizza."

"Tia?"

"Pappy's it is." Tia turned to Jason. "Once a month, we all go out to eat after church. This is that Sunday. You're welcome to join us."

He'd intended to eat then head over to his grandparents' house. But Pappy's Pizzeria was a whole lot more appealing than the cold ham and cheese sandwich he'd planned to make, and lunch out with Tia and her friends beat eating alone in his room.

"I'll take you up on that."

Tia's gaze circled the lot. "I don't see your truck. Where did you park?"

"I walked."

She addressed the others. "Jason's with me. We'll see you there."

Jason followed her to the Fiat. The stuff at his grandmother's could wait. He wasn't counting on finding anything life-changing. He'd never shared his mother's optimistic outlook.

That wouldn't stop him from taking the time to cover every square inch of the house. If his grandmother had ensured he'd inherit something more valuable than some old clothes and books, he had no intention of leaving it behind.

Tia looked over at Jason squeezed into the passenger seat of her Fiat. His head was about two inches from the roof, and his knees almost touched the dash. But it beat walking, considering the pizzeria was on the edge of town, two miles past the church.

When she'd started up the aisle and seen Jason

standing there, her first reaction had been surprise, then pleasure. Then had come guilt. She should have invited him herself.

BethAnn had probably done the honors, with ulterior motives. Though she had no interest in seeking out romance in her own life, she had no problem with using her matchmaking skills on her friends. According to Melissa, BethAnn had played a big part in bringing Chris and her together.

If Tia wasn't careful, she'd be next. BethAnn had already made the observation that Jason was good-looking. Tia hadn't argued, because he was. Today, he looked especially good in his black dress jeans and teal-colored polo. His hair rested in soft layers, full but without curl, as if he'd hit it with a blow dryer. He smelled good, too, a fresh woodsy scent detectible now that they were in the close confines of the car.

She eased to a stop at a traffic light. "I hope you enjoyed our service."

"I did. It's similar to mine at home. When I searched for churches online, I found two in Harmony Grove—my grandparents' church and Hope Community Church. Hope looked like it might attract a younger crowd."

So he'd found the church online. She'd accused BethAnn unjustly. "Hope has only been around for about six years. When I first came, it was meeting in a store front." She hadn't gone right away. It had taken several months of gentle coercion from Mrs. Garrett before she'd broken down and given the church a try. "We moved to our new location two years ago."

"How long have you been here?"

"A little over four years."

After escaping Victor, she'd spent two months in an emergency shelter in Orlando, before moving to a more permanent facility for another six months. She'd needed every bit of that time, along with the counseling and guidance that had come with it, to get on her feet—physically, mentally and emotionally. During those months, she'd made brief trips to Madison to testify against Victor, complete their divorce proceedings and make sure he was solidly out of her life. Without the support of her advocate, she wouldn't have managed even that.

It had taken her a while to find the inner strength she had possessed before Victor had stamped it all out of her. It wasn't until arriving in Harmony Grove and finally accepting Mrs. Garrett's invitations to church that she'd stepped onto the path toward true healing. That restoration had begun in earnest when she'd accepted an even greater invitation—to become part of the family of God. If Victor ever did find her, he wouldn't see the woman he'd broken and defeated. That woman was dead and buried.

"How did you wind up doing what you're doing? I mean, I'm pretty sure most young girls don't think, 'I want to be a domestic violence shelter director when I grow up.'"

"You're right. From the time I was twelve, I thought I'd be a forensic psychologist or psychiatrist." She grinned over at him. "Mom used to watch a lot of crime shows."

She eased to a stop at a traffic light. "I'd done three years of college right out of high school, then had to…" She hesitated. "I stopped for a while."

Right after she married Victor, he'd convinced her

to take a term off. It was so they could spend more time together, he'd said, to get their marriage off to a good start. Three-quarters of the way toward a bachelor's in psychology, and she hadn't recognized him for what he was. By the time the term was over, he'd dug his claws of control into her so far, she'd never gone back.

"When I first moved to Harmony Grove, I did clerical work for a medical clinic during business hours and volunteered at a Lakeland shelter nights and weekends. I also enrolled in online courses and finished my bachelor's degree during that time."

"You were one busy lady."

"The schedule was a little extreme." It had been a great way to keep the nightmares at bay. By the time she'd fallen into bed at night, she'd been too exhausted to dream.

The light changed and she stepped on the gas. "At the other shelter, I shadowed one of the advocates until I was sufficiently trained to begin taking on clients of my own. That was when I realized that this was what I wanted to do. I got the nonprofit set up and the rest is history."

That was the abbreviated version. The reality involved months of work—organizing a board of directors, completing mounds of paperwork, planning fundraisers, writing requests for grants and handling dozens of other tedious tasks.

A quarter mile ahead, Pappy's red, green and white sign stood at the edge of the road, and Tia slowed. "I've since been working on my master's. I've got two more classes and my thesis to do. I'm taking a break this term and going back after the first of the year." This time the break had been her choice.

"I really admire what you're doing."

His tone held a warmth that hadn't been there before. When she glanced over at him, that warmth was reflected in his eyes. Her stomach dissolved into a quivery lump.

She tightened her grip on the wheel. *Victor, remember Victor.* Besides, she didn't have time for a relationship, even a short-term one. What she was doing was too important to allow distractions.

She took her foot from the accelerator and allowed the car to slow. "Have you ever been to Pappy's?"

"Yeah. My grandparents used to sometimes take my mom and me there for lunch."

He and his mom, but not his dad. Maybe the man wasn't a part of their lives by then. "How does your dad feel about the will?" With an inheritance of ten dollars, he'd received less than Jason had. The ten-dollar provision had probably been to cover some kind of legal base.

"I don't know. I haven't talked to him since my mom and I left seventeen years ago."

He shrugged, a gesture that was at odds with the hardness in his tone. Apparently, his relationship with his dad hadn't been good. Maybe the man had been abusive. Or maybe he'd abandoned them.

Whatever the case, Jason seemed to have turned out all right. Though she'd known him only a few days, his actions had impressed her—his willingness to get involved when she and her residents had been in danger, his insistence on helping wherever he saw a need, his concern for a kid who rejected any form of kindness. The more time she spent with him, the worse she felt about keeping his inheritance.

She needed to get over it. She needed the house, as well as the funds to fix it up, not for herself, but for the women and children who would come through those doors. Besides, this was what Elizabeth Sloan had wanted. Who was she to deny the woman her final wishes?

Tia pulled into a parking space, and Chris stopped his Blazer in the next spot over. BethAnn parked her van at the other end of the row.

Jason rested his hand on the door handle. "I guess the shelter runs smoothly in your absence?"

"As long as no one makes any unauthorized phone calls." She gave him a sheepish grin. "Monica and Kristina, two of my staff members, are there. Every Sunday morning, I attend church, and once a month, I do lunch out with my friends."

She shoved the car into park and killed the engine. "The residents are encouraged to watch the services remotely, there at the shelter. Transportation is an issue for liability reasons, so we don't bring them to the church. In fact, they usually arrive at and leave the shelter via public transportation, sometimes Uber or Lyft."

She opened her car door, and pleasant aromas wrapped around her. "If I wasn't hungry before, I am now."

Jason smiled. "Amen to that."

Once inside, the hostess walked them toward a large corner booth. A young woman wove between tables carrying a tray holding drinks. Tia waved, and the woman nodded a greeting.

Priscilla Parker wasn't in Tia's circle of friends, but

she was a fixture at Pappy's. She was young, early twenties, but she was good. According to BethAnn, she'd started serving there Friday and Saturday nights while still in high school.

BethAnn slid into the middle of the booth. Chris and Melissa followed, leaving the other end for Tia and Jason. The hostess passed out menus, promising them Priscilla would be with them shortly.

By the time Priscilla arrived with apologies for keeping them waiting, they'd already decided to split three medium pizzas. She finished taking their orders, and BethAnn gave her one of her signatures smiles. "I'm glad you're still here."

When she walked away, Tia lowered her voice. "Is there a reason she wouldn't be?"

"Have you seen her new car? A late model Lotus Exige."

"Sounds expensive." Not being a car person, the name didn't mean anything.

"More than all of our rides put together. Hammy bought it for her."

Hammy Driggers, her boyfriend. His father owned Driggers Porcelain a short distance outside of town. Tia had met Hammy and his brother, Spike, not long after coming to Harmony Grove.

The old man was okay, but something about Hammy made Tia uneasy, as if he was guarding dangerous secrets. Spike did more than make her uneasy—he scared her. Though he'd never threatened her, he put out a tough vibe that bordered on cruel.

Priscilla Parker with either of the Driggers boys didn't make a good combination. She was the kind of woman that men like Victor preyed on—attractive, trusting and a little naive. Easy to break.

Or maybe she was smarter than Tia thought. "She might be keeping her options open, unwilling to give up her means of supporting herself."

Maintaining some independence was never a bad idea. Neither was keeping as many pre-relationship contacts as possible. With men like Victor, isolation was often their first line of offense.

Melissa looked at BethAnn. "Where's Kevin today?"

Tia had wondered the same thing. Kevin Burgess usually joined them, letting his grandfather man their bookstore for the first hour it opened on Sunday afternoons.

"He's home trying to kick a case of strep throat. Unfortunately, I think it's kicking him."

Melissa gave her a sad smile. "Poor guy. I hope he gets over it quickly." She shook her head. "You need to give in and go out with him."

"He hasn't asked."

"Because he doesn't know you're interested."

"I'm not. We're just friends."

BethAnn looked toward the entry door and frowned. "Great. Guess who just walked in."

Tia followed her gaze. It was Chief Branch. Considering he wasn't in uniform, he was apparently off duty. A lot of people didn't care for Chief Branch. His conceited swagger and patronizing attitude had a way of making enemies of good, law-abiding citizens.

Jason looked from Tia to Melissa and back again. "Who?"

BethAnn tilted her head. "See the guy over there strutting like a peacock, looking like he's spent way too much time at the buffet? He's our chief of police.

Stay in Harmony Grove for long, and you'll have a run-in with him eventually."

Jason cast her a doubt-filled glance. "I don't usually have run-ins with the police. I try to stay on the right side of the law."

BethAnn responded, her eyes still locked on Branch. "You don't have to do anything wrong to get on his bad side. Ask Tia."

Tia frowned. "Anything that requires him to put in some effort is a problem, and he lets you know it. He doesn't make any distinction between suspects and victims."

Branch scanned the restaurant. When his gaze settled on the five of them seated in the corner, his eyes narrowed.

Jason leaned closer to Tia. "I believe you now. If those daggers were real, you'd be dead."

Or maybe Melissa would be the casualty. His grudge against her seemed a lot more personal.

The hostess had just seated Branch at a table close to the opposite wall when the door opened again and Harold Reynolds entered.

Tia released another groan. "Can it get any worse?"

BethAnn heaved a sigh. "Your favorite neighbor."

His gaze circled only half the room before landing on Branch. He spoke to the hostess, and she led him away...straight to the chief's table.

"No way." Tia had silently asked if it could get any worse. Yeah, it could. What relationship did Reynolds have with Branch?

As soon as the hostess walked away, Branch leaned toward Reynolds, and Reynolds looked in their direction.

Tia crossed her arms. "They're conspiring against me."

Jason lifted his eyebrows. "Are you sure you're not overreacting? Maybe they're friends having a casual Sunday lunch."

BethAnn came to her defense. "I know it sounds paranoid, but you don't know them. Reynolds has wanted Tia and her shelter gone since day one, and something about Branch just seems shady. I've never trusted him."

Priscilla arrived with the pizzas, a stack of plates and three serving utensils. "Anything else I can get you?"

A chorus of "that's good" and "no" went around the table. After Chris said grace, thick slices of pizza soon filled the plates. Tia pushed thoughts of Branch and Reynolds to the back of her mind.

Eventually she'd be moved into the Sloan place and wouldn't have to deal with Reynolds anymore. Since the house was outside the city limits and was in the sheriff department's jurisdiction, she wouldn't have to deal with Branch, either.

When they walked away from the table an hour later, all the plates were empty. Chris held the door for BethAnn. "Give Kevin our well wishes."

BethAnn nodded. "I will. I'm planning to stop by later to check on him, maybe bring him some chicken soup."

The rest of them filed out and Chris released the door.

BethAnn pursed her lips. "Is chicken soup good for a sore throat? Maybe that's a cold or a fever. Maybe I should bring him some cold yogurt."

Melissa smiled. "Whatever you bring, I'm sure it'll be appreciated."

After saying her farewells, Tia slid into the Fiat and waited for Jason to join her. "What are you doing the rest of the day?"

"First, I'm going to hit Walmart and pick up about two dozen boxes. Then I'll head over to Grandma and Grandpa's place. If I feel really ambitious, I might get the upstairs finished."

She pulled from the parking lot and headed for the inn. "I'm glad you joined us."

"I enjoyed it. Hot pizza beats a cold ham and cheese sandwich any day. The company wasn't half bad, either."

His tone was teasing, but his smile wasn't. Another flutter passed through her stomach.

She squelched the unwanted reaction. Anything more than friendship was out of the question. Even then, she needed to stay on guard. She hadn't fully ruled out the possibility that he'd try to somehow swindle her out of what his grandmother had willed to the shelter.

She hadn't forgotten his display of anger the night Danielle's boyfriend had shown up, either. Maybe the man had a propensity toward violence. He had a short fuse, anyway. People like that were better to keep at a distance, at least emotionally.

"Wait!" The word cut across her thoughts. "Turn around."

Tia swiveled her head at the terse command.

"The vehicle that followed me, I think it just passed, going the other direction."

Tia took the next left, turned around and got back

onto Main Street. If the vehicle was ahead of them, it wasn't visible.

"Do you see it?"

He shook his head. "I can't see around the pickup truck."

"Driving a Fiat, there's not much I *can* see around."

Passing wasn't an option, not until she got away from town.

"There." He pointed out the right side of the windshield. "He just turned up there past the gas station."

She clutched the wheel more tightly, willing the pickup driver to go faster. He didn't. When she reached the corner, the SUV was two blocks ahead, the path between them clear.

She stomped hard on the gas and her little car surged forward. "Should we call the police?"

"Not yet. I don't even know if it's the same person. If we can get a tag number, though, the cops can run it."

The gap between her and the SUV gradually closed. Jason leaned forward in his seat, phone clutched in one hand. "It's a Highlander. I wasn't sure till now. Get a little closer." He touched the screen and brought the phone to his mouth. "KFV…" He rested the other hand on the dash. "One-zero-six. Or maybe it's an eight."

The SUV made a sudden right turn. When Tia followed, the driver had obviously increased his speed. The distance between them grew. Brake lights came on briefly, and the vehicle took a left turn far too fast. Tires squealed and the rear end fishtailed.

"Call the police." Tia glanced over at Jason, but he

already had the phone pressed to his ear.

She breathed a sigh of relief. Law enforcement could take it from here. She wouldn't risk hurting someone by engaging in a high-speed chase through town.

Jason explained the situation to the dispatcher, giving them both possible tag numbers. When he ended the call, he dropped his hand into his lap, still clutching the phone. "They're putting out a BOLO for the vehicle."

After making a couple of turns, Tia was again headed toward the inn. "Did you get a good look at the driver?"

"Not enough to identify him. I'd been looking at you. I glanced forward again right before he passed and got a quick glimpse of a hat and sunglasses. I was pretty sure it was him, but the way he took off confirmed it."

"If they don't catch him, we'll ask them to run the tag numbers. I'm guessing the owner of that Highlander is someone with a connection to Danielle's boyfriend."

It couldn't have anything to do with Victor. The suspicious vehicle had shown up too early—several hours before the news story aired, likely even before Victor had been released.

Tia chewed her lower lip. Jason was in danger because of his involvement with her. It was Danielle's fault, but Danielle was Tia's responsibility.

Maybe the police would find the driver and the threat would go away. Then Jason would be able to safely finish the work at his grandparents' place and head back to Connecticut.

Unless Victor found her first. If that happened, she wouldn't be the only one in danger.

Everyone close to her would be, too.

SIX

JASON PULLED ONTO Main Street from the inn's parking lot. Today should be a productive day. Yesterday afternoon, he'd purchased three dozen boxes and thirty black trash bags, then stopped at his grandparents' house. He hadn't done any more sorting, but he'd packed up what he'd already dragged out of closets and dresser drawers and stuffed the items into boxes labeled either "donate" or "take home." A few items, mostly papers, had gone into trash bags.

He was too frugal to throw away anything of value. He'd spent too much of his childhood dirt poor. His father had held onto jobs barely long enough to provide the necessities, sometimes not even that long. More than once, his mom had had to risk his father's fury by asking for help from his grandparents to keep the power on or stop a pending eviction.

As he passed Tranquility Way, he cast a glance to his right. With the inn and its fenced garden blocking his view, he couldn't say whether Tia's car was sitting in her drive, but early in the morning, chances were good she was home.

He'd enjoyed the time he'd spent with her yesterday, both at church and eating out afterward. He couldn't deny the attraction he'd felt since the moment he'd seen her standing in his grandmother's hallway, fear she was clearly trying to hide swimming in her blue eyes.

It was more than simple attraction, though. She intrigued him. She cared for the women and children in her home with a sacrificial love, while possessing the strength and tenacity needed to start and keep a ministry like Peace House going. She was vulnerable during unguarded moments, like in the park, but possessed an underlying fierceness that came out when she or her women were threatened. There were so many facets to her personality, facets he really wanted to explore.

He'd asked what had led her to set up her shelter, and she'd answered him, sort of. She'd explained how volunteering at the shelter in Lakeland had led to her desire to start her own but hadn't said how she'd begun volunteering there in the first place. Something told him there was more behind her choice of profession than simply stumbling into it.

A police car moved down Main toward him, and he squinted through the windshield as it passed. The chief he'd seen at the restaurant sat at the wheel. As Jason checked his rearview mirror, the cruiser's left blinker came on. It was preparing to turn down Tranquility Drive. Uneasiness sifted through him, and he made a right on the next street to circle the block. His sorting could wait until he'd made sure the cruiser had nothing to do with Tia and Peace House.

When he came up Tranquility from the other end, the cruiser was parked at the edge of her front yard. He pulled into the driveway and turned off the truck.

Tia stood on the porch with the chief. She glanced in Jason's direction, her jaw tight and her lips drawn into a straight line. She wasn't happy. He'd known her for four days, and he was already able to sense her moods.

As he stepped from his truck, the chief turned to give him a once-over before returning his attention to Tia. He stood in profile, hands on his hips, chest poked out in a pose of assumed importance.

"You can't leave this boarded up. It's against code. You're blocking ingress and egress. Besides that, it's an eyesore."

Jason tightened his grip on his keys. Her neighbor had likely made a complaint at lunch yesterday, and instead of allowing her time to get the damage repaired, the chief was giving her grief.

Tia matched his pose, standing almost toe-to-toe with him. He was a half head taller than she was and two to three times her weight, but what she lacked in size, she made up for in determination and grit.

"I have no intention of leaving the front door boarded. It'll be fixed by the end of the week, as soon as Andy gets back from vacation."

As Jason walked up the drive, Branch ignored him. "It should have been done by the end of last week."

Jason stopped at the bottom of the porch steps. "That would have been Saturday. This just happened Thursday night. Requiring the frame to be rebuilt and a door installed in forty-eight hours is a little unreasonable, don't you think?"

Branch turned and stared down at him, letting his gaze linger. Jason didn't fidget. He didn't even feel the urge. If Branch hoped to make him uncomfortable with those disdain-filled eyes, he was going to be disappointed. Instead of being intimidating, he came across as a small-town cop who thought way too much of himself.

Finally, he cocked one bushy eyebrow. "And you are?"

"Jason Sloan."

"A pesky outsider sticking his nose in where it doesn't belong."

"No, a good neighbor, trying to protect women and children from bullies."

Branch turned his back, effectively dismissing him. "You've got till five tomorrow. Get it done, or Mrs. Garrett will be getting a violation notice from Code Enforcement."

Tia tossed her head. "You do what you want. By the time she gets it, the work will be done. I'd suggest saving the trees, along with everybody's time doing unnecessary paperwork."

Branch stalked to his car, his gait broadcasting his annoyance. He'd lost that proud, composed air he'd had when Jason first arrived. Tia had gotten the upper hand.

As Branch drove away, she gave Jason an appreciative smile. "Thanks for sticking up for me."

"Anytime. Although, you didn't need it. You were handling things pretty well on your own."

"It's still appreciated." Her smile faded. "His threat about Code Enforcement is probably real. I'll give Mrs. Garrett a call and let her know she might be getting a violation notice. I already told her about the incident. She knows I'll take care of any damage."

She leaned against one of the posts supporting the

porch roof. "Are you headed to the house?"

"Yeah. I'd planned to put in a long day, see if I can finish the upstairs."

Except since Branch's visit, he was considering changing those plans and tackling a different project. That one would be over Tia's objections.

He nodded toward the boarded-up opening. "Is your door salvageable?"

"Yeah, it's in the shed. Since there's no glass panel, it fared pretty well."

He'd thought so, but at the time he and Danielle's boyfriend had plowed through it, he hadn't been paying much attention to the door.

"Good. So you'll just need to have the jamb rebuilt."

"Yep. Andy should be able to knock that out in a half day or less."

The soft hum of a car engine approached behind him. When he turned, a police cruiser was coming to a stop behind her Fiat.

Not again. But one glance through the windshield revealed a much younger driver. Alan White, the same one who'd responded yesterday when they'd called about the white Highlander. Maybe he had news.

As the officer opened the door, Jason and Tia approached.

"Did you find out anything?" Tia's tone held hope.

"Yes, just not what we'd hoped. The second tag number you gave us came back registered to a Toyota Highlander, but it's owned by one of the car rental companies."

Jason frowned. "They're supposed to get driver's license info."

"They did. We ran it, and it's fake."

"How did he pay for the rental?"

"Prepaid Visa card, so we can't even track him that way. He returned the vehicle yesterday afternoon in Lakeland. Judging from the time you guys called and the time on the rental place's paperwork, he must have hightailed it over there right after you called us."

Jason heaved a sigh. All that investigation, and they didn't know any more than they had yesterday.

Actually, they knew less. Yesterday, he knew that someone driving a white Highlander had a bone to pick with him. That was no longer the case. The guy could go somewhere else and get himself a different set of wheels.

Jason frowned. With no idea of what kind of vehicle to watch for, he'd be a sitting duck.

"This is where you'll be sleeping." Tia stood in the open doorway of her master bedroom, her newest resident behind her. She'd come through a referral from one of the special services agencies and arrived forty minutes ago, having taken the Winter Haven Area Transit bus from Bartow. "You'll be sharing the room with Tricia and Angela, the two ladies you met in the kitchen."

The woman followed her into the room, clutching a large tote. Tia stopped in front of a dresser. "These two drawers are yours."

This client actually had something to put in them. Some of the women escaped with little more than the clothes on their backs. Others had the time and privacy to toss together some necessities. A few had created an exit plan well in advance. If there was a class on preparedness, Tia's newest client could teach it.

Her name was Jasmine, but she preferred to be called Jaz. She didn't just have a couple of changes of clothes hidden away. She had, during a calmer time, managed to collect identification, legal documents, health insurance papers, bank account information and a long list of emergency phone numbers. She'd even socked away a few twenties to get a prepaid credit card.

Jasmine opened one of the drawers and instead of unpacking the items, laid the whole tote inside. Maybe she felt safer that way, ready to run again at a moment's notice. After pushing the drawer shut, Jasmine straightened and turned. "Thank you."

Though her appreciation wasn't reflected in a smile, it shone in her eyes. She was bigger than the other women, tall and large-boned, but a lot of her bulk was muscle.

As soon as she'd arrived, Tia had met with her for the intake interview and had gotten her story. She had a head start on some of the women. Her abuse had gone on for months instead of years. Both sides of her jaw held a yellow tint, final remnants of what were probably some ugly bruises a week or so ago. The damage to her left eye was more recent, the swelling severe enough to keep her from opening it more than halfway.

The confidence that should have come from size and physical strength was gone, likely pounded out of her. She compensated with loudness.

Tia gave her a smile. "You're welcome. If there's anything you need, don't hesitate to ask."

She nodded. "I've been thinking about leaving him for a while, but this was the final straw." She indicated the side of her head with a flick of her wrist. The gesture wasn't aimed at her swollen eye.

The woman was sporting the worst haircut ever. Katie's twins could have done a better job. The light brown strands varied in length from a half inch to two inches, with several patches cut almost against her scalp. During the interview, she'd told Tia that her husband had dragged her into the bathroom by her hair and taken scissors to it.

Jasmine brushed past Tia and stalked out the bedroom door, anger radiating from her. In the hall, she spun to face Tia. "I didn't tell you why he thought I deserved this." Judging from her volume, she wasn't concerned about who else learned her story. "We were at the grocery store, and I ran into a guy I'd known in high school. Benny had gone to get a box of cereal, and when he came back, the guy was talking to me. That's it. This was the result." She repeated the frustrated gesture.

Tia kept the placating words, "it'll grow back," to herself. That wasn't what the woman needed to hear. Her hair *would* grow back, just like the bruises would fade and disappear. But saying so would minimize what she felt right now.

As Tia followed her into the living room, the aromas coming from the kitchen hit her full force. Tricia and Angela had started lunch when Jasmine first arrived—homemade vegetable soup and biscuits.

Although it wasn't part of her chore assignment, Pam had asked for a hand spade and lawn rake and spent the morning weeding and tidying up the yard. Katie had signed herself out and, with Pam's permission, had taken the kids to the park. The three younger ones, anyway. The last she'd seen Damian was through her office window, sitting at one of the picnic tables with his Gameboy.

When they entered the kitchen, Tricia gave them a half smile. "Two more minutes on the biscuits, and lunch will be ready."

The ringtone sounded on Tia's cell phone, and a familiar name displayed on the screen. Joyce was the director at one of the Lakeland shelters.

"Y'all go ahead. I'll take this in my office."

Tia pulled the door shut behind her. She knew several of the shelter directors, staff members and volunteers in the area, had done training classes and other activities with them. Joyce was almost forty and had been working with abused women in one capacity or another for the past fifteen years. She was a wealth of information, advice and encouragement.

After the two of them had caught up, Joyce's tone grew serious. "I had a new referral to the shelter last night. She says she knows you."

Probably one of her former residents. She'd either returned to her abuser or fallen into another unhealthy relationship. "What's her name?"

"Vanessa Stephens."

The name wasn't familiar. Tia had had too many women come through her doors to remember them all, but this one would have stuck with her. Victor's twin sister was named Vanessa.

Uneasiness sifted through her, and she tried to shake it off. Different Vanessa, different last name. Unless she got married or changed her name for another reason.

If Victor wanted to find her, he wouldn't hesitate to enlist his sister's aid. He'd likely be able to get it, and it wouldn't be because of any spite on Vanessa's part. Her former sister-in-law was sweet and a little naïve. Throughout the trial, she'd vacillated between shock and disbelief. It wouldn't be difficult for Victor to convince her to help him in a way that she thought she was doing the right thing.

"What did she say about me?"

"That you guys were friends and had lost touch. She'd heard you were running a shelter for abused women but didn't know how to get in touch with you."

If Vanessa saw the news story and recognized Tia's voice... her breath hitched and her heart seized up. Vanessa Krasney was looking for her, which meant Victor was looking for her.

She swallowed hard. "Did you tell her anything?"

"I know better than that."

Of course she did. Joyce's passion for helping abused women had the same foundation as Tia's did, except Joyce had moved far enough past her experiences to actually share them.

Joyce continued. "That's something we always look for during intake, the possibility that an abuser might be using a friend or family member to gain access to his victim, but in this case, the advocate didn't pick up any signs of deviousness."

"Any visible injuries?"

"No. The abuse was supposedly all mental and emotional—taking away any means of independence, locking her in a closet without food and water, threatening to hurt her family if she left."

"Is she still there?"

"No, she left. Last night, she seemed pretty determined to track you down. Apparently, she gave up, because she didn't mention it this morning. A little while ago, she told me she had a friend who was going to take her in."

"This friend picked her up?"

"Supposedly. I didn't meet the friend. Vanessa gathered her belongings, thanked me and walked out, said the person was meeting her in the Publix parking lot a half mile away."

A noise drew Tia's attention toward the front window, a clatter from the direction of the driveway. She stood and circled her desk. When she parted the blinds, a familiar blue pickup sat in the drive. It was backed in, its tailgate down. Several boards were piled in the driveway.

Jason stood at the back, leaning into the bed of the truck. When he straightened, he'd dragged a large portable saw onto the tailgate. What was he doing?

"Anyhow," Joyce said, "I wanted to give you a heads up."

Tia thanked her and disconnected the call. After slipping out the kitchen door, she rounded the side of the house, then planted her hands on her hips. "What are you doing?"

He turned with a smile. "Getting a grumpy chief off your back and sparing you the hassle of a Code Enforcement violation letter."

"You're going to do this yourself." She didn't even try to keep the doubt out of her tone. The man built submarines. That hardly qualified him to play carpenter.

"Since your guy won't be back in town for several days, that's the plan.

"I appreciate the thought." He really was a great guy. But Mrs. Garrett likely looked for more than a good heart when choosing her repair men.

Tia pursed her lips. "No offense, but I'm pretty sure my landlady would prefer to use someone who does this for a living."

"I'm capable. The five years before going to work for Electric Boat, I did construction. I got tired of the feast-or-famine nature of the job. When I hung up my hardhat, though, I didn't do a brain dump. I still know how to repair a door jamb."

He held up the male end of an orange extension cord. "Do you have somewhere I can plug this in?"

With a sigh, she took it from him and plugged it into a covered outlet behind the wicker rocker on the porch. No sense trying to dissuade him. He had his mind made up.

She stepped down off the porch. "Let me at least help." She wasn't a pro, but she knew how to wield a hammer, along with several other tools.

"Absolutely. You can start with getting the screw gun you used Thursday night."

She raised her eyebrows. "You were watching?"

"Not watching, listening. I sat in the garden behind the inn while you ladies worked, in case someone else tried to bother you. When the news crew showed up, I was getting ready to head over here, but again, you had everything under control."

Her chest tightened in an odd mix of annoyance and appreciation. She didn't need him to step in and handle her business, but the fact he wanted to sent warmth shooting through her.

"Thanks." She gave him a half smile, dousing that warmth with the fire hose of practicality. Sweet, selfless, charming guys like Jason were too good to be true. Knights always had chinks in their armor.

"I'll get the screw gun. Anything else?"

"The door. But I'll carry that."

Good. It had taken two of them to tote it back there Thursday night. Solid core exterior doors had some weight.

When they stepped from the driveway into the grass, Damian stood leaning against the oak fifteen feet away, watching them. She hadn't noticed him. When she'd passed by him the first time, she'd been too intent on confronting Jason.

After slipping into the house to get her keys, Tia unlocked the door to the shed. "The door is resting against that wall." She tilted her head to the right. "Do you need help with it?"

"I got it. Just get the drill."

She removed the item from the tool drawer, then snagged the stepladder. Jason wouldn't have any use for it, but she'd need it if she hoped to be much help.

When she turned around, he was already carrying the door out. She followed, swinging the shed door shut with one sneakered foot. As they marched through the side yard and into the front, Damian watched from his place in the shade of the oak, his brown eyes alert. His back straightened, and a spark of interest flashed across his features, as if he wanted to be part of the activity. Maybe it was for nothing more than staving off boredom.

But even that wasn't enough incentive to encourage him to drop the attitude he wrapped around himself like a security blanket. At Jason's "hello," he grunted a response, then leaned back against the tree, arms crossed.

Instead of stepping onto the porch, Jason stood the door against the house, then headed to his truck. "If you want to remove the plywood you ladies put up, I'll get out what we'll need."

Tia stepped onto the porch and unfolded her ladder, then set to work backing out screws. Fortunately, the plywood was in two pieces, so she wouldn't have a problem handling it alone. After removing most of the screws in the upper board, she leaned against it, holding it in place with her shoulder as she backed out the final two. When she'd lowered the three-by-four-foot sheet to the porch floor, she looked at Jason.

He'd buckled a leather tool pouch around his waist and stood holding the end of the extension cord in one hand and a short cord with three outlets in his other. A long, yellow hose snaked from a portable compressor, a nail gun attached to its other end. A circular saw sat on the tailgate. He'd placed a toolbox on the ground, opened the lid and removed the tray inside.

She frowned. "I hope you didn't rent all this stuff. Or worse yet, buy it."

He plugged the three-way into the cord. "With the exception of the miter saw, I brought everything from home."

She lifted an eyebrow. "Do you always travel with a truck full of tools?"

He shrugged. "I had no idea what I was going

to run into at my grandparents' place, what repairs might be needed to get it ready to sell, so I threw in everything I thought might be useful but ran out of space before I got my miter saw in."

Oh, yeah. When he'd left Connecticut, he'd thought he'd have to get a house ready to put on the market.

When she had removed the other sheet of plywood, he joined her on the porch, a demolition bar in one hand.

He gave the air a sniff. "Something smells awfully good in there."

"The ladies made vegetable soup and biscuits. I'm sure there's plenty. Would you like some?" She'd be willing to give up her portion in exchange for all he was doing for her.

"I hit Wendy's when I was out, so I'm good." He narrowed his eyes. "Have you eaten?"

"I can wait. I want to help you with this."

"If you pass out from hunger, that sort of defeats the purpose. Get some soup. You can sit in the wicker rocker while you eat, and I'll holler if I need you."

He probably wouldn't. But at least she wouldn't feel as if she'd deserted him. By the time she returned with her bowl of soup and two buttered biscuits, he'd removed the interior and exterior trim and all the pieces of the splintered jamb and was prying out the last of the nails. She pushed the chair into the corner with one leg, making sure she was well out of Jason's way, then sat.

Damian had moved out from under the tree and stood a few feet from the edge of the porch. The way he was watching, he looked as if he expected to be quizzed on the steps and wanted to be prepared.

Jason laid down the demo bar and looked at him over one shoulder. "You good at reading a tape?"

He shrugged. "I get As in math."

"Cool. There's a second tape measure and carpenter's pencil in the toolbox."

Tia stirred her soup and took a bite, keeping Damian in her peripheral vision. As he walked to the truck, that irreverent, bored shuffle that characterized his gait was gone. So was the air of a condemned man being dragged to his death.

While Damian retrieved the mentioned items, Jason unclipped the tape from his pouch and measured the top of the opening. "See those one-by-sixes over there? I need the shorter one marked at thirty-nine inches."

Damian straightened and walked to the small pile of lumber. Besides the one-by-sixes, there were decorative trim pieces for the door casing and narrower strips of wood for the door stop. Jason gave him measurements for the side pieces, then stepped off the porch. While Damian finished his marks, Jason plugged in the miter saw, then slid it to the right-hand edge of the tailgate.

"All set?"

"Hold on." Damian stretched the tape down the length of each board again. "I'm making sure I didn't mess up."

Jason smiled, pride in his eyes. "Smart man. Measure twice, cut once."

Damian picked up the first piece of lumber and carried it to the saw. Surely Jason would measure a third time. He wouldn't trust a thirteen-year-old for an accurate mark.

But that was exactly what he did. "Can you support the other end of this?"

"Sure." He moved to the end opposite from his mark.

Jason lined up the board then brought the blade down to check the alignment. After a couple of adjustments, he depressed the trigger. The high-pitched squeal of the motor pierced the softer sounds of traffic and other midday activity, and soon the board was sawed in two. Tia hoped it was cut correctly.

She bit into a biscuit, mentally dismissing her concerns. If it wasn't, there were plenty more one-by-sixes where that one came from. The value of Jason's trust in building Damian's confidence far outweighed the cost of a couple of boards.

"Perfect. We'll get the others cut then nail them together."

Enthusiasm lit Damian's eyes. "Can I cut them?"

Tia started to object before Jason could respond, then clamped her mouth shut. The saw's plastic guard would protect his fingers. And Jason would be standing right next to him.

"I don't see why not."

As Damian laid one of the longer boards across the saw, Jason stood a couple of feet to his left, supporting the other end. "Mine at home has a laser, so you can see a red mark where the cut's going to be. We'll have to line this one up manually. You saw how I did it, right?"

Damian nodded, then positioned the board, adjusting, checking and adjusting again until he was satisfied.

Jason looked at Damian, which put him in profile

for Tia. His expression was serious. "Before you touch that trigger, always check where your fingers are. You never take chances with power tools. All it takes is a one-second distraction for an accident."

Damian nodded again, his expression likely as serious as Jason's.

After both pieces had been cut, Jason leaned into the rear driver door of his truck and pulled out a two-foot level and what looked like a pack of shims. "Let's line them up and nail them together."

He plugged in the compressor, and the pump roared to life, pressurizing the tank. "Once we finish the jamb and hang the door, we'll do the trim. We'll miter those pieces."

"What's miter?"

"Cut on a forty-five-degree angle so they finish off nicely."

"Like a picture frame."

"Yeah."

Tia sopped up the remnants of her soup with the last bite of biscuit and rose. Jason didn't need her help. He had Damian's. She wasn't sure who was benefiting more.

She stepped through the opening into the living room. Unfortunately, Pam and her kids wouldn't be there long enough for Jason to have a lasting impact on Damian. Peace House was an emergency shelter, a place for women and children to have immediate refuge from a dangerous situation. Soon Pam and her kids would be moved to a more permanent facility where Damian and his sister would be enrolled in a new school system, and Pam would get help that Tia wasn't set up to provide.

It was too bad. Damian needed a guy like Jason. But Jason had a life elsewhere, other people who needed him. Once he returned to that life, there'd be no reason for him to come back to Harmony Grove.

A sudden emptiness spread through her core, shot through with a needle-like sense of loss. Maybe Damian wasn't the only one who needed a guy like Jason.

Tia squared her shoulders. She didn't *need* any man. She had her work, and she'd made it all-consuming. For the past five years, she'd been on her own, and she'd done fine. Better than fine. She'd found fulfillment, the assurance that she was exactly where God had placed her.

Wishing for a man like Jason to become a permanent part of her life was a colossal waste of time. What she longed for didn't exist, and she was far too practical to entertain fantasies, too hardened by experience.

Any blinders she might have worn had come off years ago, falling to the ground in a heap of smoldering ashes.

SEVEN

Jason pulled a box down from the closet shelf and laid it on the antique oak library table. This bedroom at the end of the hall held special memories. It was his grandfather's hobby room, the place where he and Jason had pursued their shared passion of building model cars.

After he'd finished reinstalling Tia's front door yesterday afternoon, he'd cleaned out the third and final bedroom. This was the last of the upper-level rooms.

Jason pulled the tape from the top of the box and folded back the flaps, a sudden sense of nostalgia sweeping through him. A 1965 Mustang, complete with chrome headers and racing stripes, lay inside. He placed it on the table and took out the others one by one, projects he'd done with his grandfather. All of them were there, except for the first few. Those he'd taken home and proudly displayed on his dresser. His father had smashed them during one of his drunken rages.

He carefully packed the miniature cars and trucks, then retaped and labeled the box. These would go back to Connecticut with him.

The closet was empty. All that remained was a five-drawer chest and a library table. He approached the table. With only two shallow drawers, the task would go quickly. He grasped the handle of one and slid it open. It held the glues, paints and solvents he remembered being there. A piece of paper lay to one side.

He picked it up and unfolded it. Instead of the bold print his grandfather always used, fancy script filled the page. Unless his grandmother's handwriting had changed a lot during the past two decades, it wasn't hers, either. The date at the top was October 15th. Less than two months ago.

The next line jumped out at him—*My Dearest Jason*. He sank into the desk chair, thoughts reeling, and began to read.

If you're seeing this note, that means the lawyer was able to find you. First, I want you to know, Grandpa and I both understood why you had to leave. Even though your mother didn't tell us the extent of what was going on, we both knew what your father was.

I have left you everything inside the house except the furniture. I wish I could have left it all to you. But I wouldn't risk your father trying to take what your grandfather and I had worked for all our lives. I hope you understand. Tia Jordan is a good woman, her cause one that is close to my heart. I'm guessing, yours too.

Your models are in a box on the top shelf of the closet. When you were suddenly adamant about not taking any more home, it broke our hearts, because we knew why.

Lastly, please take this rug. It's important to me that you have it.

He looked down at the rug beneath his feet. What

was significant about it? It didn't look like anything special. It was the same one that had been there when he'd been a child—old and worn, in faded shades of brown and beige. If it was some kind of family heirloom, his grandparents had never mentioned it to him. Maybe his mom knew something about it.

He turned the page over. There was no more mention of the rug, just the closing—*With love, today and always, Grandma.*

The signature was in a different hand from the rest of the letter. It had the sharp slant he remembered in his grandmother's handwriting but with a shakiness that hadn't been there before. Had she dictated the note to someone else and signed off herself? Had she then given someone a key and had them place the note in his grandfather's desk? Or had that someone given her a ride to the house so she could put it there herself? She'd had help getting it there; based on what he'd been told, Grandma hadn't driven since entering Winter Gardens five years ago.

He rose from the desk. Why mention the rug? Of all the items he could keep, that was the one he'd least like to have to haul back to Connecticut. But if his having the rug had been that important to his grandmother, he'd roll it up and put it in the back of his truck, under the tarp that would protect all his other take-home items. Then he'd store it in his attic until he decided what to do with it.

For now, he'd leave the rug where it was. Rather than risk tearing it or loosening the legs on the heavy antique table, he'd wait and ask Tia to help him move the table to the edge of the room. In the meantime, maybe he could find out what was special about the rug.

He dropped to his knees and lifted one corner. No label. There wasn't one on the second corner, either. The next one bore the label he was looking for. The rug was made by Maples Industries, Inc. He'd never heard of them. Of course, he wasn't a rug connoisseur. He pulled out his phone and took a picture of the label and the rug. He'd research it later.

There was one more possibility to check. Maybe his grandmother had hidden something under the rug. Not likely. It was lying too flat. He lifted the front edge anyway and peered beneath, then patted the entire area under the table. Not the slightest bulge. If there was money, enough to make a difference, he'd feel it.

He rose and set to work on the chest of drawers. By the time he finished, the sun shone through the lower part of the dirt-streaked window, sending elongated shadows stretching across the room. He picked up two of the boxes he'd marked "donate" and carried them downstairs. He'd designated one end of the living room as his staging area, blocking in the Queen Anne sofa that sat against the wall. It didn't matter. He'd have everything moved out before Tia made use of any of the furniture.

When he finished his four trips up and down the stairs, he stepped outside and locked the front door. The sun had disappeared beneath the horizon and the final remnants of dusk hung over the neglected landscape.

After a five-point turnaround in the wide drive, he pulled out onto the highway. Moments later, headlights clicked on some distance behind him, and a vehicle slowly closed the gap.

The muscles across his shoulders drew taut as he studied the headlight configuration in his rearview mirror. It wasn't the Highlander. The lights were too low, the spacing different. Of course, the Highlander had been turned in. If whoever had followed him planned to continue, it would be with a different vehicle.

Jason clicked on his left signal and gently pressed the brake. When he completed the turn, he stopped at the edge of the road and looked in his rearview mirror. The vehicle sped past, heading toward Harmony Grove, a brief blip. He swiveled his head just before the car disappeared from view.

It looked like an Accord or Altima, light-colored. Maybe the driver happened to be leaving for Harmony Grove the same time he did. Or maybe the driver of the Highlander had swapped it for a sedan. He'd keep his eyes open and continue backing into the parking space at the inn, hiding his Connecticut tag.

When he reached his temporary home, instead of going inside, he headed down the sidewalk toward the corner. Tia might be able to shed some light on who helped his grandmother place the note. If not, she could give him some ideas for where to donate the boxes accumulating in the living room.

He rang her bell and stepped to the center of the porch, standing in front of the peephole. He hadn't noticed it the night he and Danielle's boyfriend had busted through, but he'd checked to make sure it hadn't been damaged after he'd finished the work yesterday.

Tia was already smiling as she swung open the door. "Come on in."

When he stepped into the living room, Damian was sitting on the end of the couch, leaning against its arm. He looked up from his game, and an involuntary smile snuck past his defenses before he wrangled it under control. The cool-and-detached mask slipped back into place.

"Hey, Damian." The kid gave him a nod and what could almost be classified as a reserved smile.

Jason looked at Tia and drew in a deep breath through his nose. "It always smells good here."

"We just finished dinner. We'd have saved you some if we'd known you were coming."

"I'll microwave a frozen dinner when I get back to my room. I stopped by to see if I could pick your brain."

Tia took a seat at the other end of the sectional sofa and patted the spot next to her. "Pick away."

As he sank onto the couch, he slanted a glance at Damian. Instead of returning to his game, he sat watching them.

"I'm going to have dozens of boxes of stuff to donate and need helping choosing a charity." Though he'd sorted and packed up plenty of stuff, nothing held enough value to bother with advertising, and the little he'd make on a garage sale wouldn't be worth the time and hassle it would involve. That hidden stash of cash he'd hoped to find wasn't looking good, either. He hadn't even come across a Pringle's can filled with quarters.

"How about three charities?"

He smiled. "That's even better."

She twisted to face him more fully. "Two years ago, a group of Harmony Grove residents started an annual spring-cleaning drive. Half the town cleans out their garages and closets and we have a huge yard sale at the community center at the end of April. The proceeds are split between the three charities."

"Sounds good." He frowned. "I just see one problem. Your monster garage sale is four and a half months away. Where do I store everything in the meantime?"

"It can stay at the house, especially if the boxes are confined to one room. The estate won't be settled for months, so it's not like I can go forward with renovations and move my clients in."

"Then it's settled. I'll donate everything I don't want to Harmony Grove's annual spring-cleaning drive and leave the boxes stacked until then."

She pursed her lips. "In full disclosure, I have to admit that Peace House is one of those three charities."

"Who are the other two?"

"One is a ministry to the homeless in Winter Haven, and the third is an animal rescue."

"All worthy causes." He paused. "I have one other thing you might be able to help me with. I found a note at the house this afternoon."

"What kind of note?"

"From my grandmother, dated October 15th of this year. It was written by someone else, but she signed it."

"How can I help? What did the note say?" She hesitated. "If you don't mind sharing."

"No, I don't." At least part of it. The rest would raise

too many questions, ones he wasn't ready to answer. "There's a rug in my grandfather's hobby room. I don't know why, but she felt so strongly about me taking it that a month and a half before she died, she went to the trouble of putting her wishes in writing and tucking the note into my grandfather's desk drawer."

"Does the rug have some kind of sentimental value?"

"Not that I'm aware of."

She drew her brows together. "Maybe it's a rare collector's item. I know there are old tapestries worth tens of thousands of dollars. Maybe the same holds true for rugs."

"I don't think that's the case with this one. It's worn out, almost threadbare in spots. Of all the stuff in the house, I don't know why she wanted to make sure I took that rug."

"Maybe she mentioned something to whoever wrote the note for her."

"My thoughts exactly. Any idea who I can ask?"

"I didn't know her well enough to know who might have helped her with business matters, but I'm sure someone at the home would. BethAnn might have some insight, too." She crossed her arms, apparently deep in thought. "I have another idea if that doesn't pan out. Winter Gardens has a log where visitors sign in. You could see who came to see her from October 15th on."

"Excellent idea. I'll check with BethAnn first, then make a trip back to the nursing home tomorrow or Thursday and see what they can tell me."

Pam stepped into the living room from the hallway

and gave him a nod of greeting, and Tia continued.

"Just a heads up, whatever you do Thursday, make sure you're back by five."

"Why?"

"The second Thursday in December, Harmony Grove holds its annual Christmas parade. It goes down Main Street, right past the inn. It doesn't start till six, but they close the roads and people start lining up around five. If you come home much later than that, you'll be parking somewhere and waiting until after the parade to get home."

"I'll make sure I'm back well before five. That'll be fun." He'd loved parades as a kid. His mom had taken him to the Citrus Festival parade every year, since it was almost within walking distance, and he'd been to Harmony Grove's Christmas parade with his grandparents several times. He'd even attended quite a few as an adult.

He looked from Tia to Damian. "Are you guys going to come over and watch it with me? We can set up chairs on the sidewalk in front of the inn."

Tia smiled. "Sure."

Damian scrunched his nose. "No way. Parades are for babies and sissies."

Jason shrugged. "You must not like candy."

"Of course I like candy. What's that got to do with it?"

"Only that it's everywhere. Most of the people on the floats throw candy as they pass. All you've got to do is pick it up. I usually come away with a pretty big stash."

"You go to parades?"

"Of course, I go to parades. They're fun and they

don't cost anything."

Damian nodded. "I'll think about it."

Jason resisted the urge to mirror the nose scrunch Damian had done. What thirteen-year-old kid had never been to a parade?

Damian rose from the couch and walked into the dining area. Moments later, the back door creaked open and shut.

Jason stood too. "I'll leave you to your evening activities."

Tia walked him outside and Pam followed. When they stepped onto the porch, Pam put a hand on Jason's arm. "I appreciate the interest you're taking in my son." Her voice was barely above a whisper. "While you guys were working yesterday, I was watching through the bedroom window."

Uh-oh. Maybe he shouldn't have allowed Damian to use the saw without getting her permission. The nail gun, either. Jason had shimmed, leveled and lined everything up and let Damian shoot it all in. He'd emphasized safety the entire time, using it as a bonding as well as a teaching experience. But still.

Instead of a reprimand, she gave him an appreciative smile. "It's making a difference. He's still giving me grunts or single-syllable answers, but he's not as angry." She paused. "I hesitate to speak for him, but I'm pretty sure you'll have his company for Thursday night's parade."

Jason nodded. "Good."

She looked past him into the front yard. "We have some good parades in Lakeland, and I've taken Julie several times. But if an activity doesn't involve sports or some other he-man endeavor, Damian's father ridicules him for even thinking about it."

"I understand." More than anyone would guess.

She dropped her arm. "Thank you."

Jason watched her disappear into the house. When he looked back at Tia, she was studying him. A gentle breeze lifted her hair, swishing it around her shoulders and sending some fine strands across her cheek. Her lips were parted in a half smile, and admiration shone from her eyes.

"You're not just doing the Good Samaritan thing, or even trying to win him over for the sake of a challenge. You really like him, don't you?"

"I do."

That admiration was still there, and he was having a hard time focusing his thoughts. Everything about her was beautiful—her soft features with the full lips and pert, upturned nose, her wispy blond hair that would probably feel like silk against his fingers and her tiny frame that held both a giving heart and amazing strength. He could fall for her so easily.

But that wasn't why he was here. He was here to clean out his grandmother's house, to locate and collect the items that had sentimental value and make sure he didn't overlook anything that might have the potential to get him out of the situation he was in. If he could help a troubled thirteen-year-old kid in the process, that would be even better.

He descended the first step, hand resting on the railing, Tia next to him. "Damian reminds me a lot of someone else."

Another angry thirteen-year-old with dark hair and brown eyes. By age fifteen, that angry teenager had been headed for a life behind bars.

Then all that changed, thanks to a powerhouse named Cory, with endless energy, infinite wisdom and unconditional love.

He'd been the church's youth pastor. Fifteen years later, Jason still viewed him as a saint. He'd looked past an angry kid's prickly exterior, ignoring the barbs that pierced anyone who got too close.

And he'd loved him anyway.

God, please send a Pastor Cory into Damian's life.

Tia pulled up next to the Ram in Elizabeth Sloan's driveway and killed the engine. Before Jason had walked home last night, she'd asked him if he'd mind if she came over to the house this afternoon. Even though she couldn't do any real work until the estate was settled, she wanted to jot down some ideas. She'd promised to not get in his way. He'd assured her he'd enjoy the company.

She stepped from her car and moved toward the porch, her purse hanging from one shoulder and a spiral-bound notebook clutched against her chest. A zippered plastic bag held a ham and cheese sandwich.

The short trek up the walkway wasn't nearly as scary as the first time she'd visited. Jason had found a weed eater in the shed and had beat back the growth that had encroached on the walk. Now if a snake approached, she'd see it in plenty of time to react.

For her, "react" meant running screaming toward the house or her car, depending on the location of said snake. She'd overcome a lot of fears in the past five years. Her snake phobia wasn't one of them.

She climbed the steps onto the porch and tried to

turn the doorknob. It was locked.

Probably smart. Jason had told her yesterday about the vehicle he'd seen pull out behind him after he'd left his grandparents' place. They were both keeping an eye out for it, but the description was so generic, neither of them had high hopes of definitively spotting it.

She fingered through the keys on her ring and inserted one into the lock. The bolt slid over with an audible click. When she pushed the door open, the prolonged creak echoed through the house.

"Hello." Announcing her presence was probably unnecessary. Until the hinges got a liberal shot of WD-40, stealth would be impossible.

"In here." The response came from the back of the house.

As she moved that direction, rustling drifted to her from the den. She'd almost reached the room when Jason stepped through the open doorway.

The smile he gave her crinkled the skin at the corners of his eyes. "Good morning." He glanced at his watch. "Or I should say 'good afternoon,' as of two minutes ago."

"Good afternoon yourself. How's it going?"

"Pretty well. I started in the kitchen when I first got here, then decided to tackle something a little less daunting. I'm almost finished with the den."

"Then I'll leave you to it. Are you sure you don't mind me roaming through while you're trying to work?"

"Of course I don't mind. It's your house."

She listened for sarcasm in his tone. If it was there, he was doing an admirable job of hiding it.

Instead of going back into the den, he followed her. "This is a good time to break for lunch. Did you bring anything?"

She grasped the zipper part of her baggie and dangled it in front of him. She hadn't planned to eat for another hour or so, but she might as well enjoy his company.

While he removed his lunch from the fridge, she took a seat at the bar that bordered the island and laid her notebook and sandwich on the laminate countertop.

"Did you talk to the folks at Winter Gardens?"

"I didn't have to. I called BethAnn's Fabrics and Crafts as soon as it opened this morning and talked to BethAnn."

He pulled his own sandwich from a plastic bag and paused to bow his head. She did the same, an unseen thread drawing her to him. Not only was he brave and protective and compassionate and selfless, as well as good-looking, he also shared her faith.

He opened his eyes and took a bite of his sandwich. "BethAnn's grandmother wrote the note."

Tia lifted her brows. "BethAnn knows about it?"

"No more than I do at this point. I asked her if she would recognize her grandmother's handwriting. She said she would, so I texted her a picture of the note. She has no doubt. I'm meeting her when she closes the store tonight, and we're going to the hospital together."

"I hope you get some helpful information."

"Thanks." He looked at the notebook lying in front of her. "Looks like you came prepared to do some work. Planning, anyway."

"Yep." She grinned. "I'm one of those people who has a six-month, one-year, two-year and five-year plan, besides my daily schedules."

Now, anyway. At one time, she'd been afraid to try to look past tomorrow. Thinking about the future required at least some sense of optimism. When all one's thoughts were occupied with day-to-day survival, contemplating anything beyond twenty-four hours could be debilitating. Too many dark, terrifying days piled on top of one another.

She unclipped her pen from her notebook and turned back the cover. "The first thing I want to do is to figure out how many people this place can accommodate. There are four bedrooms on the second floor and one on the first, along with some other rooms down here that could be repurposed."

"When you're doing your planning, you'll probably want some places where your residents can spread out, have a little bit of quiet time without having to hole themselves up in their rooms."

She nodded. "Good point."

"A play room for the children might not be a bad idea, too." His gaze circled the kitchen. "With the number of residents you're talking about, a commercial dishwasher is a must."

"Definitely. Although I've always got help, not many of us are fans of washing dishes."

"I can relate." He bit into an apple. "It would be good to have two or three separate food preparation areas, too." He paused, apparently deep in thought. His eyebrows were drawn together, vertical creases carved into the bridge of his nose.

"You've got about three feet of wasted space on

the other side of the fridge. If you remove the smaller cabinet and put the refrigerator there, you could install a cabinet that spans almost to the doorway leading into the dining room. Besides giving you another food preparation area, it would make your work triangle more efficient."

Tia cocked an eyebrow at him. What guy thought about a kitchen's work triangle? Of course, Jason had a background in construction. He'd maybe even designed a kitchen or two. Too bad he wouldn't be here to assist her with the renovations. He had some great ideas.

It was more than that, though. It was also his enthusiasm, as if he was excited about the prospects for the place, the good that would be accomplished here.

She tilted her head to the side. "Why are you so on board with this? A week ago, you were ready to fight me to the bitter end. What changed?"

He smiled, but it held tightness. "I avoid battles I can't win. Right now, I'm less than halfway through the house, only a third if you count the attic. I'm still holding out hope for that half million dollars my grandparents hid in coffee cans." The relaxed, teasing smile was back. "It's not under the beds. I already checked."

She returned his smile. He was right about one thing—it was a legal will. But the certainty of being on the losing side of a lengthy battle wasn't the only thing behind his change of heart. If it was, he'd be resigned, even a little resentful.

Instead, he seemed happy for her and what the inheritance would mean to Peace House. It was as if her cause was dear to him, as if the plight of abused women held a special place in his heart.

Her jaw went slack as a light bulb clicked on in her mind. No, not a light bulb, a whole bank of 500-watt spots casting illumination over all her confusion.

His excitement over her project. His connection with Damian. His taking time away from his own work to repair her jamb and rehang her door. Even the fierce protectiveness he'd displayed when she and the women had been threatened, an act that had put his own life in danger.

She flopped against her bar stool's back, and her hands fell to her lap. "You're sympathetic with my cause because you've been there. That's why you and your mother left, why you never reestablished contact with your grandparents. You fled for your lives and couldn't risk the abuser tracking you down."

She stared at him, waiting for confirmation. He didn't meet her gaze. Instead, his eyes were fixed on the two bites of sandwich he hadn't yet eaten. Silence stretched between them, thick with tension, and that silence confirmed that she was right more strongly than any words he could utter.

She longed to know his story but didn't press. The same as with her clients, she would listen to as much or as little as he wanted to share.

There were parts of her story that she hadn't shared with anyone, either, and probably never would. She caught herself halfway through an unconscious lift of her arm, fingers splayed, ready for the comforting touch of silk against her palm, the assurance that the outer scars were hidden behind the fabric barrier, the inner ones walled off even more securely.

She dropped her arm to let it rest on the bar, then lifted her other to intertwine her fingers. Still he didn't speak. The silence bore down on them—a heavy, suffocating blanket.

She needed to say something to break it, to punch holes that could allow in light and life and ease the torment on his face. But the emotions she dealt with on a daily basis didn't slither away defeated with mere words.

He finally lifted his eyes and fixed his gaze on the window above the sink. It looked out over the unkempt back yard. He likely wasn't even aware of the view on the other side of the dirty panes of glass.

"My dad." It was just two words, but they held a thunderbolt of emotion. She waited for him to continue.

More than once, she'd held one of her residents in her arms while the woman had sobbed, releasing months, sometimes years of pent-up grief and fear. She'd even had the opportunity to comfort quite a few children.

She didn't work with the men, though, whether abused or abusers. She left that up to people more qualified, those lacking the baggage that no matter how she tried, she'd never been able to fully cut loose.

Jason continued, his gaze still fixed on the window. "Most days, he'd hang out with his buddies after work. Then he'd come home drunk and angry. It was even worse when he wasn't working."

His tone was flat, the emotion she'd sensed earlier restrained behind a wall of control. "My mom could never do anything right. Dinner wasn't hot enough, the house clean enough, my mom sweet or compliant or smart or pretty enough. It was her fault that they didn't have enough money, even though he never kept a job more than two months and didn't allow her to work outside the home." His mouth curved into a scowl. "It would have given her too much independence."

The breath he drew in hitched, belying the lack of emotion in his tone. "Most nights were the same, some worse than others. The front door would slam, he'd bellow a while, then send me to my room. I'd cower there, listening to the thud of his fists and my mom's whimpers."

He curled his fingers into his palms and squeezed until his knuckles turned white. She rested a hand over one of his, hoping her silent touch conveyed her sympathy and support.

He turned his head until his eyes met hers. Sadness swam in their golden-brown depths, but there was something else, too—anger, maybe even guilt. His jaw was tight and his eyebrows were drawn toward his nose. His features held hardness, as if he was trying to steel himself against a devastating blow.

His gaze drifted back to the window. "One night, I couldn't do it anymore. I'd just turned thirteen. He'd lost his job again for showing up drunk, and we were in the last few hours of the five-day final warning from the power company. Mom went to Grandma to ask for help, and Dad found out. He threw his first punch, and Mom's head slammed into the edge of the refrigerator door."

A grimace of pain flashed through his features. "She was lying at his feet, and he just kept yelling at her to get up. Then he kicked her. That was when something snapped. I grabbed one of the kitchen chairs and brought it down hard over his head."

Tia pressed her lips together against a surge of emotion—sorrow for what the young Jason had had to endure, admiration for what he'd done. He'd been just a kid, Damian's age, and he'd gone up against a full-grown man, trying to protect his mother. Tia steeled herself to hear what happened next.

"I only made things worse. It didn't even slow him down. When he was finished with me, he turned on Mom with a new vengeance. After he went to bed, we dragged ourselves to a neighbor's house. She took us to the emergency room and refused to bring us back home."

He gave her a wry smile. "She was a spitfire, a little Hispanic lady about your size. That night, she was our savior. More times than I could count, Dad had told Mom that if she ever thought about leaving him, he'd hunt her down and kill her. But Maria shut down Mom's objections, insisted on buying us bus tickets to anywhere she wanted to go."

"She chose Connecticut?"

"Yep. We didn't know a soul in all of New England, so Mom figured Dad would never look for us there. Another plus was the brutal winters. We both hated the cold, so the last thing he would have expected was for us to flee north. But we did, with nothing but the clothes on our backs and five hundred dollars that our amazing neighbor withdrew from an ATM machine."

"What you did was brave. It was the impetus that got you both out of the situation."

The hardness she'd seen earlier crept back into his

eyes and his jaw tightened. "I should have done it years earlier. I let it go on far too long."

"You were just a kid." She put a hand on his shoulder and gave him a little shake. The guilt was unjustified. It was also common, kids feeling as if they were somehow to blame, whether through their actions or inaction.

When Jason didn't respond, she continued. "I'm sure he was a lot bigger than you. I doubt you were the size you are now."

He lifted one side of his mouth in a crooked smile. "I was a runt, even got picked on at school for it. My growth spurt didn't happen until I was sixteen." He dropped his head. "But I should have done something besides cowering in my room."

Grief and guilt radiated from him, and she wanted nothing more than to wrap him in her arms and try to soothe away his anguish.

She wouldn't do it. Any physical comfort she tried to offer could be misunderstood, especially if he suspected the attraction she'd fought since the night he'd played the hero and crashed through her front door with Danielle's boyfriend.

She gave his shoulder a squeeze. "There was nothing you could do. It's easy to try to take on that burden, but it wasn't your responsibility to protect your mother. It was her responsibility to protect you."

He swiveled his head to look at her, his lips curving in a genuine smile. "Are you sure you haven't been talking to my mom? I can't tell you how many times she's said those exact same words."

She matched his smile with one of her own. "Then you need to listen to the smart women in your life."

"I'll keep that in mind." He grew serious. "Thanks for listening. I haven't told many people my story."

She hadn't told many people hers, either, at least not the details. Whoever said talking about traumatic experiences made one feel better probably didn't have many traumatic experiences of their own.

Jason had, and the knowledge seemed to forge an invisible bond, which made the attraction she felt even stronger. She looked at her hand, still resting against his shoulder, then dropped it. Whatever feelings might develop for Jason over the next few weeks, she would never act on them. No matter how brave and protective and compassionate and selfless he seemed, it could all vanish in a moment, a mirage that shimmered and disappeared without warning.

All men were charming at the beginning of a relationship. Victor certainly was. Based on the stories that had been shared with her over the past few years, so were the mates of many of the women who landed in shelters.

No, relationships didn't start out violent. Usually, the abuse began gradually, with enough promises and half-hearted apologies to make the victim believe that if she just tried a little harder, he would go back to being that person she'd fallen in love with.

She didn't know Jason's whole story. Had his father hit him just that one night, or had the abuse been ongoing? Did it make a difference? No, it didn't. Both the abused and those who witnessed abuse often grew up to be abusers.

It was hard to imagine Jason being violent. He was too caring and protective. But she'd already witnessed his loss of control once. Seeing her standing there had seemed to bring him back from the brink of something dark and dangerous.

She'd known all along that a relationship with him would never work—the distance, his responsibility to his mother, her responsibility to her clients. Now she had another reason to add to the list. One more barrier.

Maybe it wasn't fair to label Jason. She was judging him for his past, putting expectations on him that might never materialize.

But she'd seen too much. Men and women too scarred to heal, their lives a destructive vortex that sucked in everyone close to them. Broken people who created yet more broken people. She would never be able to drop her guard and trust a man with her heart, her life, her secrets.

Not Jason. Not anyone.

EIGHT

TIA THANKED THE cashier at Harmony Produce and Meats and slid her wallet back into her purse. Two bulging plastic bags of fresh vegetables and salad fixings waited on the counter.

Harmony Grove didn't have any large chain grocery stores like Publix or Aldi's or Winn-Dixie. Shopping at those locations involved a trip to Winter Haven. Her twice-monthly trip to Sam's Club in Lakeland was even farther. The drive was worth it, though, to be able to buy in bulk. She usually combined the trip with lunch out with Joyce, someone who understood the challenges as well as the emotional drain of running a shelter.

Moving to the Sloan house was going to alleviate the current challenge she had with lack of space, but expanding was going to present other challenges. Like greater cost, twice as much work, more staff, and more organization needed to keep everything running smoothly.

That didn't dampen her anticipation. When she'd left Jason a half hour ago, she'd walked out with her notebook clutched to her chest, more excited than she'd been when she'd arrived. Waiting until after the estate was settled to start renovations was going to be hard, even if there wasn't any red tape.

It wouldn't come from Jason. His father wouldn't be a problem, either. According to the lawyer, the man didn't even plan to leave his home in Mississippi.

As soon as Tia stepped from the store, she looked down the street. Only the upper curve of the sun was visible above the tops of the trees in the distance. Three or four white cars were parallel parked along both sides of Main. Were any of them what could be considered sedans? Without viewing them from the side, she wasn't sure.

When she looked in the other direction, a woman stood two businesses down, on the opposite side of the road, staring at the market's front door. As Tia studied her, she spun away and moved quickly up the sidewalk. Wavy red hair flowed halfway down her back, so like someone else's. Although Victor had gotten his Italian father's jet-black hair, Vanessa had taken after their Irish mother, inheriting both her red curls and lighter skin tone, complete with a smattering of freckles across her cheeks and nose.

But the woman currently hurrying away wasn't Vanessa. Those form-fitting stretch jeans couldn't have been larger than a size seven. The blouse she wore had three-quarter sleeves, but instead of a thicker fabric that would hide any lumps, it was made of some kind of clingy material that flowed around her thighs as she walked.

Tia's former sister-in-law had always been chunky. Unless she'd shed fifty pounds in the past five years, someone else had been blessed with that same enviably thick red hair.

Tia opened the passenger door of the Fiat and dropped her groceries into the seat. Had the woman been watching her? If so, who was she and what did she want? Maybe nothing. Maybe she'd just paused in her walk and that happened to be when Tia had stepped out of the market. But why was she hurrying away as if she'd been caught doing something illegal?

Tia closed the passenger door and rounded the rear bumper on her way to the other side. As she slid into the driver's seat, the woman turned and disappeared into Harvey's bookstore. Tia pulled onto Main, then slowed to peer inside Harvey's as she passed.

The woman stood at the picture window staring out, watching her. Or maybe she was simply taking in the holiday-themed display, with its snowflake window decals and book-topped columns rising out of a rolling bed of quilt batting. Of course, window displays were much more interesting viewed from the sidewalk than inside the store.

A few blocks later, she passed the inn and turned onto Tranquility Way. If she could have handpicked an address for her shelter, she couldn't have come up with a more fitting one. Tranquility was what she hoped to offer. That and hope, the prospect of futures that were much brighter than the ones the women had faced before coming through her doors.

When she stopped in the drive, Jasmine and Katie were sitting in the wicker rockers on the front porch.

Jasmine rose as soon as Tia opened the car door. "Need any help?"

"I've got it." She reached into the other seat to snag the two bags, then slipped her purse strap over her shoulder.

As she approached the women, she did a double take. When Jasmine arrived, Tia had offered to schedule an appointment for her at a salon, but Jasmine had wanted to give the butchered locks a chance to grow out first.

Sometime during the afternoon, though, someone skilled had gotten a hold of Jasmine's hair and done an amazing job. It was cut short, but still looked feminine. The stylist couldn't do anything about the places where her husband had snipped too close to the scalp, but without all the long and medium patches sticking out, the bare spots weren't nearly as noticeable.

Fortunately, her husband had left the front alone, so the bangs had stayed. They were now feathered and made a gentle swoop over her forehead and across her temple.

"Your hair looks good."

Jasmine smiled. "Katie did it for me."

Tia's jaw dropped. "Katie?"

Pride lit Katie's eyes, but apprehension crept in. "I found some scissors in a kitchen drawer. I hope you don't mind. I put them back when I was done."

"Of course I don't mind. Actually, I'm impressed. I didn't know you did hair."

Katie's gaze dipped. "I don't, really, except my own. When I was a kid, I dreamed of going to cosmetology school. I read everything I could on cutting, coloring and styling and watched lots of videos." She grinned. "And practiced on my friends. They'd have me give them new hairstyles. Their parents weren't thrilled with some of the colors they chose, but everybody encouraged me. I still cut my own hair, but it's been years since I've done anyone else's."

Tia shook her head. "And you said you have no marketable skills."

Jasmine gave Katie's shoulder a nudge. "Girl, you're the bomb. You could open your own salon."

"No, I can't. It's not a marketable skill if I don't have the education to back it up."

"Doesn't matter." Jasmine waved away her concerns. "You have the talent and passion."

Tia nodded. "She's right. The education is the easy part."

Another smile crept up Katie's cheeks, then faded. "I can't go to school. I have no money."

"There are programs—loans, grants." Tia crossed the porch and stopped at the door. "You'll have to come up with a way to support yourself and your boys. Why not with something you love?" Once she moved to a more permanent facility, they'd match her up with the best program.

The smile returned, and she gave a firm nod. "You're right. Even if Mark got counseling and we eventually got back together, I want to maintain some independence." She looked over at her new friend. "Jaz says you always need an exit plan."

Tia reached for the doorknob. "Jaz is a smart lady."

As soon as she opened the door, the pleasant aroma of dinner hit her full force, and her stomach growled. That sandwich she'd had with Jason was long gone.

She carried the groceries into the kitchen and greeted Pam, who was sitting on one side of the dining room table. Ethan, Aiden and Pam's daughter, Julie, were clustered around the curved end, kneeling in their chairs. They were bent over the table, intent on a game of Hungry Hippo.

As Tia put the groceries away, loud taps came from the dining room, each of the kids determined to win by having their own hippo gobble up the most balls. After sliding the crisper drawer shut, Tia straightened and closed the refrigerator.

Monica appeared in the doorway. "I've finished November's bank reconciliation and gotten all the bills paid, at least everything we've received. I'm still waiting on the utility bill, which should arrive any day now." She paused. "I didn't bring in today's mail."

"Me, neither. I'll go get it."

As Tia walked toward the mailbox, she glanced to her left. A figure stood near the corner, on the opposite side of the street. It was the red-haired woman she'd seen on Main. The uneasiness she'd felt descended on her again. She'd been right; the woman was stalking her.

She removed the mail and thumbed through it, keeping the woman in her peripheral vision. She was moving slowly up the sidewalk, gaze fixed on Tia. Her gait sped up, and she lifted an arm in greeting.

Tia waited at the box. Although names got fuzzy over time, she never forgot a face. This wasn't one of her residents. The stranger crossed the street and closed the remaining distance between them.

Tia squared her shoulders. "Can I help you?"

Now that she was closer, there was something familiar about her. She removed her sunglasses and slid them on top of her head.

Tia stiffened as a jolt of recognition shot through her. The green eyes, the red hair, the freckles scattered across her nose and upper cheeks like pebbles on a beach.

Vanessa. A fifty-pounds-lighter version, but definitely Tia's former sister-in-law.

Tia opened her mouth, but nothing came out. Too many questions trying to escape at once—*What are you doing here? How did you find me? Where is Victor? Where is Victor? Where is Victor...*

"Hi, Tia." Vanessa gave her a shy smile. "I wasn't sure if you'd recognize me."

Vanessa had always been nice to her, but they hadn't been close. Of course, during Tia's three-year marriage to Victor, she hadn't been close to anyone. Victor had seen to that. The isolation had started before they'd even been married. She hadn't seen it for what it was, because he'd expertly disguised it as being so crazy about her that he didn't want to share her with anyone else.

"I didn't recognize you until you took off your sunglasses. You look good."

"Thanks. Shortly after you left, I met someone, ended up joining Weight Watchers and dropped fifty pounds in six months. I've kept it off for three years."

Vanessa gave her another shy smile. In spite of her slim, new look, she still projected an air of shy sweetness, a sense of not being sure of herself.

Not Victor. The confidence gene that missed Vanessa broadsided him, giving him a double dose.

Tia forced out one of the questions ping-ponging through her mind. "What are you doing here?"

"I came to see you. I want you to be happy."

There had to be more to it than that. "I *am* happy."

Vanessa pursed her lips, as if trying to decide how to continue. Finally, she sighed. "I told you I met someone. Two years ago, we got married. He's an amazing man. I wouldn't trade what we have for anything."

"I'm happy for you." Regardless of everything she'd gone through with Victor, she held no hard feelings against his sister.

"Thanks." Vanessa shifted her weight to the other foot. "I just want you to have the same thing."

"The same thing?" Tia narrowed her eyes. What, happiness? She was already there. Marriage in general? An asteroid wiping out planet Earth was more likely. Marriage to Victor? Hell would freeze over first.

Vanessa chewed her lower lip. "Everything you said in court was true. I'm sorry I didn't believe you at the time."

Tia shrugged. "Those weren't easy things to hear about someone you care about."

"I know, but I should have believed you." She heaved a sigh. "After Victor got out, he told me everything, admitted to everything you accused him of."

After he got out. Five days ago. After the news story aired.

Vanessa tilted her head, an earnestness in her eyes. "He's sorry for everything he did and wants to make it up to you. He's a changed man."

Tia swallowed against the panic spiraling through her body. "Does he know where I am?" *God, please, no.*

"He doesn't know anything. He saw the news story, but they blurred your face and didn't give your name. He thought he recognized your voice, asked me to check out shelters around the state."

Tia leaned against the mailbox as weakness washed

through her limbs. "How did you find me?"

"I played the part of an abused woman, got referred to a shelter in Lakeland. The lady I was rooming with mentioned staying here a couple of years ago. When I asked, she told me it was run by someone named Tia."

Tia swayed as panic pounded through her, sending a toxic current through every cell in her body. Her muscles twitched with it, her ears rang and her vision swam. She grasped Vanessa's arm. "Please don't tell him where I am. Tell him you couldn't find me. Say there are no Tias involved with Florida shelters." Yes, she was asking Vanessa to lie for her, but it was a matter of life or death—her own.

"There's nothing to be afraid of." Vanessa's tone was soothing, the voice a teacher might use to calm a frightened first grader. "Please just talk to him, hear him out."

"I can't. He'll come after me." She drew in some jagged breaths, suddenly dizzy from a lack of oxygen. "You can't believe him. He's a master manipulator. Trust me. I was married to him for three years."

"I've known him longer than you have. He's my twin. I'm telling you, he's a changed man."

Tia shook her head. "He's manipulating you. He never owned up to anything until he needed your help to find me."

"He loves you." The plea in her voice was reflected in her eyes.

No, Victor was incapable of love. Anything that resembled love was manipulation in disguise. But Vanessa would never believe her. Victor had already polluted her mind, and Vanessa was too naïve to see it.

At one time, Tia had possessed the same quality. That had been in another lifetime. Naivety, along with trust, had long since been stamped out—stamped, beaten or carved. A shudder shook her shoulders, and she buried her fingers in the silk scarf draped below her throat.

Vanessa's eyes followed the motion. She was one of a small handful of people who understood what it meant. She winced and her gaze dipped to the ground. She was uncomfortable. Good.

"Victor swore if I ever left him, he'd kill me. He's lost five years of his life, and he's not about to let it go. That threat is more real than ever, and he'll use anyone to help him carry it out, even you." She put a hand on Vanessa's forearm. "Please, promise me you won't say anything to him."

"All right." She reached into her purse and pulled out a small notepad. "I won't tell him anything until you say it's okay." After scrawling something there, she tore out the sheet. "This is my number. I'm just asking you to think about it. You guys could even start out with email, totally safe. If you give him a chance, you'll see he's changed."

She handed the piece of paper to Tia and headed back up the sidewalk toward Main. She'd evidently parked nearby, then set out on foot.

Tia held the paper against the small stack of mail. She wouldn't use it. In fact, as soon as she was back inside, she'd toss it into the nearest trashcan.

Or maybe she should hang onto it. Not for the reasons Vanessa intended. More for insurance, something to pass to the police if things started to get scary. Having an in with someone who had an in with Victor could be a good thing.

Vanessa had promised to keep her location a secret. Her intentions were probably good. But Victor could be persuasive. If he found out Vanessa had found her, he'd never let it go.

And he *would* find out, even if Vanessa repeated verbatim everything Tia had told her to say. Vanessa was a terrible liar. Her emotions always showed on her face. The woman didn't have a crafty bone in her body. She'd try, but Victor would know. He'd get the information out of her somehow.

It wouldn't be with force or threats, and he wouldn't hurt her. That wasn't how he kept his sister under his thumb. Instead, he'd use guilt, feign hurt over her lack of trust, her determination to keep secrets. Eventually, she'd cave.

Yes, he was a master manipulator, and Tia had no doubt. Once he had the information he sought, he'd come after her.

The last time she'd been threatened, Jason had come to her aid. But he wasn't going to stay forever. In fact, he'd probably be gone well before Christmas.

Chances were good that when Victor showed up, she'd be facing him alone.

Alone with her .22.

Jason pulled into a parallel parking space in front of BethAnn's Fabrics and Crafts. Tia had hung around his grandparents' place for most of the afternoon, not leaving until an hour before he had.

He'd enjoyed having her there. As she'd walked through with her notebook and pen, he'd trailed along behind her, making suggestions of his own, the same as he had in the kitchen.

He'd always been good at visualizing possibilities for spaces, and as they'd talked about her goals and dreams for the shelter, he'd shared her excitement. He knew what these places meant to those seeking refuge. They were a glimmer of light in a world of darkness, the starting point on a long path to healing.

By the time she'd left the house, she'd filled several pages of her notebook with notes. She'd also helped him with his tasks, packing items into boxes, leaving him free to keep sorting. She'd insisted, saying it was payment for his expert advice.

He hadn't intended to share the details of his past with her. She hadn't even pressed. She'd just looked at him with those expressive blue eyes, silently encouraging him to let go, and the story had spilled out. She'd listened, without judging or offering meaningless platitudes.

What she hadn't done was crack the door behind which her own secrets lay. The ladies in her home seemed to like and respect him. He'd even managed to win his way past some of Damian's defenses. But Tia kept some inner part of her locked up tight. Gaining the trust of a woman who'd experienced unspeakable horrors at the hands of a man was a lot more challenging than connecting with an angry thirteen-year-old boy.

He stepped from the truck and looked at his watch. It was almost six o'clock. One minute till closing time. Then BethAnn would take him to meet her grandmother.

When he stepped inside, she was standing at the

counter, leaning against its inside edge, her back to him. The door whispered shut, and she turned in his direction. Her face was streaked with tears. After a soft "thank you," she hung up the phone.

"That was the hospital. My grandmother passed away ten minutes ago. Massive heart attack, no warning." A sound escaped that was half hiccup, half strangled sob. "I didn't even get to say goodbye."

His heart twisted. He didn't know BethAnn well enough to give her a comforting hug. He didn't even know if she was someone who appreciated hugs, although with her warmth and friendliness, she probably was. If only Tia were here, or Melissa, the bride-to-be that he'd met on Sunday. But they weren't.

He put a hand over hers, resting on the counter. "I'm so sorry." He wouldn't even try for any of the typical words of comfort—*she lived a good long life* or *she's in a better place*. Not even *I know how you feel*.

Because he didn't. Although he'd lost his grandmother, too, it was different. BethAnn was grieving a flesh-and-blood person. He was grieving a memory.

She wiped her eyes with one hand, and he released the other.

"Would you like me to call someone?"

"I'm all right. It was unexpected; she was just cleared to have surgery tomorrow. She wouldn't want me to be sad, though. She's with Granddaddy now. And Jesus." She gave him a weak smile. "I'm guessing they both met her at the gate."

She put her purse over her shoulder, rounded the counter and headed toward the front. When she flipped the double switch next to the door, all but the frontmost part of the store fell into darkness. Though the sun had set some time ago, a nearby streetlight cast a soft glow through one of the picture windows.

BethAnn led him outside the same time the door to the business next door opened and an elderly gentleman walked out. A younger man followed. As soon as he looked their way, he flashed BethAnn a broad smile. It disappeared as quickly as it had come.

"BethAnn?" Without locking the door, he rushed to where she stood and put his hands on her shoulders. He was probably the absentee Kevin that Tia's friends had mentioned on Sunday. "What happened?"

"Granny's gone."

"Oh, no." He drew her into the circle of his arms and held her for several moments, pivoting his body to rock her back and forth. Finally, he pulled away. "What are you doing tonight?"

"Nothing. Jason and I were planning to go to the hospital until I got the phone call."

She turned to make introductions. Kevin shook his hand and muttered a "pleased to meet you," but his attention was on BethAnn. Whether their relationship was friendship or something deeper, he couldn't tell.

Kevin frowned at her. "You don't need to be sitting home alone. How about if I come over? We can order pizza and do a movie, or whatever you'd like. You choose."

"Pizza and a movie sound good."

"I'm locking up and taking Granddaddy home. Then I'll be right over."

Jason bid them both farewell and walked the short distance to his truck. If he'd have acted a day earlier, he might have been able to get some of his questions answered. Now, any light her grandmother could have shed on the strange note had been snuffed out.

He climbed into the driver's seat and cranked the engine, but before he could pull away from the curb, his phone rang. He glanced at the name on the screen, and something sour filled his stomach. Every so often, his ex-wife contacted him out of the blue. Usually it was for the sole purpose of putting him in turmoil.

"Yes?" He didn't try to inject friendliness into his tone.

She didn't, either. "I heard your grandmother passed away."

"You heard right." Though he didn't know where she'd gotten the information. His grandfather had died while they'd still been married. She'd probably been keeping an eye on the obituaries since the divorce, hoping she'd be able to con him into giving her some of his inheritance.

It didn't take her long to get to the point. "Now that you've come into some unexpected money, I need some help with buying a new car. The mileage is getting up there on my old one."

There weren't any condolences. He didn't expect any, not sincere ones.

"Sorry, I can't help you." Her *old* car was newer than his truck.

"Isn't generosity and sharing with others part of your Christian faith?" Her words held an accusatory tone.

The sick feeling in his stomach morphed instantly to anger. It was just like Ashley to use his faith against him. She'd claimed to share that faith when they'd first gotten together. Shortly after marriage, she'd dropped both the pretense and the church attendance.

He clenched a fist, then tightened and released it several times, willing the anger to drain out with the action. He shouldn't still have any buttons for her to push.

He added a silent plea for peace. "It is, but one can't share what one doesn't have."

"Don't try to con me. I know about the will."

She probably did. They were married for four years. He or his mother had probably mentioned it at some point.

"The inheritance, had there been one, would have gone for my mother's cancer treatments."

"What do you mean *had there been one*?"

She'd glossed right over his mention of his mother's cancer. He didn't expect otherwise. If it didn't affect her world, it didn't exist.

"There's a new will, drawn up this year. I've inherited the personal effects. The house, furniture and bank account have gone to Peace House and the lady who runs it."

"What is Peace House?"

"A domestic abuse shelter."

"You do intend to fight it, right?"

"There's no point. The will is legal. There was nothing wrong with my grandmother's mind."

"Oh, come on, man up." Disgust laced the condescension in her voice.

His chest tightened as that familiar heat spread through him. If he couldn't destroy those buttons, he needed to at least figure out how to deactivate them.

"You're going to lie down and let some conniving, greedy, gold-digging woman walk away with your inheritance? You're not half the man I thought you were."

Her words injected a life-giving shot of oxygen into the fire that smoldered inside. It wasn't what she'd said about him. It was her calling Tia names. Apparently, he had a new button she could push, one with Tia's name on it.

"You just described yourself." His words had a steely edge. "None of those colorful adjectives fit Tia. She's devoted everything to providing a refuge for women and children facing abuse. Of course, you wouldn't understand. I don't think there's ever been a time when you've done something without any thought of what you might get in return."

His diatribe silenced her, but she recovered too soon.

"So her name is Tia. Do I detect a note of tenderness?"

He didn't respond. If his feelings could come out in his voice, there probably *was* some tenderness there. In record time, Tia had gone from adversary to friend. She could easily become more than a friend if all the obstacles were removed—things like distance and her baggage and his baggage and a nasty ex-wife.

He ended the call, thankful that his mother's random, spur-of-the-moment decision on where to settle had taken them so far from Florida.

Because if it weren't for the twelve hundred miles that lay between Harmony Grove and Groton, he wouldn't put it past her to sleuth out the location of the shelter and show up on Tia's doorstep, just to see what trouble she could stir up.

NINE

TIA STOOD ON the sixth step of the eight-foot ladder, left hand resting on the roof near the gable's peak. White Christmas lights dangled from her right hand. Angela and Jasmine stood below, untangling and stretching out the string of lights while Pam set to work on the next strand.

They were the icicle kind, with dangling strings of lights. This was the third year in a row Tia had used them. The hooks she'd slid between the drip edge and shingles had stayed, making the subsequent years' decorating much less time consuming than the first.

She stretched to drape what she held over the next hook, two feet away, then descended. She'd have to move the ladder to continue.

They'd started at the back door, continued across the rear of the house, around to the front and were now completing the right side. An orange extension cord snaked through the yard from the outlet on the front porch, the lights Pam held plugged into the end. Her job had been to test the strands before Tia hung them.

Angela gripped the other side of the ladder and helped her wrestle it through the shrubbery that lined the foundation. "I'm glad we're almost done. You make me nervous on those gables."

"I make *myself* nervous on those gables." Heights weren't her thing, but decorating was. Anything to add a little cheer to her surroundings, for herself as well as her residents.

Right now, she needed it. She was down a resident. Tricia had left that morning, gone to a more long-term shelter where she'd receive occupational training and much-needed counseling. It was nothing unexpected. Peace House was a temporary shelter, with a typical stay lasting thirty days.

Once they got the ladder positioned, Angela helped stabilize it. "When is the new lady coming?"

"Within the hour." Someone from the crisis center had called just before they'd started the lights. The newest referral was alone, married with no kids. She sounded like she'd be a good fit for Peace House. Tia would find out for sure shortly.

Angela sighed. "I'm going to miss Tricia. We came here on the same afternoon, and we've been sharing a room for the past three and a half weeks." She pursed her lips. "She wasn't much of a talker—I still don't know her story—but she was a good listener." She paused. "I hope she's going to be okay."

"Yeah, me, too."

Tia was concerned for all of them, but she worried even more about Tricia. She'd spent almost four weeks at Peace House and had left just as fragile as when she'd come. Tia had asked her to stay in touch, to let her know how she was doing, but she didn't hold out much hope of hearing from her again. The entire time she'd been there, she hadn't opened up to anyone.

"Another thirty feet or so, and we'll be back where we started." Tia ascended the ladder and draped the white strand over two more hooks. At least the peaks were done now. The rest would be easy. Once finished, she'd plug the lights into the receptacle near the back door, ready to flip the switch when it got dark.

Tonight, the holiday activities would continue, with the annual Harmony Grove Christmas parade. She always enjoyed the parade. Actually, she loved all the Christmas activities—driving through neighborhoods to see the lights, watching the children's and youth's production at church, even strolling down Main Street to view all the window displays.

Right now, though, it was the parade she looked forward to the most. If she said her excitement had nothing to do with the fact Jason would be sitting next to her, she'd be lying. She'd invited him to dinner, too. A cookout for her residents on parade night had become tradition—burgers with all the fixings. Jason had insisted on contributing the potato salad and chips.

She wasn't the only one looking forward to the parade. Even Damian had been in a good mood all day. Okay, maybe not good, but he'd seemed a lot less miserable. For a while, he'd watched them work on the lights, had even given his mother a hand when she'd struggled with a tangled strand. She'd been smart enough to not comment on his change in attitude.

Tia finished the last stretch of the gable, but before she could move to the back, a vehicle turned into the drive, then disappeared beyond the front corner of the garage. Moments later, the engine died. Probably Uber bringing her newest client.

She frowned at the others. "We'll have to do the last of it tomorrow morning."

Pam waved her away. "Go take care of the new lady. We'll finish this."

Tia hesitated. Putting her women on ladders was probably not a good idea. "Just be careful. We don't want any broken bones."

The warning seemed almost silly considering Jason had let her son use the power saw. Of course, he'd been supervising the entire time.

Tia thanked the women and jogged around the side of the house. The rear passenger door swung open. A woman with short, dark hair stepped from the passenger side of the car, her purse and a bulging tote over one shoulder.

When Tia introduced herself, the woman held out her left hand, her right temporarily out of commission. A cast ran from mid bicep to palm.

"I'm Maggie. Pleased to meet you."

Tia accepted the backward handshake. "Me, too, just not under these circumstances." She dipped her eyes toward the tote. "Can I help you carry anything?"

"Thanks, but I've got it." She lifted her shoulder. "This is all I have. While I was in the emergency room getting my arm taken care of, I shot off a quick text to a friend. I asked her to get me a couple changes of clothes and my toiletries and meet me in the hospital's main parking lot in two hours. Then I deleted the text before my husband walked back into the room. My friend takes care of the cat and mail when we're on vacation, so she has a key to the house.

If not for her, I don't know what I'd have done."

When Tia opened the front door, childish voices came from the dining room. Katie had the three younger kids involved in some kind of game, something calmer and quieter than Hungry Hippo.

Tia glanced that direction, then led Maggie into her office. In one corner, a swivel chair sat behind a desk. She and Monica did their clerical work there. When it came to talking with new clients, Tia preferred a more relaxed setting. She indicated the loveseat for Maggie and took the adjacent matching chair for herself, snagging a legal pad and pen from the desk.

As Maggie relayed her experiences, Tia took notes, recording yet another version of a story she'd heard countless times. Finally, Maggie paused. "I had a scare a couple of weeks ago, thought I was pregnant. When I found out I wasn't, I figured I'd better get out before my life got a lot more complicated."

"Has your husband been arrested?"

Maggie shook her head. "I didn't call the police. I don't care about destroying him. I just want out. He owns a restaurant, is well thought of in the community. I figured he'd let me go quietly rather than risking disgrace, or a night in jail."

"Did he?"

"Pretty much. He was furious, but he wasn't about to make a scene. We'd just left the hospital cashier. I told him I wasn't going home with him, to get in his car and leave. He walked away, but I wasn't taking any chances. I had hospital security accompany me to my friend's car. She's keeping Fred, too."

"Fred?"

"My cat. Samuel knows how much I love that

cat, and I wouldn't put it past him to punish me for leaving by mistreating him. Someday when this is over, I'll take him back." She gave Tia a weak smile. "The cat, not the husband."

Tia returned her smile, hoping that Maggie kept that resolve in the days and weeks to come. When they'd finished talking, Tia handed her some resources on escaping and healing from domestic abuse and led her from the office.

"I'll show you where your room is. You'll be sharing it with two other ladies who are in back right now hanging the last of the Christmas lights."

She indicated the bed that had been freshly changed after Tricia left and pointed out the empty dresser drawer that would be hers. Maggie laid the tote on top and began to transfer items with one hand.

Tia crossed the room and stopped at the open doorway. "Some of the other ladies and I are going to work on dinner now." It was time to pull that five-pound package of hamburger from the fridge and start pressing it into patties. "You can take it easy, get your bearings."

"I'll help. If you don't have any one-handed jobs, I'll hang out."

They headed down the hall, and as they stepped into the living room, footsteps approached, fast and light. The twins shot into the room from the other direction, followed by Julie and finally Katie. Aiden's face filled with disappointment when he saw that it was just Tia and Maggie. The more outgoing of the two boys, he'd probably hoped the newcomer would have kids.

Ethan's eyes had locked on the stranger. "What

happened to your arm?"

"Ethan!" Pink tinted Katie's cheeks. "It's not polite to ask people things like that.

"Why not?"

While Katie struggled to formulate just what was rude about the innocent question, Ethan skipped off down the hall to join Julie and his brother, already in the bedroom the boys shared with their mother.

Katie gave Maggie a sheepish smile. "I'm sorry. I'm trying to teach them not to voice everything that pops into their heads."

Maggie held up her other hand. "It's okay. I fell down the stairs." Her eyebrows dipped downward and she pursed her lips. "I don't have to lie anymore or make up excuses, do I?"

Katie shook her head. "No, we don't. I'm still trying to get used to that."

The young mother headed down the hall, probably to check on her boys. When Maggie's gaze met Tia's, it was with surprising steadiness.

"You wanna know truth? I've never fallen down the stairs. Ever. I've been pushed down them a few times, was thrown once. But I never fell on my own. If you look at my medical records over the past three years, though, you'd swear I'm the most accident-prone woman in Polk County."

"We don't do ourselves any favors by covering for them."

"I know. I just kept hanging in there, hoping the man I fell in love with would return. But that doesn't happen, does it?"

"Not without some serious counseling, and sometimes not even then."

All too often, that man was a facade, a restrained version of what was really inside. Once restraint was no longer necessary, that man vanished.

The back door creaked open, and Pam appeared a few seconds later. "We're finished. Jaz and Angela are putting the ladder back in the shed."

For the next half hour, Katie kept the kids entertained while the rest of them worked together making baked beans and coleslaw, brewing iced tea and heating up the grill.

Angela pressed a ball of hamburger between her palms and compressed the edges, working her way around the patty. "You know, you can get these premade."

"I know, but with lean ground chuck on sale, I couldn't resist. Besides, we can make them as big or small as we want them. Kid-size ones for the young'uns, and healthy-size servings for us."

Angela winked. "And man-size ones for your guy."

Tia frowned. "He's not my guy."

"Whoever he is, he was a hero when Danielle's boyfriend showed up."

She wouldn't argue with that.

Three knocks sounded on the front door. When she looked through the peephole, Jason stood on the porch, two grocery bags dangling from each hand. She swung open the door and greeted him.

He extended a hand holding two of the bags. "Chips. I wasn't sure what flavors you ladies liked."

She peeked into the bags. "So you got four. We'll be set for the next week." Maybe not with four children in the house. For kids, chips were a staple.

He followed her into the kitchen, where he placed

the other two bags on the counter. When he'd finished pulling out the contents, four quart-size plastic containers sat in a row.

"I obviously picked these up at the grocery store. I hope when I volunteered to bring potato salad, you weren't expecting homemade."

"Publix potato salad is great."

Angela plopped the last burger on the platter and handed it to Tia, who turned to Jason.

"Would you like to man the grill while we finish stuff in here and get out the condiments and paper goods? The utensils are there and the grill should be good and hot."

"I'll be glad to."

He headed toward the door with the platter, and Maggie slipped around him to open it. Once she'd closed it behind him, Jasmine poked Tia in the ribs. "I think he likes you."

Tia slid her a sideways glance. "He's packing up his grandparents' things. In the meantime, he's putting up with me."

"If that was true, he wouldn't be joining you for dinner and hanging around every chance he gets."

"You're exaggerating." She removed the teabags from the tea, and after adding ice, put the pitcher in the refrigerator.

Establishing enough of a rapport with her women for them to feel comfortable teasing her was a good thing. But this was teasing she could do without.

Whatever Jason might feel for her, she couldn't deny liking him. He'd found a way past her protective barriers, something no other man had done since the moment she'd erected them. Of course, she hadn't met a man like Jason. He had that lethal combination of good looks, charm, protectiveness and compassion. There was also their shared faith and now his past trauma. Everything she learned about him sent another cannonball at her defenses.

Before closing the refrigerator door, she removed a pack of individually wrapped slices of American cheese. When she stepped outside, Jason was standing at the grill about ten feet away, his back to her. His phone was pressed to one ear.

"Don't even think about it."

She jerked to a stop, her hand tightening around the cheese. Was he threatening someone?

He shook his head. "Absolutely not." Though his voice was stern, it wasn't sharp or harsh.

She stood listening, feeling like an eavesdropper, but unwilling to turn around and go back inside. Instead, she closed the door behind her, the contact of wood against wood the softest whisper.

"That's not an option. I'll do whatever I have to—beg, borrow or steal."

Steal? No, that was an expression, one she'd used herself. Jason wasn't a thief.

But was there something about him that she should know? He was apparently in trouble, trouble that involved money. An unmistakable air of desperation clung to him. Had he borrowed from some bad dudes and now they were trying to collect? If so, why had he given up the fight for his inheritance so quickly?

Maybe he hadn't. Maybe he'd been playing her while he and his Lakeland lawyer worked behind the scenes to wrangle the Sloan place away from Peace House. Or maybe he'd been truthful about not fighting the will because he knew he didn't stand a chance. Either way, whatever mess he'd gotten into with the person at the other end of that phone call, it didn't sound as if his dealings were on the up and up.

She should have known he was too good to be true. She'd let down her guard, given him too much access into her life. He had free rein of the house she'd inherited, was able to come and go from the shelter as he pleased. She'd even allowed him to get close to one of the young men in her care.

His raised voice cut across her troubled thoughts. "Don't you dare give up. We're going to get you through this."

Get you *through this?* So maybe he wasn't the one in trouble. Maybe it was someone close to him. Jason had apparently taken on the problem.

He sighed. "I'll call you later tonight. If I don't get these burgers flipped, they'll be crispy, and I'll have a bunch of ladies upset at me." A pause, then, "I love you, too."

The last sentence was like a splash in the face with cold water. She'd noticed the lack of a wedding ring within two days of meeting him. But that didn't mean he didn't have a girlfriend or fiancée. Why did she assume he didn't have a significant other?

Why did it matter? She wasn't in the market for a relationship, certainly not with someone who grew up witnessing abuse. Someone who could fly into a rage at the flip of a switch. She'd seen it the night he'd tackled Danielle's boyfriend. Granted, he'd had a reason, even an honorable one, but if the police hadn't arrived when they had, he might have killed the guy.

The abused often becomes the abuser. No matter how sweet and considerate and selfless Jason seemed, it was a chance she couldn't take. Now all temptation had been removed. She'd never acted on attraction to another woman's man.

Jason lifted the grill's cover and picked up the spatula. As he flipped the first burger, she walked into his peripheral vision. He gave her a relaxed smile, the emotion of the conversation he'd just had apparently forgotten. "Hey."

"Hey." She lifted what she held. "When you get them flipped, I'll put a piece of cheese on about half of them, for anyone who likes it melted."

His smile widened. "That's the best way."

Soon the grilling was finished and all the food and paperware was spread out on the kitchen counter. The residents made their way through the line, some carrying their full plates to the dining room and others heading outside to the two picnic tables.

Finally, Jason held out a hand, motioning Tia to go in front of him. They were the only ones left, except Damian. He stood at one end of the kitchen, leaning against the wall holding his heaping plate. He seemed to be waiting for something.

Tia focused on filling her plate. If Damian needed something, he'd ask. Having any kind of fuss made over him was usually met with disdain.

After getting her food, Tia looked at Jason. "Outside or inside?"

"Outside. Sundown two weeks from Christmas and we don't even need sweaters. I'm taking advantage of it."

Jason smiled at Damian as he passed. "Wanna join

us?"

"Yeah."

The acquiescence came without a return smile, but it was more than Jason would have gotten a few short days ago. If he stayed in Florida a little longer and Damian remained at the shelter for a couple more weeks, Jason might have a shot at making a real impact on the kid's life.

Tia headed outside with both of them following her. The sun had dipped behind the trees in the distance, its upper curve barely visible. Shades of orange and lavender streaked the western horizon, and the mid-seventies temperatures they'd enjoyed all day were sticking around.

Tia took a seat at the empty table. Jason sat next to her, and Damian sank onto the bench opposite him. Katie occupied the other table, one son on each side of her, both too excited about the parade to want to sit still and eat.

Between bites, Tia and Jason's topics ranged from childhood stories to work mishaps to amateur sports. Jason included Damian in the conversation with frequent glances, but didn't push him to respond. He seemed to instinctively know how to connect with the kid. He'd make a good father.

She looked at Katie, sitting facing her at the other table. She had her left arm around Aiden and pressed a kiss to the top of his head. Tia sighed. Before Victor, she'd wanted kids. She'd always assumed she'd have at least two. After Victor, she'd been glad she'd remained childless. But during odd moments, unexpected longing hit her out of nowhere. Like now.

Marriage might be somewhere in her distant

future, along with motherhood. It was a terrifying thought. Having children raised the stakes, making escape from an abusive relationship that much more difficult. Of course, escape wouldn't be necessary if she married the right man. Someone kind and caring and selfless. *Someone like Jason.*

No, not like Jason. He was already taken. The woman on the phone might have been his wife. The lack of a wedding ring meant nothing. Not all men wore them. In fact, he was possibly even a father, and that was why he was so good at relating to Damian.

By the time they'd finished eating, darkness had swallowed the last remnants of daylight, and the temperature had dropped several degrees. The three youngest children's excited chatter surrounded the adults as they gathered up the trash and took it inside. Soon, the few dishes they'd used were washed and stored back in the cupboards.

Tia tied up the bulging trash bag. "I'm grabbing a sweater. Anyone who wants a chair for the parade, come and get one."

She snatched her sweater from the office, then swung open the hall closet door. A dozen folding chairs stood stacked against one another, leaning on the side wall. After taking a head count, Jason removed four of them, each hand hooked around two chair backs. Damian did the same. Pam's eyebrows lifted, but she limited her reaction to a smile.

After Jasmine took a chair, Ethan and Aiden each claimed one, insisting they were big enough, then relinquished them to their mother before they reached the end of the driveway. Tia relieved her of one of them for the rest of the trek to the inn. Soon eleven chairs were lined up two deep between the back of Jason's pickup truck and the curb.

Damian stood in front of one of the chairs. "Can I put mine in the back of your truck? I want to be up high so I can see good."

Jason shrugged. "Fine with me. But you'll have a harder time getting to the candy."

"Oh." He clearly hadn't thought of that.

Soon the shrill squeal of sirens cut off conversation, and in the distance, lights flashed blue and red. Branch led the parade in his cruiser, "Chief" emblazoned on the side in gold capital letters. He drove slowly past, windows down, alternating hands on the wheel as he waved to the people lining both sides of the street. Branch was in his element anytime an activity put him in the limelight.

Tommy and Alan shared the second cruiser, Tommy at the wheel. Candy sailed through the open windows, and kids on both sides ran into the edges of the street to gather it up. Harmony Grove's one and only fire truck followed, the toot of its horn competing with the squeal of two sirens. More candy flew through the air.

Then bands from the local middle and high schools marched through, interspersed with floats representing the various businesses. The Hope Community Church float featured Mary, Joseph, Baby Jesus, wise men, angels and sheep, with all except Jesus played by the church's Kidz Klub. Christmas carols streamed from a loud speaker and two church members passed out tickets to the annual chili cookoff.

Two horses approached pulling a sled, stuffed felt antlers on their heads and lighted garland around their necks. Squeals of "Santa" rose from the kids in the crowd. The bearded man in the red suit sat in the middle of the sled, waving, wrapped gifts in all sizes and shapes packed in around him.

As the next float moved closer, Tia stood and waved her hands, giving a loud whoop. As long as she'd been in Harmony Grove, Harvey's bookstore and BethAnn's craft store had shared a float, BethAnn occupying the front and Kevin the rear, a lighted archway between. Old Harvey, Kevin's grandfather, sat on the back of the trailer with his feet dangling over the edge, tossing candy both directions while BethAnn threw other objects. A beaded Mardi Gras-type necklace landed in Jason's lap.

He picked it up and put it over Tia's head. "Pretty baubles for a pretty lady."

What, was he flirting? Whoever was on the other end of that phone call wouldn't appreciate it. No, he was just in high spirits, caught up in the celebratory atmosphere around him. He wasn't the only one having fun. Damian was actually smiling, pockets bulging with candy. He'd even shared some of what he'd gathered with the three younger ones.

After the parade was over, they headed back toward the shelter as a group, Damian and Jason again carrying most of the chairs. Maggie, Angela and Jasmine walked abreast in the lead, and Tia and Jason fell in behind them.

Jason smiled down at her. "Thanks for letting me hang out with you and your folks."

"It was fun." Probably her most enjoyable Harmony Grove Christmas Parade ever. "We always do after-parade hot chocolate. It's tradition. Would you like to join us?"

"I think I'll take a rain check. I need to call my mom back before it gets too late."

"Sure."

Wait, his mom? Tia looked up at him, brows raised. "That's who you were talking to earlier?"

"Yeah, when you came out with the cheese."

His mom. The woman on the other end of that call had been his mother. Laughter bubbled up, but she gulped it back, along with the elation that came from out of nowhere. Jason's relationship status didn't affect her one way or the other.

"I thought you were talking to your wife."

He gave a little snort. "Don't have one of those anymore."

With the hardness in his tone, she almost expected him to finish with a "thank goodness." So Jason had been married before, too. Apparently, his marriage hadn't ended on much better terms than hers had, although there likely hadn't been any arrests involved.

She suddenly sobered. "Your mom, is she...all right?"

He paused before answering, lips pressed together. "She's sick, cancer. The traditional treatments haven't worked. She's trying something experimental."

Tia nodded as the pieces of the puzzle began to fall into place. "And it's expensive."

"Very. The insurance she had with her counseling job covers part of it, but the copay is astronomical."

The dire financial straits, the desperation she'd sensed, and his demand that the person on the other end of the line not give up. Now it all made sense. His mother was dying of cancer, and Jason was spending every last dollar trying to keep her alive.

"Why didn't you tell me?"

"I wasn't going to try to sway you by pulling on your heartstrings."

Tia's shoulders sagged. Could the man be any more perfect?

"I feel awful."

"Don't. This is what Grandma wanted. I've still got a lot of stuff to go through." One side of his mouth lifted in a half smile. "Those coffee cans have to be somewhere."

The teasing tone said he didn't believe his words any more than she did.

They turned the corner onto Tranquility Way, Ethan's and Aiden's excited voices drowning out Pam's and Katie's behind them. Ahead of them, the three women talked softly, their words indistinct.

Tia had fallen silent. Tomorrow she'd go back to the house and reassess her plans. Maybe there'd be a way to make the place suitable for her shelter without wiping out the bank account. Somehow, she'd make sure Jason walked away with more than some knickknacks and keepsakes.

They passed the hedge-lined fence that framed Tranquility Inn's back yard, and Maggie looked wistfully over her shoulder. "That's probably not open to the public, is it?"

Tia shook her head. "Not really. It belongs to the inn."

"Too bad. Gardens are soothing to the spirit."

"I agree. I'm planning to have a nice one at the new place."

Maggie's head swiveled. "You're moving?"

"Eventually. It'll be a much bigger place, a lot more room to spread out."

"I bet you're excited."

"Yeah." Just not nearly as excited as she'd been five minutes ago. Knowing that her gain was Jason and his dying mother's loss left her with a sick feeling in the pit of her stomach.

The three women had just started up the driveway when Maggie turned again. "What's on the window?"

Tia followed Maggie's gaze, quickening her pace. Before she'd left, she'd drawn the drapes and turned on the porch light. Its soft glow barely reached the left-most living room window. Something had been written there, red letters standing out against the white backing of the insulated drapes.

Maggie read slowly, pronouncing each word as she made it out. "Enjoy…your…Holidays."

There was another line below that, the print smaller. Tia's step faltered. Awareness tingled through her, as if something crawled just beneath the surface of her skin. No matter what she did, she could never escape it. Anyone who had ever experienced true terror knew that it was a sentient being, with a life and will of its own.

She squinted, moving closer, then jerked to a stop. Someone bumped into her from behind and spoke an apology close to her ear. Katie. Or maybe it was Pam. A chill that had nothing to do with the comfortable December evening swept through her, and her mind stalled out. Jason's presence wasn't any comfort. Neither was the fact that she was surrounded by several other women.

Now she was close enough to read the last line. It

wasn't a greeting or any kind of good tidings.

It was a threat. How serious of one it was depended on who'd made it.

I'm watching you.

TEN

JASON PRESSED HIS key fob and the Ram's locks clicked into place. As far as adult living facilities went, Winter Gardens was a nice place. He'd only been there once before, for his grandmother's memorial service, but he'd been impressed. The staff had gone all out decorating for Christmas, and instead of the stale odor he often associated with homes for the elderly, the place smelled of cinnamon potpourri.

Learning his grandmother had spent her last five years in a "home" had planted a knot of regret in his chest, but seeing the facility for himself and witnessing the affection the aides showed for the residents had soothed some of his guilt.

He made his way toward the covered drive in front of the entrance. He'd never gotten around to placing the call to his mother last night. Tia had seemed so shaken over the message on her living room window, he hadn't wanted to leave her.

She'd called the police, and Officer Willis had responded. She hadn't been able to say whether the threat was aimed at her or one of her residents, but all the women had insisted no one knew their location.

Tia had provided two possible suspects, someone

connected with Danielle's boyfriend and a Victor Krasney. Based on what she'd told Willis, she had a history with the latter. He'd been released from prison, and though his sister had made contact with Tia, she'd promised to not reveal her whereabouts.

The conversation confirmed something he'd suspected all along—that Tia had experienced abuse herself. Though she projected strength and tenacity, a hidden fragility lay just beneath the surface.

It was that fragility that had drawn him to her from the start. She kept it buried, except during unguarded moments. During those times, her eyes grew haunted and she lifted her hand to the scarf draped below her neck, as if the silk against her palm somehow brought her comfort. The action, along with the vulnerability on her face, sent his protector instinct into overdrive.

Through most of her report last night, she'd kept her right hand buried in the scarf, clutching its folds so tightly her knuckles looked white in the glow of the porch light. He'd had to tamp down his reaction to the scenarios that played through his mind. The thought of any man laying a hand on this beautiful, sweet woman almost made him crazy.

Jason moved toward the entrance, and the automatic glass door slid sideways on its track. A man stood at the reception desk talking with the young lady there, his back to the door. Jason waited several feet away.

This morning, he'd made the call that he'd promised to make last night. His mother had sounded better and was anticipating a good day. Any improvement was a cause for celebration and sent hope coursing through him. He'd raised enough heartfelt prayers that a full-blown miracle wasn't out of the question.

The man in front of him finally turned and walked toward the door, nodding as he passed. Jason stepped forward, and the young lady at the reception desk offered him a bright smile.

"Jason, right?"

"You have a good memory." Better than his. He glanced at the name plate near the edge of the counter. Carrie. He'd met her briefly when he'd signed in the day of his grandmother's memorial service.

"I never forget a face. What can I do for you?"

"I'm hoping you can give me some information, maybe shed some light on a mystery."

"I'll try." She flashed him another smile. "I love a good mystery."

"My grandmother had a friend who I understand came to see her regularly." He hesitated. He should have asked BethAnn for her grandmother's name. "Do you know BethAnn, runs BethAnn's Fabrics and Crafts?"

"Everyone knows BethAnn. She's here with her church group just about every Sunday evening. The residents love her."

"I understand our grandmothers were close."

"Yep. Jeanne Benson usually came with BethAnn but also visited alone once or twice a week."

Jason nodded. "I'm curious about a visit that might have happened on October 15th. My grandmother apparently asked her to write a note to me on that date. BethAnn confirmed the handwriting. We made plans to talk to her at the hospital Wednesday night."

Carrie's eyes widened. "Mrs. Benson's in the hospital?"

Oh, no. She hadn't heard. He hated being the

bearer of bad news. "She was. She passed away that afternoon."

Her chest deflated. "I'm so sorry to hear that. She was such a sweet lady. Your grandma was, too. I'm going to miss them both." She paused. "I take it you didn't get to talk to her."

"No. I walked into BethAnn's store right after she got the news. I was wondering if Mrs. Benson did visit on that date, and if so, whether any of the staff might have overheard anything."

"This note…" Carrie bit off whatever she was going to say.

"It's okay. She mentioned a rug, was pretty adamant that I take it back with me."

"Is it valuable?"

"Not that I've been able to determine."

After getting back to his room last night, he'd done a search with his iPad. The name of the manufacturer had turned up hundreds of rugs, all low- to middle-end merchandise. Keying in a description of the rug's design hadn't been any more helpful than the first search he'd done.

In a last-ditch effort to find something useful, he'd keyed in several other search phrases, such as *high-end rugs*, *collectible tapestries, valuable rugs* and *heirloom rugs*. The only thing he'd gotten from his efforts was sticker shock. If he spent fifty thousand dollars on a rug, he certainly wouldn't walk on it.

"I'd love to find out if anyone here might know what's so special about this rug and why my grandmother was so determined that I take it with me."

He'd even asked his mom about it this morning.

Although she remembered it, she didn't think it held any value, sentimental or otherwise.

Carrie nodded, her lips pursed in concentration. "The first place to start would be to find out when Mrs. Benson was here and who was on shift at the time."

She spun her chair and rolled toward the back wall, where several binders were lined up on top of a credenza. After turning back around, she laid one of the binders on her desk and flipped the pages until she found what she was looking for.

"Yep, October 15th. Jeanne Benson signed in at 10:37 a.m. and signed your grandmother out at 10:45."

"How long were they gone?"

Carrie followed the line across to the last block. "They signed back in at 1:35. Lunch here is served at 11:30, so that means they ate somewhere off-site."

Jason nodded. Almost three hours. Lunch wouldn't have taken more than an hour. Writing the note and putting it in the library table drawer would maybe add another forty minutes. What else had they done, and did it have anything to do with his grandmother's insistence that he haul a seemingly worthless rug all the way back to Connecticut?

Carrie closed the binder. "The manager does all the scheduling, so she can tell you who was on during that time frame."

She ushered him into an office two doors away. Over the next half hour, Jason talked to the manager and four other staff members. Except for one nurse's aide who was currently on vacation, they were the only ones working during the hours noted on the log. No one had overheard anything about a rug or what stops they had planned for the day.

After thanking everyone who'd spoken with him, Jason walked from the building not knowing any more than he had when he'd come.

He slid into his pickup and pulled Tia up in his contacts. At his insistence, they'd exchanged numbers last night before he'd gone back to the inn. He'd wanted her to be able to call him any hour of the day or night if she felt threatened, and he'd wanted to be able to check up on her.

She answered on the second ring. Her voice seemed to hold a happy lilt.

"I'm leaving Winter Gardens. No one knows anything about the rug." If only there was a way to trace the ladies' routes that day. "I have a crazy question for you. Do you have access to my grandmother's bank account?"

"I don't yet, but the attorney does. Why?"

The hesitation in her tone bordered on distrust. He didn't blame her.

"Don't worry, I'm not asking you to get into it. I'm wondering if my grandmother made any withdrawals on October 15th."

"The date on the note. I'll see what I can find out and call you back. Either that, or I'll see you at your grandmother's house."

"You're coming over?" His stomach tilted then righted itself.

"If it's all right with you. I'll bring lunch for both of us."

When he pulled into the driveway twenty minutes later, the Fiat wasn't there. Tia hadn't said what time she was coming, but it would probably be soon. Lunchtime was less than an hour away.

He stepped from the truck and started up the front walk. The yard still looked good from the mowing and weed-eating he'd done a week ago. It was no longer overgrown, anyway. Bringing it back to his grandparents' standards would require several months of irrigating, weeding, seeding and fertilizing.

Once inside, he entered the den, where several boxes were packed, taped and labeled, ready to haul to the living room. Other than that, the den was finished. He toted the boxes two at a time down the hall and into the living room. When he'd finished stacking them with the others, he surveyed his surroundings. If it weren't for the custom built-in units that occupied the entire length of one wall, the living room would be the easiest room to sort.

Other than the book-filled shelves and the drawers beneath, the room held a Queen Anne style couch, a loveseat with matching chairs and a spinet piano. A rug occupied the center of the room. It was much bigger than the one upstairs. Much nicer, too. But apparently his grandmother didn't care what he did with this one, or any of the others in the house.

He crossed the room to where a piano sat against the wall. He'd removed the sheets from the furniture a few days ago to see what was there. Already a fine layer of dust had settled on the top. He swiped a hand across the surface, leaving a wide, walnut-colored trail. Was the piano furniture? Or would Tia consider it a personal effect?

He pulled out the bench and sat. The same layer of dust had settled on the lid that covered the keys. He lifted and slid it back. This was the piano his grandparents had had when he was a child, the brand spelled out on the front edge of the lid. Cable Nelson. Maybe it wasn't as well-known as Steinway and Kawai, but it had always had a nice sound. Now it spurred some good memories.

He rested his right hand on the keys, his thumb on middle C. He depressed the key, following with the E and G, then played the three notes together to make up the C major chord.

The creak of hinges came from the direction of the entry. Jason stepped into the opening between the two rooms as Tia closed the door. He announced his presence with a soft "hey," hoping not to startle her. It didn't work. She spun toward him, alarm in her eyes, alarm that faded the moment she saw him.

"Sorry, I didn't mean to scare you."

"No problem. I'm a little jumpy after last night." She held up a plastic bag. Her other hand clutched the same spiral-bound notebook he'd seen the last time she'd come.

"Lunch. I cheated, picked up sandwiches at the Hometown Cafe. They were having a two-for-one special. I hope you like pulled pork."

"There's not much I don't like." He followed her into the kitchen. "Two things—anchovies on pizza and liver with onions. As long as you don't try to feed me those, I'm good."

She pulled the items from the bag and laid them on the island bar. Noon was still ten minutes away, but he wasn't complaining. Those two breakfast burritos he'd eaten early this morning were long gone, and the aroma of pork and whatever sauce the cafe had used had kicked up a serious hunger.

She grinned over at him. "I brought it; you can bless it."

"Gladly."

He took her hand, then second-guessed the automatic action. Joining hands for prayer was something he and his mother and several of his church friends had done for years.

Maybe Tia had, too. He bowed his head, and after offering thanks for the food, he asked for blessings on Tia and the women and children who came through her shelter. He ended with a healing prayer for his mom.

Tia repeated his "amen" with a hand squeeze, then picked up her sandwich. "I'm praying for your mom, too."

"Thanks." His heart twisted. What would it be like to have someone like Tia, a woman whose faith was as genuine as his own, a partner who would support and encourage him, someone he could count on to always be at his side?

Someday he would find what he longed for. But it wouldn't be with Tia. He couldn't bring his mother back to Central Florida, and he wouldn't leave her in New England alone. And he'd never ask Tia to leave what she'd built in Harmony Grove.

She chewed and swallowed the bite she'd taken. "I heard back from the attorney's office right before I walked in. No withdrawals of any kind. His assistant checked from the beginning of August through the end of October. No debits except the autopay stuff, like the nursing home and the electric bill and basic lawn care on this place."

Jason heaved a sigh. It would have been nice if his grandmother had pulled a large sum of money from her account and hidden it somewhere in the house. He hadn't expected it, but now he knew for sure—wherever his grandmother and Mrs. Benson had gone on October 15th, it hadn't been the bank.

Tia slid him a sideways glance. "I'm sorry. I'm still hoping there's something of value here that'll be a godsend for you and your mom."

"Thanks." But he wasn't holding out much hope. Knowing his grandmother had had the opportunity to visit the bank but hadn't, he couldn't even hope for hundred-dollar bills tucked between the pages of his favorite books.

Tia finished her sandwich and crumpled the paper that had wrapped it. "I'm reassessing my plans for the place. That's why I'm here this afternoon."

"What do you mean?"

"I believe there are things I can do more cheaply. I need to look at the must-haves versus the like-to-haves. I know I need a new roof. The shingles aren't even lying flat in places, and some of the upstairs ceilings have water stains on them. But a commercial dishwasher isn't a must, and I can make do with the cabinets I have."

"If you've got the money, do what you need to for the shelter."

She smiled. "I will, with emphasis on the word *need*." Her smile faded, but the sincerity in her gaze didn't. "I'm going to keep only what I need to get the place up and running. I want you and your mom to have the rest."

He swallowed around a sudden lump in his throat.

Could Tia and Ashley be any more different?

"Thank you." He took her hand again, this time with intention and forethought, and gave it a squeeze, hoping the small gesture relayed how much he appreciated her selflessness and generosity, because he no longer trusted himself to speak.

She climbed down from the barstool, sliding her hand from beneath his, then picked up her notebook. After folding back the cover, she turned a couple of pages. "Here are our kitchen ideas. If we double our capacity, a working dishwater is a must, but it doesn't have to be a fancy commercial one."

She opened and closed several cabinet doors. Each shelf was filled with dishes—plates in three sizes, bowls, cups and glasses. Several of the lower cabinets held pots and pans in every size imaginable.

"I have plenty of cabinets, so the wasted space on the other side of the fridge is no problem."

He nodded. "Let's go through the kitchen together. Anything you can use, I'm willing to leave here. Whatever you don't want, I'll pack it up for your yard sale."

They went through the rest of the house the same way, with Tia figuring out where she could cut corners. Finally, she turned to face him in the entry.

"What are you going to work on next?"

"I was thinking about the living room. All the work there is confined to one wall. Even that's going to be a little overwhelming."

She gave him a sympathetic smile. "I noticed. It's a nice unit, but that's a lot of shelves and drawers."

"My grandparents had quite a collection of books." He'd never looked to see what the drawers contained.

"I guess I need to clean out the piano bench, too, if there's anything in it."

Tia walked into the room, stopping in front of the piano. She extended an index finger and depressed an F-sharp. The tone lingered for some time, slowly fading to silence.

He stood next to her. "Do you play?"

"No. I'd wanted to off and on, but always changed my mind before Mom could buy a piano. Ending up cheering instead."

"I could see you as a cheerleader." She was certainly cute enough.

"Yep, top of the pyramid. I was always the shortest, lightest girl on the squad." She turned her back to the piano. "What about you? Do you play?"

"No."

"I thought I heard the piano when I opened the door."

"Well, I used to play, a little."

"Why did you stop?"

He shrugged. "Lost interest."

No, that wasn't true. His gaze dipped to the keyboard. His grandmother had paid for six months of lessons, and his next-door neighbor had allowed him to practice on her electronic keyboard for an hour after school every day.

His mother had encouraged him. His father had insisted playing the piano was an activity for sissies, that real men played sports, like football or basketball. Jason hadn't been interested in sports at the time. He hadn't been built for it anyway. His growth spurt hadn't happened until the summer he hit sixteen.

When he looked at Tia again, she was watching

him. He avoided her eyes, sure she'd be able to discern all his secrets if he allowed that perceptive gaze to lock on his.

"Why did you really stop?" Her voice was soft.

He paused before answering. He'd already told her more of his past than he'd intended. Too much deep sharing forged connections he'd have to sever in two or three short weeks.

"My dad." The words slipped out anyway. She was too easy to talk to.

"He didn't want to have to listen to you practice?"

If it had been that easy, he'd have been a virtuoso by the end of high school. The hours his father spent hanging with his friends in the local taverns would have given Jason hours of practice time.

"It wasn't that. Anything artistic, creative or musical wasn't masculine enough for my father. He was determined to make a man out of me almost from the get-go."

Tia nodded. "Like Damian's father."

Yeah, exactly. He sat on the bench, and his fingers found the C chord he'd played earlier. He moved from that to F, then G, the three major chords that contained only white keys. That was all he remembered.

"I was already at a big disadvantage." He talked over the lingering notes of the final chord. "I told you before, I was a runt, which just about made him despise me. He tried to force me to make up in toughness what I lacked in size."

He moved to the D chord, remembering to sharp the middle note. The same with the E chord, then A. He remembered more than he thought he had.

"My dad gave me such grief about playing the

piano, it was easier to quit."

"Have you considered taking it back up? You're free to do what you want now."

"Not really." The activity had too many negative emotions connected with it. He couldn't even think about it without hearing his father's voice, filled with disdain. He'd worked hard at trying to forgive the man, only because he knew that was what God required. He still wasn't there yet.

He rose from the bench and faced Tia. "What's the story with Victor Krasney?"

When he said the name, she flinched as if he'd struck her. Indecision flashed across her features, and the vulnerability in her eyes punched him in the gut.

"Someone from my past."

His chest tightened. "He hurt you, didn't he?"

"Yes." Her response was the softest whisper.

A tiny ball of heat formed in his core. He recognized the sensation immediately, because that was how it always started—a small seed that expanded until it exploded through his body, overpowering reason.

Not this time. Instead of growing, the fire sputtered and died under something far different from anger, but just as powerful. He leaned toward Tia, an invisible cord connecting them, trauma shared though miles and years apart. Both no longer victims but survivors. She felt it, too. He could see it in her eyes.

"I'm so sorry." He lifted a hand to her cheek.

When she moistened her lips, his eyes followed the motion. He wanted to kiss her more than anything he'd wanted in a long time. If it would erase the pain in her eyes, he'd do it in a heartbeat. And maybe in the process, he'd erase a little of his own.

But whatever comfort either of them might find would soon dissolve into regret. Tia apparently recognized it, too. She turned away and rested her hand on the top of the piano.

"Is this furniture or personal effects?"

He smiled, the spell broken. "I'd asked myself the same thing. I'm not taking it home, so you can decide what you want to do with it."

"I think I'll keep it." She turned to face him again. "I'm sure there'll be women staying here who play and would find the activity comforting." She walked from the room. "I'd better go so we can both get something done."

After she retrieved her keys and purse from the kitchen, he followed her to the front door. "I'm glad you came. Come anytime. Believe me, the distractions are welcome."

"I'll remember that."

After she stepped outside, he stood in the opening, watching her walk to her car, climb in and back from the drive. He hoped they'd stay in touch after he went back to Connecticut. At the thought of never seeing her again, an overwhelming sense of loneliness settled over him.

The sharing today had been...nice. She was a kindred spirit, and it was a relationship he wanted to cultivate. He needed someone like Tia in his life, even if they'd never be more than friends. Even if more than a thousand miles would always lie between them.

But if they were going to have any kind of long-term relationship, even friendship, there were things she needed to know. He'd told her about his childhood, the abuse he and his mother had experienced. He'd shared his pain as well as his guilt and regrets. But he'd held back on the one thing that could be a deal-breaker for Tia.

Eventually, he'd have to come clean—about everything. It was a conversation he dreaded. But Tia needed to know, and it was better for her to hear it from him than from someone else.

ELEVEN

TIA GATHERED THE used paper plates the others handed her from around the picnic table. After church, Jason had joined her, and all eleven of them had crowded around the two wooden tables, insisting it was too nice a day to eat inside.

Tia didn't have a garden like the one behind the inn; that would have to wait until she moved. But even with her little back yard, time in the sunshine each day went a long way in staving off the depression that plagued so many of the women that came through her doors.

Jason took the stack of dirty plates from her, then stepped through the door she opened for him. "Thanks for lunch. That was wonderful."

"It was easy." Before leaving for church, she and three of the other women had filled her big roaster with carrots, potatoes and two three-and-a-half-pound beef roasts and put it in the oven. The hunks of meat were large enough she had enough left over to make sandwiches for lunch tomorrow.

When they stepped into the kitchen, the other ladies had already begun clean-up. Jason stuffed what he held into the trash, while Tia removed a plastic container and lid from the cupboard, ready to put up leftovers.

Pam waved her away. "We've got this. You guys go on."

Tia thanked her and walked Jason to the door. He'd already announced his plans for the afternoon. After checking on his mom, he was heading over to the house.

He stepped onto the porch. "What does the rest of your day look like?"

"I've got a date with my Kindle." Sunday afternoons were lazy, an opportunity to rest up from the prior week and recharge before time to dive into the next one.

"That sounds good. That's how I'll be spending my evening. What are you reading?"

"A light-hearted women's fiction book." It was a good escape. But so was suspense, comedy and even romance. Just because her own had ended badly, that didn't stop her from enjoying reading about someone else's tortuous road to happily-ever-after. "How about you?"

"Slightly different genre." He grinned. "Aliens are trying to take over the galaxy. Lots of intergalactic battles, cool technology." He put his fingers to his brow in a farewell salute. "Enjoy your light-hearted women's fiction."

She returned the gesture. "Enjoy your aliens."

As he descended the two steps, she closed and locked the door. Then she moved to the window to watch him walk down the driveway.

When he reached the sidewalk, he looked back toward the house, as if he could sense her eyes on him. His face lit with a smile, and he lifted one hand in a wave.

Her stomach flipped over, as much from the smile as the fact she'd been caught. She'd been attracted to him right from the start—the wavy dark hair that begged to be touched, the rich brown eyes with their golden flecks, the masculine lines of his face. At first, it had been easy to ignore. Simple attraction didn't involve the emotions. With each day that passed, though, she was getting to know him better, and everything she saw endeared him to her further.

After he'd shared more of his childhood with her yesterday, she hadn't been ready yet to talk about Victor. He hadn't pushed, but the silent concern and support in his eyes had bolstered her. When he'd cupped her cheek, his touch so warm and light, she'd almost melted.

For the first time in five years, she'd wanted to be kissed, to feel cherished. Jason had been thinking about it, too. It had been written all over his face. The panic that should have come hadn't, but a voice of reason had nudged its way through her scattered thoughts. She'd turned away before she could allow anything to happen that they'd later regret.

She backed from the window with a sigh. What would her life have been like had it been Jason who'd swept her off her feet instead of Victor? She probably wouldn't be running a shelter for abused women. She also wouldn't carry the scars that marked her, both inside and out.

The more time she spent with him, the harder it was to imagine him ever laying an angry hand on her. He was too gentle, too selfless, too protective. But his history wasn't their only obstacle. His home was twelve hundred miles away. So was his job. The odds of a Central Florida transfer were nil. Almost equally distant from both coasts, Polk County didn't have any submarine plants.

Of course, Jason had a construction background, too. Those jobs were plentiful. But he'd never leave his sick mother. Bringing his mom to Harmony Grove was out of the question, too. More than likely, nothing had changed since they'd fled. As long as Jason's father was alive, his mom wouldn't be able to return to Central Florida.

Tia would never walk away from her shelter, either. Too many people had gotten behind her—supported her, sacrificed and poured their own resources into her cause.

When she returned to the kitchen, Pam slid the roaster into one of the bottom cabinets and straightened while Angela hung the dish towel on the oven door handle.

Maggie wiped the last counter with one hand and looked at Tia over her shoulder. "All finished. For a few hours, anyway."

Tia returned her smile. "The work is never done for long."

"I'm all right with that." Jasmine moved toward her. "Staying busy is good. It makes the time go faster."

Maggie nodded. "And helps keep the demons at bay."

Over the next ten minutes, everyone settled into different activities. Jasmine started a jigsaw puzzle on the dining room table. Pam joined her, and after setting the twins up with coloring books and crayons at the other end, Katie did, too. Tonight, Tia would choose a movie and anyone who wanted to watch it with her could join her in the living room. One of her goals was to make the shelter feel as much like home as possible. At least a peaceful, safe version of home.

Tia got her Kindle from her room and plopped herself at one end of the couch. Maggie sat in the center of the sectional, a book she'd taken from one of the shelves open in her lap. Damian sat at the other end, engrossed in whatever game he was playing. But neither the presence of the other two nor the beeps and dings coming from Damian's device intruded on her relaxation.

When a knock sounded on the front door a short time later, a bolt of uneasiness shot through her. She laid aside her Kindle and crossed the room to check the peephole.

A woman she didn't recognize stood on the porch. She didn't look threatening, but Tia wasn't taking any chances. She moved to the window and peered out. A Hyundai Sonata sat in the drive. No one was inside. The woman had apparently come alone.

When Tia opened the door, the stranger's gaze swept her entire length. The charcoal-colored skirt and jacket accented a perfect figure, and her hair, makeup and nails looked as if she'd just come from a salon. An air of cold haughtiness oozed from her, leaving Tia feeling frumpy in the comfy sweater and dress jeans she'd worn to church.

"I was looking for Peace House, and someone at the gas station directed me here."

"Okay." Keeping a shelter's location secret from the

people in the community was nearly impossible, but something about this woman put Tia on edge. "What can I do for you?"

The visitor looked her up and down. "So you're Tia." Based on the disdain in her eyes, the woman had found her lacking.

Tia straightened her spine. "Can I help you with something?"

"I doubt it."

When she didn't continue, Tia tossed aside any attempt at politeness. "Who are you and why are you here?"

"I'm Ashley." She paused for effect. "Jason's wife."

Tia nodded. Jason had said he'd been married before. What she couldn't explain was why his former wife was standing on her front porch.

"*Ex*-wife." Tia kept her tone flat. If the woman thought they were in competition for Jason's affections, she was wrong. From what Tia understood, Ashley would never have them. If yesterday's interactions at his grandmother's place were any indication, Tia already did, but it didn't matter.

Ashley surveyed the front facade of the house. "You run a shelter for abused women. I could have used a place like this when I was married to Jason."

Tia's chest tightened as something dark drifted over her and lingered there. No, Jason couldn't have abused his wife. Whatever the woman was hinting at, it couldn't be that. There had to be another explanation.

Arched brows lifted. "You look surprised. Apparently, you haven't seen what he can do when he's angry."

Tia swallowed hard, trying to quell the nausea churning in her stomach. The problem was, she *had* seen him angry, and she'd been scared. She'd later tried to justify it, to convince herself that the rage would never be turned on her. But if Ashley was telling the truth, it had been turned on her, apparently more than once. Had Tia really pegged him that wrong?

No, she didn't believe it. He did everything he could to protect women. He wouldn't hurt them.

Ashley snorted, the action at odds with the snooty air she was trying to project. "Of course you haven't seen it. He does a good job of keeping that side of him hidden." She paused. "Until you tick him off."

Tia opened her mouth, but nothing came out. The questions and denials circling through her mind collided and stalled out, a giant mental traffic jam.

Ashley shook her head. "He didn't tell you about the night he landed me in the hospital with a broken arm and dislocated jaw, did he? It wasn't the first time he hurt me, but it was the first time I had the guts to report it. And the guts to get out."

Her features softened, and sympathy entered her eyes, but it didn't seem genuine. When she backed it up with a hand on Tia's arm, Tia fought the urge to jerk away and run inside.

"I understand. Believe me, he duped me, too. I like to think of myself as an intelligent woman, but I was swayed by those good looks and that charm and sweetness he seems to have. Give it time. You'll see it's all an act."

Ashley dropped her arm. "I can tell you're wondering whether you can believe me. Look it up. Arrest records are public. I'll even help you out.

Groton, New London County, Connecticut." She turned, descended the porch steps and walked to her car.

For several moments, Tia stood leaning against the door jamb, unable to go in and face the others. She'd brought a man with a history of abuse into the home, let him sit at the table and share meals with her and her clients. She'd even allowed him to get close to a troubled young man, thinking he could use a mentor. The last thing he needed was another abusive man like his father. Jason was exactly what she was trying to protect her women from.

She turned toward the door and reached for the knob. Wait, Ashley had left without saying why she'd come. Had she really traveled all the way from Connecticut just to warn her? Or was she bent on creating trouble for Jason and would go to any extremes to make that happen?

Her story would be easy enough to check out. Tia went into her office and opened a search window on her laptop. The first few tries didn't give her what she was seeking. She knew her way around the Polk County Sheriff's site well, but she'd never done a jail search in Connecticut.

Finally, Jason's name yielded the result she was looking for, one she didn't want to see. Four and a half years ago, he was arrested for battery. Ashley was telling the truth.

Tia flopped back in her chair, eyes closed. She'd begun to think of him as a friend, someone she wouldn't mind keeping in her life, at least on a casual basis. She crossed her arms in front of her, suddenly chilled. Maybe there were extenuating circumstances.

No, she was grasping at straws, refusing to believe what was right in front of her. There was never a reason for a man to hit a woman, regardless of the circumstances. If events weren't as they appeared, Jason would have told her. His silence meant one thing. She'd been stupid. At least, she'd been naive. She'd put on the blinders she'd supposedly cast away years ago.

Jason was no different from Victor or Danielle's boyfriend or any of the other men whose actions had put their women in her shelter.

They were all cut from the same ugly piece of cloth.

Jason walked from Walmart pushing a shopping cart. Four bags lined the bottom. Three of them held planned purchases—some paper goods to keep at his grandparents' place and quite a bit of food, which he'd also leave at the house. The full-size fridge and cabinets held a lot more than the mini-fridge and two shelves in the hotel room.

The fourth bag held an impulse purchase. He'd loaded his cart with the items on his shopping list, then found himself in the sporting goods section. There, an official size, leather composite Wilson basketball jumped out at him, begging to be bought. Shooting baskets, maybe even a little one-on-one were sure to be activities Damian would enjoy.

After loading the bags into his truck and parking the cart in the corral, he pulled his phone from his pocket. He would text Tia and see if she could find out whether Damian might be interested in shooting some baskets.

He slid into the truck and swiped the screen. She'd already texted him a good two hours ago. His pulse picked up speed. He'd been so intent on his sorting he'd missed the notification. He touched her name. Anticipation dissolved into worry and confusion as he read.

She was upset with him, told him it would be best if he stayed away from the shelter. She'd ended the text, "You're not who I thought you were."

Then who was he? Where was this coming from? Did someone get a hold of her phone and was playing a cruel trick on him? One possibility nagged at him, like a splinter in the end of a finger—Ashley had somehow gotten to Tia.

That was impossible, at least unlikely. Tia's phone number wasn't available. Ashley would have had to physically show up at the shelter. A twenty-hour road trip one way was a little over-the-top just to try to cause trouble. Did Ashley really hate him that much? Yeah, she probably did.

She'd thought she could continue to poke and prod him and he'd keep coming back for more because he loved her. It hadn't taken him long to learn that love wasn't enough. Soon after that realization, he'd figured out the love he'd initially had wasn't even there anymore. Even then, he'd planned to hang in there long enough for her to finish her MBA. He hadn't even made it that long. Ending up in jail had been the final straw.

He cranked the truck and backed from the space. As soon as he dropped the food by the house, he was going to Tia's. If that crazy message actually came from her, she could tell him in person. She wasn't going to break up via text. Okay, it couldn't technically be considered breaking up when they'd never dated. But it was the severance of a friendship. He could at least claim that.

When he got back to Harmony Grove, he backed his truck into the parking space in front of his room. Once he killed the engine, he climbed from the seat with a bag hooked over his arm. It held the basketball and two of the bottles of water he'd purchased. If Tia really wanted nothing to do with him, he hoped that antagonism didn't extend to Damian. He was finally making some headway with the kid.

Two minutes later, Jason stepped onto the shelter's porch and knocked. The door opened just enough for Tia to step out. She closed the door behind her.

"Did you not get my text?" Her tone was cold and stiff.

"I did. I figured someone was pulling my leg." It was obvious now how wrong he was. Tia was upset and he had no idea why.

She crossed her arms in front of her, effectively shutting him out. "This isn't a joke. You're not welcome here."

"Would you please tell me what's going on?" He was having a hard time keeping the exasperation out of his voice.

"It's my responsibility to protect the women and children under my care."

"And if you remember what happened a week or so ago, that's exactly what I did."

She heaved a sigh. "Just please go."

"Why? What have I done?"

She backed up without responding. As she started

to swing the door closed, he lifted a hand to stop her, then caught himself. Any actions she could view as strong-arming wouldn't get him anywhere.

He heaved a sigh and walked back down the stairs. He might as well head over to the park and shoot some baskets alone. Or go for a good, hard run. Maybe both. Baskets first, then run.

He headed for the park. After stepping under the entry arch, he dribbled the ball down the sidewalk. Ahead and to the right was a fenced-in area, a full court inside, with a hoop at each end. Some distance past the latched gate, a park bench overlooked the playground. A figure sat hunched over a small object. Damian?

As Jason drew closer to the gate, the figure looked up, likely alerted by the thud of the ball against the concrete. Yep, definitely Damian.

Without interrupting his dribble, Jason lifted the bag holding the two bottles of water and improvised a wave, then lifted the latch on the gate. If Damian wanted to join him, he would.

Once inside, he set the water against the fence and shot a few balls from the free throw line. Then he ran in an arc, approaching the basket from the side. His hook shot hit the rim and bounced back. He was a little rusty.

The soft clank of the gate's latch dropping down drew his attention behind him. Damian stood inside the fence, one hand still resting on the latch, the other at his side, holding his portable game console.

Jason tossed the ball up, then spun it on his index finger in true Globetrotter fashion, something he'd worked tirelessly to perfect during his teen years.

"You up for some one-on-one?"

Damian shrugged, then stuffed his game console into his pants pocket. "Sure."

"We'll warm up first." He passed the ball to Damian with a hard bounce. Damian ran toward the basket, Jason shadowing him, then took a shot. It followed the path Jason's shot had earlier, bouncing off the rim.

Jason recovered it and dribbled it back behind the free throw line before advancing. When he made his shot, the ball traveled part way around the rim before falling through. Not a swish but it worked.

Over the next fifteen minutes, they both worked up a sweat. Jason had about six inches of height on Damian, but the kid was good. He would give Jason a run for his money when they started keeping score.

Jason tossed him the ball. "Take as many practice shots as you want, because I'm not gonna go easy on you."

"I wouldn't want you to, old man."

Just the response Jason expected. The banter had gone on through most of their play. Damian expected him to give it his all. If he didn't, the kid would know and wouldn't respect him.

Jason had finally won him over. Maybe Damian would even put in a good word for him with Tia. No, he wasn't going to use a thirteen-year-old kid to get back into Tia's good graces. She'd have to cool down eventually. If not, she was going to have to at least talk to him about the house.

Five minutes later, Damian recovered the ball after shooting another successful basket. "All right. I'm ready. First one to eleven wins."

"Yep, that's the way it's played."

The game commenced, and when it was over, Jason had won by two points.

Jason gave him a high five. "Good game. You know, when you get that extra six inches of height, you're gonna kill me."

"You betcha."

After a brief water break, Jason tossed him the ball to start the next game. He won again, but this time, the spread was only one point.

Jason grinned. "You're closing in."

"Next one, I'll have you."

"You might be right."

Jason lifted the ball to pass it to Damian. A fraction of a second later, a shout from nearby drew Damian's attention, and he swiveled his head in that direction.

Jason gasped. He'd already released the ball, and there was nothing he could do to stop it. "Watch out!"

The ball hit the ground six feet in front of Damian and bounced. He turned his head back, drawn by Jason's shout of warning, and raised his arms. But it was a second too late.

The ball connected with Damian's face with a sickening thud, and Damian cupped a hand over his nose.

Jason rushed toward him. "Oh, no! I'm so sorry."

Blood gushed between Damian's fingers and dripped onto his shirt. Jason stripped off his own shirt and poured water onto it.

"Here, use this." He put one arm around Damian's shoulders and, with the other, tried to raise the shirt to his bloodied face.

Damian's eyes widened, and something Jason didn't

recognize flashed in them. He twisted away, taking several steps back. "Don't touch me!"

Jason stepped forward, dripping T-shirt still raised. "I'm sorry. Please let me help."

Damian continued to back up, eyes wild. He'd reached the gate now and was going for the latch. "Get away from me!"

"Damian, please. I didn't do it on purpose. I'd never hurt you intentionally."

"Leave me alone."

He jerked the latch up and swung the gate open so hard that it clanged against the fence, then ran toward the entrance to the park.

Jason left the ball lying where it had rolled against the fence, then followed, his heart in a free fall. How could he have messed up so badly? First Tia and now Damian. Could he do nothing right?

When they reached the shelter, Pam and Maggie sat on the front porch. Great. Now Pam was going to be furious with him, too. He'd hurt her son. It wouldn't matter that it was an accident.

Pam jumped up from her chair. "Damian? What happened?"

Damian shot past her and into the house without speaking, slamming the door behind him. Pam opened it to follow. Before she could close it again, the firestorm that was Tia swept through, ready to burn him alive.

"What have you done?" Her voice was shrill. "I can't believe you hit a kid."

"It was an accident."

"I told you to stay away from the shelter. That also applies to the women and children here."

"Tia, please." It was the same thing he'd said to Damian, and it was doing just as much good.

Tia pointed at the driveway. "Get off my property."

"Tia, please listen to me."

"I don't need to hear your explanation. There's no excuse for bloodying the kid's nose. I should never have trusted you. Go before I call the police."

Pam walked out the door, and he turned his attention on her. She didn't seem to hold the anger that Tia did. Instead, there was resignation in her gaze, even sympathy. How could she be sympathetic with him when he'd just hurt her son?

"I didn't mean to hurt him. I bounced the ball toward him just as he looked away. He looked back but not in time to react, and the ball hit him in the face. I'm so sorry."

"He's all right. I'm sure nothing's broken. He gets nosebleeds easily."

Jason shook his head. "I told him how sorry I was, even took off my shirt and wet it to hold over his nose." He lifted the item, which was no longer dripping. "He was so angry with me, he wouldn't let me anywhere near him."

Pam stepped down off the porch and approached him. For a brief moment, he wondered if he should prepare himself for a punch across the jaw.

Instead, she laid a sympathetic hand on his shoulder. "It's all right. Damian's used to playing with his father."

Jason's stomach sank. "And his father would have been more careful."

Tia planted both hands on her hips. "If it was an accident, why is Damian so angry?"

Pam heaved a sigh. "His dad would have yelled at him, told him he was stupid and careless, that he should never take his eye off the ball. Damian doesn't know how to react to kindness." She gave him a sad smile. "He's in the bathroom now, cleaning up and calming down. Leave him alone for a while."

Jason nodded. "Thank you for understanding."

When he looked at Tia, she was chewing on her lower lip. Her eyes held a mixture of doubt and regret. Maybe now she would hear him out.

"We need to talk, but first, I want to get a dry shirt." Now that the sun was low in the sky and he'd calmed down from the earlier excitement, he could no longer ignore the slight chill in the air.

Tia didn't answer, but her barely perceptible nod was all the response he required. Now it made sense. Tia's anger with him and her jumping to the worst possible conclusion about Damian—Ashley had paid her a visit. He'd known he needed to talk to her. Instead, he'd put it off. He'd been a coward.

The only reason she was willing to hear him out now was because she'd been wrong about what had happened with Damian. The accident at the basketball court was almost worth it, although Damian might beg to differ.

Sometimes God worked in mysterious ways.

TWELVE

TIA HURRIED DOWN the sidewalk, purse slung over one shoulder. The shock and anger that had bombarded her when she'd seen Damian rush past upset and bloody had subsided. Having just learned about Jason's past, she'd assumed the worst. She owed him an apology.

She also owed him an explanation as to why she'd gone from friendly to antagonistic in the course of a couple of hours. She should have at least told him about his ex-wife's visit and given him the opportunity to explain. She was normally levelheaded and reasonable, the type of person who thought things through rather than reacting.

This was different, though. It wasn't just what she thought Jason had done to Damian. It was also what she thought he'd done to her—making her believe a lie, then shattering her trust.

She would hear him out, not that it would make a difference. He'd been arrested for battery. Ashley hadn't made it up. The arrest was right there in the records. The odds of him talking his way out of that were nil. He'd probably try to assure her that it was a one-time thing and would never happen again.

Other women might buy it. Not her. If there was anything that would put an instant kibosh on even friendship, that was it.

She reached the end of Tranquility and turned onto the sidewalk that paralleled Main. After stepping into the inn's parking lot, she slowed her pace to cut between his Ram and a Sunbird sitting next to it. The door three feet from the truck's tailgate was probably his. She'd dropped him off a couple of times, but hadn't waited to see what door he went in.

She stopped at the back corner of the truck, ready to text him, and the door to room number eight swung open. His eyes widened in what looked like a combination of surprise and pleasure.

"Thanks for giving me a chance to talk to you."

"I owe it to you after the way I reacted with Damian."

"It's all right. Seeing a kid running in covered in blood had to have been a little shocking."

"Yeah, but I should have known you'd never hit him." She'd watched him with Damian, and he'd acted like a model mentor right from the start. He'd handled Damian's moods and stinky attitude a lot better than she had. Her way was avoidance. "I'm sorry."

"It's okay."

"Tell me what happened with your ex-wife."

He gave her a knowing nod. "Just what I thought. Sometime between when I left you after lunch and when I came back from shopping, you had the dubious pleasure of meeting Ashley."

"I did." She wrinkled her nose. "I wasn't impressed. She made it obvious the feeling was mutual."

"What do you say we head over to the park? We can walk while we talk, and I can kill two birds with one stone. I've got a brand-new basketball still sitting on the court."

"It may not be there anymore."

"I can always pick up another one." He frowned. "If Damian even wants to play with me anymore. After today, I doubt it."

"I'm sure he will. You heard what Pam said. His anger wasn't aimed at you."

Jason nodded but didn't look convinced. They crossed Main Street in silence, then walked the short distance to the park's entrance. Jason's jaw tightened and a hardness entered his eyes. His thoughts had likely shifted from Damian to his ex-wife.

Finally, he heaved a sigh. "Ashley told you I was arrested for battery." It was a statement, not a question.

"Yeah. I didn't believe her."

"It's true."

"I know. I looked it up."

"She didn't tell you the whole story."

Actually, she had, and that was the problem. If she hadn't provided the details, Tia could have come up with some of her own, those extenuating circumstances she'd thought about earlier. Like maybe Ashley had attacked him first, and he'd simply been trying to restrain her, or some such other nonsense.

Several more seconds passed in silence. If he was searching for a palatable way to tell the story, he may as well spill it, because there wasn't one. There was no way to justify beating his wife badly enough to put her in the hospital.

Jason stopped at the basketball court. The gate was

closed, and a boy who looked to be about eleven or twelve was inside the fenced area, shooting baskets. For several moments, Jason watched him. Finally, the boy turned to see them standing at the fence.

He stopped the ball, catching it mid-dribble. "Is this yours?"

"Yeah, but you look like you're having a good time. Keep playing. I'll get it later."

The kid gave him a broad smile. "Thanks."

Jason waved and continued down the sidewalk, Tia next to him.

"What will you do if both the kid and your ball are gone when we come back by?"

"Nothing. I hope he gets a lot of use out of it. That's a small price to pay to give a kid a few hours of enjoyment."

Tia slid him a sideways glance. Shortly after meeting him, she'd wondered if he was a counselor or youth pastor. At the time, he'd laughed. But seeing how he related to kids, her guess didn't seem so far-fetched. Maybe he worked with youth in a volunteer capacity. No, with his abuse record, probably not. He'd never pass the required background checks.

"Ashley thrives on conflict."

Back to his ex-wife. He was giving her the story piecemeal. She waited for him to continue.

"She's the type who loves to stir the pot. Almost from the moment we said 'I do,' she was constantly trying to push my buttons."

Tia swallowed hard, a black cloud descending over her. So far, he was placing all the blame on Ashley. A typical trait of abusers. Victor had been able to justify everything he did. Except in court. Then he'd denied everything, claiming the wounds that scarred her were self-inflicted. Fortunately, the jury had done a better job of seeing past his charming facade than she had.

Ahead of them, the path forked to circle a small lake. Jason stared out over the water, eyebrows drawn together, mouth in a straight line. Two ducks glided across the surface, but he seemed to not see them. His gaze was fixed on some point on the opposite bank.

He continued without meeting her eyes. "She was good at it, coming up with ways to set me off. She had a knack for finding buttons I didn't even know I had. During the first three years of our marriage, we got numerous complaints from neighbors in our apartment complex, reports of fighting."

Tia swallowed hard. This was a mistake. She didn't want to hear his story, didn't want to see the images his words conjured up—the transformation from handsome to terrifying, the cold hardness in those dark eyes, his face tinted red with rage, lips curled back in a sneer.

He continued over her silent objections. "When Ashley was upset, her voice took on a shrill quality, and getting her to quiet down was almost impossible."

"So you dislocated her jaw."

"What?" He swiveled his head to meet her eyes. His own were filled with hurt.

"Stop making excuses." Her voice was raised, but she didn't even try to soften it. The situation hit home in too many ways. After being so wrong about Jason, if God ever did send the right man into her life, how would she even recognize it? How could she be confident that she wasn't being duped again, manipulated by yet another master of control?

She continued at the same volume she'd started, fists clenched. "When someone's picking a fight, you walk away. There's never a justifiable reason to hit someone, especially a woman much smaller than you."

Jason shook his head. "I didn't hit her."

"You dislocated her jaw and broke her arm."

"No, I didn't. At least not on purpose."

So now he was claiming he didn't mean to hurt her, that it was all an accident? How gullible did he think she was?

He heaved another sigh and stared straight ahead, following the path around the lake. "We were standing in the kitchen. I was cooking, and she'd just come in from one of her classes. She started in with her usual picking at me. I ignored her. After I put the casserole into the oven, I started cleaning up the kitchen, still ignoring her. Finally, she told me she was seeing someone else."

Tia nodded slowly, a sick feeling growing in the pit of her stomach. How many women had been hurt during fits of jealous rage?

He turned to look at her. "I laid the pan I was rinsing in the sink, walked out of the kitchen and headed up the stairs. We lived in a townhouse, with two bedrooms on the top floor. That wasn't the reaction she expected, but by this point, I'd have been happy to have someone take her off my hands."

He shook his head. "She didn't get the rise out of me that she'd hoped, so she blew a gasket. She stormed up the stairs behind me, and I turned in time to see her swinging a cast iron skillet at the side of my head. I raised my arm to block her swing. She was gripping the skillet handle with both hands, and when her arm came into contact with mine, it threw her off balance. She hit the side of her face against the banister. I grabbed for her but missed, and she tumbled down the stairs."

He paused and looked at Tia, brows drawn together. "Did she actually tell you that I dislocated her jaw and broke her arm?"

Tia nodded, still trying to absorb everything he'd just said. His side of the story was so different from hers.

He frowned. "She dislocated her jaw when she fell against the banister and broke her arm either on the stairs or at the bottom. Maybe it was my fault for knocking her off balance, but the only reason I raised my arm was to keep from having my head smashed in with the skillet."

He stopped walking and turned to face her. He seemed to be studying her. "You believe me, don't you?"

"I don't know what to believe." She looked away. She'd already proved that she wasn't the greatest judge of character. How well did she know Jason? Not well at all. The only thing she knew for sure was that he'd been arrested for battery, because she'd seen the proof in black and white. Or pixels.

He reached into his pocket and pulled out his phone. After a swipe and a couple of taps, he keyed in a message, thumbs flying over the screen. When finished, he slid the phone back into his jeans pocket. Then he started walking again.

Whoever and whatever he'd just texted, he

apparently wasn't going to share it with her.

"During the four years Ashley and I were together, she hit me several times, but I never hit her back. I won't lie—I wanted to. But I knew if I ever crossed that line, I wouldn't be able to go back. I was determined that, no matter what happened, I would never become my father."

Tia drew her lower lip between her teeth, his words circling through the clatter of arguments in her mind. She wanted to believe him. If she went with her gut, she *would* believe him. Because her gut told her he was telling the truth.

Of course, her gut had led her astray during the entire time she'd dated Victor. Apparently, that voice of reason wasn't always reliable. Sometimes it grew mute when it mattered most.

Jason released a sigh. "I spent the night in jail, bonded out the next day. I came back home long enough to get my personal belongings together. Ashley was only two months away from graduating with her MBA. I filed for divorce but continued to pay her living expenses until she finished school."

Warmth stirred in Tia's chest. He'd been awfully generous, considering the circumstances. Of course, with everything she'd witnessed so far, that wasn't surprising.

What had he ever seen in a haughty, spiteful woman like Ashley? Probably the same thing she'd seen in Victor. People like that could keep their dark side hidden for months. Victor didn't reveal his until after they were married. Soon his promise to love and to cherish lost all meaning and the gold band on her finger became a ball and chain.

When they reached the "Y" in the path, instead of circling the lake again, Jason headed back the way they'd come. He'd finished his story and fallen silent.

She needed the silence, the opportunity to absorb everything he'd said. She was inclined to believe him. He was too sincere, too open. All she'd gotten from Ashley was cold haughtiness and a sense that she'd go to any lengths to cause trouble.

The entire conversation had been unpleasant, from the greeting, if it could be called that, to the goodbye. *So you're Tia.* The woman had pronounced her name as if it was something base and distasteful. Almost like a swear word.

Her eyes widened. "Ashley knew my name. How?"

Jason winced. "I think I mentioned it."

"What?" Why would he talk about her to his ex-wife?

He drew in a deep breath before letting it out in a weary sigh. "The divorce has been final for four years, but every so often, I hear from her out of the blue. It's never to catch up. She only calls to see what kind of turmoil she can put me in." He looked at her with a frown. "Or if she wants something. This was one of those times."

"And?" She still couldn't fathom why he felt the need to bring her into the conversation.

"I'm guessing she's been watching the obituaries since the day the divorce was final, figuring that when my grandmother passed away, I would stand to inherit."

"But you're divorced. She wouldn't have gotten anything."

"Legally, no."

In the silence that followed, the unspoken answer floated between them, as obvious as if he'd voiced it. He would have given her something just because he was a nice guy. Tia's chest tightened in an odd mix of admiration and a desire to give him a hard shake.

He continued before she could express either. "With Mom's health, I'm no longer in a position to be generous."

And since his grandmother had left both the house and the bank account to Tia, any generosity in the near future would be out of the question. He hadn't said it, but he had to be thinking it.

They approached the basketball court and stopped at the fence. The kid Jason had spoken with earlier was still there. In their absence, he'd picked up two more players, and it looked like they had a game of one-on-one going. Or maybe it would be two-on-one, if there was such a thing.

The first kid made a basket. When he turned, his smile faded. "Sorry, game's over. This is that guy's ball."

Jason held up a hand. "No way am I going to interfere with a good game. Keep playing and you can return it when you're done."

"Where?"

"You know the inn, almost across from the entrance to the park?"

"Yeah."

"That's where I'm staying. Door number eight. You can bring the ball back when you're finished. If I'm not there, leave it in the office."

"Thanks, Mister."

They'd just walked away when Jason's phone

buzzed with an incoming text. He pulled it from his pocket again and, after a brief look, angled it toward her.

The contact name at the top of the screen was "Mom." Below that was a photograph, sent via text. When he touched the center, the picture filled the screen.

The rather official-looking document bore Jason's name and showed that all charges had been dropped. The date was two days later than the one she'd seen on the arrest record.

Jason texted back "Tx," then pocketed his phone. "When Ashley's injuries substantiated my story rather than hers, they dropped the charges. I didn't even have to go to court. Nothing shows up on an official background check. But if you're looking at arrest records, it's there. Unfortunately, those don't show the outcome."

Tia dipped her gaze to the sidewalk. "I guess I owe you a second apology."

"It's all right. You had every reason to assume the worst, in both cases."

She sighed. Quick to forgive, one to not even hold a grudge in the first place. Two more admirable qualities.

After leaving the park, Jason insisted on walking her all the way back to the shelter. When they reached the archway into the inn's rear garden area, Tia stopped. "Wait, you never told me how Ashley knew my name."

He smiled. "Since I had supposedly gotten a big inheritance, she felt I should buy her a new car. I told her there wasn't any inheritance, that the house, furniture and bank account had gone to a lady who runs a shelter for abused women. She said some not-nice things about you, which ticked me off, and I let your first name slip."

He pulled her under the wisteria-draped arch. Respect and admiration shone from his eyes, sending a shot of warmth through her. He'd gone up against his spiteful ex-wife to defend her.

"When I mentioned your name, Ashley said she detected some tenderness in my voice."

"Really?" The word came out in a high-pitched squeak.

"I couldn't deny it, because I knew it was true."

He took both of her hands in his and smiled down at her, the tenderness Ashley had accused him of obvious in his gaze. The warmth inside her expanded and intensified until the walls she'd built around her heart threatened to melt into a gooey heap.

His smile turned teasing. "Am I forgiven for my slip?"

"If I'm forgiven for my false accusations."

"Absolutely."

He squeezed her hands, and his smile broadened.

If he wanted to seal their agreement with a kiss, she probably wouldn't object.

Jason made his way toward Peace House, dribbling the basketball down the sidewalk. The kid had actually brought it back. Jason had been in the middle of warming a frozen dinner in the microwave when a soft knock had sounded on the door. He'd opened it to see the boy standing there with the ball tucked under one arm. He'd thanked Jason for letting them use it and handed it back.

The kid exuded politeness and respect. Obviously the product of good parenting. Not all good parents produced good kids, but nine times out of ten, good kids had at least one good parent, often two.

As the kid had walked away, Jason had almost called him back and told him to keep the ball. Now he was glad he'd kept his mouth shut, because he hadn't made it back to Walmart to pick up another one.

Showing up with a basketball twenty-four hours after he'd bloodied Damian's nose with it seemed heartless. But it hadn't been his idea. According to Pam, who'd told Tia, who'd told him, Damian had been asking about him, wondering when he was coming back. He'd asked Tia, who'd asked Pam if he should bring the ball with him, and she'd responded with an unequivocal yes.

Shortly after he rang the bell, the door swung inward and Damian stood in the opening. Excitement flashed across his face. Then his eyes dipped, and disappointment swept aside the enthusiasm that had been there a moment earlier. The sudden change left Jason wishing he could make the ball disappear. Like deflate it and stuff it into his pocket.

Jason stepped up to the threshold but didn't cross it. "What's up?" Other than the fact that he'd hit the kid in the face with a ball then brought said ball back the very next day.

"We're leaving."

Jason's chest clenched. "Leaving where?"

"Another shelter."

"How soon?"

"They're sending a car for us in a half hour."

A half hour? Was that all?

"Mom already has us packed." He frowned. "Not that there's much to pack up. Everything's at home." He pressed his lips together in a frown. "Think I'll ever see my stuff again?"

"I don't know. You might."

Jason hadn't seen his. The night he and his mother fled, they'd walked away from everything. He still didn't know what had happened to his toys, clothes, books—everything he'd held dear. For all he knew, his father had burned them.

"You've got thirty minutes. What do you say we go to the park?"

Damian nodded and followed him down the porch steps. Once they reached the sidewalk, Damian took the ball from him and bounced it against the concrete walk in front of him in a steady rhythm. As they walked into the park, he spoke without taking his eyes off the ball. "Sorry I got mad at you yesterday."

"Sorry I gave you a bloody nose."

One side of Damian's mouth lifted. "It's okay."

He tucked the ball under one arm to open the gate onto the court, then dribbled to the free throw line. His first shot hit the board and bounced back to him. His second throw was successful. When he'd retrieved the ball, he tossed it to Jason.

Jason stood at the same spot, hands raised and elbows bent, preparing for his throw. When he glanced over at Damian, the boy was staring at him.

He hesitated. "What?"

"Did your dad hit you?"

"What do you mean?"

"Somebody broke your nose."

Jason smiled. Since he was an avid sportsman, most people assumed he'd been hit accidentally playing sports.

He straightened his arms, propelling the ball through the air. "Yeah, it was my dad."

The ball hit the rim, and Damian ran after it. After retrieving it, he tossed it to Jason for another try and approached.

"Your dad wasn't playing like you were with me." Damian's voice held a lot of wisdom for a thirteen-year-old.

"No. He broke it when I tried to stop him from hurting my mom."

"My dad hits my mom, too. I haven't tried to stop him, because he's so much bigger than me. And I don't want him to be mad at me." His gaze settled on his feet. "But I guess I should try to protect my mom."

"I hope you won't have to make that decision. Where you're going, they'll be getting some help for both you and your mom. Your dad, too, if he'll accept it. If he won't, that's out of both you and your mom's control. Remember, whatever happens, it's not your fault."

Damian nodded. "Did your dad ever get help?"

"No, never did. The last time I saw him, I was your age."

Jason released his second throw, which followed the same path as the first. Damian retrieved the ball again and relinquished it. He seemed more intent on talking than playing. That was all right, too.

"I don't know if I want to see my dad again. At

first, I was mad at my mom for taking me away from him. He wasn't mean to me like he was Mom." His eyebrows dipped down in concentration. "I mean, he's not nice like you are. But he didn't hit me like he does Mom."

Jason threw the ball again. It sailed through the net without hitting the rim. "Third time's a charm."

"Good shot."

When Damian returned with the ball, he backed up several feet farther, to the three-point line. "Now I don't know what I want. I don't want things to go back to how they were, with Dad yelling and hitting Mom and Julie hiding in her room crying."

Jason nodded. "That's hard. I didn't have a little sister to worry about. It was just my mom and me."

After a few more shots, Jason checked his phone for the time. "We'd better be heading back. Your ride is going to be here any minute."

"I don't want to go." It was an opinion rather than an argument. All the fight seemed to have gone out of him. The attitude he'd held onto throughout most of his stay had changed. It was as if he'd admitted defeat.

"I don't want you to go, either."

When they turned the corner onto Tranquility Way, a red SUV sat at the end of the driveway. Pam stood behind it, putting three cloth bags inside. Those bags probably held everything she and her kids possessed.

Before sliding into the front passenger seat, she hugged Tia and the others who'd gathered to see them off. Julie followed suit, then climbed into the back seat behind the driver. There was a new face in the group. Apparently, someone had already arrived to fill the vacancy left by Pam's departure.

After giving Jason a fist bump, Damian approached Tia to thank her, but forewent the hug his mother and sister had given. When he reached the vehicle, he opened the door and stood motionless for several moments, a battle raging inside him. Jason shared the pain of that battle.

Suddenly, Damian spun and ran full bore into him, almost knocking him backward. His arms wrapped around Jason's waist in a hug that held a surprising amount of strength.

"Bye, Jason." His voice held a quiver.

Jason swallowed around a lump in his own throat. "Bye, Damian."

After releasing him, Damian gave his eyes a quick swipe with the heels of his hands, then dipped his head. "The sun's in my eyes."

It was low in the sky, almost directly behind Damian. Jason blinked back his own moisture. "Yeah, mine too."

Jason watched him climb into the SUV and lower the window. "Wait." He patted his pockets. "Let me give you my number. I want you to call me, let me know how you're doing." He pulled a napkin from his shirt pocket, but he didn't have anything to write with. "Pen, I need a pen."

The man at the wheel pulled a pen from the console and passed it back to Damian, who handed it through the open window. After Jason had written his cell number, he folded the napkin in half and gave it to Damian.

Damian wrinkled his nose. "That's not used, is it? Like, you didn't blow your nose on it or anything?"

Jason grinned. "Not since this morning."

Damian's mouth lifted in one of those rare smiles that were gradually becoming more common.

The vehicle's engine roared to life, and it moved away from the curb. Jason walked next to it, increasing his pace to a jog as the vehicle accelerated. "Call me."

Damian poked his head out the window. "I will."

"If you lose my number, find me on Facebook." He was shouting now, at a full run. "Jason Sloan, in Groton, Connecticut, where the submarines are."

"I'll remember."

The SUV turned the corner at the end of the road and sped away. Jason watched it disappear, then plodded back to Peace House. The other women had gone back inside, leaving Tia alone on the sidewalk. She didn't look like she felt any better than he did.

She gave him a sad smile. "You really made an impact on him."

"I hope so."

"God put you in Harmony Grove at just the right time. He knew you were what Damian needed."

Jason nodded. Maybe Tia was what *he* needed.

No, he couldn't think like that. He didn't know what traumas she had faced, but there'd been plenty, things that had changed her, things that still haunted her. She needed someone whole, someone who could give her a solid foundation, someone who could be her rock.

That someone wasn't him. He was still fighting too many of his own demons.

Tia tilted her head to the side. "What are you doing this evening?"

"I don't know." Sitting alone in his hotel room

didn't appeal to him, but neither did working at the house. "You?"

She shrugged. "We had an early dinner so we could feed Pam and her kids before they left. No plans for the rest of the evening."

"You suggested that we sort the kitchen stuff together. Do you feel up to doing that tonight? I wouldn't mind getting out for a couple of hours." His earlier sentiment of not wanting to work at the house didn't apply if Tia was going to be with him.

"I'd love to. Let me check with Kristina. I think she was planning to spend the evening."

"Kristina?"

"One of my staff, works as an advocate. She's talking to Ethan and Aiden, making sure they're handling Julie's leaving all right. She's there for any of the women who need to talk also."

"Ah, the new face. I thought you already had a new resident."

"Not yet, but I'm sure it won't be long." She paused. "I assume you haven't eaten yet. If leftover lasagna sounds good, I'll bring it along."

"That's perfect."

Twenty minutes later, he was seated at his grandmother's bar, a steaming plate of lasagna in front of him. Tia stood at one of the cabinets, two fingers looped through the handle on the open door.

"Dinner plates, salad plates and saucers." She swung open the opposing door next to it. "And cups and glasses."

Jason swallowed the bite he'd just taken. When he'd complimented her on dinner, she'd waved it aside, insisting the credit went to Stouffer's.

"I've got everything I need in the way of dinnerware. If you can use them, they're all yours."

"I can definitely use them." She counted the stack of plates. "Looks like place settings for twelve. When I add what I currently have, there should be enough to feed everyone. They even match, or at least complement one another."

She closed the doors and leaned back against the countertop. "Sometimes we use paper, but not all the time. That would be a lot of waste, not to mention expense."

He smiled. "I think you're going to need that commercial dishwasher."

By the time he was done eating, she'd finished going through the upper cabinets. She crossed the kitchen, and opened the pantry's double doors. "Hmm, five-year-old canned goods. Might be best to throw those away."

"Agreed." He pulled a black trash bag from a small box on the top shelf. "At least someone cleared out the dried goods." The shelves that had probably held items like pasta and flour were empty.

"Good thing, or they'd be full of weevils."

Jason emptied the shelves, splitting the contents between two bags. He would finish filling them with lighter-weight items, then stuff them into the green garbage can outside to wheel to the road on trash collection day.

Tia opened the doors on one of the lower cabinets, then squatted in front of it. "This is a nice set of pots and pans."

He squatted next to her. "They're all yours if you can use them."

"When I get mine over here, I'll see what I have duplicates of." She duck-walked to the next cabinet. "It'll probably be your grandma's stuff that I keep. Hers looks like better quality than mine."

A muffled ringtone sounded behind them, and Tia rose to retrieve her phone from her purse. A moment later, her lips pressed together in a frown. "It's the shelter's land line."

She swiped the screen and put the phone to her ear. "What's going on?"

The high-pitched tones of a female voice filled the kitchen. Jason couldn't make out the words, but someone was obviously hysterical.

"Katie, calm down. I can't understand you."

The tone softened, only slightly. Tia's eyes widened and her jaw dropped. Finally, she snapped her mouth shut, lips pressed into a thin line of determination. "I'll be right there." She dropped her phone into her purse and put the strap over her shoulder. "I need you to take me home. Now."

"What's going on?" Without waiting for her answer, he swiped his keys from the bar and headed for the front door. He'd driven them there in his truck.

Tia followed, running to keep up. "Maggie went out back to have a cigarette. No one's allowed to smoke inside."

Jason clicked the key fob, and she slid into the passenger side of the Ram. When he'd settled himself in the driver's seat, she continued.

"Someone came up behind her, clamped a hand over her mouth and held a knife to her throat. Then he dragged her behind the shed."

Jason closed his eyes, nausea churning in his gut.

"Did he…" He didn't finish the thought. Men who forced themselves on women…

Tia shook her head. "Not according to Katie. He just threatened her."

"Is she hurt?"

"Mostly shaken up. She panicked at first and struggled, so she got cut. But it's just a nick."

When Jason turned onto Tranquility Way, flashing blue and red lights pierced the darkness. He eased to a stop at the edge of the road. A police cruiser sat in the driveway. Officer White stood in the front yard, the four women and Kristina gathered around him.

Tia was out of the truck before he could throw the transmission into park. As he approached, Maggie was talking, telling her story to the officer. She held a washcloth against her throat with one shaking hand.

The soft glow of the porch light didn't quite reach the small group, but the illumination of nearby streetlight spilled over them. The police cruiser's strobing red and blue reflected on their faces and clothing.

As Maggie talked, the officer jotted notes in his pad, looking up only when she had fallen silent.

"Can you give me a description?"

She shook her head. "I didn't see his face. He was wearing a ski mask."

"What about height and build?"

She paused, studying the officer. "A couple of inches taller than you, probably thirty pounds heavier, muscular build."

"Any ideas of who he might have been?"

When Maggie shook her head again, Tia stepped forward. "Who knows you're here?"

The question sounded more like an accusation. If she was playing "good cop, bad cop," White was definitely the good cop.

Maggie's eyes widened. "No one. I mean I've talked to my mom and sister but I didn't tell them where I was."

Tia's stern gaze shifted to Jasmine, whose denial was as adamant as Maggie's. Angela and Katie seemed to be exempt from Tia's suspicions.

Of course, they'd been there when Danielle's boyfriend had shown up. Not only had they probably been scared half out of their wits by his threats and the crash of the door giving way, they'd both witnessed Tia's scolding and Danielle's expulsion from the shelter. Neither was likely to repeat the former resident's infraction.

White raised the pen and pad again. "Tell me what he said."

"He told me to be still, because I panicked when he first grabbed me. He said if I tried anything stupid, he'd cut my throat clean through." She closed her eyes, and a shudder shook her body.

She took several moments to compose herself, then opened her eyes. "I just remembered something. He smelled like mint—peppermint or spearmint."

Tia made a short, sharp intake of air. Her eyes were haunted, her face pale in the glow of the streetlight. What was significant about the scent of mint?

The officer lifted his brows. "His breath or cologne?"

"His breath, like he'd been sucking on mints or chewing gum."

White's eyes shifted to Tia. "Anything you can add?"

Tia crossed her arms in front of her as if trying to ward off a chill. "That name I gave you guys before, Victor Krasney. He used to go through breath mints like candy. Spearmint." She swallowed hard, her throat working with the action. "It may not mean anything. A lot of people use breath mints. Just like a lot of people chew gum."

The words sounded more like a persuasive argument than a report. Likely, the person she was trying to convince was herself.

White nodded. "From what I can remember, the height and build are right, too. We'll look into it, see if we can determine his whereabouts."

He returned his attention to Maggie. "What else did he say?"

Her eyes shifted to Tia. "He had a message for you."

"For me?" Tia's voice squeaked on the last word.

"He said to tell you…" She paused, wincing.

"Tell me what?"

The silence seemed to stretch, one second, two, maybe three. If it felt that way to him, it must seem like an eternity to Tia.

"He said to tell you he's sharpening his blade."

THIRTEEN

TIA PEERED THROUGH the peephole, then opened her front door. For several moments, she stood at the threshold, her eyes scanning the yard, her mind commanding her to step outside.

Three days had passed since Victor's threat. Although Maggie couldn't identify him, Tia knew. Everything matched—the height and build, the scent of spearmint, the reference to the blade...*especially* the reference to the blade.

She clutched the scarf at her throat and forced one foot over the threshold. The other followed, and she scanned the yard again, heart pounding. Moisture coated her palms. Three days, and the fear only seemed to get worse. If she didn't do something, it was going to debilitate her.

Her nightmares had returned with a vengeance. Instead of a rare occurrence, they were happening every night. Last night she'd awoken everyone in the house with her screaming. For the next hour, she'd lain awake, begging God to release her from the terror. It had taken Katie some time to calm Ethan and Aiden, too. Their whimpers had continued long after the others had gone to bed. How could she be a source of strength to her clients, when she was barely hanging on herself?

After several more glances around the yard, she descended the two steps. She wouldn't be caught off guard like Maggie had been. Of course, Maggie hadn't known there was any threat.

As Tia stepped onto the concrete walkway, an overwhelming sense of being watched brought her to a dead stop. She looked around again, her breaths fast and shallow. A wave of dizziness swept over her. If she didn't calm down, she was going to hyperventilate.

Yesterday, Jason had taken her grocery shopping. He'd made his wishes clear before Alan had even driven away in his patrol car. Under no circumstances was she to go anywhere by herself while Victor was still at large. She'd offered no argument—the thought of venturing away from the house alone sent panic coursing through her.

But this was a trip to the mailbox, in broad daylight. Sunset was still a couple of hours away. If she was too scared to bring in her own mail, she was pretty pathetic. After another look around, she kicked her body into gear. She'd cover the final yards to the box, get the mail and retreat back inside.

As promised, Alan had attempted to track down Victor, but hadn't had any success. Tia had even given him Vanessa's number, thankful for the second time that she'd had the foresight to keep it.

According to Alan, Vanessa had claimed that Victor was one week into a two-week wilderness camping trip and unreachable. She'd sworn she hadn't revealed Tia's whereabouts, but when Alan told her the specifics of the latest threat, she admitted that *maybe* she'd mentioned Harmony Grove.

Tia opened the door to the box and reached inside, looking around again. A black Explorer turned the corner, a familiar dark blue Ram behind it.

She'd been expecting the Explorer, or something like it. The crisis center had phoned a couple of hours ago with a battered woman needing placement. All Tia knew was that her name was Nika Scheer and she was coming alone after spending the past two weeks in the hospital recovering from injuries inflicted by her boyfriend. An advocate from another shelter had already been working with her, providing counseling and emotional support, but they'd decided Peace House might be a better fit for her.

Tia withdrew the mail and closed the box as the SUV turned into the driveway. A woman sat in the rear passenger seat, a riot of light brown curls falling down the sides of her head and over her shoulders.

Instead of pulling into the driveway, Jason brought the Ram to a stop at the curb. Tia's stomach quivered, and a warm surge of anticipation shot through her. She hadn't expected him. In the middle of the afternoon, he was supposed to be at his grandparents' place, tackling the final rooms.

When he turned to look out the back window, he was wearing a broad smile, as if he was about to burst with good news. Maybe he'd found something at the house—those money-filled coffee cans he'd joked about. Whatever he'd learned, she'd have to hear about it later. Right now, she had a new resident to meet and get settled in. She gave him a greeting wave and stepped to the SUV's passenger side.

The door swung open, and the woman lifted one

leg then the other out of the vehicle, pulling a cloth tote across the seat. Her movements were slow and cautious, as if she was sore. Or scared.

Whatever injuries had kept her in the hospital for the past two weeks weren't obvious, at least on her right side. Tia studied her profile—the small, straight nose, high cheekbones and full lips. And that enviably thick hair. The woman was beautiful.

Of course, when it came to abuse, that was irrelevant. The victims who ended up at Peace House came in all sizes and shapes and levels of attractiveness. The common ground lay in their experiences—the pain, the fear, the degradation, the scars, both inside and out. And the long road back to wholeness.

The woman straightened to her full height, about six inches taller than Tia's, and closed the door.

"Hi Nika. I'm Tia, Peace House's director."

Nika gave a slight nod, then turned to face Tia fully. Tia started to extend a hand, then froze. Her pleased-to-meet-you died on her lips. Someone should have warned her.

An angry scar ran from the outside edge of Nika's left eye all the way to her chin, new enough to still be red and puffy, but healed enough to have had the stitches removed. Without extensive plastic surgery, it would be there the rest of her life.

Tia shifted her gaze, muttering a greeting, something she hoped was appropriate. Another wave of dizziness washed through her, as powerful as what she'd felt walking to the mailbox, and she leaned on the hood of the car for support. This couldn't be happening. Not three days after learning Victor was coming for her.

He's sharpening his blade.

Movement in her peripheral vision drew her attention to the left. Jason had stepped from his truck and was hurrying toward her. The smile had disappeared, and concern now weighed down his features. She had to pull herself together. She was a professional and she was going to act like one.

She held up a hand. "I'll call you." Jason had come for a reason, and she wanted to find out what it was. Depending on how much Nika wanted to share, intake would take thirty minutes to an hour. After that, Tia needed to introduce her to the other women and get her settled in.

Or not. She could arrange to have her placed in another shelter. That was one of the things that was determined during intake, whether that location would be the best fit for the client. Someone had decided Nika belonged at Peace House. Someone didn't know what they were talking about.

After a nod of greeting for Nika, Jason returned to his truck.

Tia gave her an encouraging smile. "It's nice to meet you, Nika. Come on in, and we'll talk."

She led her onto the porch and through the front door. The last Tia had seen Katie, she was sitting at one of the picnic tables outside while her boys played a few yards away. Maggie was napping in her bedroom, and Angela and Jasmine had signed out and gone to the park.

That meant the living room was empty, giving them the privacy Tia always hoped for when bringing in a potential new client. Once she moved to her new location, it wouldn't be an issue. The separate entry door into the den would guarantee the privacy she wanted.

When they'd both taken seats on the couch, Nika began without any prompting. "This was the last thing I expected to happen." Her words were soft. "Marty and I had been dating for six months. He started talking marriage after two. I felt it was too soon. Over time, he got more and more possessive, didn't want me going anywhere without him except to and from my job. Then he didn't even want me going there. He said he made enough money that I didn't need to work."

Tia nodded. It was a story she'd heard too many times to count.

"I couldn't live like that. When I tried to break it off, though, something snapped. He grabbed a butcher knife and started slashing. This happened." She indicated the side of her face. "Several other things happened, too, like a lacerated liver and a punctured lung. And there was that little section of my intestines that had to be stitched back together."

Nika gave her a weak smile, but there wasn't any humor in it. "I was lying on the kitchen floor, bleeding out all over his tile. Then he grabbed a gun and shot himself in the head. Landed right next to me. I passed out then. Whether from shock or loss of blood, I'm not sure. But him killing himself is what saved me. A neighbor heard the shot and called the police."

She released a heavy sigh. "I woke up the next day after several hours of surgery and a blood transfusion. I felt like I'd been fed through a wood chipper and pieced back together." Another one of those humorless smiles.

"You've been through a lot." The terror of knowing she was about to die, then watching her boyfriend blow out his brains. Wait, if her ex killed himself, why was Nika at Peace House? "Is your life still being threatened?"

"Yeah. My boyfriend's brother. They were super close and he blames me. He visited me a couple of times in the hospital. Yesterday he tried to smother me."

Tia gasped. "Oh, no!" The woman was holding it together remarkably well.

"Fortunately, I had the call button lying next to me under the blanket and managed to push it. But he got away, knocked the nurse down on his way out, then used the stairs."

She pressed her lips together. "He's still at large, and he knows where I live. My friends and family are local. I didn't want to put them in danger, so I called a friend who runs a shelter. She's full but after some phone calls, she got me in here."

Tia nodded. Now it made sense. Nika's friend had sent one of her own advocates to work with Nika in the hospital, even though she didn't have the space. That still didn't mean Peace House was the best place for her. If Tia thought hard enough, she'd come up with a reason why another shelter would be a better fit.

Sometimes it was the inability to meet a particular woman's needs. Sometimes it was the suspicion that the personalities of the residents wouldn't mesh. Some reacted to trauma by becoming loud, obnoxious and manipulative, and others became reclusive and withdrawn. All of her residents fell on the continuum somewhere between those extremes.

Even Jasmine, who'd been angry and loud when she'd arrived, had mellowed. In the week and a half she'd been there, she and sweet, soft-spoken Katie had formed an unlikely friendship. What had begun as a simple haircut had developed into a bonding and self-esteem-building experience for both of them.

Try as she might, Tia couldn't come up with a single reason why Nika didn't belong at Peace House. Except one—Nika's presence made her uncomfortable, which wasn't a valid reason at all.

Nika rearranged the throw pillows behind her, then leaned back again. "I'm really fortunate in a lot of ways. First of all, I'm alive. That's a miracle in itself. Soon I'll put this behind me. Once they catch Donnie, I'll be able to go back to my old life."

She drew her eyebrows together, doubt creeping into her features. "The nightmares go away eventually, right?"

"They get less and less frequent." *Until something happens to bring them back.*

Nika nodded. The answer was probably not what she wanted to hear but seemed to satisfy her.

"They've promised to hold my position at the lawyer's office where I work as an administrative assistant. The other ladies are going to fill in until I get back, picking up the slack. So I'll at least still have a job when this is over."

She looked down at her hands, clasped in her lap. "I had another job on the side, very part-time, but I loved it—doing photo shoots, modeling clothing for a chain of boutiques. That's definitely over now."

"I'm so sorry." Another young lady with her life ruined. Maybe not ruined, but irreparably altered.

After making sure there was nothing else Nika wanted to share, Tia stood and opened the door. Voices drifted down the hall. The women who'd gone to the park were back. Based on the younger voices that were part of the mix, Katie and her boys had come in from outside, too.

"The bathroom is here." Tia pointed to the open door on the other side of the hall then led her into the middle bedroom. "You'll be sleeping in here."

Nika's gaze circled the room, taking in the double bed and the single one next to it. "I have this room to myself?"

"Right now you do. I can't speak for tomorrow."

Relief swept across her features, obvious even in profile. Meeting new people had to be difficult. She stepped forward to place her tote on the larger of the two beds, her back to Tia. When she turned back around, her gaze dipped. "I know this is hard to look at."

"I'm sorry about my reaction in the driveway. I was caught off guard, seeing you for the first time…" Tia waved her hand in a meaningless gesture. Her first priority was making her clients feel welcome and comfortable. She'd blown it with Nika and didn't know how to fix it. "It—it broke my heart." How lame was that?

Nika started to smile, then winced. "I bet you see a lot that breaks your heart."

"I do. You'd think it would get easier over time, but it doesn't." Especially when someone else's experiences hit so close to home.

Tia moved toward the door. "Let's meet the others. Then I'll let you get settled in, have some alone time if you want it."

"Thanks. I'll take advantage of that."

In the living room, Maggie offered Nika her left-handed handshake, and Angela greeted her with her usual friendliness. Jasmine gave her a wave and a smile, confident and welcoming at the same time. When they moved into the dining room, Katie followed her warm greeting with a stern glance at her boys whose gazes were shifting between their mom and the newcomer. Apparently, the silent command to hold their comments worked, because after staring for several seconds, they turned their attention back to their coloring books.

When Tia looked out the front window, Jason's Ram was still parked at the curb. He'd waited for her instead of going back to the inn. She stepped outside, and he met her halfway down the drive.

"I came to share some good news. But you look like you could use a hug." He held out his arms, palms up.

He was right. She needed a hug more than anything, someone to lean on, someone bigger than she was, who could lend her some of his strength.

But she couldn't accept what he was offering. Not now. Not until she felt ready to again stand on her own two feet. If she allowed herself to lean on him, even for a few moments, the rickety frame of self-control that she was keeping in place by sheer will would collapse, and she'd never pull herself back together.

Instead, she squared her shoulders. "Thanks, but

I'm all right."

Jason dropped his arms and nodded. "The arrival of your newest resident seems to have really shaken you up."

Tia pressed her lips together. What could she say? It had. But to admit it would require telling him why.

He rested a hand on her shoulder. "Women come to you all the time, battered and broken. Surely you've seen worse."

"Maybe." She drew in a shaky breath. "But it's different with Nika. She'll never be able to escape the reminders." Every glance in the mirror would bring to the surface all those feelings of helplessness and fear.

Tia looked past him, beyond his truck to the house catty-cornered from hers. A family of inflatable snowmen adorned the lawn, Styrofoam snowflakes hanging from the oak tree behind them.

Everywhere she looked, Christmas cheer surrounded her. She'd tried her best to bring it to Peace House, too, with her festively-decorated tree, garland draped from the valances, candles in the windows and icicle lights dangling from the eaves. But all her efforts provided little more than a temporary distraction.

She frowned. "You can push the memories to the back of your mind, but the false sense of peace never lasts, because buried things have a way of resurfacing at unexpected and inopportune times." Her voice sounded weak, even to her own ears. "The scars never go away."

"These scars, are they internal or external?" His voice was almost as soft as hers, with a noticeable gentleness.

She met his gaze. "Both."

His eyes dipped to her scarf, as if he knew, and she stiffened. Knowing was one thing. Seeing the proof was entirely another. It would never happen.

"Outer wounds heal." He continued in that smooth, gentle voice that was like warm oil over her frayed nerve endings. "They might leave scars, but they do heal eventually. It's the hidden ones that still bleed long after the outer ones scab over." He put his hand on her shoulder again and gave it a squeeze. "Whatever you've been through, tell someone. If you can't share it with me, share it with her. It'll help you both feel a lot less alone."

He lifted a hand and cupped her cheek. His palm was warm against her face, almost as warm as his gaze. There was that connection again, the mutual trauma that bound them together. She shouldn't have turned down that hug, because now she really wanted him to kiss her.

All too soon, he dropped his hand. "Think about it."

Then he walked to his truck. Instead of getting into the cab, he stood at the open door. He wouldn't leave until she was safely inside the house.

With a sigh, she started to turn away. "Wait. You never told me your news."

A smile spread across his face, and the joy she'd seen earlier lit his eyes. He moved toward her. "My mother's cancer appears to have gone into remission."

"That's wonderful news."

"They're doing some follow-up tests, but the experimental treatment seems to be working."

"I'm so happy to hear it. I've been praying for her."

She wrapped her arms around him in an impromptu hug. It was the same thing she'd do with any of her friends, a show of shared joy over answered prayer. But what if Jason misinterpreted it?

Before she could second guess herself too much, his arms came up to circle her waist, and he gave her a tight squeeze. "Thank you. God is answering your prayers…all of our prayers."

When she released him, his arms slid from around her waist, and he trapped both of her hands in his. "We won't know for sure until the rest of the test results come back, but I have high hopes that she's going to get well."

She matched his smile, his joy contagious. "I do, too."

If Jason's mother got well, would that mean they could return to Central Florida? The possibilities circled through her mind—continued regular contact with Jason, a deepening of their friendship, and getting to know his mother. She had to be a special lady to have raised a man like Jason alone, to have led him through the process of overcoming the damage done by his abusive father.

No, that wasn't what her recovery would mean. It would just mean that he wasn't going to lose her to cancer in the near future. The threat that ran them out of Florida was probably still there.

The joy of Jason's announcement carried her all the way back to the house. When she stepped inside, Katie was shooing two complaining boys toward the restroom for baths.

The young mother shook her head. "We're going

to wash off some of the grime from playing outside so they'll be ready for bed when we finish eating, but the way they're carrying on you'd think I'm getting ready to waterboard them or something."

Soon the sounds of happier voices and running water came from inside the small space. Halfway down the hall on the opposite side, the door to the middle bedroom was shut. Nika was likely inside.

For several moments, Tia stared at the closed door. It was probably hard for Nika, being in a new place, having to meet new people, her wounds fresh.

And Tia had made it harder on her. A boulder of shame and guilt filled her chest. She had no intention of following Jason's advice, but she at least owed Nika an apology. Now was as good a time as any. Dinner wasn't due to start for another half hour.

She raised a fist to knock, then hesitated. She didn't even know what to say. Nika needed to know why she'd reacted the way she had, but the foundation of why was in everything she'd experienced at Victor's hands.

A lifetime ago, she'd provided the gruesome details for the court case. Reliving those events had almost killed her. She'd survived with most of her sanity intact but had vowed to never speak of them again.

Maybe it was time to break that promise.

She raised her hand again, and this time she knocked.

"Come in."

Nika had a sweet voice. In fact, she radiated sweetness. If there was anyone who should be easy to open up to, it would be Nika.

When Tia opened the door, her newest resident

was sitting on the bed, pillows propped behind her against the headboard.

"Mind if I join you for a few minutes?"

"Not at all. I'd love the company."

Tia sat near the foot of the bed. Now that she was here, she had no idea how to start. She dragged in a deep breath and released it slowly. Drew in a second. Looked down at her hands clasped in her lap.

Nika waited, watching. Tia could feel the woman's eyes on her. She didn't sense any pressure, just that sweetness that seemed to hover around her like a cloud. Now it was mixed with understanding and patience.

Tia swallowed hard. "There are some similarities between our stories, but yours is much worse."

Or was it? Could terror even be quantified? What was worse, one massive burst where the victim knows without a doubt she'll die, or feeling trapped in a prison of pain and fear, with no end in sight?

Nika had shared her story. Now it was Tia's turn, but the words wouldn't come. Nika waited—calm, composed, patient. Finally, Tia opened her mouth to speak. Nika didn't need eloquence. She needed honesty.

"I already apologized to you for reacting the way I did. I told you that what you went through broke my heart. That was just partly true."

She sucked in a stabilizing breath. "Seeing your cut took me back to a time in my life that I never wanted to return to." Actually, Victor's warning had done that. Nika's injuries had just cemented her even more thoroughly in the quagmire of everything she'd tried so hard to flee.

She reached for her scarf and slowly unwound it from her neck. After a final tug, the silk length fell to her lap. The neckline of the blouse she wore rested about four inches beneath her collarbone. The scars extended from her waist to the bottom of her neck.

Sympathy shone from Nika's eyes, but the shock Tia had expected to see wasn't there.

"Did you do it, or did he?"

It was the same question that had come up in court, more than once. Victor's attorney had circled back to it several times, in spite of the prosecution's objections. He seemed to believe that if he asked the question enough times, phrased enough different ways, Tia would eventually break down and admit that her wounds were self-inflicted.

"I've never been a cutter. But that was the picture my husband painted. He said he'd begged me for years to get help but I'd always refused."

"Did the jury believe him?"

"No. He got five years."

"He's still in?"

Tia shook her head. "He was released. Tomorrow makes two weeks."

Nika's brows drew together. "What he did was cold and calculated, not something done in a fit of rage, without forethought."

Tia nodded, the desire to cover up pounding through her. No, Nika couldn't hide, and she wasn't going to, either. She tried to summon strength. It had to be there, somewhere deep inside her. Or maybe that was the problem. Maybe she'd tried too long to rely on her own strength. *God, please help me.*

She met Nika's gaze. "It was all about control. It

started within days of our marriage. If I wanted to so much as step out the door, I had to ask for his permission, permission that he denied more and more frequently."

"You were living in a prison."

"With a warden that could make Hitler look like Mother Teresa. Anything he saw as resistance resulted in punishment."

Tia kicked off her shoes and tucked her feet under her legs to sit Indian style. "At first it was just scratches, nicks that barely pierced the skin and healed over quickly. Then they gradually got deeper. How deep depended on the seriousness of the infraction. If I got the meat a little tough, or he found dust on the entertainment center, those were little sins. Oversleeping and not having his breakfast ready on time was a little more serious."

She didn't dare scream, either. "I got really good at biting my tongue. Since we lived in a large house situated in the middle of five acres, the only thing screaming accomplished was increasing the length and severity of the punishment."

She repressed a shudder as her mind pulled her back to that dark place. A seed of panic sprouted and spread. Screamed commands to escape bounced around inside her skull. She clenched her fists. *No.* No one was restraining her. She was free. Everything she'd suffered at Victor's hands was in the past.

"That's awful. How long were you in that situation?"

Tia opened her eyes, the soft voice pulling her back to the present. "The worst of it, almost two years. Near the end, I thought I'd lose my mind. I couldn't sleep, couldn't eat, and I had a hard time getting things done around the house. I finally called my sister. Victor hadn't allowed me to have contact with her for months."

"You told her what was going on?"

"I didn't dare. I just needed to hear a friendly voice. Big mistake. Victor had taken away my cell phone long before this, but I didn't know he'd changed our home phone to a business account, with logs listing all calls sent and received."

"What did he do?"

Tia shuddered and closed her eyes. "My deepest scars are from that night. I did scream then. I couldn't help it. He said I'd always be his, and he'd make sure that no one else would ever want me."

She closed her eyes, the mess that was now her chest and abdomen stretched across the canvas of her imagination. She'd memorized every slash. When two cuts joined it wasn't accidental. Those scars formed Vs.

"Is that why you didn't leave him?"

"No. He threatened to do terrible things to my little sister if I left him or told anyone what was going on. He said no one would believe me. He and his dad had a successful law practice in town, and my sister and I were daughters of a single mom who kept food on the table by waitressing in the local diner. With his connections, I figured he'd beat the charges then come after all three of us."

"You obviously found a way to escape."

"My sister was the brave one." And probably responsible for saving Tia's life. "She'd just turned eighteen, but she's smart. She read between the lines, and she and my mom sent the police out for a wellness check. I tried to tell them everything was fine, then dissolved into a blubbering mess. I ended up going to a shelter, a lot like this one, and my mom and sister hid out with a high school friend of my mom's who'd relocated to another state."

She clasped her hands together. "I thought I'd moved past the trauma, but recently, a single threat brought it all back."

Concern entered Nika's gaze. "He's found you?"

Tia nodded. "He showed up here. While I was out, he grabbed one of my women and gave her a message for me."

"What kind of message?"

"That he's sharpening his blade."

Nika shuddered.

"You guys are safe. It's me he's after. Besides, the Harmony Grove police are watching the house, with help from the Polk County Sheriff's Department and a couple of retired deputies who were happy to lend assistance. It's not twenty-four/seven, but it's pretty close, especially at night."

And there was no end in sight. Victor had always gotten a sick thrill out of tormenting her. Letting her live days or weeks with the terror of knowing he was close, with no idea of when or where he'd strike, was just the type of thing he'd do.

"Where are your sister and mom now?"

"Jacksonville, more than 100 miles from where we grew up. My sister's married to a cop now—a big, tough guy who will do whatever's needed to protect the woman he loves. Their house has a mother-in-law suite that Mom occupies. And if that isn't enough, one of the county deputies happens to live right next door."

"You said your ex's name was Victor."

Is. If she could put it in the past tense, she wouldn't be struggling with nightmares, too terrified to leave the house. "Yes."

"Last initial *K*?"

The other identifiable letter. Tia nodded. "For Krasney."

"He was marking you."

She nodded again, longing, as she had so many times before, to erase the physical reminders, to rid her body of everything that remained of Victor.

Nika turned to let her feet hang over the side of the bed, then stood and moved closer. Based on her grimace, the effort didn't come without pain. Tia appreciated it all the more.

Nika put her hand over Tia's and squeezed. "Thank you for sharing with me. It means a lot. When I look at you and everything you're accomplishing with this place, it helps me believe I'm going to make it."

"You will. I have no doubt." Maybe Nika would have resources Tia hadn't. Working for a law firm, she likely had decent insurance coverage. "Have your doctors talked to you about plastic surgery?"

"Yeah, we're definitely going to pursue that. I'll still have a scar, but it'll look much better than this. Some of my friends have already set up a Go-Fund-Me page to help cover the deductible and other expenses. The only downside was I had to let them take a picture of me in the hospital." She frowned. "I usually enjoy being in front of the camera, but not like this."

"That must have been hard."

Tia stood and wrapped the scarf back around her

neck. "I'm going to leave you be and go start making dinner."

"Can I help you cook?"

"I'll leave that up to you. There'll be at least two others working with me. If you'd like to join us, you're welcome to, or if you'd like a little time to yourself before jumping into activities full bore, you've got a free pass, at least until tomorrow."

Nika gave her a right-sided smile. "I'll think about it."

Before opening the door, Tia checked the full-length mirror hanging there. The scarf looked good. It covered everything she wanted it to cover.

She'd shown her scars to Nika, and she was glad she had, for Nika's sake and for her own. But she wasn't ready to show them to anyone else.

Least of all to Jason.

FOURTEEN

A PICKUP TRUCK BACKED from the driveway, *Bob and Jerry's Roofing* painted on the door and ladders secured to the rack on top.

Yesterday after church, Jason had had lunch with Tia, then finished cleaning out the two closets in the foyer. This morning, they were handling a more important task. After noticing that the ceiling stains had spread during the last rainstorm, he'd suggested that Tia have the problem looked at. He could have given her all kinds of recommendations for Connecticut roofers but didn't know a single one in Polk County. Fortunately, Tia's landlady did.

Bob had spent a half hour on the roof, assessing the condition and taking measurements before approaching them with his verdict: The roof was long overdue for replacement. Several shingles were raised or missing altogether, and in spots, the plywood decking below was soft. He'd promised to provide two estimates: One to make the repairs needed to prevent further damage, and one for a complete reroof.

As the pickup truck disappeared from view, Tia frowned. "It doesn't make sense to put money into repairs then turn around and have the whole place reroofed in a year."

"I agree. When you get the estimates, take them to the attorney. Let him know you'd rather have it reroofed. As executor, he has the authority to release the funds for work needed to preserve the asset."

She nodded. "I'll do that."

"Are you ready for me to take you back home?" He'd picked her up at the shelter and brought her to the house to meet the roofer.

"How much longer are you planning to work?

"A couple of hours, but I can come back."

"Don't make a special trip. Monica's there. She'll let me know if I'm needed."

He led her into the house and to the living room. "This is the only room left." He motioned toward the built-in bookshelves and drawers that spanned the length of one wall. "Once I get that stuff sorted, there won't be anything left to do except haul the trash to the landfill."

He should be relieved. A big project completed and off his back. No reason to have to return to Florida.

He wasn't relieved, though. Just the opposite. The thought of leaving Tia to return to his life in Connecticut tied his stomach in knots. Sure, she was being careful and not taking any unnecessary chances. The police were keeping an eye on her, too. But ever since she'd received the threat a week ago, she'd seemed to be on a downward spiral. Gone was the spitfire who'd stared him down at his grandmother's house, insisting it belonged to her. Even the woman who'd stood in her living room pointing her rifle at the two men who'd charged through her front door seemed to have disappeared.

The woman that now filled that spot wore fear in her posture, her drawn features and the dark circles under her eyes testimony to lack of proper rest. Was the sleep she was getting wracked by nightmares?

He trudged to the bookcase and scanned the spines of the books lining the shelves. "I don't have room for a quarter of this."

Tia moved to stand next to him. "Are there any you especially want to keep?"

"Yeah." There were several books that held a lot of sentimental value, titles like *Twenty Thousand Leagues Under the Sea*, *The Hobbit* and the *Lord of the Rings* trilogy.

He brushed his hand across a row of books. "This is the full set of C.S. Lewis's *Chronicles of Narnia*. Grandma and Grandpa got it for me as a Christmas gift for my tenth birthday."

"You definitely need to take that home."

He nodded. Christmas and birthday gifts from his grandparents always included at least one or two books, which ended up back here, on these very shelves. Jason had learned early on to keep whatever book he was reading in his school backpack and leave the others at his grandparents' house. Things at his own place had had a way of disappearing. Books especially hadn't lasted long, because reading was another activity for sissies.

"Could the shelter use any of these?" He'd noticed the small library in her living room, housed in a three-foot-wide by four-foot tall bookcase. He'd even seen a couple of the women reading books they'd taken from there.

"Absolutely. Reading is a popular activity at Peace House. It's a great escape." She scanned the shelves. "I'm guessing titles like *A Complete Guide to Renovation* and *The Home Cabinetmaker* wouldn't be super popular with the ladies, but you never know."

"That's true. Sometimes exposure to random things can spur a lifelong passion for an activity someone never considered."

Damian would have probably found the books fascinating, based on how enthusiastic he'd been about the door repair. Jason's chest squeezed at the thought of the boy he'd gotten so attached to in such a short time. He hadn't heard from him yet. Of course, Pam and her kids had only been gone a week.

Tia indicated the books in front of her with a nod. "There's plenty of fiction here, too."

Yeah, there was a little bit of everything. His grandmother had always been an avid reader. Even Grandpa could often be seen with a book in his lap in the evening.

While Tia prepped some boxes, he scanned the shelves. There were four in all, split into three sections by wooden dividers. Photo albums occupied the bottom shelf on the far right-hand side. Those would go home with him, too.

He pointed out the two shelves above them. "These are the books I want to take home."

She pulled them from the shelf two or three at a time and packed them into the first box. "This is a lot of books for a kid. Did you read them all?"

"At least once. Most of them two and three times. Like your women, I needed the escape."

She nodded, understanding in her eyes. She finished

filling one box and started on the next. The next several minutes passed in silence as she packed up books and he finished scanning the shelves, making sure he wouldn't leave anything precious behind.

While he worked, he cast frequent glances at Tia. There was tension in her features. He hoped she'd taken his advice and talked with the new lady. He'd met her yesterday, had spoken with her over lunch. She seemed nice enough. Quiet and sweet, a pretty girl, self-conscious about what her boyfriend had done to her face.

When he'd first seen her standing in Tia's driveway, he'd reacted, too. Anger. He'd been better at hiding his reaction than Tia had been, because he'd had so much experience. Injustice and cruelty did it to him every time, especially when it was aimed at women and children.

Tia knelt to tape the two boxes. "That's all of them from these two shelves, unless there are others you'd like to take."

"That's it on the books, but I definitely want to take these." He pulled down the photo albums and stacked them on the deep bottom shelf that formed the top of the drawer units. He would enjoy looking through them when he got home.

Maybe "enjoy" wasn't the right word to use. He'd get to see all the activities with his grandparents that his father had robbed him of over the past seventeen years. Actually, longer than that, because before he and his mother fled the state in the middle of the night, his father had forbidden contact with his grandparents

Tia straightened and stood beside him. "I love

looking at old pictures." She put her hand on the edge of the top album. "Do you mind?"

"Not at all."

On the first leaf, a piece of paper bearing the words *1998 Europe trip* was trapped behind the plastic sleeve.

"Europe." Tia's tone held a wistful quality. "I've always wanted to go there. Victor promised, but we never made it."

Jason pressed his lips together. He remembered that trip. Not the trip itself, but his grandparents planning it. That had been at a time when Friday night family dinners were still a regular thing, before his father distanced himself, along with Jason and his mom.

"Grandma and Grandpa invited me to go with them."

"Wow, what an opportunity. You would have been what, eight or ten?"

"Nine. But my dad wouldn't let me go. My mom even tried to convince him when we got home that night, insisted it would be a great educational experience."

And Jason had listened around the corner with his fingers crossed, wishing with every hope his nine-year-old heart could muster that his father would give in and let him go.

"And?"

"She couldn't sway him. He said he wasn't going to let anyone spoil his kid by giving him things that he couldn't afford to provide."

His responses had gotten louder and angrier with every second that passed. He'd finally told his mom that if she didn't shut up about it, he was going to shut her up. Then Jason had wished with every hope his nine-year-old heart could muster that his mother would quit before fists started flying.

While Tia looked through the album, he started on the first drawer. He knew what the album held. His grandmother had shown him the pictures when they'd gotten back from the trip.

He pulled some items from the drawer. This one held supplies for gift-giving, things like wrapping paper, bows, gift totes, tissue paper, boxes of cards. It would all go in the "donate" stack. He was more of a gift card kind of guy.

Tia prepared another box and put the Europe album in the bottom. By the time he'd packed up the items small enough to fit into a box and laid the rolls of Christmas paper across the top, she'd flipped through another three albums.

"I think this one's your baby album."

He stepped up behind her and looked over her shoulder. A picture of a newborn baby occupied the top half of the page, a birth announcement beneath.

"No, wait." Tia pointed at the name on the announcement. George Wilburn?"

"My father."

"Your father's name is George Sloan. It says so in the will."

"My dad's birth father was killed when he was young, and Grandma remarried. Grandpa Sloan adopted him."

He looked down at the announcement, trying to reconcile the sweet innocence displayed in the picture with the cruel, angry man his father had become, then gave up. It was too much of a stretch. As the subject of the pictures progressed from baby to toddler to preschooler, sweetness gave way to sullenness. His father was clearly not a happy child.

Tia turned another page. With each new picture, Jason's stomach tightened. One of the albums in the stack would have pictures of him, and if the boyhood photos in each were laid side by side, the resemblance would be striking. As much as he wanted to deny it, he'd gotten his looks from his father.

But that was all he'd gotten. He wasn't like his father, never would be.

Tia turned another page and another. By adolescence, sullenness had given way to anger. Even in decades-old pictures, it was obvious in the narrowed eyes, pinched lips and tight set of his jaw. Just like someone else he knew.

He clenched his teeth. He'd had a reason for his anger. Growing up in Elizabeth and Daniel Sloan's home, his father hadn't.

Jason snatched the book from Tia and snapped it closed, ignoring her gasp. "You can put this in that black trash bag over there." His tone held an icy hardness. He didn't try to soften it.

Tia looked up at him, her eyebrows forming delicate arches. "Are you sure?"

"Why wouldn't I be?"

"This is part of your history. You might regret it later, especially if you and your father…" Her voice trailed off.

"If my father and I what, make up? If he suddenly has a change of heart all these years later and apologizes for everything he did to my mother and me? If I actually grant him forgiveness?" *Not gonna happen.*

A needle-like twinge of guilt stabbed through the rage building inside him, and he tightened his fists. His father didn't deserve his forgiveness, and he was nowhere near offering it. Now Tia was judging him for it.

"How many pictures of Victor do you have lying around?"

The instant the words left his mouth, he regretted them. Her eyes filled with pain, and she seemed to deflate in front of him.

"You can take me home now." Her voice was paper thin.

"Tia, I'm sorry, I didn't mean it." How could he have used her relationship with Victor against her, with the threats she was currently facing?

Like father, like son. As much as he'd tried to overcome his past, he still sometimes lashed out in anger. He didn't use fists, but words could wound just as deeply, even more so.

"Please take me home." She'd managed to put some strength behind the request this time.

With a brief dip of his head, he strode toward the front door. He'd do as she asked, then try to figure out a way to make it up to her later, maybe after the sting of his words faded.

He had a day and a half. This afternoon and tomorrow morning, he'd finish the drawers. Tomorrow afternoon, he'd make a trip or two to the landfill. Then Wednesday morning, he'd load up the items he was taking home and hit the road. He still had two weeks of vacation left, but Christmas was Friday, and he wasn't about to leave his mom to spend the holiday alone.

He opened the Ram's front passenger door for Tia, then closed it behind her. During the drive back to town, silence stretched between them, heavy and oppressive. He drew to a stop in her driveway. "I'm going to check on you tonight."

She slid from the truck without comment. Since she didn't tell him to not bother, he took her silence as acquiescence.

As he watched her walk to the house, shoulders curled forward, he kicked himself yet again. Wednesday afternoon, he'd have to say goodbye. Maybe he could delay his trip by a half day. If he headed out in the wee hours of Thursday morning and drove straight through, he'd be home shortly after midnight.

And Victor would likely still be out there, his threats as real as ever. Jason sighed. He'd have to trust the police to do their job. And trust that God would give Tia the emotional strength she needed in the meantime.

Back inside the house, he pulled open the second drawer and knelt in front of it. Maybe he should consider a third alternative for travel plans. If he flew home instead of driving, he could leave Thursday afternoon and come back Saturday. That would buy him an extra week. By the time the new year arrived and he had to be back to work, maybe Victor would have been caught. Then he would feel better about leaving Tia.

Who was he kidding? Nothing would make him feel okay about leaving Tia. He'd finally found someone special. Someone who understood his scars, because she bore her own. Someone genuine who said what she felt without pretense or manipulation.

Someone who shared his faith. Soon he'd head back in the dead of winter, to dreary days and cold nights, because his sunshine was staying in Florida.

Why would God bring them together when it could never be? Tia was tied to Central Florida, and Central Florida was the one place in the country he could never live. Not as long as his father was alive.

He lifted a shoe box out of the drawer, and rummaged through the screwdrivers, wrenches, scissors and other items there. These would go in the "donate" stack. His place at home was well-stocked with miscellaneous tools.

When he finished that drawer, he opened the bottom one, then positioned himself on the floor in front of it. It held several photo albums. Why weren't they on the shelves with the others?

He pulled out the top one. It was his grandparents' wedding album. But it wasn't the grandfather he'd known. It was his dad's birth father. His grandmother never talked about him, except to say that he'd been killed in an accident when Jason's father was young. Then she'd married Daniel Sloan who'd adopted his dad and given him his name.

Jason's father had never mentioned his birth father, either. Depending on how young he'd been at the time of the accident, he probably didn't remember him. Could the trauma of losing his father at a young age have turned him into the man that Jason knew?

No, he wouldn't make excuses for him. A lot of children suffered loss without becoming abusers.

Jason flipped through the pages of the wedding album, then picked up the one beneath it. He'd never seen pictures of his father's real dad. His grandmother had kept them hidden away for decades. His dad obviously had this man's genes. If the man didn't remind him so much of his father, he would have wanted to know him.

Jason laid the second album on the floor beside him. A journal lay in the bottom of the drawer, and he picked it up to fold back the cover. His grandmother's slanted script filled the page. He read the date of the first entry and did the calculations in his head. His father would have been about ten.

I'm writing this with a split lip and swollen eye. I blame it on clumsiness, and no one is any the wiser. I can't shatter the image of the happy wife and doting mother.

Jason looked up. What was she talking about? He turned the page. The next entry was made a week later.

Every day it gets harder. The facade is crumbling. When I was checking out at the grocery store today, Wilma asked me if everything was okay. I wanted to scream, "No, it's not."

But I didn't. He has his public face, and I help him preserve it. If the truth got out, I don't think I could bear the gossip, the whispers, the looks of pity.

Jason lowered the book to his lap and shook his head. She couldn't have been saying what he thought she was. His grandfather had never been abusive. Mild-mannered, soft-spoken, the kind of man that nothing riled, he was so different from Jason's father.

Jason hadn't been naive or ignorant. He'd had his eyes opened at a young age. If his grandfather had abused his father or his grandmother, Jason would have seen the signs. No, he couldn't believe it. Wouldn't believe it.

He turned the page and read the next entry.

Business is tough, so competitive. He comes home tired and frustrated. He keeps up the front for his customers then comes home and takes out his frustration on me. George and I are the only ones in the world who see what he really is.

But as long as I can keep his anger channeled away from George, I will bear whatever I have to. Lately, he's been yelling at him a lot more, has even sent him to his room without supper for minor infractions.

For the first time ever, I'm scared.

Jason released a breath he hadn't realized he'd been holding. Bile followed the air up his throat. It couldn't be. But there it was, in black and white. His grandmother wouldn't have any reason to write falsehoods.

He returned his gaze to the journal. He didn't want to read any more, didn't want the image of the man he'd idolized as a child shattered any more than it already was. But he couldn't stop himself.

The next entry was two weeks later. The script looked different from the other entries, the curves jagged, as if the writer had been nervous or upset. The first two sentences sent a wave of dread crashing over Jason.

Dear God, what do I do? It has started. After years of watching his father hit me, George got his first beating tonight. Instead of fists, he got the belt, leaving welts all over his back and legs. I begged his father to stop, even tried to stay his hand. But I'm no match for his strength when he's enraged. I paid for my interference later.

What was George's crime? He accidentally knocked over his tea glass reaching for the salt shaker.

Jason closed his eyes, the words bringing back a similar incident. *He'd* been the culprit that time, spilling his milk. He'd been about six. His mother had stepped between him and his father and sent him to his room before his father could hit him.

Instead, he'd hit his mother. Over and over. Jason had lain in bed with the pillow pressed over his head, trying to block out the thud of fists and his mother's cries. It hadn't helped.

He opened his eyes, swallowing hard. His dad had lived through the same experiences that haunted Jason's memories. A bond he had no desire to feel tugged at him. No wonder his dad had turned out to be such a monster.

But how had Daniel Sloan made the transition from the cruel man in these journal entries to the gentle, loving grandfather Jason had known for the first thirteen years of his life? Change that drastic didn't happen, short of a miracle. Would the journal provide the answer?

He continued to read. Though written only a week later, the script was much more relaxed.

He's gone. Forever out of our lives. I am devastated. That's what I keep telling myself and the face I show the world.

But the thought that keeps circling through my mind is that it's over. Never again will I have to be the target of his fists.

Jason looked up. Where had his grandfather gone? He'd apparently come back a changed man. Jason dropped his gaze back to the page.

What he was will remain a secret. Eventually, I will destroy even this, wipe out the last trace of the ugly story that has been my life for the past fifteen years.

Wait, fifteen years? Something wasn't adding up. Jason's dad was only ten. His real father died when he was young. Or maybe ten did classify as young. Maybe it wasn't his grandfather that Jason had been reading about after all. At least not the grandfather he'd known.

A final paragraph finished off the page.

But for now, I keep this journal as a reminder, in case I should ever contemplate allowing another man access to my child and home. I am closing the book on this chapter of my life. I will never speak of him again. Neither will George. With time, the memories will fade, and with them, the pain.

Jason thumbed through the remainder of the journal. The rest of the pages were blank, but a folded-up newspaper clipping was tucked between two of them. When he opened it, a bold headline stretched across the top—"Harmony Grove Man Killed in Head-On Collision." He skimmed the first paragraph. The victim's name was Gerard Wilburn.

After scanning the rest of the article, he tucked it back inside, and closed the journal, his thoughts still reeling. His father had suffered abuse at the hand of his own father, and it had gone on for ten years. Maybe he hadn't been beaten the entire ten years, but being yelled at, put down and denied food, having to see his father's punches and hear his mother's cries, it was abuse all the same.

It had stopped at age ten. After that, he'd lived in a home that couldn't have been any more loving. But the harm had already been done. He'd been so damaged that even a man like Daniel Sloan couldn't fix him.

Jason rose and pulled out his phone. He had to call his mom. It wouldn't justify anything his father had done. But it would help explain it. Sometimes understanding could bring a measure of healing.

Then he would go see Tia. He shared a connection with her. He'd known it almost from the start. This revelation had nothing to do with her, but he needed to tell her what he'd learned. He didn't know why.

He just did.

FIFTEEN

TIA STOOD CLUTCHING the front doorknob, palms sweating and heart slamming against her ribcage as if trying to escape. It was an automatic rerun of two days ago. When was she going to reach the point where she could walk to her mailbox without terror descending on her?

She should have brought in the mail when Jason dropped her off. She'd been upset and had forgotten about it. Now it would be dark in another hour, and her mail was still sitting in the box.

Maybe she could check the yard, then sprint to the box and back before Victor, if he was watching, had an opportunity to react. Or not. She pulled her phone from her pocket. Since the police were keeping an eye on her place, chances were good someone was nearby.

She shot off a text to Alan. *Where R U?*

2 blocks away. Why?

Forgot to bring in mail.

B rt there.

She pocketed the phone. She was such a chicken. But no one would witness her cowardice except Alan and any of her women who may watch him drive up.

For Alan, it was his job, and the women… If anyone understood fear, it was them.

She opened the door and poked her head out in time to see the police cruiser make its way down Tranquility Way. She descended the porch steps, and the cruiser eased to a stop at the edge of the road, just past her mailbox. A few seconds later, a blue Ram appeared from beyond the inn's hedge.

Her stomach flipped, then clenched. She was still upset at him about the photo comment and wasn't ready to let it go. Or maybe she *had* let it go, and all that lingered were the remnants of what she'd felt when Victor's name had unexpectedly fallen from Jason's lips.

The comment had been cruel, like pouring salt into an open wound. It was so unlike the Jason she'd come to know.

The regret that followed had been just what she would expect. So had his heartfelt apology, as if in that moment he would have done anything to make up for the pain he'd just caused.

No, she couldn't hold a grudge. She wasn't the only one fighting demons of the past. If the mere mention of Victor's name could leave her feeling as if she'd been punched in the gut, what memories had those photos dredged up for Jason?

As he pulled into her driveway, she waved the officer on. No sense pulling him away from his duties.

Jason stepped from his truck and cast a glance over his shoulder. "Harmony Grove Police just checked on you?"

"Sort of. Alan's stop just then was to make sure I made it to the mailbox and back safely. I forgot to get the mail when you brought me home. Didn't think I should walk out alone to get it."

"Absolutely not. If they're unavailable, call me." He grinned. "I'll even deliver it right to your door."

"Thank you. That's service."

He sobered. "I came to tell you again that I'm sorry."

She gave him a weak smile. "No need for another apology. I've already accepted the first one."

Relief filled his features, proving how important her forgiveness was to him. "I also have another reason for stopping by. I made an interesting discovery when I returned to the house."

Her heart lifted, along with her eyebrows. "The elusive coffee can?"

"'Fraid not. I'm as broke as I was an hour ago. But I found my grandmother's journal. It shed some light on some things I'd never considered before."

"What kind of things?"

"Abuse. My dad's father."

"Daniel Sloan?"

Jason shook his head. "His birth father."

She pursed her lips. "Had you had any hint of this before?"

"Not at all."

"Your dad never talked about it?"

"Not a word. I'd always known that Daniel Sloan was his adoptive father, but had thought the accident that killed his birth father happened when he'd been much younger. Instead, he lived with that for ten years." He sighed. "I'm not justifying what he did. He was mean and cruel and made our lives miserable. But looking at his childhood pictures and seeing the anger and sadness in his face, I'd felt a connection. It made me mad, because I didn't want to feel any sympathy toward him."

He gave her a sad smile. "I've had to work hard at not hating him, and the only reason I've done that is because I know it's what God requires."

She nodded. She'd faced the same struggle. Every time she thought she was almost there, she would relive an event through another memory or nightmare, and the hatred would bombard her once again.

He pressed his lips together for several moments before continuing. "Reading my grandmother's journal gave me a different perspective. I've always resented my father for not giving me the same kind of home that he grew up in. I had no idea what his life had been like for the first ten years. My grandfather was an amazing man, but even he couldn't undo the damage my dad's birth father had inflicted."

He shook his head. "I can't help wondering, if my grandmother would have sought help instead of keeping quiet, if things would have turned out differently. But back then, there weren't the resources there are now." He looked at her hard. "Resources like Peace House. Do you have any idea how important your ministry is, how many lives you're changing?"

His gaze locked with hers, and the warmth and admiration in his eyes sent a flutter through her chest.

"Thank you." She liked to think that, anyway. On occasion, she received a card in the mail from a past resident, thanking her for providing help when it was needed, with an update about the client's progress in her new life.

"Although I'm not justifying anything he did, I

understand it a little better now. It's like the backdrop of my life had holes, and I've suddenly found the missing pieces." He wrinkled his nose. "Do you think I'm crazy?"

"Not at all. It's normal to try to make sense of our circumstances, to try to formulate explanations for why things are the way they are, even if knowing doesn't do anything to fix them."

She'd never been able to do that with Victor, had never understood what had turned him into the monster he was. He'd come from a stable family, upper middle class. He and his father had been close, even worked together. Unable to pin his faults on nurture, she'd gone with nature—he seemed to have been born defective, imbued with a cruelty gene that was lacking in normal people.

She glanced toward the house. The curtains were pulled aside at one of the living room windows, a small face pressed into the opening. The face disappeared immediately, but a few seconds later, the front door swung open.

Aiden charged through as if shot out of a cannon. "Mr. Jason!"

When he hit the second step, he stumbled and toppled forward, landing on his hands and knees on the sidewalk.

Tia gasped and rushed toward him. Several seconds passed in silence, that inevitable span of time between when a child fell and the moment the pain registered.

The wail she expected started, softly at first, then grew in volume. She scooped him up, and he wrapped one arm around her neck, pressing his face into her shoulder. His other hand gripped the folds of her scarf.

Katie ran through the still open door, navigating the steps with ease. "Aiden, what happened, buddy?" She held out both hands, but he still clung to Tia.

His cries settled to shaky sobs, and he pulled away to show his mother both of his hands. The heels of his palms were red, bits of sand embedded in the skin.

He twisted to extend one leg. A hole was worn in the denim just below his knee. Fresh blood caked the frayed edges.

Katie extended her hands again. "How about if I take you inside and get you cleaned up? We'll run some cold water over your hands and bandage the booboo on your knee."

He drew in a quivery breath. "'Kay."

Tia passed him to his mother. It wasn't until Katie had turned that Tia realized Aiden had once again tangled his hand in her scarf. The slippery fabric loosened and slid from her neck.

Panic shot through her as she grabbed for the scarf. Aiden finally released his grip to wrap his arms around his mother's neck. By then, Tia had a wad of silk clutched in one fist, ends draping down in front of her.

Katie spun back to face her. "I'm sorry. I didn't realize he had hold of your scarf. Can I help you fix it?"

"No." The single word came out sharper than she'd intended. She softened her tone. "I've got it. Thank you."

Katie nodded, climbed the two steps and disappeared inside, while Tia fought the overwhelming urge to bolt. But where could she go? Not inside, where two children and five women might be lurking about, only one of whom knew her story.

She couldn't stand here with Jason staring at her, that dark gaze filling with concern as it shifted between her eyes and where she was holding the scarf. Did she have herself amply covered, or was there a scar or two peeking out between the wadded-up silk and the edge of her blouse?

Why had she never learned to wear turtlenecks? She knew why, but she should have tried harder. If she could have ignored the sensation of knit or nylon circling her throat and the feelings of claustrophobia it induced, she would have grown accustomed to it. Instead, she'd given up too soon, thinking she could hide behind flimsy silk.

She spun away from Jason and strode toward the oak tree a short distance away. Facing the large trunk, she pulled the scarf from her neck with shaking fingers and held it up. She needed a mirror. No, it didn't matter. She was going for concealment, not style.

A rustle sounded behind her, and she tensed. A moment later, gentle hands touched her shoulders.

She swallowed the panic rising inside and closed her eyes. Jason's would hold concern; she didn't even have to turn around. If he saw how Victor had marked her, that concern would turn to revulsion, and that would be more than she could bear.

What Jason thought of her mattered. It shouldn't, but it did. She wanted his respect and admiration, but she also wanted to be beautiful in his eyes.

Victor's words circled through her mind. *I'm going to make sure no one else will ever want you.* She squeezed her eyelids shut more tightly. No, she would never be beautiful, in Jason's eyes or anyone else's.

With gentle pressure on her shoulders, he slowly turned her to face him. Her feet obeyed, but she crossed her arms in front of her, fists pressed against her shoulders as she hid behind a thin shield of silk.

He tilted his head, his features pleading. "Tia, please don't hide from me."

"I can't." She shook her head. "Please don't ask this of me. I just…can't."

"I know you've been hurt, but no matter what he did to you, I'll never look at you differently. I already know what's in here." He pressed a hand against the silk, over her heart. "Here there's love and compassion and selflessness. Those are the things that matter, not what's on the surface." He covered her hands with his, then curled his fingers into her palms.

She searched his eyes. The pleading was still there, underscored by sympathy and understanding. He was a good friend. If there weren't so many obstacles in their way, he could become much more. Honesty and trust were crucial to every real friendship. Could she trust him with her secret?

She worked her hands free of his, then lowered them one painful inch, then another. She couldn't look at him, couldn't bear to witness the moment he first observed what Victor had done to her, how he'd marked her. She closed her eyes and let her hands fall to her sides.

In front of her, Jason sucked air through clenched teeth, and her tension ratcheted up even further. *This was a mistake.* She willed her eyes to open, forced her gaze to climb, up his chest, to the hollow at the bottom of his throat, past his chin to settle on lips drawn into a straight line. When she met his eyes, they were hard, even tortured.

Her stomach filled with lead, and bile worked its way up her throat. She'd been right. "You're repulsed. I knew you would be."

"Not repulsed, angry. Angry that any man would hurt you. Angry about the fear and pain and degradation you faced. Angry that you're still suffering years later." He cupped her cheek with one hand. "But repulsed? Never."

His hand moved downward, brushing the side of her neck and coming to rest on her shoulder. His thumb traced the ridge of her collar bone, moving back and forth over the scars there, his touch featherlight.

He leaned forward to press his cheek softly against hers. "Nothing about you could ever repulse me."

His warm breath brushed her ear, and she suppressed an involuntary shiver.

"You're beautiful, and your scars don't change that." He pressed a kiss to the side of her neck, then moved around to her throat, still trailing kisses. She tipped her head back and released a sigh.

When he continued downward, toward her collarbone, she tensed. Beginning there, her skin became an ugly roadmap of abuse. But the scars didn't deter him. He kissed one side of the bony ridge, then dropped below.

That was where she bore the remnants of her last night of terror, after the call to her sister but before the visit from the cops. Those cuts had been deeper than Victor had intended. He'd had to make an emergency trip to the drug store for wound closure strips. He'd even released one of her arms so she could apply pressure until he returned.

No. She shut out the memory. She wasn't going back to that dark place.

Jason straightened to look at her. His eyes held determination, intensity. "When I look at you, I don't see a victim. I see a survivor. And what I see is beautiful." He leaned closer, his eyes drifting closed.

When his lips met hers, the kiss was as gentle as the others had been—soft, respectful, without demand. She leaned into him, her eyes misting. For the first time in years, she felt cherished. And beautiful.

The last of her defenses fell, leaving her heart exposed. The fear that should have swamped her wasn't there, and she gave herself fully to the sensations swirling through her—joy, contentment and love. The latter was probably a mistake, but now wasn't the time for those doubts. Not while Jason was holding her and giving her everything her heart needed.

When he finally broke the kiss, her eyes fluttered open. "Thank you." The words escaped on a soft exhale. It was an odd response to a first kiss. But that wasn't what she was thanking him for.

He seemed to understand. He lifted his hand to her cheek, lightly brushing her lower lip with his thumb. "For too many years, Victor has stolen your happiness, your self-esteem and your peace of mind. Don't let him steal your future, too."

She nodded. "I'll try." She handed him the scarf. "I can do this without a mirror, but I have no idea what it'll look like."

For the next minute, Jason's lips were pursed in

concentration as he wrapped, poofed, tucked and rearranged. Finally, he stood back.

"You might want to double check this before you go anywhere public. I'm no fashion expert." He grinned. "Do you have any idea how long it took me to learn to tie a necktie? I'd always mess up the knot or have one end way longer than the other or mess it up in some other way. Then my dad would reiterate to me what an idiot I was."

"It's hard to do anything well when you're being put down."

"He never figured that out. Unfortunately, my coordination didn't develop until around the same time I had my growth spurt."

Jason walked with her toward the house. "I'm guessing it's getting near time for you to start dinner."

When they stepped onto the porch, he started to reach for the doorknob, then dropped his hand. "Didn't you originally come out to get the mail?"

She laughed. "I did, and it's still in the box."

"Wait here."

He bounded off the porch, and returned a half minute later holding a small wad of envelopes. "Is it all right if I check on you this evening?"

"Sure." Sometimes he checked on her via text, other times in person. Either would be fine.

"By the way, I'm staying till Thursday afternoon."

"Then you'll be on the road for Christmas."

"I'm flying."

She tilted her head and lifted her eyebrows. "And your truck is going to drive home by itself?"

"Nope, it's going to wait patiently for me at the airport."

What? He was coming back? Her heart did a somersault.

"I'm on vacation until January 4th, and I'm taking advantage of every second of it." His smile faded, and his expression grew serious. "I want to spend as many of those seconds as I can with you."

Warmth filled her chest, but there was a cold, hollow spot in the center. By returning to Florida, he was only delaying the inevitable. Whether now or a week from now, goodbye was still goodbye.

A sense of loneliness swept through her, so powerful it stole her breath. *Why, God?* Why would He send a man like Jason into her life, knowing he would have to leave?

Jason exited the Polk County Landfill, the bed of his truck empty except for the big green trash can lying on its side. He'd filled it twice for the trash collection people to take, which had saved him a little on dump fees. Then he'd filled it a third time and loaded it, along with numerous black lawn bags, into the back of his Ram.

Now that the trash was gone, he was finished at the house. The stuff he was donating to the shelter occupied almost half of the living room. What he planned to take back to Connecticut was stacked on the other side of the room—eight boxes the size of copy paper cases. They would have easily fit into the Ram's cab if he hadn't packed the back full of tools. Instead, they'd ride in the bed under a tarp, along with the rug.

He pulled the trash can from the bed of his truck

and wheeled it around the back corner of the house. The lawn still looked good, but he'd hit it with the mower and weed eater again next week. He'd also see if he could make himself useful at Tia's. In a women's shelter, there had to be plenty of things that needed to be done. He'd never been good with being idle.

Once inside the house, he headed up the stairs. He'd forgotten to ask Tia to help him move the library table when she'd been there. Now he'd have to try to manage it without damage to the table or the rug. After staring at the table for several moments, he squatted and rolled the rug until the wooden legs stopped him. Then he stood and tipped the table enough to roll the rug farther with one foot.

He dropped to one knee. Something didn't look right. There was a thin crack in the floor, as if the hardwood planks hadn't been locked together properly. He followed the line to one end, where it turned ninety degrees and disappeared beneath the rug. The other end did the same thing.

His pulse picked up speed. Had his grandparents built a secret compartment into the floor? Heart pounding, he rose to lift the front edge of the library table, then rolled the rug the rest of the way free with one heel.

He'd been right. There was definitely a panel inserted into the floor, measuring about two feet by one foot. It was constructed of the same planks that made up the floor, but a distinct line ran all the way around its perimeter.

Anticipation bubbled up inside, spilling out in a combination of relief and joy. His grandmother had made sure, in the event he could be found, that he'd inherit more than some personal effects. She hadn't cared anything about him taking the rug. She'd just wanted to make sure he found what was underneath. It had to hold some value; she'd gone to too much trouble to hide it and lead him to it.

And she'd done it in a way that guaranteed that, in his absence, Tia would be the one to discover the secret compartment when she began renovating the place for her shelter. Even if his father would have returned to fight for part of the inheritance, he wouldn't have cared enough about his parents' possessions or his mother's wishes to have bothered with an old rug.

Jason dropped to his hands and knees and ran one hand along the panel's surface. It lay completely flat, with a recessed space at each end, barely large enough to insert two fingers. He lifted out the panel and set it aside.

Two small boxes lay in the space between floor joists, dark plastic with clear lids. Both held some type of thin, flat objects slid into grooves in the side of the box so they stood on edge. He placed one of the boxes on the floor in front of him, removed the lid and pulled out the first item. It was a plastic case, tamper-evident according to the print near the bottom. It held a thin gold bar, The Perth Mint logo molded into the upper portion, "99.99% pure gold, 100 gram" beneath.

He removed two more items from the box, then checked the others. They were all identical, a total of ten. The other box held the same.

What did 100 grams translate to in ounces? He keyed the question into the search bar on his phone.

A little over three and a half ounces. Times twenty. He released a low whistle. He didn't have to know what gold was going for these days to realize that he was looking at a small fortune.

Had his grandparents always kept this kind of wealth hidden in the bedroom floor? Or had it been tucked away in a safe deposit box until October 15, when BethAnn's grandmother had written the note about the rug?

The latter was possible. They'd left Winter Gardens together and been gone for three hours. Could they have managed the table and the panel? Between the two of them, probably. BethAnn had said both women were in good shape for their ages. That had to be it. If the gold had been there all along, his grandmother would have had someone write the note in July, the same time she executed the will.

He picked up one of the bars, ready to tuck it back into the box. Sunlight streamed in through the window, glinting off the precious metal protected behind the clear plastic. A sudden sense of vulnerability swept over him. A lot of people would kill for a find like this.

He tamped down the uneasiness. No one knew what he had. The house was locked, and since he was on the second floor, no one was likely to observe him through the window.

After putting the lids back on both boxes, he rose and placed them on the table. His heart pounded, and a quivery weakness had settled in his limbs. Whether or not the treasure came from a safe deposit box, that was exactly where he was going to take it. Preferably not without police escort. Tia wasn't the only one being watched. It hadn't been too many days since someone had followed him.

He picked up his phone again and placed a call. "Is one of those cops that watches your place handy?"

"I'm not sure." Tia's voice held a note of alarm. "Why?"

"Nothing bad. I need some police escort."

"For what?"

"You know the coffee cans I keep joking about?"

"You found some?" The alarm had turned to anticipation.

"Something like that."

"Is it a lot? I mean…" Her voice trailed off.

Yeah, it sounded like a prying question. But he knew her reason for asking it.

"Enough to take care of my mom's medical expenses and then some."

"That's awesome!" Another pause. "So where are you going with it?"

"To the bank. I'm putting it in a safe deposit box, because it's not exactly cash."

"Now you've got me curious."

"100-gram gold bars, twenty of them."

"How are you going to change them into something you can pay the bills with?"

"I've got to research that. That'll be my project when I get back. I'll have a week to figure it out."

"I'll get a hold of Alan, see if he's available or if he can round someone up." I'll let you know.

After ending the call with Tia, he phoned his mother. Maybe he should have called her first. But he was thinking about safety. He'd been watched and was currently sitting on tens of thousands of dollars.

He needed a way to transport it safely, and Tia was friends with Officer White.

At least that was what he would keep telling himself.

He shook his head. What did it mean when he got good news, and Tia was the first person he wanted to share it with?

It meant that things were moving far too quickly. He'd allowed her to become a much too important part of his life.

He was falling fast and had no parachute to slow his descent.

SIXTEEN

THE AROMA OF chicken divan trailed Tia from the kitchen. According to the timer, it would be ready to come out of the oven in twenty minutes, the same time the rice would be ready. Casseroles were a staple at the shelter.

Nika and Katie followed her into the living room and sat on the couch with her. Christmas music streamed from the TV, a soothing backdrop, and in the corner, silver garland draped the tree. Ornaments stood out against an array of tiny multi-colored lights. The figures on the lower half of the tree had obviously been hung by little hands. Some spots were bare, and in other places, two hung from the same branch. But none of the adults had attempted to correct what the children had done.

Squeals sounded from the hallway, and a second later, two boys streaked into the room.

"No running in the house."

Both boys skidded to a stop at their mother's scolding, and Aiden knelt in front of the tree to pick up a wrapped package. After Tia had added the gifts, it hadn't taken the boys long to discover that their names appeared on some of them.

Aiden gave what he held a squeeze then a shake. It didn't depress or rattle. The dump truck inside was well-packaged, any loose parts secured with plastic ties.

"Uh-uh." Katie's tone was scolding. "No peeking till tomorrow."

Ethan disappeared down the hall, but instead of following, his brother stared longingly at the present he'd returned to its spot under the tree.

There were other gifts, too, one for each of the two women who'd be spending their holiday at the shelter. The others had gotten theirs early. Maggie's sister had picked her up that morning to spend Christmas with her family, and Jasmine had taken a bus south to be with friends. Angela's cousin in Ohio had booked an airline ticket and secured a ride to the airport. Angela had left yesterday afternoon, all excited about seeing snow for the first time.

Besides the gifts Tia had placed under the tree, another gift had shown up, one with her own name on it. Likely Jason had slipped it to one of the women, but none of them would own up to it.

He was currently in the air, somewhere between Florida and Connecticut. He'd stopped by the shelter early that afternoon to wish her Merry Christmas and tell her goodbye. She was still fighting the sense of loneliness that had swept through her as she'd watched him drive away. This time, he'd only be gone for two days. What was she going to feel like when he left for good?

Aiden rose and followed his brother to their room. Outside, the wail of a siren drew closer, temporarily competing with the strains of "Joy to the World" before falling silent. A second approached right on the tail of the first.

Tia frowned. "I hope no one's hurt. There's never a good time for an emergency, but Christmas Eve is one of the worst."

"I agree." Nika sighed. "A month ago, I'd have never guessed this is how I'd be spending Christmas."

"For sure." Katie looked at Tia. "But I'm glad we're here."

Nika nodded. "Me too."

Tia gave them all a wry smile. "A lot can change in a month." A month ago, she'd thought Victor would be in prison for another three months. A month ago, she'd had no idea Peace House would soon be the recipient of a huge home and a good-size bank account.

A month ago, she'd never laid eyes on Jason.

Having him in her life these past three weeks had been a comfort. Most of the time, he hadn't been close enough to make a difference in an emergency. That was what the cops were for.

But she needed more than physical protection. Ever since she'd learned Victor was being released from prison, she'd fought against the fear. The sense of being watched and the message on her window had unsettled her even further. The final threat had almost sent her over the edge.

Regardless of what she was going through, she had to be strong for the women in her care. They were going through their own traumas, fresh ones, and needed a refuge. Over the past three weeks, Jason had increasingly become that for her. The bond she'd felt almost from the start had strengthened, and she'd confided in him, had given him a window into her past. She'd even allowed him to see her scars.

It was one of the hardest things she'd ever done. She'd expected him to turn away, repulsed. Instead, he'd done just the opposite, assuring her with each kiss that she was worthy, beautiful, cherished. Something had happened in those moments. All her defenses had fallen, and she'd tumbled headlong into love.

"What all's on the menu for tomorrow?" Nika's question cut into her thoughts.

Heat rushed up Tia's neck and into her cheeks, as if Nika could see where her thoughts had gone.

She drew in a stabilizing breath. "Turkey and all the trimmings." Of course, they knew about the turkey. It had been thawing in the fridge for the past two days. "We're doing broccoli casserole and cranberry salad. My sister and her husband are bringing sweet potato souffle and Mom's baking two pies." The prospect of seeing her family tomorrow helped to numb some of the disappointment over Jason's leaving. "I'll be up at six to finish thawing the bird, then stuff it and put it in the oven."

Nika twisted to face her. "Anything you want to get a jump on tonight?"

"I was thinking about making the cranberry salad and getting the stuffing ready." That way, once the bird was thawed, she could spoon the dressing into the cavity and have it ready to put in the oven.

Her jaw sagged. She'd bought celery and onions and walnuts, but the most important ingredient hadn't made it onto her grocery list. "I forgot the stuffing mix for the dressing."

Katie gave her a worried frown. "I don't think you

should go out alone."

"I agree." But she wasn't about to endanger anyone else. It wasn't dark yet, but it would be by the time she came out of the store.

"I'll see if Alan's available."

Several minutes passed with no answer to her text. "I'm guessing that one of those sirens might have been his. Meanwhile, I've got a fifteen-pound turkey thawing in the fridge and nothing to stuff it with."

"Maybe someone can pick up the dressing mix for you." The suggestion came from Nika.

"How about BethAnn?" Katie said. "I'm sure she wouldn't mind."

"I hate to ask anyone to battle the crowds the day before Christmas." But Katie was right—BethAnn wouldn't mind.

Before she could locate her friend in her contacts, her phone rang in her hand.

"It's my landlord."

She swiped the screen and put the phone to her ear. After they'd exchanged greetings, Mrs. Garrett asked if Tia was home.

"All evening." Regardless of her need for dressing, she wasn't leaving the house.

"Good. I'm on my way over with some home-baked goodies for you and your guests."

"That's sweet of you." She'd done the same thing for the past three years.

"I'm leaving Winter Haven now. See you in a bit."

Tia thanked her and started to wish her farewell. "Wait. Since you're coming here anyway, I wonder if I could impose on you for a small favor. I've got everything I need for Christmas dinner except stuffing for the turkey."

"I don't have any, but there's a Publix on the way."

After disconnecting the call, she returned to the kitchen to stack plates and lay out silverware and serving spoons on the counter. Katie called her boys, and soon the four long beeps of the timer announced that the food was done. Tia's ringtone sounded from the living room at the same time, competing for her attention.

She looked at the two women and two boys who'd gathered. "Y'all go ahead. I shouldn't be too long."

After a sprint into the living room, she grabbed her phone from the end table and glanced at the screen. *Jason?*

Her "hello" held confusion. "You're supposed to be somewhere over the Carolinas by now."

"My flight got delayed, so I'm stuck at the Orlando Airport. What are you up to?"

"We were just getting ready to eat."

"I don't want to bother you then."

She sat on the couch. Talking to Jason was never a bother. "It's okay. I'm expecting a visitor in the next ten minutes or so."

"In that case, do you mind keeping me company until your visitor arrives? I'm bored."

She grinned. "Poor baby. Didn't you bring anything to read?"

"I did, and that's what I've been doing. I guess I just wanted to hear your voice."

An appropriate comeback eluded her.

"So who's coming to visit?"

"My landlady."

"Collecting rent on Christmas Eve?"

"Just the opposite. She's bringing goodies. She's made it a Christmas tradition, home-baked treats for the residents and me."

"I left a few hours too soon."

"I'll try to save you a cookie." The sounds of soft conversation and the ting of serving spoons against plates drifted to her from the kitchen. "I might have to keep it under lock and key."

"If you get down to the last cookie and anyone wants it that badly, let them have it. I'm willing to make the sacrifice." His tone grew serious. "I wish I could have brought my mom down here for Christmas instead of having to fly back home. I'd love for her to meet you. You two have a lot in common."

Tia swallowed hard. He wanted her to meet his mother. In her experience, when a man brought a woman home to meet his parents, that was a milestone in the relationship.

No, she was making something out of nothing. He'd said it himself—they had a lot in common. Tia ran a shelter for abused women, and had been abused herself, just like his mother. It was no different from someone wanting to introduce friends who shared like interests. Granted, he'd kissed her under the oak tree, but she couldn't even make a big deal out of that. He'd been trying to encourage her, assure her she wasn't hideous, no matter what Victor had done to her.

Everything he'd done had worked. It had also turned her world upside down. Longing she'd never planned to feel again had made itself her constant companion. Jason was even weaving his way into her dreams. So much better than the nightmares they'd replaced.

But she had to admit that the experience under the oak tree had moved her more than it had him. He hadn't tried to kiss her since that day, not even when he'd left for the airport. Of course, Nika and Katie had been sitting on the porch in the wicker rockers at the time. But there'd been other opportunities, ones he'd ignored.

She guided her thoughts off the track they'd taken. "You remember that long grocery list you helped me with?" He hadn't made the list with her, but he'd scoured the shelves, helping her find the items on it. "Nika and Katie and I were talking about the Christmas dinner menu and what we might want to get a jump on tonight. Guess what wasn't on the list."

"What?"

"Stuffing."

"You're not considering going out alone, are you?"

"Nope. I was going to call BethAnn to pick it up, then learned Mrs. Garrett is on her way over with the goodies. So she's stopping at Publix for me."

"Excellent. You can't be too careful."

A few minutes later, the ring of the doorbell echoed through the house. "There's Mrs. Garrett now."

"I heard. Just make sure it's her before you unlock the door."

"*Cautious* is my middle name." Even more so in the past couple of weeks.

She ended the call, then crossed the room and flipped on the porch light. Standing on her tiptoes, she peered into darkness barely touched by the glow of the Christmas lights hanging from the eaves. The porch fixture's bulb was out. It had been ages since she'd had to replace it. Uneasiness sifted through her.

"Mrs. Garrett?"

A muffled "yes" came through the door. "Cookie delivery."

She reached for the lock, then hesitated. One more check. She moved to the window and drew the curtain aside. A car sat in her driveway, at the edge of the circular glow emanating from the pole light catty-corner from her yard.

Tia dropped the curtains with a sigh of relief. Definitely Mrs. Garrett's silver Malibu. It was one-of-a-kind, almost as old as Tia was. She threw the deadbolt, then opened the door, casting an angled glance in that direction. Something moved in her peripheral vision.

With lightning speed, someone jerked her through the opening and spun her around, simultaneously clamping a hand over her mouth and trapping her against a hard body. Above her silk scarf, the cold blade of a knife rested against her throat.

Her heart pounded against her ribs, sending the blood roaring through her ears. There was no one to help her. Her muffled cry wouldn't have carried to those eating in the dining room a few yards away, and Mrs. Garrett was nowhere in sight.

Behind her, her assailant lowered his head and put his mouth next to her ear. His warm breath rustled her hair, and the scent of spearmint wrapped around her.

"You make a sound or fight me in any way, I'll slit you from ear to ear right here on your porch."

Her knees gave way, and he tightened his hold. The pressure of the blade against her throat increased, penetrating the soft skin there. The pain barely registered.

Her brain spun as if stuck in a centrifuge, thoughts slung to the outer edges of her mind. Victor. He'd been waiting, watching for the perfect opportunity to strike. Mrs. Garrett's visit had given him that. So had the fact that the police were likely tied up somewhere else.

He took a step toward the house, dragging her with him. "Close the door."

She reached for the knob. The soothing notes of "O Holy Night" flowed through the opening. The music helped to ground her, and she closed her eyes, hand hovering over the doorknob. Her thoughts gradually slowed. *God, please protect me. Give me wisdom.*

A drop of blood trickled down her neck and under her scarf. She opened her eyes. Light from the lamp inside spilled out of the room and onto the porch. If only one of her ladies would peer through the kitchen doorway, see she was in trouble and call the police.

Victor pressed his face against her hair. "I said close it."

She pulled the door shut, and the porch fell into darkness. Now she knew. The light hadn't burned out. Victor had unscrewed the bulb.

The final faint strains of "O Holy Night" died, and another carol began, unidentifiable now that she'd closed the door. As Victor dragged her down the steps, even those soft notes disappeared.

Was she going to survive long enough to see Christmas? Would she live to see Jason again? He would blame himself, convinced that if he'd been there, he could have prevented Victor from taking her. One more mistake to pile onto the guilt he'd already heaped on himself.

Victor led her down the concrete path toward the driveway, and she scanned the area. The car was definitely Mrs. Garrett's Malibu, but where was Mrs. Garrett? The woman had shown her nothing but kindness. If Tia's affiliation with her got her seriously injured, Tia would never forgive herself.

Oh, God, please let her be all right.

She squinted at the driveway. Something lay on the concrete next to the Malibu, almost invisible in the shadow cast by the car. As she drew closer, her stomach sank to her knees, leaving a trail of dread.

It was a large plate, cookies shifted to one side. The cellophane was no longer sealed on that edge. More than half of the contents had escaped and were strewn about the concrete and into the grass. They were little more than crumbs, likely trodden under Victor's feet, maybe even Mrs. Garrett's own in what was likely a futile attempt to get away.

A thud came from nearby, and Tia jerked one ear toward the sound. Mrs. Garrett? She peered into the Malibu as they approached. Light spilled in through the back window, illuminating the interior. No one was inside.

Victor led her past the front of the car, then between her Fiat and Mrs. Garrett's vehicle. When he reached the Malibu's front passenger door, he stopped.

"Open it."

Tia swung the door back on its hinges, and another thud sounded. A muffled shout accompanied it. Both came from the direction of the sedan's trunk.

Victor released her, and a fraction of a second later, rough hands against her back sent her tumbling into the car's interior. She landed with her arms extended, palms down in the driver's seat, the edge of the console jammed into her ribs.

Before she could draw in a full breath to scream, Victor pressed the point of the blade into her side. "If you even think about screaming, I'll carve you up right here. So let's just be a good girl and not make a mess of your friend's car."

Renewed thuds came from behind her. Victor had stuffed Mrs. Garrett into the trunk. Not only was she still alive, if her energetic efforts were any indication, she wasn't severely injured.

Tia sat up. Victor was apparently going to take her somewhere using Mrs. Garrett's car. Since he'd be occupied with driving, she might have a chance at escape. But could she think only of her own safety and let him drive away with Mrs. Garrett in the trunk?

She had no choice. Escaping and running for help would offer both of them the greatest chance of making it through the night alive.

Victor held up a ring of keys, recognizable by her landlady's palm tree keychain. "Slide across. You're going to drive."

Her heart fell. She should have known Victor wouldn't make it that easy. She wriggled her way across the console and into the driver's side bucket seat.

Victor settled in next to her. "Drive toward Main, then turn right."

She did as instructed, looking around for anyone

she might be able to signal for help. There was no one. The stores along Main were closed, and the Christmas Eve candlelight services that were being held at both churches wouldn't start for another forty-five minutes.

There weren't any police out and about, either, at least not in Harmony Grove. She couldn't even try to make a covert 911 call. She'd left her phone in the house.

She glanced in her rearview mirror in time to see a dark SUV turn from Tranquility Way onto Main. As it followed her through the next turn, she tightened her grip on the wheel. Was someone tailing her? By the time they reached Highway 17, she had no doubt.

She continued south, Bartow some distance in front of her. The light ahead turned red.

"Get in the left lane."

She turned on her signal and eased to a stop. The SUV slowed, maintaining a distance that wouldn't raise red flags with the typical person. Tia wasn't the typical person, hadn't been for more than five years. Looking over her shoulder was second nature. So was not trusting anyone. How could she have fallen into Victor's trap?

She'd made some stupid mistakes tonight. The first had been assuming the porch light had burned out rather than been tampered with. The second had been calling out her landlady's name instead of asking who was there.

She'd made it easy for Victor to respond in the affirmative rather than having to produce a name. Then he'd added "cookie delivery" to make it even more convincing. With the music streaming through the surround sound system and the door muffling his response, she'd let his falsetto fool her. A series of stupid mistakes, and she was likely to pay with her life.

The light changed and she accelerated into her turn. Less than a half minute later, the SUV followed. Soon the small housing developments that lay on both sides of the street gave way to open fields and woods.

"Slow down." Victor lowered the knife to lean forward and peer into the darkness. "Right here. Pull off the road."

She did as instructed. Ahead of her, fresh tire tracks marked a path veering into the woods.

Victor lifted a hand, pointing. "Follow that trail."

She turned the wheel and pressed the gas. Before disappearing into the tree line, she cast a glance back in the direction from which they'd come. The SUV's headlights clicked off. The driver was going to follow.

Tia maintained her speed at a crawl, but roots jostled them back and forth, once so violently, she almost cracked her head on the window. Overhead, the trees blocked out much of the moonlight, leaving the swath of illumination created by the Malibu's headlights. The desolate surroundings intensified her sense of aloneness.

Eventually, she came nose-to-nose with a van, a silver reflective material coating the windshield. Either there was another way into the woods, or someone had backed the van all the way in. Should she distract Victor so he didn't see whoever had followed them until it was too late to react? Which threat would she rather face, known or unknown?

"We're here." There was something ominous about Victor's words. "You can kill the engine. Once I get you situated, I'll dump the car."

Situated? Her heart stuttered. He was going to get her situated, then leave. That could mean only one thing. He was going to restrain her.

The panic she'd fought since the moment he grabbed her at her front door exploded past its bonds and raged unchecked through her body. Her pulse pounded in her head, sending blood roaring through her ears. A vice clamped down on her chest and her breaths came in fast, shallow gasps.

"Turn off the car."

The command held a lethal note of warning, but she couldn't have obeyed had she wanted to. She held the wheel in a death grip, every muscle in her body frozen. Why couldn't he just kill her right here? Stab her and leave her to bleed to death in Mrs. Garrett's front seat. Throw her out and run over her with the car. Strangle her.

Anything but restrain her.

He twisted toward her, the action sudden, and she swiveled her head in his direction. The knife swung around and stopped to rest against the base of her throat, its point pressed into the indentation between the two halves of her collar bone. There was movement outside the front passenger window. A fraction of a second later, the world exploded.

The window was a road map of cracks, extending outward from a central hole. Someone stood just beyond, a pistol pointed into the car. Victor was slumped over the console. His head rested against her arm, and a gurgling sound came from his throat.

Something dripped onto her thigh and soaked into her jeans.

The passenger door swung open, and a man leaned into the opening, face illuminated in the glow of the vehicle's dome light. She didn't have to ask who he was. She was looking at a sixty-year-old version of Jason.

"Get out of the car, and I'll take you somewhere safe."

She released the wheel one finger at a time and dropped her hands to her lap. Victor's head flopped farther to the side. The seatbelt still held him partially upright. He was dead, or soon would be. He was no longer a threat.

She reached for the door, but before she could grasp the handle, it seemed to open on its own. Jason's father stood there, hand outstretched, palm up. He'd managed to circle the car without her realizing he'd moved.

"It's okay." His voice was soothing, so unlike Victor's. "I'm not going to hurt you."

How could she believe him? He'd just killed Victor. Maybe he'd done it to protect her. Or maybe it was all about the inheritance. She lowered her gaze. Dark splotches in varying sizes marked her sweater the entire length of her right arm. Her jeans had the same splotches.

She pressed her hands to the sides of her head. Her right came away wet and sticky. The panic started to build again, and a need to flee roared through her, but George Sloan was standing between her and safety. Who knew what he had planned? The only thing certain was that she had Victor's blood all over her, and she was one brittle thread away from losing her sanity.

She dragged in several jagged breaths, struggling to tamp down the panic. She had to keep her wits. She'd avoided the fate Victor had planned for her. Now she had to escape George Sloan, not just for her own sake, but for the sake of her landlady, still locked in the trunk. Her car was old, manufactured long before interior trunk releases were mandatory. Days or weeks could pass before someone found her.

She looked up at Sloan, who still stood with his arm outstretched. "Let me help you out of the car. I'll take you home."

Home? Had he really been following her just to rescue her from Victor? No, she didn't believe that for a moment. But staying in the car wasn't an option. With his SUV behind her, and the van in front of her, she had nowhere to go.

After a final glance at her ex-husband's lifeless body, she put her hand in Sloan's and allowed him to help her from the car. Would her odds be better if she broke free and tried to run for help now, or would escape be more likely if she waited until they got to a more populated area? *God, please give me wisdom.*

Sloan led her away from the Malibu and to the passenger side of the SUV. When he opened the front door, the interior remained dark, the dome light still off from his stealthy approach. Moonlight filtered through the trees, throwing scattered patches of soft, faint light into the interior. Something lay in the back seat.

She squinted, trying to identify the two items. One was round and dark in color. The other would blend with the pale leather if not for the patches of color on the clear packaging. A roll of duct tape and…she stared at the long, narrow package. Zip ties?

Terror ricocheted through her, scattering all thoughts except one: Escape. She jerked her hand from his and sprinted into the darkness. Heavy footsteps sounded behind her almost immediately and pounded closer. She'd never be able to outrun him, and help was too far away. She needed somewhere to hide.

She lunged to the side and skidded to a stop behind an oak tree. Sloan pounded past, then halted, looking around. He'd drawn his weapon. As he slowly pivoted in her direction, she sidled to the other side of the large trunk. A branch snapped under her foot, shattering the silence and sending her heart into her throat.

"Come on, Tia. I know you're close." His tone was deceptively soothing. "There's nothing to fear. Let me take you home."

Dried leaves crunched under his feet as he moved closer. A few more steps, and he'd be just on the other side of the tree. There was no chance he'd overlook her. The limb she'd stepped on had given away her exact location.

She squeezed her eyes shut against the image intruding into her thoughts—Victor slumped in the seat, blood pouring from a wound in his neck. If she ran, she'd end up just like him.

No, George Sloan wouldn't shoot her. Whatever he wanted with her, she wouldn't do him any good dead. She spun and charged away, sprinting toward the road. Maybe a vehicle would be passing by and she could flag it down. *God, please send someone.*

Her steps almost faltered. If Sloan had killed Victor to get to her, he wouldn't hesitate to shoot anyone who might try to help her escape.

Before she had an opportunity to ponder further, a hard body slammed into her from behind, sending her toppling forward and wrenching a scream from her throat. A tree loomed in front of her. She turned her head in time to save her face, but the side of her head slammed into the trunk, sending stars shooting across her vision. She rolled to the side, and Sloan landed on top of her.

A fist moved toward the uninjured side of her head with lightning speed, connecting a fraction of a second later.

More stars joined the ones that had started to fade. Then those dimmed, too, along with the moonlight filtering through the canopy over her.

Consciousness lingered just enough for vague awareness—arms sliding beneath her back and legs, jostling as he lifted and carried her away, pain through her body when he dropped her on the ground.

A car door slammed closed and another one opened. Thin plastic circled her wrists and ankles and tightened. A rip sounded beside her head. A second later, duct tape was pressed to her face, trapping in her screams, had she been strong enough to utter them.

Somewhere deep inside, terror collided with hopelessness, both muted like an old photograph in faded shades of gray.

SEVENTEEN

TIA'S BODY SHIFTED to the side as the SUV rounded a corner. The zip ties cut into her wrists and ankles, and her shoulders hurt from the awkward position of her arms behind her back.

They'd been on the road for fifteen or twenty minutes. Maybe longer. How much time had actually passed was sketchy, because she'd faded in and out. She probably had a concussion. That was the least of her worries.

The SUV slowed, made a sharp turn and stopped, gravel crunching beneath the tires. Sloan shoved the vehicle into park and swung open the door but left the engine running. Tia lay on her side listening to his retreating footsteps. The clang of a chain followed, then the grating sound of a metal gate rolling back on its track.

Where were they? Sloan hadn't brought her home as he'd promised. Of course, she hadn't expected him to, with or without her attempt to flee.

He pulled the vehicle forward a few yards and stopped again. The same metallic sounds reached her. He'd apparently closed and re-chained the gate. When the SUV resumed moving, he left the gravel and bounced along in what felt like a grassy field. The next time he stopped, he killed the engine and exited the vehicle.

A minute passed, then two. Being bound and gagged, she couldn't escape. She couldn't even scream. Finally, the SUV's back door lifted and Sloan reached inside to pull her out by her ankles. The ties chafed even more. He placed her on her feet long enough to slam the back door, then hoisted her over one shoulder. The tape swallowed her startled shriek.

She raised her head to look around. A three-quarter moon illuminated the landscape. Everything bore the signs of long-term neglect. Patchy grass hid under tall weeds, and two discarded chairs and a rusted-out dishwasher joined the other trash strewn about. Some distance away, a chain link fence lined both sides of the yard, woods beyond.

A dilapidated house stood in front of them, windows all boarded. Faint light flickered through the open door. As Sloan ascended the three steps leading inside, Tia cast a final glance at the sky. Was Jason up there somewhere, on his way to Connecticut, or was he still stuck at the airport? Was he thinking about her?

Sloan kicked the door shut with his heel then plopped her into a chair, her arms trapped between its back and her body. They'd entered the kitchen from the back. The light she'd noticed came from one of those old-fashioned hurricane lamps, a flame inside its tall, narrow globe. It was sitting on a rickety table on the other side of the door.

The inside of the house was worse than the exterior. Upper cabinets hung lopsided over countertops warped with moisture. At the wide doorway into the next room, scuffed and ripped vinyl gave way to carpet that bore the stains of months, maybe years of abuse. A mattress lay beyond the doorway, and everywhere the glow of the light reached, trash littered the floor.

Sloan retrieved his weapon from where he'd tucked the barrel into the waistband of his jeans, then laid it on the counter. When he reached into his pants pocket and withdrew an object, her eyes widened. *No.*

At the press of a button, a blade sprang from its casing. Sloan moved toward her, gripping the knife in his right hand.

No, no, no. She shook her head back and forth, ignoring the pain that seared her skull with each movement. *Not again.*

She screamed against the tape. Violent shudders started in her shoulders and spread throughout her body. Tears squeezed past her clenched eyelids to run down both cheeks.

"It's okay. I'm not going to hurt you."

Her eyes snapped open. He was right beside her now. His gaze didn't hold the cruelty that Victor's always had when preparing to mete out his punishment.

"Lean forward." He rested his left hand at the base of her skull. "And hold still so I don't cut you."

The terror dissipated. He was going to slice through the plastic ties and release her. His hand moved lower, and she complied with the light pressure against her upper back. The blade slid between the zip tie and her wrists, cold and smooth against her skin. Her heart stopped, then resumed an erratic rhythm. *Stay calm.* He was cutting the tie, not her.

He jerked his hand upward, and the band tightened painfully. A fraction of a second later, it fell away. With her hands now free, she reached across her chest to massage each of her shoulders, then gently rubbed her wrists. Red streaks marked each one where the ties had been.

She watched Sloan lay the knife on the counter next to the gun, then pull a new zip tie from his pocket. Wait, what was he doing? He'd just released her hands. Why would he restrain her again?

He stopped in front of her. "You understand why I can't just turn you loose. But you'll be more comfortable this way."

He guided her forearm until it rested against the wooden arm of the captain's chair. Renewed panic circled through her. *No, not like this.* Wrists shackled to the arms of the chair. Ankles restrained against the chair legs. Teeth clenched against the pain as Victor wielded his blade.

She jerked her arm away, clasping her hands together and holding them against her chest. Her muffled protests went no further than the tape. The terror of being zip tied to the chair had replaced the fear of being cut.

"Settle down."

There was no gentleness in the command. She jerked her gaze to his face, but it wasn't George Sloan she saw there. It was Victor. She clasped her hands more tightly and shook her head, sending silent pleas with her eyes.

He ignored every one. His jaw tightened and his nostrils flared. "Don't make me hit you again."

He pried her hands apart and forced her right

palm against the end of one wooden arm. Her left hand curled into a fist. *No.* Alarms blared through her mind, and her heart slammed against her ribcage. She swung for his jaw, but he avoided the blow with a sudden jerk of his head.

His face reddened and his lips curled back in an angry sneer. Veins bulged in his neck. The reality of what she'd done hit her immediately. It had the same effect as a dowsing with ice water. She'd made him furious enough to kill her. She couldn't even try to escape, because her ankles were still bound.

She gripped both chair arms so hard her knuckles turned white. *Do what you need to do.* Whatever his plans, her chances of survival were better if she remained conscious.

He slipped a tie around one wrist and tightened it. When he had both arms restrained, he released her ankles and secured them to the two front chair legs.

"I'm going to pull the tape from your mouth. We've got a phone call to make." He grasped one end of the tape, then hesitated. "I doubt anyone is close enough to hear you, but don't even think about screaming. You got it?"

She nodded. When he ripped the tape from her mouth, a small cry of pain escaped.

He ignored it. "We're going to give Jason a call."

"I don't know his number. It's saved in my phone, which is at home."

"You'd better figure out a way to get it."

She swallowed hard. She'd have him dial the shelter's land line and pray that Katie or Nika answered. Then she'd ask them to retrieve the number for her.

Her stomach tightened around a knot of dread.

Now she knew why George Sloan had taken her. He didn't want anything from her. She was simply a pawn in an decades-old grudge, a way to draw out Jason and his mother.

If it was only Jason that George wanted, the decision would be easy for him. Jason would sacrifice himself for her without a second thought. He was that kind of guy.

But having to choose between her and his mother would tear him apart.

Jason looked up from his book and heaved a sigh. If he'd known he was going to be stuck in Florida, he'd have stayed with Tia.

The passengers around him didn't look as though they were handling the wait much better than he was. A young mother faced him, juggling a fussy toddler on her knee. A businessman two seats down drummed his fingers on the armrest, nervous energy radiating from him.

The delay wasn't the airline's fault. Weather conditions in Providence were what was keeping them all grounded in Orlando. Regardless of the cause, it was beginning to look as though he'd be spending the night at the airport.

His phone's ringtone broke into his thoughts. Probably his mom checking on him. He'd already called her before he'd called Tia and let her know his flight had been delayed, and he'd told her he'd text her once he boarded.

She'd insisted on picking him up at the airport, which had both surprised and pleased him. Groton to Providence, Rhode Island was a straight shot up 95, just under an hour, but the fact his mother wanted to do it was a good sign, proof of how much better she was feeling.

He pulled the phone from his pocket. Instead of "Mom," a strange number displayed on the screen.

He frowned at the 863 area code. No one in Polk County had his number except Tia and the lawyer in Lakeland. And since he'd saved both in his contacts, the call wasn't coming from either of them. Uneasiness descended on him, a premonition. Whoever was calling, it wasn't with good news.

"Hello?" His greeting held a lot of hesitation.

"Jason!" A flow of unintelligible words followed then ended on a sob.

"Tia, what's going on?" Where was she and why wasn't she using her own phone?

"He's got me tied up, and he's got a gun, and I'm so scared." Hysteria tinged each word.

"Who?" Even as he asked the question, the answer loomed heavy in his thoughts. Victor. Where were the cops who were supposed to be watching her?

But the police didn't have the resources to provide around-the-clock protection. He'd known it all along. If she expected to have someone standing guard twenty-four/seven, she would have had to engage the services of a security firm, something neither of them could have afforded.

He grasped the handle of his carry-on, then headed toward the shuttle that would take him away from the terminal. "Tell me where you are."

"I don't know. Mrs. Garrett's in the trunk, and Victor's dead, and he's got me tied up and—"

"Sweetheart, slow down." She wasn't making any sense, but each word out of her mouth kicked his heartrate up further. Wait, Victor was dead? So who had her tied up? "Are you alone?"

"No, she's not."

It was a man's voice that came through the phone, cold and controlled. Jason jerked to a stop as the strength drained from his limbs. More than seventeen years had passed, but he'd never forget that voice—sometimes indifferent, sometimes brooding, sometimes cold and cruel, and sometimes loud and angry and threatening.

Now it was icy, with the underlying promise of cruelty. It was the calm before the storm, the thin thread of control that existed before the rage took over.

"What do you want?"

"You. Your mother."

Jason moved to the nearest gate and sank into one of the seats, no longer sure he could support his own weight. The white Highlander he'd seen following him, the other vehicles, even the times he'd sensed he was being watched but had seen no one—all along it had been his father.

"Mother's not here. I'll meet you."

"That's not good enough. I'll have both of you, or your girlfriend's dead."

The knot of dread grew into a boulder. "Mom can't get out. There's a snowstorm going on, and all flights are grounded. That's why I'm still at the airport."

"No problem. I've waited a long time for this reunion. What's another day?"

Jason turned his back to the other passengers sitting

nearby. "Mom's got cancer. She's not well enough to travel." Anything to keep her in Connecticut. He hoped God would forgive him for the little white lie. Just two weeks ago, what he'd said would have been true.

"If she's not dead, you'd better find a way to get her here. I'm keeping this phone on me. Call me when you've got her and not before. I'll give you further instructions then."

He swallowed hard. "Okay." He'd agree to whatever his father asked, then get White's and Willis's advice. Not only were they Harmony Grove Police officers, they seemed to be Tia's friends.

"Jason?"

Something in his father's tone made him feel thirteen again. "Yes."

"Don't even think about trying to involve the police. It won't turn out well for anyone, especially Tia." He paused. "Speaking of Tia, you'd better hurry. She's not doing well."

His stomach dropped like a bowling ball, and he curled his other hand into a fist. "What have you done to her?"

"Nothing yet. I told her I wouldn't hurt her, but she apparently has issues with being restrained."

Jason closed his eyes as a lead weight settled in his gut. His father's promises that he wouldn't hurt her meant nothing when she was reliving the other times she'd been restrained.

A tone sounded indicating the call had been dropped. His father had probably hung up. Hands shaking, Jason scrolled through his recent calls and redialed his mother. She answered after the first ring.

"You're finally getting ready to take off?" Energy filled her tone, mixed with a good dose of Christmas cheer. He was about to squash it.

"Dad has Tia."

"What?"

"He's kidnapped her." *And killed her ex-husband.* But he wouldn't share that detail yet.

"What does he want with her?"

"An exchange. You and me for her."

"It's snowing pretty hard here, but I'll be on the first available flight." She spoke in her usual decisive, no-nonsense tone. That decisiveness was something that had taken her time to develop after they'd escaped Florida.

"You can't come. He said if you ever left him, he'd kill you."

"And he'll kill Tia if I don't. This isn't her battle. It's mine."

He rose and resumed his trek toward the shuttle, wheeling his carry-on behind him. "Call me as soon as you get your flight booked."

"I will. I'll check both Tampa and Orlando."

"Good." With Harmony Grove about halfway between them, either of the two airports would be fine.

Ten minutes later, he exited through baggage claim and took a bus to parking. His father had put him in an impossible position—having to choose which of the two most important women in his life to sacrifice. His mother had made the decision for him. It would be her life for Tia's. She wouldn't have it any other way.

He exited the bus and climbed into the Ram.

Instead of cranking the engine, he touched the weather app on his phone and keyed in Providence, Rhode Island. White filled the screen. According to the hourly forecast, the storm had settled in for the night and most of the morning. His mother wouldn't be going anywhere. He might as well return to the inn. He'd need a good night's sleep for whatever he would have to face tomorrow.

His father had warned him about talking to the police, but he needed advice. He knew where to get it. After doing a search for Harmony Grove Police Department, he placed the call and left a message to have Officer Alan White phone him. He didn't have to wait long.

When White called, his tone was anxious. "Have you heard from Tia?"

"Yes." Apparently Alan had, too. At least he knew something. "What do you have?"

"One of the women at the shelter reported her missing at 6:05. She said they were eating while Tia was in the living room talking to you. They heard the doorbell ring, and when she didn't join them within a few minutes, one of them went to check on her, and she was gone."

"My father has her. She opened the door, expecting her landlady." Except she'd promised to make sure it was her before answering the door. "I just had a thought. You might want to check on her landlady. I don't know her name."

"Sonya Garrett. Her husband reported her missing. She was delivering Christmas goodies to friends and never came home. She didn't give him a list of where she was going, though. Thanks for the info. That gives us a starting point."

Jason related to Alan the conversation he'd had with his father and promised to check in with updates. As he ended the call, his chest clenched.

He'd done exactly what his father had told him not to—involved the police. He hoped he hadn't just sealed Tia's fate.

But he had no choice, because the more he thought about it, the more confident he became. Even if he did exactly as his father asked and turned over his mother, there was no way the man was going to let Tia walk away unharmed.

EIGHTEEN

JASON HEAVED A sigh and let his head fall back against the headrest. Once again, he was sitting in a parking lot near the airport, but this time it was Tampa. He did drive back to the inn last night. For all the sleep he'd gotten, he might as well have not bothered.

His ringtone sounded and he retrieved the phone from where he'd dropped it into the cupholder, waiting for the news that his mom's plane had landed. The caller wasn't his mother.

He swiped the screen. "Hey, Alan. What have you got?"

"A couple of updates. They've found Sonya Garrett's Malibu." His tone held an ominous note.

Jason stopped breathing as a sense of dread sifted through him. "Is she…?"

"She's fine. Some teenagers were exploring the woods this morning and came across her car. Victor was dead in the front passenger seat, shot through the neck. When law enforcement arrived, they heard some weak thumps coming from the trunk. Mrs. Garrett was inside, shaken up and bruised, but otherwise unharmed."

Alan paused, and there was tension in the silence, a weightiness, as if he wasn't sure whether to continue.

Jason clutched the phone more tightly. "There's more, isn't there?"

"A gold Aerostar van was parked in front of the Malibu. It was locked and had foil taped over all the glass, even the windshield. The police gained access and…" He paused. "Your father kidnapping Tia was a blessing."

Jason closed his eyes against the images flashing through his mind. He didn't want to know, but the question spilled out anyway. "What did they find inside the van?"

"The two back seats had been removed, and a chair had been bolted to the floor. Lying next to it were gags, duct tape and a variety of knives. He'd set up a mobile torture chamber."

Alan's voice was tight, as if he was struggling to rein in his emotions. Jason understood. Alan was young, fairly new to law enforcement. Working for a small town like Harmony Grove didn't expose him to the most gruesome cases. It was probably more than that, though. Tia wasn't a random victim. She was someone they knew well, someone they both cared about.

Alan continued, his tone professional. "They ran the tag on the van. It was titled to Victor Krasney. The tag and insurance had lapsed more than four years ago, but he renewed both two and a half weeks ago."

Jason nodded. The man had likely let his anger simmer for the past five years, each month that passed further stoking his need for revenge. He'd conned his sister into helping him find Tia, then waited for the perfect opportunity to act.

Except neither he nor Tia had seen the vehicle. Granted, they'd been on the lookout for a white SUV, then a light-colored sedan. But if anyone had been watching her, regardless of the vehicle, they would have noticed. "There hasn't been a gold van hanging around."

"Maybe he's kept it parked in the woods. Where it was found is only about a fifteen-minute drive from Harmony Grove. This morning, someone found a bicycle hidden in shrubbery a couple of blocks from the shelter. It had been reported stolen in Winter Haven two weeks ago. On a hunch, I suggested that Tommy dust it for prints."

"Good idea. If Victor's prints are on that bike, it would explain how he was able to keep a close eye on Tia without us seeing the van."

His phone vibrated in his hand, sending a buzz into his ear. "I just got a text. I think my mom's plane has landed. As soon as I have her, I'm supposed to call my father for instructions. I'll get back with you when I know what's going on, and we'll go from there."

Jason disconnected the call and sent a return text to his mother. After waiting ten minutes, he followed the signs to arriving flights. As he crept along behind those picking up friends and family members, he scanned the passengers standing and sitting to his right. Finally, a slender arm raised, and his mother stepped forward. He pulled to the curb, but before he could exit the vehicle to help her, she'd already opened the rear passenger door and lifted her carry-on into the seat.

After she climbed into the front, he leaned across

the console to give her a quick hug. She looked good, much better than she had when he'd left three and a half weeks ago. The dark circles beneath her eyes had begun to fade, and her cheeks held more color than he'd seen in a long time.

The thread of worry he expected wasn't there, just a calm resignation, wrapped in peace. Finally, she was winning the fight against the cancer that had raged through her body. Had she fought that battle for nothing? Was that hard-gained future going to be stolen from her by an evil man nursing a seventeen-year grudge? Not if Jason could help it.

He eased back into traffic, but before leaving the airport, he pulled into one of the parking lots and redialed the phone number he'd saved last night.

His father answered two rings later, skipping the greeting. "You have your mother?"

"Yes."

"Put me on speaker phone."

Jason lowered the phone to press the icon. "It's done."

"Tammy, are you there?"

"Hello, George." Her words didn't hold any bitterness. She'd moved past all that years ago.

For Jason, it hadn't been that easy. Maybe it hadn't been easy for his mother, either. But she'd mastered the whole forgiveness thing much more quickly than he had. He was still struggling.

"I'm going to give you some instructions." His words were obviously directed at Jason. "You'd better follow them explicitly."

"I will." Except for calling Alan. No way was he handling this alone. Not when his mother's and Tia's lives were at stake.

"Write down this address."

He scrambled to find a pen and piece of paper in the console, then scribbled the information his father gave him. He'd said yesterday that Tia wasn't doing well. Jason tried to block out the images that played through his mind—Tia restrained, bound and possibly gagged, fear and hopelessness in those blue eyes.

"Drive around to the back." His father's words cut across his thoughts. "Then call me. I'll expect you in one hour."

"I'm in Tampa. It might take longer than that." His father had given him a Polk City address. It was a small town some distance past Lakeland, with lots of wooded, unpopulated area surrounding it. An hour might be reasonable, but he wasn't taking any chances.

"You've got mostly interstate driving. On Christmas Day, traffic won't be heavy. If you take much longer than that, I'll think you're scheming something, and it'll be Tia who'll pay."

Jason cranked the truck. "I'm headed that way now." He'd call Alan while driving.

"One hour." The stern words held a note of warning. "I told you last night that you'd better not even think about calling the police. If I see or hear anything that makes me suspect that you're pulling something, your precious little Tia is dead. Do you understand?"

"Completely."

As he disconnected the call, he fought the anger rising up in him. Determination was much more productive. If he had any choice in the matter, he wasn't going to lose his mother or Tia today. He backed from the parking space and headed toward the exit. His mom could bring up the address on his GPS app later. First, he had a phone call to make.

He stopped at the exit, and since no one was behind him, he pulled up his recent calls. The second one down was the one he'd made to Alan.

His mother frowned at him. "What are you doing?"

"Calling a friend."

"You heard what your father said."

"I'm not doing this alone. You'll have a much better chance of making it out of this alive if we get Alan on board."

Her eyes narrowed. "And what does Alan do for a living?"

He sighed. "Police officer with Harmony Grove."

She reached across the cab with lightning speed and swiped the phone from his hand. "If you involve the police, he'll kill Tia."

"If I don't, he'll kill you."

"You don't know that. Now get going. We're already two minutes into that hour. When we get there, he'll be focused on me. I'll talk to him, try to reason with him. Meanwhile, you do everything you can to get Tia to safety."

His mother used the voice feature to read the address into the GPS, then clipped his phone into the holder on the dash. He looked at the anticipated arrival time. Fifty-three minutes. He'd ended the call with his father less than five minutes ago. They'd arrive well within the hour his father had given them.

His mom had told him to get Tia to safety. He would do his best. He'd also do everything in his power to protect his mother. But he might be carrying her to her death.

Maybe he was even walking into his own.

Tia tipped her head from side to side and rolled her shoulders. Her neck ached, and she couldn't even reach up to massage out the kinks. She couldn't complain to Sloan, either, since as of thirty minutes ago, he'd once again taped her mouth.

He'd apologized last night for having to leave her in the chair. He'd even slid it back against the wall so she'd have something to rest her head against. Then he'd rolled out a sleeping bag a few feet away, extinguished the lamp, and not made a sound till morning.

Well into the night, she'd sat in pitch blackness, tamping down waves of panic, until exhaustion had finally taken over. She'd dozed for brief periods, but without support on either side, she'd awoken with her head tilted toward her shoulder and the side of her neck locked in a painful spasm.

Assuming that the protein bar Sloan had given her earlier was breakfast, the time was likely nearing noon. A few hours ago, he'd cut her loose long enough for her to use the bathroom, then down some water with the protein bar.

After restraining her again, he'd started to pace. As his agitation had grown, so had her fear. All morning, one question had circled though her mind, on an endless loop: *What if Jason doesn't come?*

Almost an hour ago, Sloan's phone had rung. He'd stepped outside to take the call. When he'd come back in, anticipation had replaced the agitation. A half hour later, he'd re-taped her mouth.

Sloan sank into a chair similar to hers and opened a bottle of water. He didn't offer her any. That was all right. She wasn't thirsty. She wasn't hungry, either.

For the fourth time in the past few minutes, he looked at his watch. He was getting antsy again. He tossed the empty water bottle onto the floor behind him and rose from his chair. A moment later, a knock sounded on the back door.

Tia's heart leaped into her throat. Jason? Or had someone noticed something suspicious and called the police?

Sloan picked up his pistol from its place on the counter and approached the door. "Who's there?"

"Jason."

Tia's breath escaped in a rush as relief collided with dread. Jason had come, but his mother would be there, too. That was the arrangement. If the older woman sacrificed her life and Tia somehow managed to escape, that act would haunt her for the rest of her days.

Sloan opened the door farther, pistol raised. "Why aren't you parked in the back?"

"Let me see that Tia's okay, and I'll take you to Mom."

"Where is she?" Sloan's left hand curled into a fist. The adult Jason was doing something the child had never been able to—defy his father.

"She's close. Let me see Tia."

The elder Sloan stood his ground for a few more seconds, then moved back, the pistol still aimed at his son. As soon as Jason stepped into the room, his gaze circled the space, then stopped to rest on her. His nostrils flared, and color crept up his neck and into his cheeks. His chest rose and fell several times while a vein throbbed in his temple. He squeezed his eyes shut, visibly fighting for control.

George took two more steps back and tightened his grip on the weapon. "Is your mother here, or do I just go ahead and shoot you both right now?"

Jason slowly raised his hands. "She's here. But you don't want to do this. It's been seventeen years. Let it go. Move on with your life."

"Shut your mouth, boy." He charged at Jason, giving him a one-handed, backward shove through the open doorway.

Tia gasped. Jason was out of her line of sight, but the thud and "oomph" that followed his exit confirmed he'd landed on his back at the bottom of the steps.

Sloan charged out after him, pistol still raised. Moments later, fists met flesh. No, not fists. Boots. George was kicking Jason, each blow eliciting a grunt of pain. A cry rose up Tia's throat, and she struggled against the ties until her wrists started to bleed. It was no use. Zip ties didn't stretch and break.

The blows stopped, and Jason's father stepped back inside. He hooked one foot under a leg of the table that held the lamp and kicked upward. The table toppled, and the lamp fell with it, its tall, narrow globe landing a couple of inches from the fuel-filled base. A moment later, George slammed the door.

Tia gasped, eyes wide. The lamp lay on its side, the now open flame licking at the carpet. It caught quickly, aided by whatever fuel was likely leaking from the lamp body. She released a long scream into the tape, a muffled plea that wouldn't carry outside the house. Jason didn't even know she was in trouble. With the doors closed and windows boarded, no one would discover the fire until it was too late.

Panic screamed through her body. She tipped the chair back and forth, side to side, but the joints didn't loosen. The fire was spreading. A one-by-two-foot section of carpet was already in flames, dark gray smoke rising into the air.

Sloan had had no intention of releasing her. He was letting the fire take care of her, then going after Jason and his mother. Tia struggled with renewed vigor, but the only thing she accomplished was bruising and bloodying her wrists even more.

God, help me. If she had any hope of escape, she had to calm down and try to think rationally.

Maybe she could tip or lift the chair and possibly free her legs. She leaned to the side and looked at her ankles. Decorative ridges routed into the lower three inches of each chair leg wouldn't make the task easy. She tipped the chair to the right and worked her left foot back and forth against the chair leg, lower and lower until the tie slipped past the bottom of the leg, then did the same with the right.

Smoke billowed into the air around her, stinging her eyes and nose. The mattress had caught fire, and what she could see of the living room was now engulfed in flames. A coughing spasm overtook her, and tears streamed down her face. She blinked to clear her vision and searched for something she could use to free her hands.

Maybe one of the kitchen drawers held a knife or pair of scissors. It was a long shot. Even if the prior residents had left such an item behind, retrieving it from the drawer and using it successfully with both arms restrained would be a challenge.

Maybe there was another option. It was an even longer shot. Some time ago, she'd seen something online about cutting through zip ties with a shoelace. She'd ignored it, dismissing the claim as a gimmick to get clicks. She should have watched the video.

Another coughing spasm ripped through her, and her sinuses filled. She leaned forward, lowering her face toward her right hand, then picked at the tape covering her mouth. Once she'd ripped it loose, she sucked in some frantic breaths. Halfway through the third one, her throat closed up and her lungs rejected the polluted air she'd tried to draw in.

Whatever attempts she made to get free, she needed to act quickly. She was out of time. Maybe it was already too late. If she could get to the back of the house and close a door, she could buy herself some time. She leaned forward, tipping the chair with her, and straightened her legs. Then she hobbled down the dark hallway, bent at the waist, chair on her back, her progress painfully slow.

When she reached the back bedroom, she put the chair on the floor and kicked the door shut. The air was cleaner here. It was also pitch black. Whatever she did, she'd be doing it completely by feel.

She crossed her right foot over her knee and, with shaking fingers, worked the lace loose. Then she tied the end to that shoe. She would have to feed the other end through the zip tie and come up with a way to saw through the plastic. She knew that much without seeing the video.

Where was Jason? Was he all right, or had George badly beaten him? What about his mother? There'd been no gunshot, so that had to be a good sign. Or would she even hear it, closed up in the house, flames crackling and roaring closer?

She struggled to squelch the fear and worry. She needed to reserve all her mental energy for getting free and trust God to take care of Jason and his mom.

If she didn't remain focused and succeed in her escape, she wouldn't live to see either of them.

Jason trudged through knee-high weeds, his father at his rear. With every step, pain stabbed through him. He'd tumbled out the door and landed hard on his back. About the time he'd been able to start breathing again, his father had charged down the steps and driven a series of kicks into his side. Besides some serious bruising, Jason likely had some cracked ribs. By tomorrow, he was going to feel as if he'd had a run-in with a bulldozer. If he even saw tomorrow.

Jason rounded the corner of the house and stepped into the front yard, the soft crunch of his father's footsteps a short distance behind him. He didn't need to turn around to know that the pistol was pointed at his back.

He'd left the Ram sitting in the gravel drive, not far from the road. He hadn't bothered to close the gate and dummy-lock the chain, in case he needed to make a quick getaway. Another one of his father's instructions he'd refused to follow.

When he'd exited the truck, he'd left his mom sitting in the front seat. She'd balked at first, insisting that he remain safely out of sight and she be the one to meet his father. The only thing that had swayed her was that he'd have a better chance of rescuing Tia if he could size up her situation before his father saw his mom.

Once fully into the front yard, Jason's step faltered. The Ram's front passenger seat was empty.

The crunch of footsteps behind him ceased. "Where is she? Two seconds, or I pull this trigger."

Jason looked around, heart pounding in his throat. This wasn't part of the plan. Actually, his mother hadn't let him make a plan, beyond cooperation and trying to keep him and Tia alive. So where was she?

Movement in his peripheral vision drew his gaze toward a scrub oak about thirty feet away. His mother stepped out from behind it and moved toward them. Her sweater clung to her thin frame, and her flared skirt swished around her calves in the light breeze. She'd taken her hair down, and it flowed over her shoulders, liquid silver in the noonday sunlight.

She stopped walking and held up a hand. "I'm here. Don't shoot our son."

His father moved forward until he was a few feet to Jason's left. Though he still held the weapon on Jason, his eyes had locked on his former wife.

Jason shifted his gaze between his parents. They were seeing each other for the first time in almost two decades. What was his father feeling? Was there even a sliver of tenderness? He had to have loved her at one point. Maybe he had all along, even through the beatings, feeling remorse but never learning how to chain the beast.

Jason studied his father. Was now the time to act,

during these brief moments of distraction, or would he force his father into hasty action that would get both him and his mom killed?

The man's features hardened, and his eyes filled with hatred. "You never listened."

As he swung the pistol in her direction, Jason's heart almost stopped. His mother wasn't going to have the opportunity to use any of her persuasive arguments. His dad had said he'd kill her if she ever left him. Now he was following through with that promise.

Jason lunged and slammed into his father. An explosion rocked his world, accompanied by a distant cry. A heavy silence fell, a sudden unnatural absence of sounds he'd only become aware of now that they were gone.

He'd landed on top of the old man, the weapon pinned between them. His father bucked Jason's weight off of him and rolled him onto his back, swinging the weapon around in a smooth arc. Before the other man could take aim, Jason wrapped his hands around those gripping the handle of the gun and forced it away from him, both of them straining with the effort. They were evenly matched in both size and strength, unlike when his father had broken his nose seventeen years ago.

His father jerked forward, butting his forehead into Jason's. Pain exploded through his head, and his grip on the other man's hands relaxed for a fraction of a second. The weapon discharged again, the shot narrowly missing Jason's arm. For the next minute or so, they both fought for control of the weapon, arms shaking. Jason was tiring, but so was his father.

Far away, the high-pitched wail of sirens drifted on

the breeze and grew gradually louder. Jason continued to press, forcing the barrel toward his father. All he needed was a few more degrees.

He slipped the end of his finger between the trigger and the guard and pressed. Another explosion rent the air, the weapon jerking backward with the recoil. His father released the handle with a squeal of pain. A red stain spread in an ever-widening circle on the sleeve of his polo shirt.

Jason sprang to his feet, weapon clutched in his hands, breath coming in labored pants. The sirens were closer now. Were the emergency vehicles coming for them?

His father released a grunt, one hand pressed against his injured shoulder. "You think you've won, but at what price?" Pain underscored each word. "Your mother is bleeding out in the front yard, and your girlfriend is trapped in a burning house. Who are you going to try to save?"

What? His head pivoted toward where his mother had walked away from the scrub oak. She was lying on the ground, an object clutched in one hand. *God, no.* He stumbled in that direction. She'd been shot. The cry that had sounded so far away had been hers.

Behind him, a series of creaks and groans rose in volume, culminating in a massive crash. He spun in time to see part of the roof collapse and flames shoot into the sky.

"Tia!"

He took two steps toward the house, then spun back around to look at his mother. His father was right. Who would he try to save?

His mother was conscious, one hand pressed to

her abdomen, the other still holding the object he'd seen earlier. Was it her phone? Was she the one who'd called for help?

Tia was probably gone. If she was where she'd been when he'd last seen her, there was no way she'd survived. The grief that stabbed through him almost brought him to his knees.

He turned toward his father, hatred bubbling up inside. The man was dragging himself to his feet. Jason raised the weapon. "Face down on the ground, now. Or the next shot will be much worse than a shoulder wound."

Indecision flashed across his father's features. Then his eyes narrowed. "You won't kill me. You don't have it in you." He spun away and stumbled toward the open gate.

Jason laid down the weapon. No, he wouldn't kill his father. But he wouldn't let him walk away, either. He closed the distance between them at a full run and slammed into his father, knocking him to the ground. A punch to the side of the head rendered him unconscious. Jason tried not to find satisfaction in the action but wasn't successful.

A thud came from other end of the house, and he jerked his head in that direction. A second thud followed and a third. The lower edge of the board covering the last window bounced as if struck from inside. *Tia?*

He glanced at his mother.

"Go help Tia." Her voice sounded weak.

"You let me know if he moves."

After retrieving a pry bar and screw gun from his truck, he ran to the window, where Tia was continuing to strike repeated blows but not making any progress.

"Hang on." He put his face close to the plywood, voice raised. "I'm getting you out."

A quick inspection of the board showed a series of Phillips head screws installed every foot and a half around the perimeter. As he worked to back them out, Tia's frantic pleas blended with the whine of the drill. Two minutes after he'd started, he laid aside the sheet of plywood, then helped her through the window she'd already opened.

Her arms went around his neck, and she clung to him, her grip surprisingly strong. As he held her tightly against him, emotion swamped him—relief and gratefulness for the miracle they'd been given, and love for the sweet, beautiful, compassionate woman in his arms. He cut the hug short to lead her to where his mother lay in the grass.

He dropped to his knees and took his mother's hand. "How are you?"

She gave him a weak smile. "I've been better." When her eyes shifted to Tia, the smile widened. "You must be Tia. I've heard a lot about you."

"It's nice to meet you." She sank to the ground and hugged her knees to her chest. The zip ties around her ankles were still intact. All that remained of the ones securing her wrists were bloody red lines.

His mom's eyes were still on Tia. "You're the miracle girl. When the roof caved in and flames shot into the sky, we didn't expect you to walk out of there."

He hadn't even realized the place had been burning. Everything had been fine when he'd checked on her before his father had pushed him out the door. "How did the fire start?"

"With the windows boarded, your dad was using an old-fashioned hurricane lamp for light. He kicked over the table he had it sitting on."

"Intentionally?"

She nodded.

Of course it was intentional. His father had planned to kill Tia all along. He'd tried to do it in a way that even if Jason had managed to thwart him in his plans, Tia would be gone by the time he got to her. Except it didn't work.

"How did you get loose?"

"Sometime back, I saw something online about escaping from zip ties with a shoelace, a video on Facebook or YouTube."

He lifted his brows. "A YouTube video saved your life?"

"Yes. Or maybe I should say the title saved my life. I never clicked on the video."

He shook his head. "You're a smart lady."

"Probably more desperate than smart. But definitely blessed."

An ambulance stopped at the road, two police cars behind it. The paramedics rushed toward them.

Jason rose. "My mother's been shot." He cast a glance behind him. "My father, too."

While the paramedics tended to his parents, the officers talked to him and Tia individually. As Tia explained her ordeal of the past twenty-four hours, Jason cast frequent glances at her. She seemed to be holding up fine, at least for the time being. The events of the past twenty-four hours were likely to bring on some terrifying nightmares.

Tia was finally free. Victor could never hurt her again. Eventually the nightmares would fade. The fear would dissipate. The inner scars would heal as completely as the outer ones had.

Maybe she'd even lower the protective walls enough to allow a special someone access to her heart.

He released a sigh. He really wanted that someone to be him.

NINETEEN

TIA MADE HER way down the hall at Lakeland Regional Medical Center. She was finally in the right wing and on the right floor. According to the last person she'd asked for directions, Jason's mother's room should be halfway down on the left.

Ms. Sloan wasn't the only one who'd spent the night there. After the ambulance had sped away from the scene with her inside and a second ambulance had shown up to transport Jason's father, Jason had insisted that Tia be checked for smoke inhalation. She'd argued that she was fine.

Now she was glad she'd conceded. By last night, some shortness of breath had set in. Then the mucus had started to accumulate, triggering a persistent cough. The doctor had kept her under observation all night and throughout the morning, but as of thirty minutes ago, she was free to go home, with strict instructions to phone if her symptoms worsened. She'd already put Joyce on standby to pick her up.

She clasped the pendant hanging a few inches below her throat and slid it back and forth on its chain. Sometime between when Victor had abducted her from the shelter and George Sloan had carried her into the abandoned house, her scarf had disappeared. The gold lion with the emerald eyes had made a nice replacement.

An hour ago, BethAnn had shown up with a get-well card signed by Katie and Nika. Ethan and Aiden had added their childish print below, along with two hearts, a candy cane and a smiley face. BethAnn had also brought the small wrapped box that had sat under her tree for the past few days. Besides the pendant on its gold chain, the box had held a handwritten note— *The lion symbolizes strength, courage, dignity, wisdom and goodness. To a special lady who possesses all of these. Jason.*

She dropped the pendant to let it rest against her chest. Several scars peeked out over the neckline of her blouse, but she pushed aside her self-consciousness. If she wanted to cover up when she got home, she'd do it. Maybe she wouldn't feel the need.

As she approached Ms. Sloan's room, a soft male voice drifted into the hall. Tia couldn't make out the words, but that warm, smooth baritone slid over her like a soft caress.

"I know." His mom sounded better than she had yesterday at the house. "All these years, and I still hate the northern winters."

Tia's pulse picked up, and she stopped outside the door. Was Jason's mom just making an observation, a frequently-voiced complaint about the Connecticut cold? That wasn't what it sounded like. The conversation had a sense of going somewhere.

She was almost afraid to hope. A month ago, a long-distance friendship would have suited her fine. Not anymore. Sometime between when Jason had burst through her front door and when he'd kissed her under the oak tree, she'd fallen hard.

A soft rustle behind her drew her attention. She turned to watch an older gentleman shuffle down the hall toward her, holding onto the handrail. Hospital-issued socks covered his feet, and his gown hit him mid-calf.

She nodded at him then stepped into the room before anyone else could observe her eavesdropping. Jason sat with his back to her, chair pulled close to the bed nearest the window. His mom lay beneath a white lightweight blanket, the back of the bed raised slightly. As Tia approached, her head rolled to the side, and a smile lit her face.

Tia lifted a hand in greeting. "I hope I'm not interrupting."

"Not at all."

Jason rose to face her. His smile held its usual warmth, but something else was there, too, something she wasn't sure how to interpret. Whatever it was, it sent a flutter through her stomach.

She greeted his mother, then lifted a hand to touch the pendant. "Thank you for the necklace. It's beautiful."

"You're welcome." His eyebrows dipped. "You weren't wearing it yesterday, were you?"

"No. BethAnn came to visit while I was eating lunch. She brought your gift and a card from the ladies."

He took the second chair from its place against the wall and moved it next to the one he'd been sitting in. "Have a seat. I take it you've been released, since you're back in your regular clothes."

She sank into the chair he offered, and a poof of

smoke-scented air rose around her. "Yep. I almost hated to part with the hospital gown. I stink."

Grinning, he took a seat next to her. "If it's any consolation, you look better than you smell."

"Thank you. I think." She looked at his mother. "How do you feel?"

"Better than last night, thanks to whatever they've got in that IV bag up there."

Tia smiled. The lady was blessed to be alive. While she had spent almost three hours in surgery during the early morning hours, Jason had sat in Tia's room. They'd prayed together, and she'd consoled him and worried with him.

Jason shifted in his chair. "The bullet grazed her stomach and lodged near her spine but didn't do any serious damage. The surgery was successful. The doctors expect her to make a complete recovery. God answered our prayers."

God had answered a lot of prayers over the past two days. The fact that any of them had survived seemed nothing short of a miracle.

Jason took Tia's hand and squeezed it. "Thank you for being there for me and helping me hold it together. You were my rock."

Warmth flooded her. She'd never thought of herself as anyone's rock. Throughout her marriage, she'd been the weaker one, always the victim. She'd been broken and pieced back together so many times that the strength she showed to the world, even now, was nothing but a facade.

Jason's gaze held hers. That invisible connection she'd felt so many times was a bond that couldn't be broken. Respect and admiration flowed between them, a sense of oneness and unity, as if they stood on equal ground.

Maybe that was what a loving relationship was all about, each being there for the other, neither one always in submission nor always in control. Each sometimes the leader, sometimes the follower, at times the weak one and at other times the one providing strength and encouragement.

She left her hand in Jason's but tore her gaze from his to look at his mother. She lay smiling at them, her features holding joy, approval, acceptance. Had Jason and his mother been discussing her before she walked in?

It didn't matter if they were. What possibilities could there be for their futures when their lives were twelve hundred miles apart? Jason would never expect her to leave Peace House, and she would never ask him and his mother to walk away from their lives in Connecticut. But if their reasons for fleeing Florida were no longer relevant, would that make a difference?

"Have you heard anything about your father?"

Jason nodded. "After leaving your room this morning, I learned Mom was just being moved to recovery and wouldn't be awake for some time, so I checked on him. The doctor was with him. My shot went through his shoulder, did a lot of damage to the joint."

He frowned. "But that's not his biggest problem. The years of heavy drinking have finally caught up with him. He has such severe cirrhosis of the liver that he was recently given six months to live. I'll be surprised if he makes it long enough to stand trial."

He shook his head. "He didn't want to end his time on earth with unfinished business, so he came all the way here from Mississippi to make good on a seventeen-year-old promise. The entire time I was in his room, he shot daggers at me, but he did allow the doctor to talk with me."

Tia released a sigh. She was finally free. Victor could never hurt her again. Although George Sloan was still alive, he was no longer a threat to Jason or his mother. Kidnapping, arson, murder and two counts of attempted murder…sick or not, there was no way a judge would allow him to bond out.

Were Jason and his mother considering coming back to Florida, now that the threat was removed? Was that the reason for Ms. Sloan's comment about still hating the northern winters?

When Tia looked at her again, her eyelids were half closed. She put her hand over the other woman's, as small as her own. "I'm going to go and let you get some rest."

Jason stood. "Do you need a ride home?"

"Yes, but I've already lined up a friend who's a shelter director over on the south side. She's ready to head out at a moment's notice."

"I'll wait with you. Once you call her, you've got what, twenty minutes to kill?"

"Something like that."

After wishing Jason's mother farewell, she headed for the door.

Jason followed her out. "What do you say we go to the cafeteria and let me get you something to eat?"

"I just had lunch."

"Coffee, then."

"I'm not much of a coffee drinker, but I think I'll make an exception."

"And a dessert. You deserve it after everything you've been through the last two days."

She smiled up at him. "So do you."

They stopped at the elevator, and Jason pressed the down button.

Tia pursed her lips. "Are you going to see your father in prison?"

"I haven't decided, but I'm thinking about it."

"Good." He wouldn't be free to pursue a satisfying future until he escaped his past. Part of that process would be releasing the resentment he still felt toward the man who'd been so cruel to him and his mother. It wouldn't be easy. No one understood that better than she did. Maybe the two of them could find that freedom together.

She heaved a sigh. She couldn't stand not knowing any longer. "Now that your dad is out of the picture, is there any chance you and your mom might come back to Florida?"

The elevator dinged and the door opened.

"A pretty good chance, actually." They stepped on, and Jason selected floor number two, the location of the cafe. "We just have a few things to work out."

"Like finding jobs."

"That's one thing." He grinned. "I'm also wondering what your ladies would think of a man hanging around all the time."

She tilted her head to one side. "That depends on the man."

The elevator dinged and the number two lit up, notifying them they had reached their floor.

She hesitated. "Can I change my mind about the coffee and dessert?"

"What did you have in mind?"

"A walk."

"A romantic stroll through the halls of the hospital or down Lakeland Hills Boulevard?"

"Neither. If we go out the side and head straight down Parkview, it ends at Lake Parker."

As soon as they stepped into the sunshine, he took her hand. "For two weeks, I've dreaded going back home. I was worried about leaving you, knowing Victor was a threat, but that was just part of it."

She waited for him to continue, her heart pounding and her insides a quivery mess. Was there a chance that his feelings for her went beyond friendship? Had what transpired under the oak tree meant more to him than she'd allowed herself to believe?

He didn't speak again until they reached the corner, where they waited to cross the four-lane boulevard.

"I was attracted to you from the moment I saw you step into the hall at my grandparents' place. Alone in that big house with a stranger, a whole head shorter and sixty or seventy pounds lighter, you stared me down like you weren't afraid of anything."

She smiled. "I guess I did a good job of covering up my nervousness."

The white "walk" signal came on, and they stepped into the street. When they'd reached the other side, he continued.

"Then I found out what you did, how you'd devoted your life to helping victims of domestic abuse. Watching you manage the shelter, seeing you interact with the women and children under your care, it didn't take me long to realize that what's inside is as beautiful as what's outside." He squeezed her hand. "I've tried hard to not fall for you. I was sure there was no way a relationship would work. I couldn't leave Connecticut and you couldn't leave Florida."

"The obstacles did seem insurmountable."

"It wasn't just the distance. With everything you've been through and my own messed-up past, I was convinced that I could never be what you need. But with God's help, I really want to try."

He released her hand to put his arm around her. She slid her own around his waist. Nestled against his side, she'd never felt safer or more content. This was where she belonged.

But she couldn't just think of herself. "What about your mom? With all she's going through with her health, is she really going to want to share you?"

"Are you kidding? Ever since things blew up with Ashley, she's been hoping I'll find someone and doesn't mind telling me so every chance she gets. I told you she would love you, and I was right. Of course, with all the times I mentioned you during our phone conversations, she feels like she already knows you."

They reached the end of Parkview and stepped onto the sidewalk that wove along the shore of the lake. A gentle breeze blew across its surface, and several ducks glided along, leaving a fan-shaped path in the ripples. She released a contented sigh. She wasn't in any hurry to call Joyce. Jason didn't seem anxious to see her leave, either.

"Before Mom got sick, she volunteered with a

couple of shelters up north. She's excited about the prospect of helping out at Peace House."

"I'd love that."

He looked past her toward the lake, then smiled down at her. "When I asked you what the ladies would think of a man hanging around, you said it depends on the man. What kind of man do you think would be suitable?"

She stopped walking, and when she turned to face him, there was a teasing glint in his eyes. She lifted her arms to clasp her hands behind his neck, and his encircled her waist. "A suitable man for Peace House would be someone heroic, who would go to any extreme to protect the women inside."

"Even if it involves charging through the front door?"

"Even then." She matched his smile. "A man who is willing to lend a hand when needed."

"Such as making repairs to said door."

"Exactly." She tilted her head. "Someone strong and handsome, too, with unruly dark hair and golden-brown eyes."

"A crooked nose?"

"And straight, white teeth and a masculine jaw." She let her smile fade. "Someone who is gentle and kind and compassionate. A man who puts others first instead of just looking out for his own interests. One who follows the best Leader of all, then leads by example."

"Your standards are high."

"And you surpass them all." He probably had no idea how special he was. "It's helpful for women who've lived in abusive situations to see positive male role models. It helps to reinforce the fact that not all men are evil, that there are wonderful, kind ones out there. It's good for the kids, too."

"Like Damian."

She nodded. "Like Damian."

"And what about you?"

"I think a man like that might be good for me, too."

He lifted a hand to cup her cheek. "I love you, Tia, and I want to be that man. Your guard is up. I understand that. You can't experience the things you have and not build some serious walls. I'd never intentionally do anything to hurt you. I hope you'll give me the opportunity to show you that you can trust me with your heart."

"You already have. And those walls you mentioned? I'm afraid their rubble is lying somewhere beneath the oak tree next to Peace House."

She stood on her toes, and he leaned forward to meet her halfway. The first time he'd kissed her, he'd shown her what it meant to feel loved and cherished. Now she tried to return that gift, to pour into the kiss all the love and appreciation swelling in her heart.

A new year was right around the corner. Each January was a fresh start, with the potential to be the beginning of a bright future. Though it was something she'd often told the ladies spending their holiday season at Peace House, she'd never claimed those dreams for herself.

The moment God sent Jason into her life, that was exactly what He had blessed her with—a new start. Hope for healing.

A bright, happy future filled with love.

The End

SNEAK PEEK!
Here's a sneak peek at book three in the
Harmony Grove series,
Pay the Price

ONE

THE HOUSE STOOD silhouetted against a cloudless sky, the landscape frozen and still under the onslaught of one of Central Florida's infrequent cold fronts.

Just like the last time she had stepped foot on this property.

Jessica Parker threw open the car door, stopping short of dinging the shiny red Lotus sitting next to her Bug. As she stepped into the frigid night air, she pulled her coat more tightly around her, the cold outside mirroring the chill within. Eight long years, and nothing had changed. The same huge oak shadowed most of the front yard. The same potted plant waited by the front door, hiding the key to the house. And as she made her way up the cracked cement drive, she was hit with the same lack of warmth she had always associated with home.

She squatted to tilt the pot, then heaved a sigh. The key was gone. Priscilla was still messing with her, even from beyond the grave. She straightened and walked back to her car. It had been years since she'd picked a lock. But that wasn't a skill easily forgotten—like riding a bike.

The sliding glass door was her best bet. It had been her most frequent middle-of-the-night point of entry after her sister had locked her out. Priscilla's favorite pastime had always been thinking of ways to get her in trouble. Of course, Jessica had given her plenty to work with. But those days were over. She was a law-abiding citizen now.

She rounded the back of the house. Good, no Charley bar. A sliding glass door without it would be no match for a screwdriver in practiced hands. She squatted and slipped the flat tip under one of the doors. A twig snapped a short distance away. Her senses shot to full alert, and she eased to her feet, gripping the tool like a weapon. But all was still. Eerily so.

Of course it was. This was Harmony Grove, not Miami. At two a.m., all its citizens would be home in bed, fast asleep. Shaking off the last of the uneasiness, she resumed her work on the locked door, then slid it back in its track. She hadn't lost her touch.

Her confident smile faded the instant she stepped into the kitchen and flipped the light switch. Every cabinet door was open. Dishes and utensils filled both sinks and covered the countertops in haphazard stacks. Pots and pans littered the floor, and the overflow occupied the four-person table. Her sister had grown up to be quite the slob. It would take days to get everything clean and back into the cabinets. Especially with no dishwasher.

Irritation surged up inside her, with guilt on its tail. She had tried to set aside her animosity toward her sister, now more than ever. But this was so typical of

Priscilla. Acting with total disregard for anyone who might be affected by her selfish decisions.

A closer look, though, shattered her initial assessment. These weren't dirty dishes. In fact, there wasn't a dirty plate, glass or piece of silverware in the bunch. What had Priscilla been doing? Why empty all the cabinets?

Jessica pushed a stack of pans away from the edge of the table to clear a spot for her purse, then hung her jacket over the back of a chair. When she reached the end of the counter, she stopped in the open doorway of the living room. Decorative throw pillows littered the floor, and couch cushions rested at haphazard angles, as if someone had been looking for something. She moved further into the room. A photo frame lay face down on the end table, and she reached to stand it up. Priscilla stared back at her, sending an unexpected jolt coursing all the way to her toes.

Jessica drew in a steadying breath. She had buried the past and moved forward with her life. And she had done well. Then she got that phone call. And now she was back. It was hard to keep the past buried when she was surrounded by it, memories dogging her at every turn, a blond-haired princess accusing her with those crystal blue eyes.

She picked up the frame for a closer look. Priscilla had grown up to be quite pretty. She had been a chubby-cheeked thirteen-year-old when Jessica left, with a lingering childishness and an angelic innocence that fooled ninety percent of the people she met. The woman in the photo looked neither childish nor innocent. Though she wore a pleasant half smile, her features held hardness, hinting at a life that had knocked her around and the barriers that had gone up as a result.

What had happened? What could be so bad that she believed she had nothing to live for? Why does anyone take their own life?

She set the frame back on the table and kicked a pillow aside. Two bedrooms waited for her down the hall, likely in the same shape as the other rooms. She stopped at the first open doorway, and dread washed over her. No, this was much worse.

It was her and Priscilla's room, frozen in time—the twin beds and their whitewashed headboards, the chest with five drawers, three of which Prissy had always managed to claim, and the mismatched vanity, which Prissy took over from day one. They had always had to share a room. And Jessica had hated every minute of it.

But the mess made the room almost unrecognizable. Every dresser drawer had been pulled out, clothes scattered from one end of the room to the other. The contents of the closet contributed to the disarray. Cloth-covered hangers, even a pair of crutches, jutted up from the chaos at odd angles. This wasn't Priscilla's doing. Someone had ransacked the house.

She backed into the hall, ready to call the police. But she didn't make it far. As she reached the living room, a muffled squeak sounded in the kitchen. Like the rubber sole of a tennis shoe against the vinyl tile floor.

Apprehension sifted over her, raising the fine hairs on the back of her neck. She stood frozen, ears cocked for any sign that she wasn't alone, mind ticking through her options. Her phone was in the kitchen with her purse. So was anything she could use as a weapon. If she had to defend herself, it would be through hand-to-hand combat.

A face appeared around the wall separating the kitchen from the living room, then disappeared a nanosecond later. Her heart began to pound and her muscles tensed as adrenaline pumped through her body. Someone was in the house. And not knowing whether he was armed or had brought buddies, standing her ground and fighting was a last resort.

She bolted toward the front door. Heavy footsteps sounded behind her. She would never get the door open before he reached her. Her best weapon was the element of surprise. At five foot three and a hundred twenty pounds, no one expected her to pack a hard punch.

Or a devastating kick.

She spun to face him, disconcerted at how much ground he'd covered in such a short time. She had less than a second to respond. She raised a knee and thrust outward with a boot-clad foot. It contacted with a thud and a whoosh of forcefully exhaled air. The impact sent him flying backward onto his rear. But he didn't stay there. In fact, he didn't really land there, just used the whole experience as a launch into a backward somersault that brought him effortlessly to his feet.

At least he wasn't armed. Not that she could see, anyway. She couldn't vouch for what might be hiding under that black leather jacket.

Whatever it was, she wasn't going to give him a chance to reach for it. She charged forward, feet flying.

A well-placed kick to the gut doubled him over, but he managed to turn and deflect the majority of the follow-up punch to the face. A steely hand clamped around her wrist, thrusting her forward and flinging her to the floor in front of the entertainment center. He hurled himself toward her, but before he could pin her, she was back on her feet, ready with a kick to the chest.

His body slammed backward into the coffee table with the crack of splintering wood and the crash of shattering glass. One more kick should put him down for the count. But she never got the opportunity. In one smooth motion, his hand swept inside his jacket and emerged with a pistol. It was pointed at her chest.

"Sit. Over there. On the couch."

His voice was husky. She liked to think it was from the blows she'd delivered. For several moments she stood unmoving, except for the rapid rise and fall of her chest. Her heart pounded and her mind churned. A low crescent kick would probably send the gun flying. It could also get her killed. Not worth taking a chance.

But she wasn't ready to back down. If he intended to shoot her, he would have done it already. "Who are you?"

He raised himself to a seated position, eyeing her cautiously. "How about if you talk first, considering I *am* the one with the gun." He flashed her a smile that would have appeared amicable without said gun. "Tell me what you're doing sneaking in here in the middle of the night."

She stared down at him, trying to size him up. She'd never seen him before. If she had, she would have remembered him. If not the sandy blond hair that fell around his face and neck with careless abandon, then those warm green eyes with their golden flecks. Or his perfect white teeth.

He was exactly the type she would have gone for a few years ago—wild and carefree, with just enough bad boy to keep things exciting. But she'd learned her lessons. And she wasn't going there again, well-fitting dress jeans and black leather jacket aside.

"So are you going to answer me?"

His eyes held hers a moment longer. Then she threw back her head and laughed. She had known that the town of Harmony Grove wouldn't roll out the welcome mat for her. But she hadn't expected to be greeted like this, either.

Welcome home.

You can find purchase information here
https://caroljpost.com/my-books/pay-the-price/

ACKNOWLEDGMENTS

A huge thank you to Elizabeth Carroll for tirelessly answering a zillion questions about the workings of a domestic abuse shelter. If there are any inaccuracies in this book, they are mine rather than yours.

Thank you to my sister Kim for providing encouragement and great plot ideas and for helping to keep this directionally-challenged author from getting hopelessly lost during research expeditions.

Thanks to my amazing mother-in-law, Martha Post, editor extraordinaire. You have a knack for finding the mistakes no one else can see. I'm so glad you wield that figurative red pen so ruthlessly!

Thanks to my amazing critique partners, Sabrina Jarema and Karen Fleming, for always being there, whether it involves plotting, reading, letting me pick your brains or just helping me keep my sanity. You're not only my writing partners; you're my dear friends.

Thank you to my husband Chris for your unending encouragement and support. I couldn't do this writing thing without you.

And thank you to all of you who read my stories.

OTHER BOOKS BY CAROL J. POST

HARMONY GROVE SERIES:
Flee the Darkness

~

CEDAR KEY SERIES:
Deadly Getaway (novella)
Shattered Haven
Hidden Identity
Mistletoe Justice
Buried Memories
Reunited by Danger

~

Murphy Series:

Fatal Recall
Lethal Legacy
Bodyguard for Christmas

~

Trust My Heart
Dangerous Relations (The Baby Protectors)
Trailing a Killer (K-9 Search and Rescue)

ABOUT THE AUTHOR

Carol J. Post is an award-winning inspirational romance and romantic suspense author who splits her time between sunshiny Central Florida and the mountains of North Carolina. She's also a popular speaker, presenting workshops on a variety of craft topics. Besides writing, she works alongside her music minister husband singing and playing the piano. She also enjoys sailing, hiking, camping—almost anything outdoors. Her two grown daughters and grandkids live too far away for her liking, so she now pours all that nurturing into taking care of two sassy black cats.

Thank you for reading *Shatter the Silence*. Please let other readers know what you thought of it by posting a review.

For exclusive content, news and fun contests, sign up for Carol's newsletter by clicking on the link below:

https://caroljpost.com/newsletter/

CONNECT WITH CAROL ONLINE:

http://www.CarolJPost.com

Twitter:

http://twitter.com/@caroljpost

Facebook:

http://www.facebook.com/caroljpost.author

Goodreads:

http://www.goodreads.com/author/show/6459748.Carol_J_Post

Made in the USA
Middletown, DE
25 September 2023

39368836R00220